CUBAN DEEP

WALLACE AND KEITH

Severn River
Publishing

Published by Severn River Publishing.

ALSO BY WALLACE AND KEITH

The Hunter Killer Series

Final Bearing

Dangerous Grounds

Cuban Deep

Fast Attack

Hunter Killer

Coming Soon:

Fast Attack

By George Wallace

Operation Golden Dawn

By Don Keith

In the Course of Duty

Final Patrol

War Beneath the Waves

Undersea Warrior

The Ship that Wouldn't Die

As our enemies have found we can reason like men, so now let us show them we can fight like men also.
-Thomas Jefferson

PROLOGUE

Admiral Juan Valdez rolled the fat, brown-green cigar ceremoniously, using only his fingertips. The tightly packed tobacco felt firm and just slightly out of round, exactly as an expertly hand-rolled cigar should. He passed it beneath his nose and inhaled the sweet yet pungent aroma.

Nothing like a fine cigar. Nothing.

Valdez used his filigreed silver cigar guillotine to clip the end before rolling it in the fire of the matching desk lighter, pointedly ignoring the three men who waited on the other side of his immense desk, patiently watching him. Finally, the long-practiced ritual completed, he placed the end of the tobacco tube in his mouth, carefully lit it, and inhaled deeply. He held the smoke in his lungs for a long time to achieve its maximum benefit.

As he slowly exhaled, the admiral gazed deliberately around the big room. His palatial hacienda, located high in the hills overlooking Caracas, was a long way from his boyhood haunt, the slums off to the west. They were still visible from his office window on the hilltop should he ever desire to consider his origins. He rarely did.

Just the hint of a smile flashed across his craggy features as he remembered the hard, driven youngster who had fought, stolen, and murdered his way up from those slums, rising in rank and stature until he could afford such glorious experiences as the first inhale from a perfect cigar. And the other benefits of wealth and power.

The three men continued to stand in a semi-circle around Valdez's heavy mahogany desk, waiting expressionlessly for the old admiral to speak. None of them were accustomed to waiting for anyone. However, they made an exception for Admiral Juan Valdez.

These three powerful men represented the interests that truly controlled the country of Venezuela. President Cesar Gutierrez may have captured the world's attention, but this group was the real power behind the throne. Even as the figure-head strutted about, proclaiming that he alone held the reins of power in his geographically well-positioned country, the inside track to all of Latin America, from the Rio Grande to Tierra del Fuego.

The first man was Manuel Gotas de Gotario, who ruled Venezuela's largest labor union. Always a portly man, many years of high living—financed with the valiant and dedicated toil of the workers he so brutally controlled—had left him with several chins folded under his slack jowls. His belly was massive, and even the expensive Italian suits he typically wore were ill-fitting, the buttons on his tailored dress shirt straining to contain his immensity. His naturally dark complexion was not enough to hide the gray pallor of his sagging skin, and his eyes were weak and yellowed. He wheezed when he breathed and limped when he walked on feet so badly swollen at the ankles that he no longer bothered to tie the laces of his Jimmy Choo shoes. Gotas de Gotario was clearly a man with a voracious appetite, and one that might well bring on his demise.

The man in the middle was Simon Castellon, who looked exactly like the *revolucionario* that he was. He wore tattered green fatigues, sweat-stained at the armpits, and always had several days' growth of beard, as if he'd just returned from battle. He never went anywhere without his Dan Wesson Valor 1911 .45-caliber pistol and a razor-edged Filipino bolo—the gun on his belt near his right hand, the machete strapped to his left side for immediate access. But the fighter's most notable feature was his steely eyes. Almost hidden under bushy, dark brows, they radiated an intense fire that burned right through anyone foolish enough to stare back. A livid red scar reached from high on Castellon's right brow, continued across his forehead, and then trailed down below his left ear. The brutalized flesh was a visible reminder of the warrior's time spent in one of Colombia's secret prisons.

The third man in the room was notably out of place. Bruce deFrance was dressed in an even nicer suit than de Gotario, the best that Savile Row could offer. Unlike Castellon and Valdez, his skin was white-on-white with no evidence of recent sun exposure. deFrance assumed an effete stance, almost as if he was acknowledging the necessity of dealing with men inferior in class to himself. Even so, the Brit expatriate looked every bit the top executive. His dove-gray, double-breasted suit jacket accentuated his shoulders with some discreet padding before sharply tapering to his slim waist. The pale lavender shirt and pink silk cravat were just a little too much for others in the oil business. However, his company, Samson Petroleum, owned exclusive rights to develop and export Venezuela's huge oil reserves. That made deFrance a major player in the world's oil economy. deFrance and Samson Petroleum had placed their bets early on Gutierrez and Valdez, before they had been the clear winners in their country's continual struggles for power. Now, having chosen correctly, he and his company would continue to prosper

—that is, so long as they maintained the guise of a government-owned company, an enterprise that supposedly belonged to and benefited the citizens of Venezuela. And, of course, so long as Samson continued to pay huge bribes and kickbacks.

After another long draw on the cigar, Juan Valdez slowly rose from his seat behind the desk and sauntered over to an ornate sideboard. He splashed a generous amount of cognac into a cut-glass goblet, held it up to consider the liquid against the daylight that radiated in from the window, and finally turned to face his guests.

"I continue to believe that a good cognac and a fine *habana* are the best ways to celebrate a triumph," he said pointedly. "I trust you agree. Please join me, gentlemen."

The others joined the admiral at the sideboard, each allowing Valdez to fill his glass with the amber liquid. Then they reached into the proffered Spanish-cedar-lined humidor and extracted a cigar.

"What exactly are we drinking to, Admiral?" de Gotario asked, the first man willing to venture the question they all wanted to voice. "A triumph? I assume you called us here for more than a casual drink and a fine smoke. You know it is not prudent for us to be seen together without the diversion of others also being present."

Valdez frowned slightly. He did not want de Gotario to spoil the mood of the moment. He took a sip of the cognac and then impatiently waved off the fat man's concerns.

"Manuel, my old friend, no one saw you come here except my man, Jorge. And you know that he can be trusted implicitly."

Valdez took another puff and then blew a perfect smoke ring. de Gotario shrugged.

"If you say so, Admiral."

To the mild surprise of the other two men, Valdez ignored the fat man's impudent response. Instead, he motioned them to the conference table and chairs at the far side of the huge office. When all were seated, the admiral pointed to the revolutionary with the glowing-ember end of his cigar.

"Simon, my old friend, please give us a report on how it goes in the mountains. And you know I do not refer to all the 'playing army' you and your ruffians conduct. Even you will admit that the way to liberate our neighbors and repel the *yanquis* is through commerce, not with rifles and bayonets. Tell us, will our crop be as rich as you promised?"

Castellon swallowed hard, the cigar between his lips trembling noticeably. The irony of this military man's jumpiness was not lost on the admiral. It was never easy—not even for a man like Castellon—to bring bad news to Admiral Juan Valdez. The Navy man had a long history of—how did Shakespeare phrase it?—"shooting the messenger." And quite literally doing so.

Castellon cleared his throat.

"Frankly, Admiral, I regret to report that it has been difficult of late. The Colombians dare to ignore the border and conduct raids on our camps, even though they are clearly located in this country. 'Terrorist interdictions' they call their trespassing. We have had significant personnel losses, and thus recruitments are down. Worse still, we cannot trust the Colombian army officers anymore. Once bribed, they refuse to remain bribed."

The tough old rebel hesitated, taking another swallow of the cognac, idly massaging the butt of his pistol with his thumb.

Valdez allowed Castellon to squirm for a moment and then looked directly at him, shooting at the rebel the question that he most dreaded answering. "What about the crop? Please tell me that this effort, at least, will not fall short. We need the cocaine revenue to finance our other operations. You and your people are obligated for one hundred metric tons this year. So far, we have seen, I understand, less than ten."

Castellon was in a very tough spot. There was every possibility that he would not leave the room alive if he was not very clever with his answer. There was no way to lie successfully to the admiral. Chances were that the wily old man already knew what was happening up in the mountains before he ever asked the question.

"Admiral," Castellon started, but his voice cracked. He swallowed hard and tried again. "Admiral, we have only just now discovered that our growers were selling to another buyer. Combined with that damnable US-financed eradication program, our supply has almost dried up. We have already taken care of the disloyal growers, but that also contributed to the shortfall since it will take time to gain new suppliers. Then, as soon as we find who our competition is, we will resolve that issue as well."

Castellon breathed deeply. He was aware that it could be his last breath.

Impossibly, Valdez's face broke into a broad grin. He puffed the cigar then held it in his teeth.

"*Gracias,* Simon, *mi amigo*. I understand that this must be as difficult a report for you to make as it is for us to hear. But it is also most truthful, honest." Without even taking notice of the relief on Castellon's face, the admiral turned next to the dapper Brit. "Bruce, what new information do you bring us this morning? But before you deliver your report, I desire a favor."

deFrance smiled, showing perfect white teeth, and answered in a very precise Oxford accent, heavy with a pronounced lisp. "But of course, Admiral. You have only to ask."

Admiral Valdez smiled slightly, then went on, almost thoughtfully, "We require an underwater robot, what the *Americanos* call a UUV. It must be no larger than fifty-three centimeters in diameter and no longer than six meters. And it must be able to operate down to at least six thousand meters. Is such a thing possible?"

deFrance smiled. "Of course. Not in our usual inventory, but I think we can procure such a device. And I assume you want this acquisition to be, shall we say, 'discreet?'"

Valdez nodded and waved for the unctuous Brit to continue with his report.

"My dear Admiral, our geologic survey reports are most promising, and I understand you and the other partners will visit our research vessel soon to see for yourselves. Based on the data gathered during the latest cruise from our survey ship as well as the updated computer models, we estimate over a trillion barrels of sweet crude and as much as ten trillion cubic feet of gas in the Deep Cuban Passage Field. If we can tap it, there is enough petroleum there for fifty or more very lucrative years of extraction."

Valdez interrupted with a wave of his cigar. "My friend, I hear a 'however' in your voice."

"Actually, two," the oilman answered. "First, it is in very deep water, well over ten thousand feet. Drilling will not be easy or inexpensive. But more difficult still is the political situation. Cuba claims nominal rights to the area based on their EEZ rights—Exclusive Economic Zone. Both the USA and Mexico maintain that the basin is in international waters, and they still have no concept yet of the bounty that awaits. We do not have any prior claims there. And with the Cuban government swaying in the wind, I do not know how much we can count on them to maintain a tough stance."

Valdez stood and stepped over to the old framed map hanging on the wall. In ornate detail, it depicted the Caribbean and the countries ringing it. With a finger, he traced out the area to the south and west of Cuba. It did not look any different on the map than any other area.

"What do you mean by 'not inexpensive?'"

"We estimate an expense in excess of one hundred thousand

million American dollars to drill the extraction field and build the necessary infrastructure," deFrance answered. "Of course, that is after we have iron-clad rights to the field. It would be foolish to proceed otherwise."

Valdez looked up and muttered, "Maybe we can use some of the hard-won leverage we have acquired in Cuba. If we could—"

"One hundred billion dollars!" Gotas de Gotario suddenly shouted, his jowls flushed and quivering. "And a lifetime in court before we ever see a drop of oil. If there is any oil!" He whirled toward deFrance. "You crazy Brit! How many of those billions go to purchase more queer clothes for you and your herd of boyfriends...?"

The enraged union man lunged at deFrance. Before the executive could even move, de Gotario had him by the neck, shaking him, choking him until he went limp. In that moment, de Gotario was once again on the docks, assaulting a shop steward who had the nerve to question the way he ran the union, showing everyone the man dare not insult or show lack of faith in him.

As the one-sided struggle quickly played out, Admiral Juan Valdez casually turned from the map, opened the middle drawer of his desk, and withdrew the Navy Colt he kept there. With the glass of cognac still in one hand, he lifted the revolver, pointed it at the two scuffling men, and pulled the trigger.

Valdez did not blink at the gun's loud report.

The shot ripped apart de Gotario's left kneecap. The fat man dropped to the floor, grasping his leg, his eyes wide as blood spurted from between his fingers.

"You, sir, are a thieving liar," Valdez said calmly. "And you dare attack a guest in *mi casa*. A member of our team?"

Gotas de Gotario writhed on the floor, sobbing in pain. He clutched his shattered leg, trying vainly to stop the stream of blood that gushed onto the admiral's fine Turkish carpet.

"Do you take me for a fool?" the admiral continued, his voice amazingly calm. "I am well aware of the game you have been playing, and I appreciate your lack of control here this morning that allowed me to bring it to a convincing halt."

de Gotario shook his head wildly and attempted to shout out a denial, but all that emerged was a wail of agony.

Valdez stepped closer. He raised the Colt and put a bullet into the fat man's other knee, then knelt down and grabbed a handful of oily hair from his head. He held it firmly so that he could whisper into de Gotario's ear, loud enough for the other two men in the room to hear, "You greedy, stupid old fool. Did you think that you could steal all those drugs from Castellon and I would not learn of your betrayal?"

Valdez stood. Jorge, his assistant, had appeared silently and now stood at his boss's side.

"You require my services, Admiral?"

"Yes, Jorge. Take this piece of *excremento* down to the river. Dump him where the really big caimans play. They will be the hungriest. But first, bandage his legs. I don't want him bleeding to death before he feels their teeth ripping into his rather ample flesh."

The other two men in the room sat at the table, watching wide-eyed—Bruce deFrance still trying to get his breath back—as the scene played out.

"The president is aware this cancer would have to be excised. Jorge, please inform this *bastardo gordo*'s second-in-command that his boss suddenly decided to retire. We have no reason to suspect that he knows what de Gotario has been doing or was involved himself."

The admiral settled back into his chair at the antique conference table and pointedly placed the Colt down in front of him. He glanced at both men.

"Gentlemen, please try to enjoy your cigars and cognac," he

told them. "We have much work to do in order to secure the wealth of that oil field. For the citizens of Venezuela, of course, but I doubt they will begrudge our being rewarded for our perilous investment and foresight. But first, we must take time to savor the perfect *habanas* and the elixir of the successful. Enjoy, *mis amigos*. Enjoy the fruits of our labor."

Valdez had a big, satisfied smile on his face as the smoke from the perfect cigar formed a distinct halo above his head.

1

One of the best-trained killers in the world was, at that particular moment, doing all he could to avoid cutting short a life. He used both feet and wished he had three hands as he stood on the Peterbilt's brake pedal and clutch, sawing away at the steering wheel. He slammed the gearshift down to the lowest gear the transmission would possibly take without blowing apart like a bomb. In his mirrors, it looked for certain that his hefty load was either about to pass him or end up inside the cab on top of him. A cloud of blue smoke trailed behind and, no doubt, left twin streaks of smoking black rubber on the pavement.

And all this because a momma duck had decided to cross the thoroughfare at that very moment. Her half-dozen babies happily bobbed along behind her in a perfectly straight line, blissfully unaware of how hard the truck driver was struggling to keep from flattening them all.

"Aaaiyeeeee!" he shrieked. Maybe screaming would help him get the rig stopped without murdering the ducks or ending up in an overturned tangle of wreckage in the middle of the roadway.

Something worked. The truck shuddered to a halt beneath

him. When he looked down, he could see the mother duck waddling nonchalantly from under the front bumper, followed by her babies, inches from his huge front tires. Miraculously, the flatbed trailer load of steel beams had stayed strapped down and in place. And even more miraculously, no other vehicle had plowed into him as he made the panic stop.

TJ Dillon Jr.'s mind had been a thousand miles away, on his wife and boy back in Clearwater. That and the fact that he would not see them again for at least five days. On his mom in Norfolk, too, and the bad report he had just gotten about her from his stepfather. And the impossible schedule the dispatchers had slapped on him, simply because they knew he could and would do the impossible for them one more time.

After he left military service, Thomas Jefferson Dillon Jr. had several reasons for choosing long-haul trucking for a career. It was a lot like soldiering—a man knew his objective from the get-go. If he performed his mission the way he was supposed to, he usually came back alive. But trucking had some of the same negatives, too. A driver was too often away from those he loved, for far too long a time. And sometimes things happened that were impossible to describe to civilians, the uninitiated. The ones who would never understand.

Dillon had loved being in the military. Maybe it was something he had inherited from his father, a cement-solid career Marine, as surely as he had his dad's dark, expressive eyes and vise-clamp jaw. His mother told him all the time how much he resembled his dad. Or at least the way his father looked the last time she saw him pull himself away from her embrace on the air base tarmac, look back, give her his patented wink and be-back-soon wave. TJ had inherited other traits as well. A rock-solid sense of duty and honor, if such things could be passed down genetically, even if he never really got the chance to know the man who had bequeathed all these characteristics to his boy.

But love serving his country or not, when shapeless wars in the Middle East began to look more like the pointless Vietnam war that his dad described, when the administration tried to turn the military he loved into a social experiment, when Reserves and the National Guard were expected to do the chores previously performed by well-drilled enlisted men and Academy-trained officers, TJ knew it was time to take the retirement that was so strongly recommended to him by his CO before a lucky bullet or IED left his own boy and bride forever abandoned. Besides, it seemed like a good idea to see how the rest of the world—the civilized civilian world—lived.

As the last duckling emerged from beneath the truck, Dillon carefully eased the gearbox back into first, hoping that the gears would still mesh smoothly, that the clutch still engaged as it should, that all was at least still right with this tiny sliver of the world once the clamor and smoke settled. Everything felt okay. His pulse was returning to normal. No damage from the sudden stop, to him, his truck, or his load.

TJ knew he really needed to get moving now. He had an unloading slot booked at a barge dock in St. Louis in just a few minutes shy of two hours that he simply had to make. As of now, he was technically two and a half hours away. Even if no more ducks out for an afternoon stroll got in his way.

He worked his way back up through the gears and soon spotted his entrance back onto I-24. As he merged with the other big rigs and the whines and staticky voices on the CB radio picked up noticeably, he once more considered the twisting road that had brought him to this point in his life, to this section of freeway in flat, humid West Tennessee.

Unlike his late father, the Naval Academy graduate and career Marine, TJ Dillon had chosen to enlist in the Navy and volunteer for SEAL training. Also unlike his father, TJ had managed to stay alive long enough to put in his twenty years. He had an impressive resume. Master Chief Boatswains Mate. Picked up a bachelor's degree in international studies along the way. Fluent in four languages and an expert with a dozen or more different weapons. Master diver and free-fall parachutist. TJ had a lot of tickets punched and he had used them all in one place or another. Iraq and Afghanistan were a couple of adventures he could actually talk about. There were plenty of others he could not.

He did his job and did it well. When the time came, he walked away from it all proudly, assuming he would never be on the first line of defense again. But TJ Dillon knew on some level that he was not really ready to quit, even as he signed the papers and mustered out to begin the rest of his life. A sedate and restful one, he imagined.

Oh, he had been looking forward to permanently moving Vicki and "TJ3" down to what had been their getaway home in Clearwater. There were plenty more beaches and seascapes and picturesque marinas down there than Vicki could ever commit to oil paint on her beloved blank canvases. And way more crabs at the edge of the surf at sunset than he and his boy could ever possibly net.

Before the ink was dry on his paperwork, TJ had an attractive offer from a security firm and another even better one from a defense contractor. He could have taken his pick. One meant moving to the sprawl south of Los Angeles. The other was in the middle of Nebraska somewhere.

But he, Vicki, and the boy were looking forward to watching thousands of Gulf of Mexico sunsets together off their deck. And TJ's mom and Vicki's folks were on the East Coast. So it was that TJ was tentatively hired for a part-time teaching gig at a local college and settled in to see what happened.

Two weeks after separation, he got a call. A plane ticket to

D.C. and a reservation in the Crystal City Marriott soon followed.

Joshua Kirkland would have made a great used-car salesman. Or an even better television evangelist. He had just a bit of a con-man attitude—a little too slick, a little oily—but the man seemed to know all of TJ's hot buttons. Maybe even the way to his soul. Duty, honor, country. He even knew when to play the long-lost-dad-killed-in-the-defense-of-his-country card. Few knew the circumstances of that sacrifice, but Joshua Kirkland had done his homework and knew exactly how and when to lay down the chit.

"Dillon, I'm not going to bullshit you," Kirkland said, almost immediately after "Good morning." They were in his office at Langley. It was the third time TJ Dillon had been inside the CIA Headquarters, but it still awed him as few other things in his life had. "Something tells me you aren't ready to walk away from your country and raise tomatoes in a little garden somewhere. We need men like you. More than ever, we need men like you. Like your dad. Look, I know in your...umm, travels...you've seen some Agency people out in the field who weren't exactly top-line. Maybe some operations that weren't run the way they should have been. We're changing that as quickly and effectively as we can. 9/11 and everything that happened afterward did look like a cluster for the Agency...well, we'll see with the new guy in charge, but I'm thinking we take advantage of his inexperience and do all we can without letting him in on what's going on."

Kirkland leaned forward and poured more hot coffee into Dillon's cup, which had the US Navy SEAL Trident insignia —"The Budweiser"—stenciled on it. Another trick Kirkland had not overlooked.

"Master Chief, the momentum is there. We're finally turning this agency into what we've all wanted it to be from the very beginning. We've proved ourselves in Syria, Somalia, and a hundred other places. We took a beating on the 9/11 thing, but that wasn't deserved. Someday everybody will know what we were telling the administration for years before. We'll come out of Afghanistan and Iraq okay, too, once we can toot our own horn. We'll have more hero stories in North Korea, China, Cuba, the Middle East, even with the drug cartels down south. We'll do all this one way or the other, but we need your help to do it right. I suspect you have the heart of your old man. He knew we sometimes had to do things in a way the talking heads on the eleven o'clock news or the liberal elitists at *The New York Times* wouldn't approve of or even understand. He knew we had to get the dirty job done, and he was only too proud to do it. Or die trying."

Thinking back on that fateful meeting in Kirkland's office, Dillon grinned as he checked his mirrors and steered his big rig around a creeping RV on westbound I-24. It had been one hell of a sales pitch all right. TJ had an idea during the meeting about the kind of job Kirkland was recruiting him for. He soon had it confirmed. TJ had quickly done several turns in Somalia, dropping in for the first two weeks of the US engagement there. He helped train guys for Mali but never got around to making that trip. Lord knows there were still plenty of potential hot spots to keep the CIA occupied and him on the payroll. TJ certainly knew that.

But during that Langley meeting, TJ kept wondering why the Agency wanted him so badly that they put one of their top dogs on his trail. Why this top-floor, corner-office dude was the one to recruit a just-about-used-up SEAL for such apparently non-taxing duty.

"I was a classmate of your dad's at Annapolis," Kirkland had told him, answering the unasked question. "He was as fine a Marine as this country has ever produced. It's a shame he was lost on a mission that never should have happened. At least not at that place and at that time and in that damned screwed-up way. I've never known another man as dedicated to his country, to what was right. Until you. Regardless of your decision, I know your father would be proud of the man you've turned out to be, TJ. I know I sure as hell would be if you were my boy."

Vicki understood his decision when he explained it to her. Her father was a retired Army colonel. She had been a Navy wife for better than twenty years. She understood that there was so much more that she did not need to know. She simply maintained "Worry-level Five," as she termed it, exactly the same as she had since marrying TJ the week after BUD-S graduation. Then there had only been another week before he left for some mysterious billet for the first time. They honeymooned in Tijuana. Later, she confessed their honeymoon had been the last splinter of time she had spent with no worries at all about her husband. And it was also the last time she knew for certain what he did and where he did it.

His new job was no big deal for TJ3 either. Even though he was only two when TJ began working with the Agency, he was already used to his dad disappearing for months at a time, then coming home, quiet and serious for his first few days back. Like his mom and dad, the kid mastered the knack of making up for lost time when they were together.

Dillon blinked hard. God, he missed them so much! But he would see them in less than a week. TJ3 would soon be five and was lobbying for a small sailboat. Now that the boy had mastered cleaning his room and loading the dishwasher, maybe it was time to learn the difference between jibs and mainsails.

The signs on the doors of TJ's Peterbilt tractor proudly said: "Land O' Liberty Truck Lines, Jacksonville, Florida, Toting Freight from Sea to Shining Sea." The other truckers called it "LOL" on their CB radios. Or even termed it "Lots of Luck" at times, but it was all good-natured.

"LOL" was one of the major lines, a legitimate concern, making a decent income contracting with independent owner-operators to haul freight to and from the docks in Jacksonville. And they were only too happy to accept a still-young military retiree who wanted to indenture himself and his brand-spank-ing-new Peterbilt to their company while he double-dipped for a while.

Jacksonville was a military town. Lots of folks decided to retire there and take on a new job to make up for the shortfall in their meager pensions. And many of them, already well-accus-tomed to travel, chose the nomadic lifestyle of the long-haul trucker.

But there was another reason that Land O' Liberty was so accommodating, more than willing to waive, in TJ Dillon's case, their usually demanding requirements for minimum number of loads per month that were in place for most of their O-and-Os. If he needed to be away for extended periods of time, and if he might be unavailable for load assignments on short notice, and if he sometimes showed back up unannounced and ready to make a run, then that was perfectly all right with LOL. The generous government contract the company had recently received to haul tanks and armored personnel carriers back from Detroit and Peoria to the ports in Jacksonville and Bruns-wick, Georgia, more than made up for the inconvenience and squelched any company curiosity about what their driver might be doing for a hobby.

It was, when it came right down to it, the perfect cover.

So far the assignments Kirkland had brought him were innocuous, never more than a few weeks in duration, and paid more per job than a SEAL Master Chief brought home in a year. They were neatly sandwiched between trucking runs. To neigh-bors, distant relatives, or anyone else who took an interest in his comings and goings, it looked like the typical erratic schedule of another "knight of the highway."

The Agency jobs hardly tapped the more basic skills acquired by a SEAL. He did a written analysis of troop preparedness for the government in Cambodia to assure they were ready for whatever the last of the Khmer Rouge might try to throw at them. He did a study of the most efficient way to train the Filipino military to combat guerrilla attacks and terrorist activities. And he made a half-dozen trips back to the Pentagon to peruse dust-dry data and dim satellite photos, all to help give the Agency an understanding of unusual troop movements and festering insurrections at various potential flashpoints in the world.

Not really cloak-and-dagger stuff, TJ thought as he steered into the first slowdowns of the St. Louis rush-hour quagmire.

Josh Kirkland simply left a voicemail at LOL when he and the CIA needed TJ to do something for them. TJ then drove the rig to any of a dozen Florida or Georgia truck stops that were near an airport, left his bobtail tractor there, and made sure no one was taking any particular interest in his presence before flying out to wherever his government requested.

The checks came through Land O' Liberty and cashed beautifully. Found money. He almost felt guilty taking it. But so far, the cash had paid for a seawall and dock, a new pair of Seadoos, and a long-delayed second honeymoon to the Virgin Islands. It had swelled TJ3's college account considerably, and even paid for a couple of cemetery plots at Sunset Gardens. And the biggest danger he had faced so far was a paper cut or Washington, D.C., rush hour traffic.

TJ was savvy enough to know the other shoe was certain to drop someday. He was being tested. Any low-level Department of Defense wonk could have accomplished what he had done so far.

As he pointed his hood emblem toward the dock and the drop-off of his heavy load, he wondered when the call would ultimately come. The call for something serious, a job for which he could actually feel that he was accomplishing something positive for the good guys.

A part of him could not wait.

Another part of him dreaded that call like a son of a bitch.

2

Commander Joe Glass peered intently through the eyepiece of his submarine's periscope. Out there somewhere on this muddy, yellow sea, someone was trying to locate him and his ship. Trying to find him and possibly kill him. As far as he could see, the water was millpond-smooth and empty, barren of even a fishing boat.

Still, the WLR-9 kept up its incessant chirping. Someone was out there boldly using a 4.5-kilohertz active sonar. The only reason to use active sonar this close to the Venezuelan coast was to find a submarine. And Joe Glass knew for a fact that he commanded the only submarine that was supposed to be within a thousand miles of this spot on the globe.

"Sonar, Conn," Glass said into the open microphone dangling above his head. "Classification of the WLR-9 contact?"

The reply was immediate.

"Conn, Sonar," Master Chief Randy Zillich calmly answered in his deep baritone. "WLR-9 contact equates to Sierra Two-Seven on passive broadband. Looks to be an old Soviet-era Feniks-Artika ASW sonar. Probably one of those antique Krivak frigates that the Russians palmed off on Gutierrez a couple of years ago. Best range estimate in excess of thirty thousand yards."

Joe Glass nodded even though Zillich could not see him. At least fifteen miles away and his sonarman could discern all that info. It was a given that Master Chief Zillich was the best sonarman in the whole US Navy submarine fleet, but he was also distinctively taciturn. He had just spoken, for him, what amounted to volumes. The most important message was that this guy making all the racket, whoever and wherever he was, did not yet have contact on Commander Glass and the USS *Toledo*.

"Sonar, Conn, aye," Glass answered.

The skipper glanced around the USS *Toledo*'s crowded control room. His Improved-688-class submarine, the most advanced ship in the US Navy, was the stealthiest spy platform ever built. It was ideally suited for snuggling up close to someone's coastline to suck up every bit of intelligence available in the electromagnetic spectrum. And to do it for months on end without anyone being the wiser, which was exactly what they had been doing for the past three months, floating within spitting distance of the sunny beaches of Caracas. The string bikinis were just barely over the horizon, but so were the quickly growing Venezuelan military installations with their requisite communications facilities.

"XO, keep a close eye on Sierra Two-Seven," Glass called out as he stepped away from the Type 18 periscope. "If SNR gets up to forty, give me a call. We certainly can't afford to get our asses detected this close to shore. CNN would have us as their lead story for a week, and you can't imagine the amount of heartburn that would cause our bosses."

Brian Edwards, *Toledo*'s tall, cocksure, and athletic executive officer, nodded in agreement with his skipper. Glass kidded him about stepping out of a recruitment poster to take his job on *Toledo*. Turned out it was no joke. Edwards's male-model good looks had actually been used in a series of TV commercials and magazine ads aimed primarily at female recruits.

"Yes, sir. Get some rest. We'll stay on the ISR mission until 2000. Then we'll head out to international waters for our daily report. When do you want to be awake?"

Glass strode to the back of the control room and bent over the navigation chart. The boundary between international waters—the open ocean—and Venezuelan territorial waters was plainly marked with a broad green line. *Toledo*'s current position was almost two miles on the wrong side of that line. Even with a Presidential Finding, official US permission to disregard the niceties of an indistinct, watery border, Glass knew that he and *Toledo* were technically committing an act of war just by being there.

Only a handful of countries in the world would make a big deal of such a minor breach. One of them was a couple of miles due south of their current position.

"Wake me up by Christmas," the skipper answered with a sideways grin. "But call me when you have the daily SITREP ready to release. And let me know if the spooks back in ESM get anything interesting besides listening to some cabbie trying to get lucky for the night."

Glass wearily walked toward his tiny stateroom. It sure would be nice to get more than a few minutes of uninterrupted sleep. The mission was almost finished. The National Security Administration riders—the "spooks"—aboard his boat had not shared any great revelations from the last thirty days of inter-cepted radio traffic. That was normal. In a day, *Toledo* would turn north for the run back to Norfolk and home. That meant a full night's sleep in his bed at home and an opportunity to remind Marilyn—Mrs. Glass—that she was still a married lady.

Glass stepped into his stateroom and dropped into his chair. He stared blindly at the message boards. Somewhere back in the humdrum, day-to-day world of the US Navy, bureaucrats were demanding myriad routine reports. People were generating paperwork, issuing orders, making decisions that clearly were deemed important to them. Out here on the frontline, such mundane nonsense did not seem to matter.

As he was contemplating the nature of his job these days, Joe Glass's head fell forward, his chin on his chest, and he dozed off.

"Torpedo in the water!"

The 1MC report blasted Glass awake. He raced toward the control room before his eyes were fully open, still wondering if this was a vivid nightmare.

"Ahead flank! Make your depth six hundred feet!" Edwards was yelling, his voice barely under control. "Left full rudder, steady course north. Launch both evasion devices! Snap shot tube one!"

The big nuclear submarine heeled over and angled down as it raced to escape the incoming ball of destruction swiftly hurdling its way.

"Torpedo bearing two-two-seven!" Zillich's voice was up a couple of octaves, confirming that this was no drill, no dream. "Zero bearing rate!"

Death was aiming a surprise haymaker straight at them, and they could do little to duck the punch. At least Edwards already had them doing that little bit.

Glass stepped next to Edwards and put a hand on his XO's shoulder.

"Captain, it came out of nowhere!" Edwards all but shouted. "We didn't have any contact in that entire quadrant. The target we've been watching is way over—"

"Torpedo bearing two-two-seven!" Zillich reported again. "Second torpedo bearing two-two-six! Forty kilohertz active, best classification Russian ET-80A, submarine-launched torpedoes."

Glass was completely mystified. Even with Zillich's solution on the odd target more than thirty thousand yards away, whatever it was, the bastard was much too far away to be a threat. Much too far away to know *Toledo* was there. Much too far to launch such an accurate and deadly attack. But somehow, someone had snuck up on them and was in the process of shooting them in the back.

"Solution ready," Jerry Perez, the navigator, yelled out. "Matched bearings with incoming torpedo."

"Weapon ready," Eric Hobson, the Weps, chimed in. *Toledo* was ready to shoot back. They just did not have a clue who or where their attacker was, if the lone mysterious target was the one that had just launched hellfire in their direction.

Glass quickly ordered Hobson to stand down.

"Check fire tube one. Shut the outer door tube one." Under his breath, the skipper muttered, "XO, not a good idea to shoot someone inside their territorial waters. Something like that might get their government upset."

"But they've launched an attack…"

"Torpedoes bearing two-two-six and two-two-seven," Zillich called out. "Still closing!"

"Sounding?" Glass yelled out.

The fathometer operator barely squeaked out his report.

"Depth one-two-five fathoms."

Toledo was racing along at better than thirty knots with only 150 feet of water between her and the rock-hard bottom of the Caribbean Sea.

"Diving Officer, get me twenty feet off the bottom and stay there," Glass ordered.

The big sub slid down a few more feet, until her giant screw was churning up a huge, unseen cloud of mud and silt as she raced along the bottom toward open water.

Toward open water and the only possible chance they had to not die this day.

Ψ

"*Almirante*, this new submarine is pure magic," Captain Alejandro Ramirez said, beaming. The lights from the control panel before him glinted off his two gold front teeth. The submarine commander's tone was slimy, so obviously attempting to play to his superior that the admiral would surely see it. "We snuck up on the American submarine and shot it without it even knowing we were here. Amazing! Our Russian friends really outdid themselves with this boat."

Admiral Juan Valdez, the commander of the Venezuelan Peoples' Navy, grunted and then smiled broadly, revealing his satisfaction with what had just happened. So self-satisfied that he did not even allow his irritation with his officer's usual fawning demeanor to bother him.

"Yes, Captain Ramirez," the admiral told him. "We chased the interlopers out of our home waters. But to really do something important, we need to carry it to America's front door. And believe me, that we will do, once we are convinced that you and your crew are ready. We know this vessel certainly is." Valdez turned and started toward the control room doorway. "Oh, and now, if you would, Captain, please turn off those torpedoes. We would not want the Americans to detect us as they have our 'fish' and do something crazy like fire back at us."

As he left the control room, the admiral stopped and added, "And make sure that your sonarmen do not tell anyone how well the pinger we tracked on the American submarine has worked this day. We cannot risk having our most helpful friend in Norfolk discovered."

3

"What the hell was all that about?" Glass thundered as he stood there in the conn, slowly rocking from one foot to the other, clenching and unclenching his fists to bleed off the tension. "One second I'm in my stateroom, contemplating the joys of life. The next, I'm running for it. Then, there's nothing. Everything's as quiet as a graveyard at midnight. What the hell happened?"

No one had an answer. The submarine's carefully controlled environment was in disarray after the mad dash to get away from the phantom torpedoes. *Toledo*'s crewmembers were slowly re-stowing their battle-stations gear. They knew how truly close they had come to dying. There was no way to hide the whine and ping of the incoming torpedoes from the close-knit crew. Neither could they miss their sudden disappearance, as if someone, his point well made, called off the deadly dogs. Nor could any of them in the conn avoid seeing the perplexed, frustrated look on their CO's face.

Joe Glass was rarely frustrated. The man simply did not rattle easily.

His XO, Brian Edwards, shook his head and commiserated with the captain.

"Skipper, I don't have the slightest idea. We didn't have a single threat contact. That was a shot totally out of the dark."

"Well, that out-of-the-dark shot could have damn well sent us to the bottom!" Glass raged. "How could anybody have a shooting solution on us without us even having contact? That cannot happen, XO, but it sure as hell just did. I don't know what they are trying to prove, but they certainly proved they could shoot us from far enough away that we couldn't see them, and if they had wanted to, they could have almost certainly sent our butts on eternal patrol."

Master Chief Zillich, just emerging from the cave-like sonar room, wore that same puzzled, frustrated look.

"Skipper, you got me. I know those *Kilos* are quiet. But so is *Toledo*. We would have to hear them well before they could get a shot on us. But if we were making noise, we'd know it, right? I just don't understand how they could get the first shot." The big sonar chief shook his head in disbelief. "There wasn't anything there before they shot. It's like they knew we were here, they knew we couldn't detect them, and they knew exactly where to shoot."

Glass nodded toward the sonar repeater where the melee was only then beginning to disappear from the long-time averaging display. "I don't know how these bastards got the upper hand and got the first shot, but we'll 'field day' all the way back to Norfolk until we figure it out."

Glass took a few steps toward the sonar room. "Master Chief, key up those tapes and replay them. Let's go through them until we get something better than a wild-ass guess. Somewhere on those tapes is a clue. I mean to figure out how that bastard got a drop on us so we can make sure it does not happen again."

Over the next few days, life on *Toledo* slowly returned to normal. The crew's racing pulses slowed. The Southern Caribbean receded behind the sub as it headed north, toward home. Field day followed drill, which in turn followed training. The Operational Reactor Safeguards Exam, waiting off Chesapeake Light, was reality. The thoughts of the warshot torpedoes that had chased them away from the Venezuelan coast like a scared rabbit slowly faded.

But not completely. Joe Glass would never allow that to happen.

Ψ

The submersible ship *Almirante Villaregoz* steamed slowly on the surface up the mud-brown river, deliberately churning toward the broken-down pier the crew called home. The submarine's black hulk was barely visible in the dim evening light as it knifed through the polluted river water. A scattering of small fishing smacks lay astern, bobbing in the river's estuary, meager evidence of *el Presidente*'s new economy. The type 876 *Kilo*-class submarine was the most modern in the Russian inventory, but the rust and sea growth streaking its steel sides belied the technological wonders that filled her interior compartments.

Caracas's raucous nightlife beckoned the few sailors standing topside. The flashing neon, so irresistible to *turistas Norteamericanos,* lay only a few hundred meters away, promising instant escape from the country's notorious poverty, as yet untouched by the president's reforms. Out on the river, all was dark and quiet. The solitude was broken only by the occasional wave slap against the warship's unyielding steel hull. Two tugs, their red and green running lights piercing the gloom, slowly made their way toward the center of the channel to meet them.

Admiral Juan Valdez stood apart from the others—or at least as far apart as he could in the submarine's narrow sail. It had been a good day, Valdez reflected. A very good day.

Soon, he would be able to share the details of this day with the man he served, and that would further cement his position within the president's inner circle. And from that rarefied place, he would be able to continue his bold ambitions. Bolder and more far-reaching than merely scaring the shit out of some cocky American submarine crew. Historical changes were coming to the hemisphere, and the admiral was more certain than ever that he, of all those with a front-row seat, was the best positioned to gain the most from it.

He must remain patient. Patient and ready. The time for decisive action was quickly coming.

Valdez took great delight in knowing that the American submarine was running north as fast as its nuclear reactor would carry it, retreating from his torpedoes. And he was confident the captain of that vessel had no idea where the torpedoes originated, or how anyone could have made such an accurate shot without first being detected.

Valdez slowly sipped from his tiny cup of rich dark coffee and smiled. It was only a matter of time before the Americans were screaming in panic as gasoline prices skewed northward from five dollars a gallon. The oil-starved fools would inevitably turn south to find the only escape from economic doom. Venezuela's oil fields were nearly exhausted and would last only a few more years before it became too expensive to recover the last drips. Even so, the deep-water fields that lay off Cuba's southern coast, mostly unknown to the rest of the world, were a tantalizing prize promising far greater riches than the home fields ever provided.

Whoever controlled those fields would ultimately control the Western Hemisphere. And Valdez meant to be that man.

Captain Ramirez sidled up alongside his commander and leaned nonchalantly against the bridge enclosure.

"Admiral, *el Presidente*'s barge is pulling alongside," the diminutive submariner reported. "He requests your presence at his palace as soon as possible. I suspect he wants a full retelling of how you made the sneaky Americans run away like frightened children."

"Yes, Captain, I suspect he does. And I look forward to telling him the story," Valdez said, but his voice was far away.

The captain of a plunging boat—even one as advanced as the *Villaregoz*—would never understand the world's complexities.

No, this incident, no matter how glorious, was only the first chapter of a far, far greater story.

4

The young Navy SEAL-team commander grunted as much in frustration as in pain from the daggers of freezing-cold spray whipped by an angry wind that lashed his exposed face. Jim Ward and his team were exhausted and still had another two miles to paddle before they made it to the island. The submarine that had regurgitated them into the elements over by Kodiak Island was long since gone, sinking back down to the calm, quiet depths. The tall, lanky ensign tried to stretch his cramped legs in the tiny combat rubber raiding craft—a CRRC —but there was just not enough room. Not with three other SEALs and all their gear filling every inch of space.

Shelikof Strait was breathtakingly beautiful to those few adventurous tourists who dared visit the wild, remote reaches of Western Alaska in summer. Winter, on the other hand, was downright dangerous for anyone crazy enough to be on these waters, no matter the type of vessel. A CRRC at night was just barely short of suicidal.

Takli Island loomed ahead, the surf crashing in huge, roaring breakers that pounded the rocky shore. The SEALs' night vision goggles illuminated the forbidding scene in shades of green on green. Ward was finally able to catch the barest glimmer of the IR ChemLight on the tiny island's far western tip. He was waiting for that signal. Safety—and hopefully warmth—was just a short paddle away.

"I see it," he murmured, as if his whispered voice would carry across the roaring surf. "On the headland. The landing should be right around the corner." Ward dug his paddle deeper into the icy, churning sea and yelled this time. "Come on, guys. Another ten minutes."

The SEALs put their backs into rowing the little boat toward the faint, flickering signal light. The CRRC heaved high with each passing crest only to race down into the following trough. Every wave threatened to capsize the rubber boat and pitch them into the water. Thirty seconds in these seas would leave a man unconscious. Ninety would likely kill him, even in his high-tech dry suit.

It had all seemed so easy when he briefed it back onboard the *La Jolla*. Surface the submarine out in the channel, far enough from the shore that there was no chance of being detected. Then paddle in the CRRC across a few miles of open water to the narrow, protected inlet on Takli's western side. Once they landed, they only had to climb Takli Mount to their final objective.

The timeline worked out to two hours on the water followed by an hour of climbing. Should have been a leisurely day in the park for a fit young team fresh out of SEAL training. But Ward had not calculated in the cold, the wind, or the pitching sea and the effect on their bodies or their will. They were already two hours behind schedule and, truthfully, the headland was probably still an hour away.

The freezing cold was quickly sapping their strength. Ward could feel it. The realization that he had led his team into a dangerous position slowly dawned on the young officer. These men were his responsibility. They were depending on him to lead them through this exercise and then get them back home safely.

Ward caught a glimpse of his team's anxious expressions. The sense of fear was spreading. Calling for rescue was not an option. Simulation exercise or not, no one was standing by to rescue them.

After the team reached the lee of the headland, the howling wind finally died off a bit. At least they could hear themselves think now. Jed Dulkowski, Chicago-born and the team wit, piped up, his voice quivering in the cold.

"We need to package this and send it to Disneyland. It's a better ride than 'Small World.'"

"Yeah," Sean Horton chimed in. "At least we don't have to listen to that damned annoying song." The big black man from East Los Angeles could barely control his chattering teeth. "Great ride if we don't turn into SEAL Popsicles."

Tony Garcia, the swarthy Latino who called Philly home, shot back, "In your case, don't you mean Fudgsicle?"

Then suddenly the swirling current that raced through the narrow reach between Takli Island and the mainland spun the CRRC around, sending the little raft into rapid circles. It was almost impossible to keep the boat headed in any one direction, let alone make headway. The tiny IR light was no longer getting closer.

"Sean, Jed, you two paddle. Tony, use your paddle like a rudder. Keep us pointed just to the left of the headland," Ward ordered as he checked the waterproof GPS one more time. Incredibly, it showed that they were almost even with the headland. Just a few hundred more yards and they could make the final run toward the beach.

A wave caught him totally off guard, sweeping over the CRRC and shoving Ward off the stern. He desperately clutched at something—anything—that would keep him inside the boat. Just as the raging water jerked the lifeline out of his grasp, Ward felt a strong hand grab his shoulder harness and stop his plunge into the sea.

"Got you, Skipper," Garcia shouted as he manhandled Ward back into the CRRC. "We can't have you slipping out for a swim just because you see a sunny beach."

Ward shivered uncontrollably, although he could not tell whether it was from fear or the numbing cold. He forced himself to sit quietly while he calmed his racing heart and willed the shivering to stop. He had come so very close to being chum for the killer whales that frequented these waters. Then Ward smiled to himself when he realized that Garcia had just become the first person to ever call him "Skipper."

The team had just paddled the CRRC into the tiny cove when they saw that the calm beach they expected was, in reality, a foreboding collection of jagged rocks. Landing here would be all but impossible. Still, the racing current drove them directly into the cove and straight toward the unforgiving rocks. Their only hope was to steer with all their strength and pray that they could avoid being pounded. Like a whitewater raft team hurtling down a class-five run of rapids, Horton and Dulkowski threaded them through a narrow cleft between two semi-submerged boulders while Garcia used his paddle to shove them clear of a third, all the while trying to avoid broaching.

Without warning, the surf thrust the boat high in the air before a gust of wind caught it and flipped them end for end. With the raft suddenly out from beneath him, Ward saw the steel-gray water rushing up at him. Then he felt the icy-cold sea slam into his chest, hammering all the air out of his lungs. The whole world became an impossible jumble of darkness as the churning surf drove him downward, deeper and deeper. The vise around his chest quickly tightened, and the pounding in his head was more pain than he had ever felt. He was disoriented, with no sense of bottom or surface. No idea which way was up or down.

Somewhere in his head, he knew that he had to get back to the air. He could not die like this. His men needed him. Where were they and how were they doing?

He felt like he had been underwater for hours, but it could only have been a dozen seconds. Every molecule of oxygen was gone because he had not been able to gulp in any air before he went under, and the pounding sea had knocked loose any residual air in his lungs.

Ward felt the fuzzy blackness seep around the edges of his consciousness. A vision of his mother flicked into view.

"Mom, I'm sorry," he murmured.

Blackness closed into the very center of his vision.

"You won't give up this easily, Jimmy," he heard Ellen Ward's soft but commanding voice say. Then he felt her hands lift him up, just like when he was a baby and he had gotten himself into some place where he should not have been.

Miraculously, his face was out of the water. Great gasping breaths filled his empty lungs. For just a moment, he wondered if he was dead, if he had popped into the next world. But then he realized how incredibly cold he was.

A wave broke over his head. He came up again sputtering saltwater.

The next wave shoved and tumbled young Ward onward. Another spun him around some more. There was nothing he could do but go where the frothy sea took him, hoping it did not dash him against a rock or send him too deep to come back to the surface before he was too cold to care anymore.

Eventually, he realized that he was lying like driftwood, sprawled awkwardly on his back, halfway wedged between a couple of rocks. He knew he needed to get out and make his way toward the sandy beach before the waves grabbed him again and snatched him backward. When he succeeded in slipping between the rocks, a wave shoved him hard to his hands and knees, depositing him well up on the rocky beach.

He coughed hard and spat out seawater and sand, trying to blink to clear his eyes.

"That was about the worst example of a covert penetration I have ever seen!" a man growled into young Ward's ears. He looked up to see Bill Beaman towering over him, shaking his head sadly from side to side. "If I didn't have a top-priority mission for you and your misfit team, I would make you do it all again and do it right this time."

Ward jumped to his feet and stood at attention, as best he could manage, his knees weak and the shivers still wracking his body. Beaman, the legendary SEAL captain and old family friend, was running this winter exercise. But he was supposed to be back at the nice, warm command center on Adak, not out here on the cold, wet beach with a close-up view of the ugly way the exercise had ended.

"My team?" Ward sputtered. "Where is my team, Captain?"

He looked in the direction that Beaman pointed. Horton, Garcia, and Dulkowski were scattered along the edge of the surf, quickly gathering up what was left of their gear.

"Come on! We haven't got all day!" Beaman growled. "Admiral Donnegan is expecting us at the Pentagon in ten hours."

Admiral Donnegan? The Pentagon?

Jim Ward shook his head again, trying to clear it. Was he hallucinating?

The young SEAL did not have time to wonder. He willed his numb legs to move without giving way as he followed his senior officer toward the coveted warmth of the command center.

5

With a smooth turn of the truck's steering wheel, TJ Dillon expertly inched the big rig into the narrow slot. He had to get it exactly right, otherwise the gantry crane would not be able to off-load his cargo. The yardmaster would make him park again, and that took time. He was late already.

The sprawling Long Beach Port Facility glistened golden in the early-morning California sun. Dillon tried to rub the grit out of his bloodshot eyes as the Peterbilt's trailer shuddered to a halt squarely under the huge yellow crane. He stretched his tired muscles as he watched the crane lift the Conex box as if it were a tiny toy. In reality, it was fifty thousand pounds of aircraft parts on their way from the Boeing factory in St. Louis to an assembly plant in Osaka, Japan.

Thirty minutes and a stack of signed paperwork later, he was heading out of the port facility toward the freeway and his next job—and the real reason he had made the mad dash to the West Coast. St. Louis to Long Beach in thirty-six hours flat had earned him some hard looks from some of the round-hats who manned the weigh stations along the way. It had to be some kind of record, although the stretch of I-40 through the Texas Panhandle had nearly killed him with its moonscape boredom.

Dillon shook his head. There had better be a really good reason for this high-speed trek across most of the continent.

The rig was certainly a whole lot easier to handle in the heavy traffic now that the load was gone, but he kept forgetting the trailer was no longer following him. The first glance or two at the empty mirrors on each side of the cab gave him a start. He eased out onto the I-710 northbound and carefully blended into the rush-hour swirl.

TJ thought about the latest voicemail message from Kirkland, the one he had listened to after unloading in St. Louis. There was something different in the spook's voice. Was this the big one, the kind of important assignment he had signed on with the Agency to do? Was that why Kirkland had sent him all the way to the Pacific side of the continent, far from his usual dodges and parking lots? Or was he bound for another grad-school-type assignment, holding somebody's hand in a humid jungle somewhere?

Dillon turned onto the I-10 and followed the broad freeway east for a while before sliding off at the exit for the Ontario Hilton. He drove around back to the truck lot and pulled into a spot between a Diamond Reo towing a stainless tanker and another big tractor hooked up to an empty Volvo car hauler. His rig was just another one of several dozen long hauls—about half of them bob-tailed—sitting in the huge back parking lot while their owner/drivers waited for the next load. No one would question a rig sitting here driverless for a few days.

TJ swung the truck's door open, carefully set his gray Stetson on his head, and eased down out of the cab. He paused to stroke the hand-painted owner/operator notation high up on the door, just below the window. "TJ Dillon and Son," it read. For a moment, he thought how great it would be when TJ3 could join the family business. He shook off the brief pang of homesick-ness as he strode across the parking lot, making his way to the rear entrance of the sprawling hotel.

He sauntered down the hallway to the Hilton's main lobby. The glass and marble reminded him of a thousand other places, all different but all still the same. The taps on his handmade snakeskin boots clicked on the gleaming tile as he walked to the desk. No one paid attention to the trucker. He was just one more working stiff, making his living aiming a big rig toward the next pile of freight with his name on it.

The room reservation was waiting for him, as was a sealed envelope with his name neatly typed on it. The pretty desk clerk flirted boldly with him. There was little doubt he could have company for the evening if he so desired. He was used to it, but he pleasantly flirted back and then politely—expertly—brought the dance to a courteous halt before it went very far. TJ Dillon had plenty of opportunities, and the animal desire was certainly there, but he never partook. Never. He was loyal to anybody and anything to whom or to which he had pledged to be. His coun-try. His SEAL teammates. The Agency. His wife, Vicki.

Besides, at that moment, he was hungrier than he was horny. The last time he could remember eating was at the truck stop in Buckeye, Arizona, just west of Phoenix. He decided to heed the growling coming from just below his ribcage and have breakfast before he checked the envelope's contents. The local non-chain diner across the street looked far more promising than the hotel coffee shop.

It was a good choice. Dillon forked the last of the *huevos rancheros* into his mouth without regard to manners. These little East County places sure knew how to do Mexican. He swirled what remained of the dark black coffee and took a swallow. The pert little waitress bent forward to refill his cup and, at the same time, reveal her deep and ample cleavage. He held up his hand.

"No more, honey," he told her. "No more."

She instinctively knew he was talking about more than the coffee, but she returned his smile anyway.

"Just let me know if you want anything," she told him, and he knew, too, she was not really talking about *huevos rancheros* or black coffee.

He watched her walk away and disappear into the kitchen before he slit open the white envelope with his butter knife. Inside was a computer printout of a boarding pass and first-class airplane ticket to Washington-Dulles Airport for a flight from LAX leaving that night. There was also a slip of paper that simply said "NC-3, 201, 1400."

Dillon sipped the last of the coffee without tasting it, paid his bill with cash, and left an especially generous tip for the waitress with the impressive cleavage before stepping out of the diner into the brilliant morning sun. Not even the usual smog that bunched up against the mountains to the east could blunt its brightness.

Dillon was still puzzled. He could not imagine why he had been required to drive from St. Louis to Southern California only to hop a red-eye back east, retracing his exact route but doing so at forty thousand feet.

One thing he did know. He had a meeting at a typical spot in Crystal City—on the other side of the continent—the next morning at 1400Z, 0900 local.

And that could only mean he once again had himself a mission.

Ψ

El Presidente Cesar Gutierrez was not having a good day. It had all started badly when his current mistress awoke in a bad mood. Juanita's shouted, ranting curses had the servants cowering outside the bedroom door, afraid to come in but too curious to leave. It was hard to believe that so much noise could come from one petite woman's mouth.

Gutierrez beat a hasty retreat, choosing to hide in the bathroom until Juanita's hot Latino temper cooled a little. This only heightened her rage. She threw her bone-china coffee cup at the closed door, where it shattered, spreading a large blotch of steaming brown liquid across the white woodwork. All this because he had paid too much attention to some girl at the previous night's party.

Gutierrez shook his head. He had vainly tried to explain that the woman at the soiree was his constituent, a voter, the head of her local party committee. He had to treat party leaders with interest.

Putas! He would never understand them.

He clicked on the television set that was mounted above the bathroom door within easy view of anyone seated on the toilet. Might as well catch up on what was happening while he allowed Juanita to consider how lucky she was to occasionally share the bed of such a powerful man. After all, the same passion she demonstrated when having one of her tantrums also applied when her long, tapered legs were open wide for him. He smiled as he contemplated that logic.

The local morning news was filled with stories about the mysterious death of a man named Manuel Gotas de Gotario. Fishermen reported that they had found remnants of his fat, partially devoured body floating in the river last night. Rumors flew around wildly. One had him the victim of a plot by the American CIA. Or the casualty of a feud with a rival union organizer. Or, most improbable to Gutierrez, he was caught in the act by an irate husband. He found it hard to believe that any woman would willingly submit to the gross old union boss.

The reporter's speculation didn't even hint at the scum

paying the ultimate price for daring to cross Admiral Juan Valdez. The admiral had done a good job of spinning the story, an amazing testament to how far the old Navy man's tentacles reached. He could as easily assure the perfect cover story in the news as he could order one of his submarines or gunboats to sea. From whatever helm he manned, he could manipulate anything and everything in this part of the world.

El Presidente ignored Juanita's continuing squalls and grinned. Admiral Valdez was smart and very ruthless. It was a very good thing that he was also loyal to his president. Otherwise, he would have to be eliminated, too, and that would be a terrible loss of a valuable asset. Gutierrez thoughtfully rubbed the stubble on his chin. Valdez and his submarines were vital elements in his grand strategy. With Russia's finest technology at his fingertips and Valdez's best-trained crewmembers running the amazing vessel, the entire Caribbean Basin would soon be his personal swimming pool. He could leverage his oil money directly into power that would finally bring him the strength beyond the borders of his country that he craved.

But still, Gutierrez knew instinctively that it would be prudent to have a contingency plan, just in case the old admiral was playing games of his own. Gutierrez grabbed the phone from its perch next to the commode and punched in a very special number. A man's voice came on the line halfway through the first ring.

Cesar Gutierrez had long dreamed of extending his reach beyond Venezuela's shores. Bolivia, Colombia, Panama—even Peru to the south—were well within his grasp. But the real victory lay to the north. He would have to be ensconced right on the USA's doorstep to prevent Washington from sticking its imperialistic nose into his revolution.

That made Cuba the key. And this particular individual whose number he had just dialed was already heavily involved in making certain the right person was in control of the island. All the chaos with the passing of the Castro regime and the on-again, off-again relations with the US had made Gutierrez a power broker to be reckoned with.

The huge oil reserve that Bruce deFrance and his company had found in the deep Caribbean Basin off Cuba's south coast was, of course, within Cuba's Exclusive Economic Zone. The reserves there were so massive that they dwarfed anything else in the hemisphere, including his own Venezuelan fields. If the Free World gained access to this oil, prices would plummet, cutting Venezuelan oil's worth in half. Without that leverage, Gutierrez would lose his place on the world stage.

On the other hand, with Cuba in his pocket, the grant of exclusive access to the reserves would, in effect, be his. He alone would be able to control world oil prices. Those haughty Arabs could choke on their OPEC. The Americans would have to come to him—him with his boot on the supply line of oil that fueled that decadent nation—with hat in hand and their so-called "free enterprise" forgotten. Cesar Gutierrez would be the next Simon Bolivar.

Gutierrez spoke briefly with the person on the other end of the telephone line. The plan was underway, he was assured. At least one operative would soon be en route, and others were already in place. There were rumblings already about the unrest and serious power plays underway within the island nation, details of warring factions in the country and outside it who were poised to seize power or control now that Fidel was gone.

Thinking of such plans always excited Gutierrez. When he finally dared to venture out of the bathroom, he was positively aroused. He knew one way to silence the woman's foul mouth. He unbuttoned his pajama bottoms as he stepped into the bedroom.

But Juanita was gone.

Frustrated, he hurriedly selected one of the Italian designer suits from the scores that hung in his walk-in closet—a room the size of the hovels in which most of his people lived—and then dressed and ventured down to his immense first-floor office. He snapped at the staff members as he passed, ordering his breakfast, his array of morning papers, the summary of the world's news and economic happenings.

The president was now convinced that this day was about to become much, much better than it had begun.

6

Joe Glass strode into Commodore Jon Ward's office on the third deck of Submarine Squadron Six headquarters. The big square metal building sat at the head of Pier 22, the submarine pier at Naval Base Norfolk. Ward's commodious office filled the entire southwest corner of the upper floor.

Ward looked up from the mound of paperwork on his desk when he heard Glass's footsteps in the hallway.

"Joe, great to see you! Grab a cup of coffee and a chair at the conference table, if you can find anything not covered with file folders." He waved toward the sideboard next to the large oak conference table. "Give me just a minute while I finish this damn report."

Glass knew from long experience that the commodore hated the paper burden that the modern-day Navy generated. Ward's motto was to attack it immediately. Touch it once and get it off his desk. But he would much rather still be at sea, commanding his own submarine, just as he had been when he and Joe Glass served on the same boat, the old *Spadefish*, long since decommissioned. Ward the skipper, Glass his XO.

Glass was pleased to see that his old CO looked as fit as ever, his hair still dark, his face unlined despite the pressure this job had to be putting on him. Jon could probably still jog all the way from Norfolk to the Pentagon and back if he needed to, and never break a sweat.

After procuring and filling his cup, Glass stepped to the broad picture window that looked out over the bustling pier and the three submarines tied up there. He sipped the steaming coffee and gazed out at the busy scene before him.

A semi-truck was working its way through the security checkpoint just below him while another was backing up to his boat. *Toledo* was all the way down at berth Sierra-Six, the outermost parking spot on the south side of the pier. The pier itself was crowded with crates and pallets of equipment and a swarm of workers trying to get onboard to start their workday. Glass appreciated all the attention directed at his boat and quickly surmised that they would not be long for Norfolk. And he also suspected the reason for that quick turnaround was about to be shared with him.

"Quite a view, isn't it, Joe?" Jon Ward observed as he looked up from the thick document he had just signed. "I can really keep an eye on you from up here. I don't even need to walk down for a monitor watch."

Glass smiled easily.

"You know that you are more than welcome on *Toledo* anytime. Only thing is, I'd be afraid you would stow away just to get yourself back at sea." He hesitated for just a second and set his half-empty mug on the conference table. "You didn't call me up here to discuss a monitor watch, though, did you?"

Ward plopped down in the chair at the head of the table. As Glass slid into the one to his right, the commodore slid a heavy manila folder across the table to him. The folder had red and white checkers printed around its edges and "TOP SECRET, SPECIAL HANDLING REQUIRED" in bold red letters across it.

"Your last patrol report, with endorsements," he acknowledged. "We need to discuss it."

"Pretty dry and routine," Glass deadpanned. "Right up to the end, that is, and then five minutes of sphincter-squeezing terror. I sure would like to know how that bastard sneaked up on us. The tapes show anything?"

Not really tapes anymore, though they were still usually referred to that way. *Toledo*'s ARCI sonar system recorded every bit of raw and processed data that it saw onto a removable computer hard drive for post-patrol analysis of every move the boat and crew made during their run. Weeks and weeks of work transformed into trillions of zeros and ones that were then stuffed into a bit of plastic no larger than a deck of cards. It all fed the super computers at Johns Hopkins Applied Physics Lab up in Columbia, Maryland. The scientists and acoustic engineers there used some very advanced algorithms to tease out any information that *Toledo*'s sonar team might have missed.

Ward shook his head.

"The boys at APL have gone through the tapes from every angle. They could find a fish fart at a thousand miles and tell you species, age, and sex of the fish. But there was no sign of any other boat beyond that one distant target you guys saw."

Glass shook his head and squeezed his lips together. He was not surprised. Disappointed but not surprised.

"Pretty much what I expected you to tell me. If Master Chief Zillich and his team didn't detect anything, it just wasn't there."

Ward nodded. Zillich had a very well-earned reputation as the best ears in the submarine force. He trained his sonarmen so that they were very nearly as good as he was and demanded extremely high standards from them.

"I'm betting that you have a sonar team that will breathe a lot easier tonight. But that means we still have a very big problem."

The room was quiet for a moment.

"I'm not nearly as worried about finding that son of a bitch as I am in figuring out how they got the drop on us," Joe Glass finally said, tapping his fingers on the table nervously. "I've got a real quiet boat. We work hard to keep her that way. *Toledo* should have looked like a black hole in the ocean. Somebody went to a lot of trouble to scare the shit out of us, to let us know they had whatever it took to find us and could have just as easily sunk us if they had been of such a mind."

"Exactly my worry," Ward said with a soft blow on the table with his fist. "Your self-noise monitoring and the delousing we did as you came up the coast didn't find a thing. We're worried that the Russians have some secret new toy. We've had hints and snatches for years that they were playing with non-acoustic stuff, some way to detect a sub without using sonar. Maybe magnetic or hydrogen bubbles. Some of the science weenies are even talking neutrinos. Real Buck Rogers stuff."

Glass stood, stepped to the coffee carafe, and refilled his cup. "You need a refill, Jon?"

Ward stuck out his mug. Glass poured it full.

"Thanks. Anyway, maybe the Russians made a breakthrough and shared it with their good buddy, Gutierrez. Or maybe Gutierrez is just being cooperative and the Russians have a safe haven in a swimming pool we've always considered to be ours."

Glass took a sip of the coffee.

"Makes sense for what we saw. But why? Why would the Russians risk our knowing they were operating in our backyard if they didn't have to? Better to stay quiet and watch us instead of giving us such a fright and blowing their cover. Or why would they sell a secret new toy to a big-mouthed blowhard like Gutierrez? He'd be bragging about it on CNN. And why haven't our spooks sniffed it out already if they have something that revolutionary?"

Ward shrugged.

"Good questions, buddy. We have no idea, not even educated guesses."

Glass, unable to sit still, stood right back up and stepped over to the window once more.

"I'm not buying it. At least not yet," he said firmly, his breath fogging the glass. "There has to be some other explanation. Those lab coats have been predicting a transparent ocean since you and I were minnows."

Ward glanced at the back of his old shipmate, then past him to the state-of-the-art submarines resting at the pier below.

"Well, therein lies your next run. I want you to find out. I'm sending *Toledo* down to AUTEC. The guys at NUWC have some new toys of their own that they want to try out and we just upgraded the noise monitoring facility there. We'll sniff out if there is something detectable about your boat that we don't already know about. Anyway, it's about time you had a little Bahamas vacation. But don't tarry. We've got something else cooking where we need your help, too. When can *Toledo* be underway?"

Glass did not even try to suppress his grin. Sea time was always far better than being tied to a pier. And he was eager to see what the mad scientists from Newport's Naval Undersea Weapons Center—the Navy's premier submarine lab—had cooked up. There was no better place to find out than AUTEC, the Navy's super-secret underwater test range hidden among the islands of the Bahamas.

"As soon as we finish the stores load and button up number two motor generator, boss. Figure 0800 tomorrow."

"Send me a T-shirt...and something cold and wet with lots of rum in the recipe."

Commander Joe Glass bounded down the pier on the way back to his boat. His mind raced, putting together a list of details that needed addressing before he could get underway. It would be a very busy day and an even busier night for him, his wardroom, and the rest of the crew.

As he stepped aboard his vessel, he nodded to several civilian workers and thanked them for what they were doing. Had the skipper glanced to his left, he likely would not have even noticed a dark-featured technician doing something to the TB-34 towed array fairing.

But he did not, and the man continued his work, hurrying to finish the job before his shift ended and it was time to go ashore.

7

Ensign James Ward followed SEAL Captain Bill Beaman down yet another nondescript gray corridor. Paint peeled from the walls and dust bunnies danced away from them as they passed. Many of the side corridors were stacked with storage boxes and unused government-issue office furniture. Ward had long since lost his sense of direction after entering this maze. The Pentagon was certainly a "five-sided puzzle palace" in more ways than one.

As he and his guide passed a doorway marked OPNAV N67, he glanced inside and overheard a snippet of conversation. A Navy captain was on the receiving end of a rather loud "professional development training" session on how the rear admiral took his coffee and preferred his newspaper folded.

Captain Bill Beaman heard it, too. He grinned as he hurried on, taking a left and then a right, until they were in a corridor marked "E Ring." Beaman finally pulled to a halt in front of an unmarked gray door. He hesitated only an instant before opening it without knocking and quickly stepping into the midst of a veritable beehive of activity. Thirty or forty people manned desks around the big room, chattering on red phones or typing away at secure SIPRNET terminals.

Without even slowing his stride, Beaman walked down a cluttered aisle toward a dark oak door at the back of the room. The young, fresh-faced lieutenant who was guarding the door to the inner sanctum looked up from his desk.

"Captain Beaman, welcome back. The admiral is expecting you. You and Ensign Ward, too. Go right in."

"Thanks, Steve," Beaman responded, smiling easily and shaking hands with the young officer. Still hardly breaking stride, he opened the door and walked in.

Jim Ward, wide-eyed, nodded to the lieutenant as he followed Beaman into the room. Somebody inside the Pentagon actually knew his name. Imagine that.

The office was bare-bones except for the massive beaten and worn oak desk that dominated the room. It had followed its owner around for years, from one duty station to another, and was not about to be replaced by generic Navy-issue furniture just because his latest office was inside this fortress-like structure.

Vice Admiral Tom Donnegan rose as they entered and stepped from behind the desk to greet them. Tall and imposing, the black man's graying hair and deeply furrowed brow gave him the air of someone who spent a great deal of his time in deep thought. But his broad smile and the friendly twinkle in his brown eyes radiated sincere delight at welcoming the pair.

"Bill! Jim! Great to see you two," he roared. He grabbed Beaman in a massive bear hug, and then Ward. "Damn, Jim! You sure have grown. It seems only yesterday that your daddy was your age. Time flies when you're stamping out brushfires and taming bad people."

Despite their differences in rank, the young SEAL and the vice admiral had much in common and a long history. Tom

Donnegan—or Papa Tom, as Jim Ward knew him—had been his grandfather's executive officer and best friend. He had all but raised a young Jon Ward—Jim's father—after Bill Ward failed to return from a mission that was still highly classified. He had always served as the missing dad for Commodore Jon Ward and the missing grandfather for Jim and his sister.

But now the roles were different. Donnegan was the Commander of Naval Intelligence at the Pentagon. Jon Ward commanded the submarine squadron based in Norfolk. Jim Ward, the third in line in his family for a Navy career, was a newly-minted SEAL.

Of course, Bill Beaman was one of his dad's best friends, too. Beaman and Jon Ward had been through many hairy scrapes together and—so far, at least—had actually survived to talk about them. That is, so long as they only talked to each other and the few people with the appropriate highest-level security clearance.

After a very non-military bear hug for young Ward, Admiral Donnegan stepped back and slipped immediately into his role. Friendships and shared family history were abruptly shoved aside. Admiral Donnegan had a mission for the young SEAL and his seasoned tour guide.

"Pull up a chair, you two," Donnegan ordered. He sat down at the head of the little conference table that filled a corner of his office. It was beside the office's only window, one that afforded the admiral a view of the Potomac, but he rarely took the opportunity to enjoy it. He slid a thick file across the table to a spot between the two. "I need some help. We're having an unexplained problem in Cuba. It may be nothing, but for some reason pretty much all our comms intercepts have dried up in the last couple of weeks. There is almost nothing on the air, and that has never happened. At least since they became our new best friends to the south. Something's up. I can feel it and I don't like it. Most of all, I don't like not knowing what I don't know."

He motioned for Beaman to open the folder. Several photographs, obviously taken from a hidden camera, showed various men climbing in or out of vehicles outside what looked like a large government building. Except for the palm trees in the background, the pictures could have been taken anywhere. Along with the blurry images were several pages of closely typed text.

Beaman leafed through them and passed them to Ward.

"Admiral, you saying the Agency is not telling you what might be going on?" the older SEAL asked.

"Not a hell of a lot. Even their sources are having trouble getting any news. At least, that is what they are telling me. That raises my curiosity even more. I hear they are looking to insert some more assets, but who the hell knows who, when, or where? They're still a jealous bunch sometimes and don't like to share their travel plans until they know for sure they'll come out looking good or can claim all the credit without accepting an ounce of the blame. So, bottom line, I don't really trust 'em."

Jim Ward glanced through the photos, then stopped and studied one before holding it up for the other two men to see.

"Who is this guy?" he asked, pointing to a well-dressed Anglo who was stepping out of a 1957 Cadillac. "He doesn't fit."

Donnegan smiled.

"Just like your old man. No finesse at all. Right to the tough questions. The answer is that we don't know who the guy is. And as previously mentioned, I don't like being so damned ignorant."

Donnegan paused as he took a sip of his coffee, then grabbed a sheet of paper and scooted it to the center of the table. Ward could see that it was a small-scale chart of the Caribbean Sea.

"Lots of things have been happening in Havana, but the

most interesting to me is out here," Donnegan began, tapping on a position in the southern part of the island. "Over around the Zapata Peninsula and down to Cienfuegos, we are getting hints of unusual activity. What looks to be a large, deep-sea survey vessel has been in and out of here several times. We are also getting some signs of Venezuelan naval activity. It is even possible that one of their *Kilo* submarines has visited and has been doing operations in the region, and I don't think they were sightseeing in that hellhole. They've even been messing with one of our submarines down there, and you know how that kind of monkey business would get stuck in my craw."

Beaman nodded as he scrutinized the chart.

"That is a pretty isolated piece of real estate out there," he said, massaging his chin as he thought. "Nothing but sand and scorpions. Isn't that where we determined that they held the Bay of Pigs prisoners back in the sixties? And, of course, by 'held' I mean 'tortured and murdered.'"

"Yep." Donnegan put his finger on a tiny peninsula off the main island west of Cienfuegos that pointed like a finger toward the Isle of Pines. "Right here. It is still an active penal facility, although I doubt if any survivors of that cluster-freak are still there. Mostly guys there now who had the audacity to question something Fidel did or said. Or just dozed off and snored during one of the bastard's speeches. We hear there may be a few guys who got crosswise with some of Fidel's plans in Latin America. Maybe in the Iran-Contra crap."

Donnegan pointed a finger at the young SEAL. "Jim, here's the deal. We are going to insert you and your team in here to see if you can tell us what is going on down there. We will put you ashore, then we want you to set up and spend a few days leisurely watching whatever is coming and going before we extract you. A simple in-and-out. Find out about this survey ship and the submarine, if you see them. We're really interested in that survey ship. Who is it and what are they doing there? And though we are pretty sure where the warship is coming from, any confirmation would help us."

He smiled and added, "Your dad's old XO, Joe Glass, will be standing by offshore in his submersible yacht *Toledo* and will relay comms and give you a hand if you need it. That is, if you behave and manage not to get your asses caught. Which you best not do, by the way, since I have deemed your little mission to remain a secret to the CIA, the rest of the US Navy, and the Joint Chiefs of Staff for the time being. Because, if you really want to know, I don't trust a couple of the bastards. But if you do —get your ass caught, that is—I don't know you, your daddy, or your beautiful mother and sister. Any questions?"

Young Ward shook his head. He knew there would be plenty of briefings and stacks of intel coming that would tell him much, much more, and that he would find out what Captain Beaman had to do with this little trip to the beach other than showing him the way to Admiral Donnegan's office in the Pentagon. But he was savvy enough to understand this mission had to be very important. Otherwise, Vice Admiral Donnegan would not be willing to risk putting combat troops ashore in Cuba, potentially rubbing salt into one of the most tender, sore scars on the face of the planet.

"No, sir. Pretty straightforward. Slip in, take a look, make plenty of notes, slip out." Ward knew all about special allowances and processes under which personnel such as SEALs could be inserted into sovereign nations, but he doubted Cuba had signed off on any such accords. It would be a major international blow-up if things went screwy. But it was not his place to question the politics of the situation.

"Son, seriously, be careful," Admiral Donnegan told him, and there was no mistaking the gravity in his deep brown eyes. "I tell all my boys that when I send them off to jump into the middle of a pile of dog shit, but you know I mean it just a tad more when I tell you. I never burped those guys or changed their dirty diapers. But as much as I love you, you know as well as I do that I wouldn't be putting you in there if I didn't believe you were the best man and had the best team for the job."

"I know, sir. I appreciate it."

The two SEALs stood and shook hands with Donnegan, then turned and walked out of the office just as briskly as they had approached it.

Beaman remained markedly quiet as they strode through the warren of gray, dusty passageways. He did not speak, even as they exited the building near where the terrorists crashed the passenger airplane against the Pentagon's façade on September 11, 2001. Several bouquets of fresh flowers and a wreath or two were lying about, recently placed there by family members and others who still felt the need—approaching two decades later—to pay their respects to those who died so needlessly that awful day.

Ψ

Joe Glass took a half step back as Brian Edwards, his XO, pored over the electronic chart table in front of them. In Edwards's left hand, he firmly clutched the UQC underwater telephone microphone. The aft section of the submarine's control room was a blur of activity centered around the two glass-topped chart tables. There was barely room to turn around in the crowded space.

Edwards was intently studying a very detailed bathymetric survey of Tongue of the Ocean, the small deep-water extension of Exuma Sound tucked between several tiny islands and broad coral reefs in the Southern Bahamas.

Jerry Perez, the *Toledo*'s navigator, stood beside the port chart table, watching closely as Dennis Oshley, his best quartermaster, plotted the latest position fix. Range Control, in a blockhouse over on Andros Island, was monitoring *Toledo*'s every move using a very sensitive sonar array implanted on the ocean bottom. They were sending a position report over the underwater telephone about every five minutes.

As Oshley laid down his fix, the BQN-17 fathometer operator standing in front of his complex bank of equipment on the port side of the narrow passageway read the output from his covert depth-finding sonar.

"Depth one-two hundred fathoms," he called out. Just over seven thousand feet.

The quartermaster checked the charted depth against the fathometer operator's report.

"Depth checks."

All was well. There was a very good likelihood that the submarine really was where they thought it was, or at least within a couple of hundred yards.

The Tongue was an ideal place for these classified experiments. Located way down in the southeast corner of the Bahamas, far from cruise ships and party boats that floated over from Florida, it was isolated enough that the waters were very quiet. Even migrating whales seldom strayed into the tiny bay. The scientists could use their most sensitive sensors without too much worry about interfering noise. And the reefs meant that there was only one way in, past the Navy's Acoustic Training Range Exuma Sound. It was all but impossible for a submarine to sneak in to monitor what might be happening in the Tongue. But the problem was that the Tongue was small. The steep granite walls loomed menacingly, ready to smash the unwary submarine that ventured outside the tiny safe box.

"How we doing, XO?" Glass queried.

The young commander looked up, rubbed the little patch of

blond hair on top of his head, and smiled.

"One more run past the buoy, Skipper," he answered. "We're winding this one up now. I figure another couple of hours and then we can head on out of this little fish bowl."

Glass looked at the chart. Electronic traces recorded *Toledo*'s activity for the last forty-eight hours, innumerable runs back and forth past a buoy planted dead center in the middle of the Tongue.

"I'll be as glad to get out of here as you will," Glass told him. He agreed with Edwards's discomfort with steaming in such restricted waters. "I sure hope those eggheads topside are getting what they're looking for."

"And that would be what, exactly?" Edwards asked.

"I haven't a clue," Glass answered. "You were at the same test brief that I was. They just said to run past the buoy at the ranges and bearings in that test plan. I'm assuming that they are gathering whatever data they want. Otherwise I figure they would tell us to keep swimming in circles for a while."

"Just another case of the old Navy way," Edwards snorted. "Ours is not to question why, ours is but to do or die."

Glass chuckled. "Let's not dwell on that 'die' part."

He stepped forward, onto the slightly raised periscope stand. The slim silver tubes of the Type 18 and Type 8B periscopes protruded from the deck and extended through a maze of piping into the overhead. At this ship's depth, the periscopes were lowered and housed in a well that extended all the way down to the submarine's keel. Only scope barrels were visible in the control room.

Eric Hobson, the officer of the deck, had staked out a position leaning against the low stainless-steel handrail that separated the periscope stand from the ship's control station. Hobson, *Toledo*'s weapons officer, was casually watching as Master Chief Sam Wallich, the on-watch diving officer, was expounding to the young helmsman and planesman about the finer points of driving a *Los Angeles*-class submarine.

The two kids, Fireman Apprentice Josh Stedman and Seaman Will Brownson, were barely old enough to drive their dad's car, yet today they were guiding a billion-dollar nuclear submarine with one hundred and fifty people onboard.

Stedman, the helmsman, sat on the starboard side facing a control wheel that closely mimicked the one on a B-52 bomber. When he turned the truncated wheel, the submarine's rudder nudged the big boat to the right or left. When he pulled or pushed the stick, the bow planes caused the boat to rise toward the surface or dive deeper into the ocean.

Brownson sat to the port side and faced a control wheel just like the one Stedman held. When he pulled back or pushed forward on his stick, a massive hydraulic piston all the way back in the after-most part of the engine room shoved the stern planes up or down, which caused *Toledo* to angle in either direction.

The big difference between flying *Toledo* and flying a B-52 was the bomber pilots could look out a window to see where they were going. Brownson and Stedman faced a panel filled with gauges and digital displays that indicated depth, speed, course, and ship's angle but afforded no view whatsoever of their outside environment.

Together, the two, under Wallich's careful guidance and an occasional rap on the back of a head, steered the submarine and maintained the ordered depth and angle.

Just outboard of Brownson, tucked into the corner of the compartment, Bill Dooley sat in front of the ballast control panel. The *Toledo*'s leading torpedoman, he was much more at home two decks down with his beloved torpedoes than he was up here in the control room being the chief of the watch.

From the mass of dials, switches, and knobs that filled the

BCP, Dooley maintained the ship's trim by pumping water between various tanks located around the boat. At the after part of the BCP were the controls for the submarine's hydraulic plant, the lifeblood for controlling the vessel. Above these controls was a maze of gauges and dials to feed Dooley information about air pressures, hydraulic pressures, and levels in various tanks and flasks around the submarine.

Just above the BCP were two large brass handles. These were the emergency blow valves, or "chicken switches." If Dooley pushed these handles up, the entire contents of the sub's 4,500-pound air flasks would immediately be dumped into the main ballast tanks. *Toledo* would be bobbing on the surface in seconds.

Joe Glass flipped down the little seat outboard and aft of the Type 18 scope. Seated here, he could watch the entire control room while easing his aching back. He did not remember it hurting so much when he was a young junior officer or even when he was Jon Ward's XO on *Spadefish*. But it sure ached now. Getting old was a bitch.

"Skipper," Edwards called out. "Range Control wants us to come to PD. There is high priority message traffic we need to copy."

Glass could just hear the exchange over the UQC.

"Sierra November, this is Range Control. Come to papa delta on corpen two-one-niner. I say again come to papa delta on corpen two-one-niner. Range is clear of all surface contacts."

Glass nodded to Edwards.

"Acknowledge them and tell Range Control that we are coming shallow. Mr. Hobson, come to one-five-zero feet and clear baffles."

Glass listened as Edwards told Range Control their intentions and Hobson brought the boat nearer the surface of the green sea.

"Sonar, Conn," Hobson said into the 21MC microphone. "Coming to one-five-zero feet. Clearing baffles to the right in preparation for coming to periscope depth."

"Clearing baffles to the right, Conn, Sonar, aye," Master Chief Zillich boomed over the 21MC speaker.

Hobson turned to the ship control team. "Dive, make your depth one-five-zero feet."

Master Chief Wallich glanced at the ship control panel. "Make my depth one-five-zero feet, aye. Seven-two-five feet, coming to one-five-zero."

He turned to Stedman and Brownson.

"Five-degree up angle, full rise on the bow planes."

The two kids pulled back on their control columns, putting rise on the bow planes and stern planes. The deck tilted up as the depth gauge reeled off the change. The huge black denizen of the deep easily rose toward the tropical daylight.

"Depth one-five-zero feet," Wallich reported.

"Very well. Helm, right full rudder, steady course two-one-nine. All ahead two-thirds," Hobson ordered Stedman.

"Right full rudder, aye. Zero-nine-five, coming to two-one-nine. Answers ahead two-thirds," Stedman said as he turned the wheel to the right. The large compass repeater on the ship control panel spun around to the right, the only indication anyone onboard the submarine had that *Toledo* was changing course.

The entire operation resembled a well-choreographed dance accompanied by a choir singing lyrics perfectly on cue and in tune.

As the boat swung around, Zillich and his carefully trained sonarmen searched the depths around *Toledo* to make sure that they were all alone in this bit of ocean. They paid particular attention to the quadrant that had previously been behind the sub. Popularly known as the "baffles," this area was masked to the submarine's sonar by her own bulk and the noise from her screw.

Finally Zillich reported, "Careful search of previously baffled area. No new contacts. Only contacts held are sierra two-one, range buoy pinger, bearing one-two-three, past CPA drawing aft, estimated range seven hundred yards. Sierra two-two, classified range support craft, bearing three-two-seven, past CPA and opening, best range estimate two-seven thousand yards. Sonar holds no other contacts."

"Sonar, Conn, aye," Hobson answered. In rapid, well-practiced sequence, he ordered, "Silence in Control, proceeding to periscope depth. Helm ahead one-third. Dive, make your depth six-two feet. Raising number two scope."

"Speed seven," Dooley called out, verifying to Hobson that it was safe to raise the periscope.

Hobson reached into the overhead and grabbed the large red ring encircling the scope, then snapped it a quarter turn counterclockwise. The scope slid smoothly out of the well. He squatted down, and as the eye box emerged from the scope well, he flipped down the control handles before putting his eye to the eyepiece. Rotating the right-hand grip shifted the scope's prism so that he was looking up into the blue water outside.

The control room had suddenly become very quiet. Everyone onboard knew that coming to periscope depth was the most dangerous evolution that a submarine did on a routine basis. Even with all the modern, sophisticated sonar sensors, there was a very real possibility of the submarine finding an unknown hazard the hard way. Whether it was a quiet sailboat, a ship hidden by an unexpected sonar layer, or just a log floating on the surface, it could do damage. They could and had all ruined a submariner's day. The tension in the tiny room was palpable.

"One-two-five, coming to six-two feet," Wallich called out,

his voice the only sound in the control room.

"One-one-zero, coming to six-two feet."

Hobson walked a slow circle, "dancing with the fat lady" in submariner jargon. He peered intently through the scope, watching for the dim gray shape of an undetected ship's underwater hull. Not a sound from the gathered team.

Glass stood, casually stepped closer, and whispered into Hobson's ear, "You see a hull close aboard."

Hobson yelled, "Emergency deep!" as he slapped the scope handles up. Even as he reached into the overhead to lower the scope, he heard the engine order telegraph ring up, "All ahead full."

As Sam Wallich was ordering full dive, Bill Dooley started flooding water into the depth control tanks with one hand while yelling "Emergency deep!" into the 1MC general announcing system microphone that he had grabbed with the other hand.

The big boat pitched over and angled down. It shot forward, heading back to the safety of the dark-blue depths. Within seconds, they were leveling off at one-five-zero feet, safely clear of the imaginary hazard.

Glass glanced at his watch. Not bad, fifteen seconds from his first whispered words in Hobson's ear until they leveled off at a safe depth. But every second wasted might be the difference between life and death, a well-run operation or disaster.

The crew had done well, but maybe they could shave off another couple of seconds, Glass thought.

Edwards, still red-faced and breathing hard from the unexpected excitement, stepped up beside Glass.

"Damn, Skipper! You could tell me when you're going to pull stunts like that!"

"Woke you up, did I?" Glass kidded the XO. "You gotta be ready all the time, every time. That means you and me, too." In a more serious tone, he continued, "Fifteen seconds that time, and they were caught totally off-guard. Not bad, but we can do better. Now, let's go see what the outside world wants with us."

"Mr. Hobson, proceed to periscope depth and copy the broadcast."

The choir and the dance resumed as if nothing had interrupted their performance.

Five minutes later the submarine's periscope pierced the surface. Eric Hobson looked out onto a bright blue sea and an even brighter blue sky. He spun around quickly, looking for anything that might be close to *Toledo*.

"No close contacts. Raise the HDR mast."

People in the control room took a deep breath and then resumed their normal business. Once more the submarine had made the transition safely. *Toledo* always had, but it only took one time.

Bill Dooley reached up on the BCP and flipped a switch.

"HDR mast coming up."

Just as Hobson caught a glimpse of the odd-shaped antenna rising above the surface, he heard a voice crackling on the 21MC circuit.

"Conn, Radio, in sync on the broadcast." That was followed seconds later by the report: "Conn, Radio, all traffic onboard and receipted for."

The whole process was very different from the old days when a radio operator had to copy by hand traffic sent in Morse code groups. Now they arrived by digital packet and receipt was almost instantaneous, regardless of message length.

Hobson made one last sweep around, enjoying the tropical sea view, then ordered, "Lower the HDR mast. Dive, make your depth one-five-zero feet. Number two 'scope coming down."

The sub angled downward on his command as he reached up to snap the control ring to lower the periscope.

"Depth nine-zero feet, coming to one-five-zero," Wallich

called out.

"Conn, Radio, request the captain lay to Radio."

Glass had been expecting this request and was already heading to the aft control room door. He slipped past the ESGN housing hanging from the overhead before sliding open the radio room door. The space inside, barely the size of a large closet, was crammed full of electronic equipment, with an array of blinking LEDs and LCD displays.

Radioman First Class Sam Seidiman handed Glass an aluminum clipboard prominently labeled TOP SECRET.

Glass flipped up the cover and quickly scanned the message. Without hesitation, he grabbed the 7MC microphone, cleared his throat, and pushed the "talk" button.

"Officer of the Deck, come to six hundred feet, course west. Ahead flank. XO, tell Range Control that we are departing on a higher priority mission. Please clear the training range for us and route us to the Exuma Passage."

As Glass walked back into the control room, he felt the boat tilt down toward six hundred feet. He also felt the bump as the reactor coolant check valves slammed shut as the huge pumps shifted to fast speed. *Toledo* leaped ahead exactly as commanded.

The skipper handed the clipboard to Edwards.

"Looks like some SEALs over in Cuba may need a lift." The skipper ignored his second-in-command's puzzled expression. "Plot the fastest course to the Zapata Peninsula on the southern coast of Cuba. SUBFOR has given us all the waters from here, through the Windward Passage, and down to the workers' paradise."

Edwards glanced up from the clipboard.

"You mean Gitmo."

"No. No, I mean Cuba."

"Jesus."

8

The sweet-rotten smell of a tropical island rode the warm offshore breeze far out to sea. Jim Ward almost laughed as he pulled on the wetsuit. A swim in these Caribbean waters would be a whole lot more pleasant than Alaska, where he had taken his unexpected dip the previous week. That little adventure now seemed like months ago.

"Here, Skipper, let me help." Sean Horton grabbed the back of Ward's stubborn wetsuit and yanked it up. The big black SEAL almost lifted Ward off the little fishing boat's deck as he pulled the tight-fitting, one-piece black suit up over Ward's broad shoulders.

The moon had set hours before. The night was inky black. No sign of another boat anywhere out to the horizon, only brilliantly bright stars and the soot-black water. Ward knew that the southern coast of Cuba was just a few miles to the north, but he couldn't see even the glimmer of a light in that direction.

The charter boat's motor hushed down to a burbling idle. The captain leaned out of the tiny wheelhouse.

"This here be as close as we gone wanna get, mon," he muttered in his singsong Jamaican accent, so heavy that Ward could hardly understand him. Despite the inflection, Ward had every reason to assume that the man was a CIA agent. Why else would he take a charter from Kingston to within spitting distance of Cuba's southwest coast? A charter in which the fishing rods and tackle aboard were never touched by the four-man party that brought aboard diving gear and mysterious black bags. And the charter captain never questioned them when they covered their gear with ice in the hold where fish would normally be stored.

"Any closer and we gonna be one pretty picture on they radar," he went on, his nerves making him even harder to understand. "I'd just as soon not have me no discussion with one of they patrol boats, if you please. They have demselves one bad habit of shootin' through the wheelhouse to get a cap'n's attention, you know?"

That sentiment Jim Ward understood perfectly. The young SEAL quickly checked his GPS.

"No, this is good. We can go swimming from here."

Jed Dulkowski lowered their gear down to Horton, who stood on the diving platform just inches above the water. Tony Garcia was already in the Caribbean, steadying one of the diving sleds as the other team members loaded the bags onto it.

The diving sleds were a very useful bit of technology. Officially named the 4500-100 Diver Propulsion Device, or DPD, they were ideal for situations such as this. Lithium ion battery-powered, they could silently tow a diver at about three knots for a couple of hours. It greatly extended the SEALs' range and allowed them to arrive on the beach relatively rested and—if everything else went okay—undetected. Equipped with two propulsion batteries, these units were good for better than fifteen miles. And the RNAV Recon Navigation System gave the SEALs both a relatively accurate inertial navigation system and a GPS on a folding mast.

Ward checked his positioning again, just to be sure.

"I figure about three miles on a bearing of three-two-five," he stated. "Should be ashore in fifty minutes, given the reported current. That should give us plenty of time to cover our tracks and get settled in before daylight."

Horton called up from below, "Sleds are loaded, Skipper. We'd better get a move on. Time's a'wastin'." Ward glanced up at the boat captain. "Pick us up at this location in three nights, same time as now, as planned," he told him. "If we aren't here on the third night, try again on the fourth. If we aren't here then, we probably aren't coming. You may want to watch CNN and get the rest of the story. Thanks for the lift."

The charter captain touched the brim of his oily cap with a casual salute and a broad smile, showing a gold tooth with a gemstone embedded in it.

With that, Ward put his regulator in his mouth and calmly stepped over the side. The warm Caribbean waters immediately surrounded him, bath water compared to his most recent swim. He popped to the surface and grabbed the sled that Garcia shoved over to him. After taking a quick bearing, he dropped below the surface again.

Trimmed to be neutrally buoyant, even with the SEAL's load of gear, the sled glided easily downward. Ward twisted the control yoke to bring the little unit up to a good cruising speed and swung around to line up on the RNAV's suggested heading.

Horton, Dulkowski, and Garcia formed a line behind him, each following the tiny infrared beacon from the diver ahead. The team slipped down to twenty-five feet and headed for the shore. Bits of bioluminescence flashed by the team like tracer fire.

Welcoming fireworks. What could be nicer? The young SEAL thought to himself how much more he enjoyed this, being on the move, swimming stealthily toward an objective, leading his team toward a mission that was, finally, for real and not just another exercise. It was much better than the last few days had been, stuck in stuffy briefing rooms, poring over maps and satellite photos and identification manuals.

But he was unable to stop thinking about just how critical—and dangerous—this assignment they had drawn would be. Or the consequences if it went bad. He had so far tried to forget what the international ramifications would be if he and his team were discovered "invading" a place like Cuba.

Ward checked his RNAV every couple of minutes and kept his sled headed on a precise course of three-two-five. Sticking the mast above water to use the GPS when they were this close to the coast would only invite detection. He could only hope that he had guessed right on the current and that his bearings were accurate. The RNAV's inertial system should compensate for the current, but the operative word was "should." A mistake of only a few degrees could put his team out in open water, heading for New Orleans. Or worse still, they could pop up right in the middle of the fishing boats at Cienfuegos. Being an unwilling guest of the Cubans was not on young Ward's social agenda.

After forty-five minutes of swimming, the white sandy bottom emerged out of the gloomy darkness beneath them. Ward led them on, cruising just a couple of feet off the seabed, just high enough not to kick up a cloud of silt as they were forced closer to the surface.

Ward spotted a huge brain coral just in time to miss crashing into it. He whipped the control yoke to the left, but the coral still scraped down the tiny sled's side. Better slow down and be a little more careful. There was no telling what might be sticking out of the bottom now that they were entering the tiny, shallow bay. He eased back on the throttle, swung the sled back on course, and motored on toward the beach.

Finally, the team lay on the bottom just beyond the surf line.

Three of them stayed fully underwater while Ward stuck his head up, but only high enough to take a quick look around. All four men gripped their M-4 carbines, anticipating possible bursts of gunfire from the tree line or a nearby patrol boat. That would be a decidedly bad way to learn that they had a warm-welcoming party.

The SEAL team lay there like that for what seemed an eternity, checking, watching, observing, hiding. The sun was just making a pale glimmering glow on the eastern horizon when they finally rose from the surf and scurried across the white sand beach. The sleds, so light and easy to handle in the water, were a real load for the SEALs now that they were on land. At 170 pounds each, lugging them across the soft sand was a chore. Three of them quickly buried the sleds and dive gear while Garcia swept the sand with a palm frond, removing all traces of their passage. Then they crouched in the thick vegetation at the edge of the beach until they were reasonably sure nobody but the sand crabs had seen them come ashore.

"Time to move out," Ward told them in a low voice, pointing toward the northeast. "We need to get up over that hill before we hole up for the day."

Thankfully, the terrain looked exactly as they expected from their briefings, a deserted stretch of sand quickly giving way to dunes and thick pines. The biting sand flies and bloodthirsty mosquitoes were so prevalent here that no beachgoers frequented the area. Now, if the SEALs were where they were supposed to be, they would find plenty of cover a few hundred yards inland while easily observing the comings and goings in the little patch of protected water to their east.

The SEALs shouldered their packs and silently slipped off through the jungle.

Ψ

Slowly, cautiously, the submarine *Almirante Villaregoz* rose toward the surface. The *Kilo*-class Russian-built ship leveled off at seventeen meters, deep enough that the periscope would just protrude above the surface of the Caribbean when it was fully extended.

Captain Alejandro Ramirez had been patrolling just offshore from Cuba and the Cape Zapata base for the past week. He was still not certain what Admiral Valdez wanted him to find here, but he was very sure that he would stay in position until he found it. Ramirez had never been one to question or disappoint his immediate superior. Still, he was especially grateful to no longer have *el almirante* aboard his submarine, watching his every move with those cold, dark eyes of his.

Ramirez and his submarine crew had slipped into a routine. Every night they would head out to deep water fifteen miles south of the coastline. No chance of the Cubans seeing them there. He had the crew snorkel to recharge the giant batteries while he slept. His Russian instructor had hammered into Ramirez that a smart submariner took every opportunity to keep his main batteries fully topped off.

In the morning, they resumed patrolling a few hundred meters off the Cuban coast. Back and forth, back and forth. It was incredibly boring work. Ramirez hated every minute of it. Occasionally a patrol boat would come out of the harbor and putter around lazily for a few hours before going back home. Once, the big survey ship that Ramirez guessed belonged to—or was working on behalf of—*Presidente* Gutierrez's government-controlled oil company had steamed out and over the horizon to the west. Other than that, nothing.

The boredom left Ramirez even more irritable and short of patience than usual.

"Raise the periscope," he snapped.

The young seaman standing against the bulkhead pulled the handle. The periscope slowly glided up from its well.

When it was fully raised, Ramirez stretched up on his toes, making himself as tall as possible. He placed his eye to the eyepiece and slowly gazed at the sea around them, trying to hide his anger. Damn insolent crew! They never could get the scope adjusted so he was comfortable using it, almost as if they were making light of his short stature. Even now, he thought he heard them snicker behind him, amused at his discomfort.

He saw nothing new out there, pretty much the same view that had greeted him every single morning since they arrived. Plenty of blue water all around. To the north, a narrow slash of white beach separated the water from the deep green jumble of pine trees that rose up toward the hills. The narrow seaward entrance to the Zapata Base cut a channel through the beach to a clutch of buildings barely visible a kilometer or so inland. The only thing new today was a rundown fishing boat that eased along nonchalantly a couple of miles out to sea.

The submarine captain yawned and settled down to another boring day.

"A cup of coffee," he growled. "Damn it, get me a cup of coffee! By now, I should not have to ask. Here, First Officer," he barked to Lieutenant Armando Vasquez, his second-in-command. "You get a headache staring out that damned pipe. I am going to enjoy my coffee, if it ever appears. These godforsaken peasants! How do they expect me to run a submarine effectively with a crew like this?"

Vasquez, tall and dark with Latin good looks, ignored his captain's grousing. He stepped up to the periscope and raised it another six inches so that he would not have to bend over quite so far to use it.

The crew stared intently at their panels and gauges, not daring a glance toward the periscope stand, trying desperately to put as much distance as possible between themselves and the sawed-off little tyrant that commanded their vessel. Anytime he was in the con, those who could not find an excuse to be somewhere else shrank back into the piping and did all they could to look extremely busy. No one wanted to get on the captain's bad side. Tough as it was, this was a far better job than picking coffee beans or manhandling loads of cocaine down from the mountains.

The seaman handed Ramirez the steaming hot coffee. The poor man's hands were shaking so badly that he spilled a few drops onto the deck. The irascible commander took the cup and then backhanded the seaman, slamming him backward into the wall that lined the outboard bulkhead. The seaman hit his head hard on one of the pipes, opening a gash on his forehead.

His face blotched red with rage, Ramirez shouted, "On the deck, you incompetent fool. Lick up every last drop! Coffee and blood both!"

The crewman, his face dripping blood, dropped to his knees as ordered and obediently began licking the deck. Ramirez kicked the man hard in his ribs. Glancing over at his first officer, he yelled, "Vasquez, you can keep that look off your face. You are no better than the rest of this incompetent crew with which I am saddled. Do you see anything up there or are you asleep?"

Vasquez looked up from the scope, trying not to clench his fists or allow his disgust to show on his face.

"Captain, I have been searching the sea as you ordered. Nothing out here but that rusty old fishing boat. Not a thing stirring at the base. The *Cubanos* probably have not even awakened yet."

The first officer returned to the periscope, speaking low enough that no one—and especially his captain—could hear him.

"Piece of shit. Thinks he is *Dios* just because his mother-in-law sleeps with the admiral."

Ψ

TJ Dillon was a few minutes early arriving at the coffee shop near Washington, D.C. Starbucks in the Crystal City Underground was an ideal place to meet someone without causing much notice. The coffee shop served thousands of office workers who daily populated the towers that stretched skyward. Two friends bumping into each other during their coffee break was the perfect cover. There were far too many people and too much foot traffic to raise suspicion. They would be hiding in plain sight, which was, after all, usually the best place for such a thing.

Nevertheless, Dillon had learned many years ago to do his homework and fully scout out the environment before ever conducting a covert meeting. He stood back in the shadows deep inside the newsstand, idly browsing through the latest edition of *The New Yorker*, even smiling at the cartoons as he watched the crowds surge and ebb, looking for any patterns, anyone who looked out of place. He scoped quick exits where it would be easy to blend in with the morning crowd and disappear should something not smell right to him.

Josh Kirkland was clearly visible as he walked in from the South Street entrance. He strolled nonchalantly into Starbucks and took a place in the long line, waiting to order his coffee.

Dillon watched for a while from his hiding place across the pavilion. The newsstand kiosk owner glanced over occasionally, his demeanor slowly changing from helpful to surly as he assumed that Dillon was not a paying customer, just another office drone killing time before slumping to his cubicle for the day.

Kirkland bought a cup of black coffee and then sat sipping it and browsing the *USA Today*, occasionally checking his watch as if burning time before going upstairs for a meeting.

After fifteen minutes, TJ Dillon finally put down the magazine, touched a few more titles on the rack as if he were going to pick one up, and then sauntered over, picked the shortest line, and bought his own cup of coffee before approaching Kirkland's table.

"Mind if I join you?" Dillon drawled. He plopped down before the CIA man could answer.

"Sure," he said with a smile. "But you're ten minutes late."

"Can't be too careful," Dillon shot back. "Never know when the IRS might be checking to make sure your business expenses are legit."

"True, true," Kirkland answered as his eyes wandered to an attractive young secretary in a particularly short skirt ordering some kind of complicated concoction at the counter. "Wouldn't mind checking out her business expenses."

TJ took a sip of his coffee. He hardly tasted it.

"I don't think you brought me all the way across the fruited plain to admire the local scenery. And by the way, you ever heard of FedEx? I hear they do a decent job of getting packages to people. So. What've you got for me this time?"

"The problem with you is that you're always in a hurry," Kirkland shot back. "Impetuous youth. You don't take time to savor life's unexpected little pleasures." He continued to eye the woman's long, slender legs as she poured sweet chemicals into her coffee and tasted it. "Or appreciate the intricacies of what we do and why we do it."

He folded the newspaper carefully and laid it precisely in the center of the small twisted-wire table, inches from Dillon's coffee cup. He then took another deliberate sip of his own coffee. The fun and games were over. Time for business.

"We need you to take a little Caribbean holiday," he started, keeping his cup at his lips, as if taking sips between sentences. "Havana is particularly nice this time of year. Go in on commercial air through Mexico City. Something is happening that has the Cubans all a'twitter, and it's not just all the warm feelings from our current executive branch. Okay, so we re-opened the damn embassy. We haven't seen this much activity at the highest levels in years. Or had so many sources suddenly go deaf and blind on us. And we have no idea what is going on."

"So you want me to slip in, snoop around a little, and slip back out," Dillon answered, his own hand nonchalantly shielding his mouth with a napkin.

"And a bit more. It seems that Marco Esteban has dropped out of sight," Kirkland added.

For a split second, TJ Dillon's world closed around him. His vision darkened and his mind spun. This was a name never spoken in his family. Here was pure evil.

Marco Esteban, Cuba's answer to the devil and their master spy. He had also been the man who tortured and apparently murdered TJ's father, TJ Senior, after he was captured in Nicaragua. The elder Dillon had been assisting Contra fighters in their battle against that squalid country's corrupt and evil socialist government.

The details the military shared publicly were hazy. A simple, routine training exercise had gone bad. Official word was that during that training mission—supposedly in far friendlier Costa Rica—there had been an accident. A parachute failed. TJ Senior's body had never been found.

Then there had been a remembrance ceremony. A 21-gun salute. A folded flag. But no grave, no marker, nothing.

Then, ten years later, there had been a knock on the door in the middle of the night. A pair of Marines stood in the dim porch light, apologizing for the late hour, for the interruption, but they could no longer sit on their secret. They needed to tell

TJ's mother and him what had really happened. Something, they emphasized, that none of them could ever share with anyone else. Otherwise, those Marines would have been in deep trouble.

That long night, over cups of coffee that grew cold before being tasted, beneath the dim light at the tiny kitchen's cheap Formica-topped table, was where TJ Dillon learned to hate the name "Marco Esteban." And where he vowed to himself to enlist and become the most efficient and effective fighter since...well... TJ Dillon Sr.

"Let's see. If I remember correctly, Esteban is the head of the Cuban DINA, their answer to the CIA. Now you're telling me he has suddenly decided to go on holiday?" Dillon quipped. He hoped Kirkland had not seen the dark shadow cross his face at the mention of the man's name. "And you want me to go down there to search all the beach cabanas at Melia Varadero to see if he is applying his sunscreen?"

"That's about it in a nutshell." Kirkland suppressed a smile. The kid had swallowed the bait, just as Kirkland had known he would. Soon he would be hooked, reeled in. "Actually, we just need you to contact in person some of the usually helpful sources to see what they'll tell you that they are suddenly so demure about sharing through the usual channels. You should know that Don Marco has been jockeying for position to climb to the top rung in our favorite rogue island now that Fidel is gone and Raul has so quickly abdicated. He may just be off somewhere planning his coup. Or somebody just as powerful and hell-bent on being boss got wind of Esteban's career plans. We just don't know. And that is not acceptable. The boss would really like answers to his questions before our Cuban friends pull off some surprise. An operative will make contact and take you to the right places so you can see the right people and ask some questions."

"But why send me? I'm better trained for other types of far dirtier duty," Dillon said. He leaned back and took a sip of coffee. To any casual observer, the two men might be discussing the previous night's Redskins game.

"We're not real comfortable with our Cuban assets right now. Too many unexplained things have happened in the last little while. Only a couple of our most trusted guys in Cuba will even know that you are there, and I'm the only one here that knows. That's why we financed your little trip on the red-eye from LA and not by the usual route. I don't want to take any chances on this. We have a cover story. You are representing your employer, looking for a way to import Mercedes-Benz trucks through Havana and not have to pay that big tariff. Believe me, they would do a deal with Satan himself if it meant some revenue for their little fiefdom."

Kirkland shoved back his chair and slowly rose. "You'll receive all instructions and documentation the usual way. Buy yourself a couple of nice suits. You are a ruthless but successful businessman. Just be careful. Like I said, there are a lot of things happening that we don't understand. Help us get a clearer image of what the hell is coming down and I'll put your picture on my mantel."

Kirkland grabbed his coffee cup and took a last swallow, then raised his voice so anyone nearby could hear him. "I told you to take the 'Skins and the points! They beat the spread better than sixty percent of the time at home on Monday night. Serves you right for ignoring the 'swami.'"

With that, he sauntered away down the promenade, a mid-level bureaucrat off to start his dull, boring day.

Dillon took a final swig of his coffee and pretended to read the story about the football game. Something about Kirkland still bothered Dillon. Something he could not even come close to identifying.

Then, shaking his head as if to show his displeasure with how he had blown his wager against the 'Skins, he grabbed the newspaper Kirkland had forgotten, stood, and walked purposefully toward another exit farther down the promenade.

Of course, the newspaper seemed heavier than it should. Somewhere in the "Money" section was a passport with his picture but a name he had never heard before. And an airline envelope with tickets booked under that same fictitious name.

Rudimentary instructions were in there somewhere, too.

And TJ could not wait to read them.

It appeared he finally had a real job, one where he could at last earn his generous paychecks provided by the American taxpayers.

But, he had to wonder, would it be worth the wages?

Ψ

Simon Castellon stepped out from the shadows as the black car slowed near him. He looked carefully up and down the deserted street before stepping through the open door and sliding into the back seat.

"Good to see you, Simon." Admiral Juan Valdez smiled as he shook the old guerrilla's hand. "My apologies for calling you out so late at night, *mi compadre*."

Castellon waved away the apologies. "In my line of work, and as you so well know, most business is transacted late at night in quiet, out-of-the-way places. Now, how may I be of service?"

"I need some assistance," Valdez answered. "I require someone who is very good with explosives, especially remotely-detonated underwater explosives."

Castellon thought for a moment. "I may know a few people who could do such work."

"Good, good," Valdez replied. "But most importantly, he must be very discreet and not traceable back to either you or me or the nation to which we are both so loyal."

"I know just the man," Castellon said. "He's Chechen. I met him in the mujahidin camps. He is known only as Buorz, the Wolf. He had a reputation even then with explosives. A real master with C-4. But he is a rabid, idealistic revolutionary, as are so many of his ilk. You cannot hire Buorz for money. He will need a cause."

"Get him," Valdez ordered. "Have him bring at least five hundred kilos of C-4. Tell your *Lobo* that it is his chance to strike a great blow against the imperialist *Americanos*. I want him and his wares aboard the submarine *Almirante Villaregoz* as soon as I can recall the vessel from its current operations."

Valdez signaled for Jorge to pull the car to the side of the street. Castellon swung the door open and stepped out into the dark, humid Caracas night.

The old jungle warrior would immediately do his commander's bidding. Once his loyalty was decided, Castellon would die to assure the success of whatever mission was his to complete.

This would not be the first time he had found the most expedient way to annihilate something important to his commander. And do it with no idea of what it might be or how many people might die in the process.

9

Joe Glass allowed himself a good stretch and a long sigh of relief. He brushed back his uncombed hair with his fingers. His mouth tasted gritty and foul. Two solid days in the submarine's control room did not allow for personal hygiene. He had passed most of the time in the little fold-down seat, snatching only a sandwich and a coffee when his growling stomach reminded him that it was time to eat something.

Toledo's run around the Bahamas, down the Florida Channel, and along the south side of Cuba was now just about complete. The dangerous navigation past all the reefs, rocks, and coral heads, dodging pleasure craft, deep-sea fishing boats, and ocean liners, was now behind them. They were safely in good, deep water. Edwards, Jerry Perez, and the navigation team could finally stand down and get a little rest while Master Chief Zillich and the sonar team searched out the patrol box, just to make sure that they were all alone in this little patch of Caribbean playground. Then they would commence the slow, boring duty of just hanging out, waiting, remaining ready if the SEAL team that had gone ashore needed a hand.

"Officer of the Deck, come to ahead one-third. Commence a slow sonar search of the patrol box."

Glass slowly stood and allowed the blood to race back into his aching muscles. He could feel the big nuclear submarine beneath his feet as it slowed from its flank-speed run. The narrow cot in his stateroom sure sounded appealing. He took a step aft and looked down at the plot that Edwards and Perez were eyeing, each man doing his best to appear alert and awake.

"XO," Glass started, "you and the Nav need some rack time." He looked at their faces, covered with several days of beard stubble, their eyes so red that it was a wonder they did not bleed right out onto the chart table. "You both look like shit, if you don't mind me saying so. Get out of here, and I don't want to see either of you for at least eight hours."

Edwards looked over at his captain and shook his head.

"Skipper, you ain't exactly gonna win any beauty contests either. You should go get some rest. I caught a couple of hours a bit ago."

"Bull!" Glass shot back. "That was fifteen hours ago. And you were slumped over the gyro for maybe twenty minutes. If you got any rest out of that, you're a better man than I, Gunga Din."

"Conn, Sonar. Array is stable." Zillich's voice, amplified by the 21MC, rang reassuringly through the conn. "Commencing a sonar search on all frequencies. Currently hold one sonar contact, sierra three-seven. Bearing three-two-seven. Classified small craft, probably a fishing boat. Distant."

"Sounds about right," Glass said. "Tell you what, XO. Let's both hit the skid. It'll take at least four hours to search this box. I'll get us set up in patrol mode, then you relieve me at noon."

The two senior submariners walked out of control and down the passageway to their respective staterooms. Joe Glass did not even remember his head hitting the pillow as he collapsed on the narrow cot.

He was instantly in a deep, deep sleep.

Ψ

Captain Alejandro Ramirez proudly watched the ballet play itself out before him. He could not believe his luck!

Once more the American submarine, with its distinguishing but unsuspected pinging device chiming away, had stumbled across his path. He would once again prepare to launch his torpedoes just seconds after the special receiver on his submarine told him that the American vessel was close enough for the likelihood of a successful shot. This time, though, there would be no one to tell him to disarm the weapons before they did their intended work.

He would claim that the other submarine made threatening moves, opened its torpedo tube doors, and that his only choice had been to fire in self-defense. That this same submarine had threatened his vessel before, that particular provocation occurring within his own country's territorial waters. With a successful kill of this interloper, the world would know that Captain Alejandro Ramirez, his Navy, his submarine, his crew were not to be trifled with. That they would defend themselves if threatened, regardless of the size and the bluster of the bully who did the brandishing.

Admiral Valdez had predicted that he would hear the telltale pinger when the American was within five thousand meters. That was well within the lethal range for his deadly undersea bloodhounds yet far enough away that his quarry would not be able to launch a likely successful counterattack.

His two gold front teeth flashed as he grinned broadly. The silly Americans would barely have enough time to taste real fear before they died. And soon, his admiral, his president, his people would give him credit for what he had done, showing the belligerent lion to the north that it no longer ruled the warm waters that lapped his homeland.

Ψ

Joe Glass was surrounded by the mists of dreamless sleep when something pulled him out of its pleasant warmth. For a moment, he was not quite sure of where he was or what he was doing. Something in his subconscious had kicked him awake.

Slowly, unsteadily, he rolled out of bed and grabbed the fold-down desk to steady himself as he got to his feet. There had been no sound from the speaker, but he knew instinctively that something was going on aboard his submarine.

"Conn, Sonar. Picking up transients on bearing zero-one-five or one-seven-five. Towed array broadband." Master Chief Zillich's voice now came clearly over the 21MC. "Just now picking it up on the sphere, too. On the edge of the baffles. Classifying."

"Damn!" Glass said, shaking his head once more to clear the fog and reaching for the door handle.

The 21MC boomed again. Zillich's voice was at a notably higher volume and pitch.

"Launch transients, bearing zero-one-four!"

Glass was instantly fully awake, sprinting to control still wearing only his skivvies. He was barely out of his stateroom door when he heard the awful words over the 1MC.

"Torpedo in the water! Snap shot, tube three. Man battle stations! All Ahead flank! Make your depth eight hundred feet. Right full rudder. Steady course south."

Glass grabbed for support as he felt *Toledo* shoot ahead. The throttleman was pouring steam into the big main turbines as fast as he could whip open the throttles. The deck pitched downward as the boat sought the relative safety and maneuver-ability of the deep.

As Glass ran toward the conn, he had an odd thought. Most submarine skippers spent their entire careers without getting shot at. He was about to get his second opportunity in less than a month!

"Torpedo bearing zero-one-five!" Zillich's voice boomed out. "On the edge of the port baffle drawing into the baffles. Torpedo is in active search!"

"Lost the torpedo in the baffles."

There was no doubt now. They were in a race with death.

Did they have one chance in hell of getting out of the torpe-do's acquisition cone before it locked onto *Toledo*? Locked on and did what it was aimed to do? Or would this one disappear in the murky depths after scaring the hell out of the *Toledo* crew, as the previous ones had done? Waiting to find out was not an option.

"Tube three ready in all respects." Eric Hobson had slid into the firing panel seat. "Set on the original launch bearing."

Glass knew that an ADCAP torpedo did not have the best chance of hitting whoever had ambushed them, but it would do its dead level best. Besides, it could become a very large, very dangerous evasion device. And they needed to defend them-selves. If nothing else, the bastard shooting at them might decide to run off and hide without sending any other deadly fish their way.

"Shoot on generated bearings," Glass ordered, without hesitation.

He watched as Hobson threw the switch that started the launch sequence of one of *Toledo*'s own lethal weapons.

The electrical pulse from the firing panel energized circuits that sent the latest target solution to the ADCAP torpedo's onboard processors. Another pulse ported 1500 PSIG air to the backside of the ejection pump piston, shoving it forward. Water from the front of the piston, now highly pressurized, shot out of the cylinder and, through a series of slide valves, to ports aft of the torpedo.

The ADCAP was flushed at high speed out of the torpedo tube. When the feeler at the top of the torpedo sensed that it was out of the tube and the accelerometer said that the weapon was rushing along at better than three G's, a tiny explosive squib ignited to start turning the Otto Fuel-powered rocker plate motor. The two-ton weapon immediately shot forward at better than sixty knots, on its way to search out, find, and attempt to destroy whoever had shot at them.

The whole sequence took less than fifteen seconds.

"Torpedo coming out of the port baffles. Best bearing three-four-two. On ship's unit in high-speed search, running normal."

"Torpedo bearing three-four-zero. Drawing left. Recommend coming right."

"Launch two countermeasures," Glass calmly ordered.

The chief of the watch reached over and punched two buttons on the countermeasure panel. A three-inch-diameter noisemaker ejected from each of two dihedrals that projected from the sub's hull, just below the stern planes. The counter-measures tumbled in the screw's churning wake. Their job was to create enough chaos in the water to try to jam the incoming torpedo's sonar.

"Right full rudder, steady course one-one-zero," Glass ordered.

With the torpedo heading generally to the south, maybe they could slip off to the east enough to lose it before it could figure out how to get past the evasion devices. Glass's mind was working quickly, trying to compute the complex three-dimensional geometry of this deadly game.

"Torpedo in the baffles. No good bearing," Zillich called out.

"Own ship unit bearing three-five-four. Still in high-speed search."

"Loud explosion on the bearing of the incoming unit!" Zillich called out, relief dripping from his voice. "I think it went for the countermeasures."

"Master Chief, do you still hold the incoming torpedo? I don't want to slow down until I know it's gone," Glass responded.

The sonarman only hesitated for seconds, though it seemed like hours.

"Captain, no longer hold active sonar on that bearing. No longer hold the torpedo."

Glass turned to Lt. Pat Durand.

"Slow to ahead two-thirds. Do a search on this course, then come around to the north. Listen for more rocks he might throw, but let's go find the bastard that shot at us!"

The sub slowed noticeably to a speed where her very sensitive passive sonars worked best for seeking out whatever was trying to hide from them in the ocean.

"Conn, Sonar. Loud explosion on the bearing of our weapon. We hit something."

More than a hundred souls had likely just been dispatched to glory.

Ψ

Back aboard the *Almirante Villaregoz*, Captain Alejandro Ramirez snapped, "First Officer, report time to torpedo impact." He did his best to sound like the American submarine captains he had heard in the movies. He could feel his excitement rising. He certainly did not want to miss a single second of this adventure.

Lieutenant Vasquez glanced up from his fire control panel,

swallowed hard, and shouted, "Best estimate is one minute twenty seconds. Torpedo has contact and is homing on the American ship."

The Russian-built torpedo spooled out in its wake a hair-thin copper wire, still connected to its mother submarine as it charged after its prey. The wire allowed Vasquez to see everything that the torpedo saw. And it saw the huge American submarine trying vainly to speed away. Vasquez awaited his captain's orders to disarm the weapon, to once again call it off after it had done its job of frightening the Americans. But time was running out. The torpedo would likely find its target very, very soon, and men—flesh-and-blood brother submariners —would die.

In his excitement, Ramirez was dancing a jig without even being aware of it, hopping from one foot to the other. Those in the conn turned their heads to keep from laughing at him, even in the tension that permeated the compartment.

The captain could already picture his triumphant return and the report to Admiral Valdez that he had defeated in a vicious battle the belligerent American nuclear submarine, left its broken hull on the bottom of the Caribbean. He would be the hero of all the homeland. The admiral would surely have no option now but to choose him to lead the entire submarine fleet.

It never occurred to the sawed-off sub commander that what he had just done could result in all-out war or cause his supreme leader extreme embarrassment on the world stage. After all, Admiral Valdez himself had fumed about the American submarine being in the Cuban Deep, had remarked that it should be chased away before its crew observed the secret activities involving the survey vessel.

Ramirez had every reason to sink the cocksure American submarine.

Though he was a more than competent submarine officer,

Ramirez had no concept of politics or, for that matter, much of anything beyond the control room on his boat. In his simplistic view, he assumed the USA would do nothing rash when they lost the submarine. Instead, they would publicly assign the loss of the vessel to a terrible mechanical failure, remaining quiet about such a devastating attack on one of their supposedly invincible submarines.

No, the Americans would have no choice but to take their medicine, file the usual diplomatic squawks through secret channels, and, in the future, avoid provocative missions such as the most recent one, the blatant eavesdropping of this very submarine that had hovered so near the homeland's coast. No, the bully of the hemisphere would no longer feel safe anywhere in the Caribbean Basin. Not with Captain Alejandro Ramirez and his fabulous warship *Almirante Villaregoz* bravely and competently patrolling these waters.

Just then, Vasquez pressed his headphones to his ears, a cloud of deep concern crossing his features that quickly changed to fear. He mumbled into the microphone, and then, certain of what he was hearing, shouted out, "Captain, sonar reports another torpedo. The Americans have launched a counterattack."

Ramirez's dance ended immediately. The diminutive skipper appeared to shrink down even smaller. This was not what he expected at all. Shooting the unsuspecting Americans in the back was virtually without risk. In international waters, the American captain would hesitate to fire at an unknown foe until it was too late.

But now, somehow, the American was shooting back. What should he do? His mind had instantly gone blank. How could he hide his ship from the wrath of an American torpedo?

"Captain, the torpedo is bearing one-two-zero degrees. It is coming right at us!" Vasquez called out. "Should I...?"

The sonarman and the rest of the crew stopped, awaiting orders from their captain. They could all hear the sonar intercept receiver chirping away. The American torpedo was active and working, determinedly sniffing them out. And doing it in one big hurry. The chirping grew louder and louder but Ramirez stood transfixed, his face frozen.

"Captain, we must do something or we are dead! What do we do?" Vasquez shouted, no longer considering the consequences of embarrassing the diminutive skipper in front of the others in the conn.

Ramirez still said nothing. Did not move. He seemed unaware of the pleas of his executive officer, the wide eyes of his crew, the incessant chirping of the sonar intercept that counted down the seconds until their certain death.

Vasquez suddenly shouted, "Right full rudder, course north. Ahead flank!"

The exec threw off his headset, half-shoved his captain out of the way, and hopped over to the periscope stand. If the captain was incapable of giving orders, it was up to him.

The officer's first thought was to get them to shallow water and attempt to hide from the torpedo in the Cuban mud. It was their only chance—and a truly small one—to escape an American ADCAP torpedo. Vasquez knew very well how good the weapon was. It almost never missed.

The submarine responded to his order and leapt ahead. It had the capability of racing at better than thirty kilometers per hour for almost an hour before its batteries would be completely drained.

They would either die from the torpedo blast or run headforemost into Cuba long before that.

"Torpedo is bearing one-two-one," the sonar speaker squawked. "It's going into our baffles."

Vasquez knew that was not good. The torpedo would now be

hidden from their sonar while it ran after them, but this did not change his survival instincts. Racing toward the shallow water was still their only hope.

"Launch the evasion device!" he shouted.

One of the seamen dutifully pulled the lever that sent the noisemaker tumbling aft into their wake. Maybe it would confuse the American killer weapon.

"Steer course zero-two-zero," Vasquez ordered. Maybe coming a little to the right would keep the torpedo from getting lost in their baffles while he tried to outsmart the damned thing.

There was no hope of outrunning it. Vazquez knew that. The American weapon could charge along at over one hundred kilometers per hour while the *Almirante Villaregoz* could barely make thirty. The only escape, the only way to stay alive, was to convince the torpedo that its target was somewhere else.

"Sir," Gomez, the quartermaster, screeched, "we must turn more or we will run aground. We must turn now!"

Vasquez risked a quick glance at their chart. Yes, they were very near the reefs that rimmed the mouth of *Bahia de Cochinos*, the Bay of Pigs.

"Right full rudder!" Vasquez shouted. "Steady on course zero-nine-zero."

Glancing again at the chart, Vasquez saw that the new course should allow them to clear the headland. Just barely, though, if they were truly where they thought they were.

"Torpedo bearing one-seven-five. Drawing into our baffles again!" the sonar speaker blared. "Water depth by fathometer at ten meters! We are going to run aground!"

Vasquez looked over at Ramirez. A broad, wet stain had appeared on the front of his captain's uniform trousers. Urine was running down the commander's pant leg. The little man continued to stand there, frozen except for the pronounced shaking of his knees.

Vasquez nodded his head in disgust.

"Depth eight meters! We are all going to die!" the crewman cried.

Vasquez leaned against the periscope barrel. There was nothing more to do. Either they ran past the headland and the American torpedo hit the rocks or they died.

It was all in God's hands now.

The submarine suddenly jolted violently upward as its belly scraped along the rocky bottom, the impact instantly ripping a ten-meter-long tear in the relatively thin steel outer hull. Vasquez and most of the crew went careening to the hard steel deck.

The explosion came a split second later, lifting the massive vessel up before slamming it back down again.

Vasquez slowly stood, his body aching from every bruised inch. A quick glance around surprised him. He fully expected to see a wall of in-rushing water inundating a mass of tangled wreckage. Instead, everything appeared shockingly normal.

Except for his crewmen, who were slowly regaining their senses. The big depth gauge above the ship controls showed that *Almirante Villaregoz* was on the surface. They appeared to be bobbing there, dead in the water, less than a mile off the Southern Cuban coast.

Vazquez idly rubbed a pronounced knot on his forehead. Apparently, the American torpedo exploded in the mud, just close enough to shove them up from the bottom but not close enough to do damage.

Captain Ramirez slowly rose from behind the locker where he had been thrown by the force of the impact.

"I think we did that rather well," he said with only the hint of a tremor in his voice. "Admiral Valdez will be very pleased when I tell him how I killed the Americans and escaped his torpedo, the one he fired at us first before we defended ourselves. He will probably award me the Order of Bolivar."

The tiny control room was completely silent. Ramirez looked around, his face growing redder. After a few seconds' pause, he growled, "This ship looks like a pigsty! First Officer, you and your crew are neglecting your duties again. Get us underway and submerged before the Cubans see us out here. Then clean this place until you can eat off the deck."

He turned and walked forward, yelling over his shoulder, "I will be in my stateroom writing the report of my great victory in the face of this atrocious attack by the Americans. Call me when this ship is ready for my inspection. Otherwise, I am not to be disturbed."

10

Bruce deFrance emerged reluctantly from the limousine's cool, dark interior. The sweltering tropical heat of Cienfuegos hit him like a hamper full of hot towels. By the time he had strolled the length of the Southern Cuban city's long cement pier, perspiration was trickling down his forehead, forming rivulets across his face, and dripping off his chin. He could already feel the fine, white Egyptian-cotton tropical shirt clinging to his back.

deFrance railed under his breath. Damn Cubans! This was not really the way that the CEO of one of the world's major oil companies should be treated. Pier security was one thing. It was meant to keep the riff-raff away, not to prevent his car from delivering him right to his ship's gangway.

Despite the discomfort, the oilman smiled as he walked the pier and approached Samson Petroleum's pride and joy. The *R/V Deep Ocean One* was the latest thing in deep-water seismic exploration. At almost thirty thousand tons, she was a huge ship, stuffed with the very latest technologies for discovering the wealth veiled underneath seawater, no matter how many miles deep it might hide.

Her after deck was totally dedicated to stowing, handling,

and deploying massive very-low-frequency towed streamer arrays and the towed air cannons that started the whole process. The air cannons were large stainless-steel cylinders, almost ten meters long and a meter in diameter. They used high-pressure air to generate a hugely powerful, high-intensity, low-frequency acoustic pulse. At well over two hundred decibels, the pulses literally shook the rock beneath the seabed far below. *Deep Ocean One* could tow and operate twenty of these cannons simultaneously.

Behind her, the research ship pulled a streamer array made up of twenty-five individual streamers. Each array was a single four-inch-diameter garden hose over fifteen miles long. The hose protected a line of hundreds of geophones, each sensitive enough to hear a mouse fart at ten miles. If the ship were alongside the Statue of Liberty, the streamers would stretch all the way north to the Bronx and from the East River to the Hudson. The highly sensitive streamer array listened for the faintest of acoustic reflections, turned them into digital pulses, and sent them to the banks of very-high-speed computers in the ship's survey center. The system was just like active sonar on a submarine, but rather than listening for submarines, it detected money —in the form of petroleum—that might be hidden deep beneath the ocean waters.

Captain Julian Savoir, dressed in a spiffy white tropical uniform, greeted the oil executive—his boss—at the brow with a hearty handshake.

"Mr. deFrance. Welcome aboard the *Deep Ocean One*," he said, with a lilting Brittany accent. "We are very glad to have you aboard for the next few days. I hope that you enjoy your time with us. Your special shipment arrived yesterday. We stowed it in the after cargo hold as you directed."

deFrance glanced around to make sure they were alone before he nodded acknowledgement.

"Very good. The crate is not to be disturbed without my direct instructions. And make sure all mention of it disappears from any ship's manifests."

Captain Savoir answered, "I understand perfectly. It will be as you ordered."

Turning on his heel and motioning for deFrance to follow him, the captain stepped over the transom and into the ship's gleaming interior. The petroleum executive could not suppress a shiver when the cool blast of air hit him.

"I will personally show you to your cabin," Savoir said over his shoulder as he briskly walked down the narrow passageway and up a ladder to the next deck. He pointedly glanced at his guest's sopping wet shirt. "You will be pleased to note that it is air-conditioned."

Captain Savoir deposited deFrance at a door opening into a spacious and well-appointed stateroom at the very forward end of the passageway.

"I'm afraid that I must leave you for a few moments. We get underway in an hour. There are many details that I must attend to before then. Please freshen up. My first officer will escort you to the bridge when you are ready." Captain Savoir pointed to the telephone. "If you need anything in the meantime, please just pick it up and ask."

The captain bowed slightly, turned, and disappeared up the ladder to the bridge.

deFrance glanced around the stateroom. The gleaming mahogany and brass contrasted nicely with the deep-pile, rose-colored carpeting and tan leather furniture. Clearly, this room was not meant for an ordinary seaman. No, this room was set aside for the most important of guests, from executives to heads of state. He knew it had already hosted its share of both.

A silver coffee service with several heavy china mugs were set out on the coffee table. An air-conditioning unit on the far wall purred quietly, filling the room with welcome cool, dry air. Though, in reality, he owned this vessel, deFrance was still duly impressed with her appointments.

He poured himself a cup of dark, fragrant coffee, adding two sugars and a heavy dollop of cream.

Large portholes on the forward and starboard side afforded a good view of the ship's forecastle and the harbor. The oil executive sipped his coffee as he watched the scene outside, the bustling activity as they prepared for departure.

Fascinated by the maritime ballet, deFrance barely heard the gentle knock on the door. It tentatively swung open a bit, just enough for deFrance to see a short, olive-skinned man dressed in a white tropical uniform similar to the captain's.

"Good morning, Mr. deFrance," the officer said, his voice both deferential and laced with a heavy Sardinian accent. "Please excuse the interruption. Captain Savoir sends his respects and requests the pleasure of your company on the bridge. Please follow me."

The immaculately-dressed officer turned and walked down the passageway. deFrance had just enough time to grab his cup and follow him out the door. The man turned left and climbed a steep ladder up to the next deck. The oilman, balancing his cup, scurried to follow and caught up just as the officer went up the next ladder.

The passageway forward opened onto a large room that stretched the entire width of the research vessel. A desk with myriad controls, LCD screens, and blinking lights stretched across the entire breadth of the forward bulkhead. Above the desk, glass windows gave an unobstructed view of the main deck and the dirty, nondescript little harbor beyond.

deFrance was confused. Although this was quite obviously the ship's control center, no one was sitting at the desk. Who was driving the ship? This room should be crammed with people shouting orders or rushing to carry them out. The room was empty, save for him and his escort.

Then deFrance spied Captain Savoir and another officer standing out on the port bridge wing. The officer was clutching a small box that looked very much like a computer game controller.

deFrance stepped over the high transom and joined them. A gentle breeze, tinged with the smell of saltwater and a faint, sweet tropical odor, ruffled his hair.

"Greetings again, Mr. deFrance," Savoir said. "Beautiful day for an underway." He turned his head slightly toward the other officer and ordered, "Come left two degrees and increase speed to five knots."

The officer played with the "controller" for a second before answering, "We've come left two degrees, making five knots."

"We'll be out in open water in a few minutes," Savoir said, smiling broadly. "And then, we will make way for the survey fields. Enjoy the voyage, sir!"

Ψ

Navy SEAL Jim Ward lay with his eye firmly in place on the scope. From his vantage point on what passed for a hill in this swampy terrain—one of his men joked they were, in reality, reclining on the bodies of millions of dead mosquitoes—the harbor and the small Cuban naval base at its deepest point inland stretched out before him. The only thing stirring down there at the pier was a gleaming white ship making its way toward them as it headed down the only channel through the shallow bay toward the deep blue Caribbean.

This was the first activity worth watching since they had found a suitable hiding place. They were sprawled on a small rise just inland from the narrow channel that marked the

entrance to Cienfuegos's large but shallow harbor. The heavily
wooded headland gave the team plenty of cover and the thick
tropical vegetation dissuaded any casual discovery. Ships
coming and going to Cienfuegos were forced to take the deep-
water channel between their headland and Cayo Carenas. Populated by a few ramshackle huts, the tiny island lay less than five
hundred yards away. The few ships that they had seen came
almost close enough for Ward and his team to reach out and
touch them.

Ward did not really need the spotter scope to read the ship's
name as it steamed past. "R/V Deep Ocean One" was inscribed
in large, dark-blue block letters on its high, jutting bow, just
below the main deck. The after deck was a maze of huge cable
reels, cranes, and complex handling equipment.

He focused in on the bridge. The man standing there looked
familiar. It took a few seconds before the young SEAL remembered where he had seen that face and out-of-place wardrobe
before.

Of course! In the grainy photo that he had handled in Tom
Donnegan's office at the Pentagon. He snapped a series of high-
resolution images.

"Sean, set up the SATCOM," he muttered to his teammate as
he slapped away a huge mosquito that hovered over his hand
like a Blackhawk chopper. "I think that we finally have something to call home about besides the size of the bugs and our
loss of blood since we hit the beach down here."

11

Jon Ward read the message again. It still did not make any damn sense.

Joe Glass was reporting that he and *Toledo* had been attacked for the second time in a month. Totally out of the blue and, once again, unprovoked. But this time he had shot back.

What in hell was happening? Did someone down in the Caribbean have some secret new way to find submarines? Who? Whoever it was clearly did not like US submarines, and they sure didn't want them snooping around in what they might consider to be unfriendly territory.

Ward glanced around the SUBFOR OPCENTER. Hidden deep in a windowless cement fortress within the Fleet Forces Command Compound, the normally bustling space was a beehive of activity. Large flat-screen monitors covering every available square inch of vertical space flickered with real-time satellite imagery covering everything from Alabama to Brazil. Groups of people huddled around the desks that filled the room. Sailors scurried about, updating status boards or whispering in one or another flag officer's ear. Every phone seemed to have someone hanging on to it and jabbering away incessantly. The

Commander of Fleet Forces and his battle staff were huddled in a tiny corner on a secure VTC with the CNO and the Joint Chiefs.

It had been a long time since someone had taken a shot at a US submarine in international waters. The incident had everyone's attention.

Never mind the attack had been aborted the first time. And unsuccessful this time, thank God. Torpedoes had been fired—by both vessels involved in this latest event—only a few hundred miles from the United States. And a few hundred yards from Cuba.

Ward's first instinct was to order the *Toledo* out of there in case the bastard tried to shoot them yet again. Joe Glass had outrun this last deadly fish. There was no guarantee that he could outrun the next one. But there were considerable complications. Tom Donnegan had overruled Ward when he told the admiral what he was thinking. *Toledo* was still busy boring holes in the ocean a few miles south of the Cuban coast, waiting to extract the SEAL team if needed.

A SEAL team skippered by Ward's own son.

Jon Ward had considered for a moment how he would have felt if he actually had given the order to yank *Toledo* out of the area, leaving his son and his team on Cuban soil to fend for themselves. To make matters worse, he could not have told his wife—Jim's mother—about it. Thankfully, Tom Donnegan had saved him from that no-win.

A young lieutenant that Ward did not recognize made his way through the orderly chaos and approached him.

"Excuse me, Commodore," he said. "They want you on the VTC. Please follow me."

Ward followed the fresh-faced kid over to a tiny alcove walled off from the rest of the room by a bank of flat-panel screens.

Admiral Westy Greene, COMFLEETFORCES, was sitting there already, sucking the stub of a cigar. He waved Ward to a seat beside him at the table.

"Jon, glad you could make the time to join us," he drawled, and winked broadly. Although Westy Greene had not been back to El Paso since high school, his voice still carried a big dose of West Texas. He waved a huge, calloused hand toward the center flat-panel. "The chairman has some questions about that little dust-up down yonder in the Caribbean."

An Air Force general filled the screen, his normally florid face livid, making the monitor look as if it were in dire need of color correction. General Arthur Schmidtmegan, the current Chairman of the Joint Chiefs of Staff, was well known for his dislike of the Navy, and particularly what he considered to be their overpriced toys. Toys such as nuclear-powered submarines.

"Bill, what is this mess of dog crap your boys have stepped in this time?" he growled. "I seem to spend all my time listening to the exploits of your cowboy submarine skippers. I don't think you have a good handle on them, and now one of them may have really gone and screwed the pooch."

Westy Greene's jaw clenched. He took the cigar butt out of his mouth to keep from biting it in half. The efforts to control his tone were obvious to all the men sitting around him at the table, and when he spoke next, he might as well have been spitting bullets, not words.

"Art, I'm not going to waste my breath reminding you once again that we are all on the same team. You're the Chairman of the Joint Chiefs, not the Chairman of the Air Force." The air in the room grew noticeably more frigid, as if someone had cranked down the thermostat. Jon Ward tried to merge into the maze of lights and monitors behind him. Mere captains could easily get smashed when caught in the middle of these kinds of bull-elephant tussles. His point made, Greene went on, with barely a pause to allow his retort to reverberate, "One of our boats was on station in international waters south of Cuba. It was attacked by an unidentified submarine that fired at least one torpedo at it. Our boat fired back in self-defense and, thank goodness, successfully evaded the torpedo."

"You sure your guys aren't imagining this," Schmidtmegan shot back. "An unidentified submarine is awfully convenient if one of your guys got a case of the yips after being out there swimming around too long smelling each other's butts. What does National Reconnaissance say?"

"Nothing conclusive," Greene responded, shaking his head. "Of course, we are dealing with submarines, so the chances of seeing anything are slim. Heavy cloud cover over the area, so no good imagery from any of our birds. Infrared got a couple of anomalous heat sources that could be anything. Imaging radar is temporarily down on that particular bird. Bottom line? Nothing. Just as we would expect, I might add."

"Of course," Schmidtmegan retorted. "Because there is nothing. Pretty damn convenient, I say. Get that boat into port and fry the skipper for seeing spooks and wasting expensive ordnance. Let's just hope those damn Cuban politicians don't make like their ancestors and try to fry us in the world press for this dust-up."

Jon Ward was on his feet before he had time to even think about what he was going to say or to whom he was about to say it.

"Just a minute, General," he fired. "No one is going to hang one of my skippers out to dry. Especially not one as good as Joe Glass!" Jon Ward leaned toward the monitor and pounded the table with a doubled-up fist. "If Joe says he was shot at, you can damn well bet he was. And if he launched a torpedo, you can bet your ass he felt it was the right thing to do to protect his boat and his crew. You don't have a shred of evidence to the contrary.

You aren't even waiting to investigate what happened and you're ready to convict him of having a bad dream."

Ward saw the expression on the face glaring back at him from the monitor screen and eased back down into his chair.

"And just who the hell are you, Captain?" Schmidtmegan growled, eyes squinted and face even more red and blotched than before.

It might have already been too late, Ward considered, but once an attack was underway, it was usually best to continue to press the assault without hesitation.

"I'm Captain Jon Ward. I'm the commodore of the squadron that *Toledo* is in. We need *Toledo* on station down there for another week." Ward's voice was as calm and even as it ever had been, even on the IMC in some of the tightest moments any skipper could find himself. Maybe he could defuse this situation and salvage both Joe and his own career. And keep *Toledo* down there in place to rescue his kid. But only if he pressed on very carefully.

"And why is that?"

Jon Ward did not know whether to answer or not. It was not unusual for the highest rung of the military to not know all the details of what their troops were doing. Schmidtmegan clearly was not in the loop on the SEAL team on Cuban soil. And, even if he were, not even the chairman would be likely to know that Ward's own son was one of them.

Westy Green spoke up before Ward had to.

"Art, she is supporting a special operation in Cuba, providing backup extraction for a SEAL team we have on the beach. The sub is their emergency extraction if the primary route doesn't work."

The general's mouth fell open and his eyes widened.

"I can't believe what I'm hearing. You mean to tell me that you Navy sons of bitches have a combat force inside Cuba?"

Schmidtmegan sputtered, his eyes growing even wider. "What the hell are you doing? No wonder somebody's shooting at your asses. You damn *McHale's Navy* clowns are about to cause a war down there. I'll spend the rest of my life ignoring the calls from the cable news channels and testifying my ass off to every congressional committee there is and a damn sight more they'll create just for shit like this. Get your damn SEALs and that sub out of there immediately. I don't care about any emergency extraction plan. I want that boat tied up in port—one of our ports, if you don't mind—inside of two days. And then report to me who ordered this screw-up in the first place and how the hell it ever got approved! Do I make myself perfectly clear, Captain Ward?"

The VTC screen snapped dark before anyone on Jon Ward's end of the circuit could answer the general's final question.

Greene smiled wryly, sitting back and spreading his big hands across his chest in a sign of exasperation.

"Well, Jon, you heard the boss man. We'd better get them all out of there." The admiral turned to his aide. "Let Kirkland at The Company know that we may need to use his backup rendezvous and extraction point if we can't get the little boat in there on time. Oh, and get Tom Donnegan on the horn. He'll want to be putting on his asbestos underwear right about now."

Ψ

Jim Ward yawned and stretched out on the sand as best he could. Two days hiding on this tiny hill sure left the muscles tight and stiff. He thought how great a nice, long run along the beach would be right about now.

Maybe Admiral Donnegan was getting the information he needed, but the only thing that Ward had seen worth reporting had been the survey vessel the previous day. Who knows?

Maybe no news was good news and that was exactly what they needed to know. That what was going on down here was... well...squat.

"Skipper, you'd better see this," Tony Garcia whispered just then, handing the team leader a small screen that looked very much like a camouflage smart phone. "Message from home. They want us to hightail it out of here soonest. Maybe they heard us bitchin' about this particular Club Med experience all the way to the Pentagon."

Ward read the message and mumbled, "Wonder what this is all about? We haven't done a thing yet and we're scheduled for at least another day."

He looked around the little hummock that they had made home for the previous couple of days. Jed Dulkowski was sleeping, quietly snoring in the meager shade of an acacia bush. The fourth team member, Sean Horton, was hidden in the thick brush a couple of hundred yards further inland, guarding against someone sneaking up on them from the rear.

"It'll be dark in an hour. Tony, go shake Jed and then get Sean. We'd better get packed."

The short Latino slipped off to gather the rest of the team while Jim Ward started to police their tiny encampment. It was important not to leave any trace.

Slipping down to the beach took a couple of hours longer than they expected. They had to wait while a lone fisherman in a tiny skiff tried vainly to catch his supper a few yards beyond the languid surf. Two hours after sunset, the weathered old man finally gave up in disgust and poled his skiff around the low point, heading across the bay.

The SEALs dug their diving gear and sleds from their hiding place, lugging everything down to the water's edge before disappearing under the dark sea. Once again Jim Ward checked his GPS and took a careful bearing to the rendezvous point where they were to meet up with the Jamaican and his battered old fishing boat.

Ward's first indication of trouble was the churning whine of high-speed screws. At first the sound was barely audible over their shoulders, back toward the naval base. Gradually the howl built to a crescendo as the fast coastal patrol vessel screamed by them, almost directly overhead, then faded away as it headed farther out to sea. In precisely the same direction in which the SEALs were traveling.

The patrol vessel was making a direct line toward their ride home. This did not look good. Maybe they were just heading out on a routine patrol. But something in Ward's gut told him that he was wrong. He had seen no such activity during their time on the beach, certainly no naval vessels in any particular hurry to get someplace. How much of a coincidence was it that such activity had started just now?

By Ward's estimate, they were five minutes from rendezvous when they heard the first shell splash, followed by a jarring explosion. Several more blasts followed in quick succession. Ward needed to see what was happening. He slid up to the surface, lifting his head just above the waves. The patrol boat, an old Soviet-era *Nanuchka*-class gunboat, was slowly circling the Jamaican fishing boat, staying a few hundred yards away. The huge spotlight mounted atop the gunboat's wheelhouse illuminated their target in an eerily bright glow, as if the sun had come back and concentrated its radiance on the little vessel. The forward 23mm cannon popped and spat a continuous stream into what was left of the sinking hulk. The gunboat's crew was obviously taking great delight in blasting the boat to pieces.

Ward could just make out the old Jamaican fisherman sprawled across the gunwale, more outside than inside the boat, one arm almost dragging in the water. A dark red streak, slowly widening, streamed down the craft's dirty, rusted side.

Ward dropped below the surface again. There was nothing left for them up there. They could not help the old man, and he certainly could no longer be of any help to the SEALs. Ward signaled his little team and headed off to the alternate extraction site, praying that Joe Glass and his nuclear-powered underwater bus would be there waiting. Otherwise it was a hell of a long swim to Montego Bay, Jamaica.

Ψ

"We've got a problem, Skipper," Doug O'Malley said as he burst into the *Toledo*'s wardroom. "Temperature is still going up on the final reduction bearing. It's one-eighty now."

Glass glanced up from the message board he was reading.

"Did your guys find anything in the purifier?"

Brian Edwards rose from his chair at the burgundy Naugahyde-covered wardroom table, put down another file from his never-ending pile of admin paperwork, and grabbed his coffee cup. The XO found the wardroom table a great place to work; plenty of room to spread out. And the junior officers seemed to never hang around when it was obvious that he had work to do.

"Pour you a cup, Eng?" he grunted as he filled his own cup.

"Thanks, XO." O'Malley grabbed the offered cup and plopped down in the chair to Glass's right. He pulled a wad of cloth out of his greasy, sweat-stained coveralls.

"Thought you fellows might like to see this," he said as he unrolled the cheesecloth. Tiny bits of metal flashed in the fluorescent light. "Looks like babbit to me."

Glass picked up one of the metal bits and looked at it closely. The sliver had a dark blue streak along its edge, fading to a silvery-yellow color. Of course, a spectrographic analysis was needed to precisely determine the metal's composition, but all the evidence pointed toward babbit, the soft metal used in the main engine bearings.

"Doug, I'm afraid that you're right," Glass grumbled. "What are you recommending?"

The submarine's engineer rubbed his stubbly chin as he gathered his thoughts.

"I've already stationed a watch on the bearing to continuously monitor lube oil outlet temperature and flow. We could replace the bearing at sea, but it would mean operating single main engine for a day or so. Speed would be limited to twelve knots."

Glass shook his head.

"I don't like that at all. Not with someone out there who doesn't seem to mind shooting at us. Anybody got a better idea?"

Edwards flipped open his laptop and clicked through a few files before he found the one he wanted. He pushed the screen around so that Glass and O'Malley could see.

"Let's see what the NAVSEA Tech Manual for main engines and reduction gears says." Edwards flipped through several links until he found one titled "Hot Bearing."

"It says here to increase oil flow and check all the other bearing temperatures," Edwards read.

"Done that," O'Malley reported in a drone.

"Increase local ventilation and consider applying wet rags to the casing," the XO read on.

"Done that, too," the Eng answered, his voice rising an octave in irritation.

"Shift, clean, and inspect lube oil purifiers at least hourly."

"XO, I can read the manual just as well as you can," O'Malley retorted.

Glass decided the exchange had gone on long enough and held up his hand.

"Boys, boys, play nice," he ordered. "XO, Eng, what's left? Have we forgotten anything? Any really good ideas?"

"Head home and pray that the bearing doesn't seize before we get there," O'Malley replied. "Baby her as much as we can until then."

Edwards rubbed his chin a moment and then hesitatingly nodded.

Glass shoved the message board over to Edwards.

"Glad we're all in agreement, then," he said as he shoved back his chair and stood. "Because our boss wants us home ASAP. The SEALs are on their way out, thank goodness, and they won't be needing us." He reached over to grab the JA phone from its cradle under the table. "Officer of the Deck, come to course zero-nine-zero, maximum speed ten knots. Call the navigator and have him plot a course for the quickest way home."

12

The night was a black hole with just a bare glimmer of gold on the far eastern horizon where the sun would soon be. The moon and stars were hidden by a dense deck of dark clouds. The inky water rose and fell easily, gently pitching the SEAL team. They were all alone in this stretch of sea, and considering recent events, that was a damn good thing.

Jim Ward checked the sled's navigation readout. He had his team exactly where they were supposed to be. Still, the skipper raised the sled's antenna to grab a GPS fix. That only served to confirm what he already knew. They were at the rendezvous. But there was no trace of Joe Glass and *Toledo*.

Ward checked the sonar pinger. The little device emitted a high-pitched tone, well above the frequency for human hearing but easily detectable by *Toledo*'s sensitive sonar systems. It seemed to be operating fine; at least the green light was on.

First the unexpected ambush and murder of the Jamaican fishing boat captain, then the long swim to the emergency extraction point. Now this—all alone, seemingly abandoned in an empty sea. They needed to figure out their next move.

"What now, Skipper?" Sean Horton spat saltwater out of his mouth. "Time to swim home?"

Ward shook his head.

"Not much chance of that. My sled is showing about twenty-percent charge. That won't even get us back to the beach."

Jed Dulkowski, floating easily to Ward's left, chimed in, "Sun's gonna be up in less than an hour. Ain't no way we're gonna be ashore by then."

"I'm showing fifteen percent," Tony Garcia piped up. "I think we'd better stay out here today, then head for shore this evening. Never can tell when someone might happen by."

Ward raised his hand.

"Hold on a minute, guys. We've got a message coming in."

He read the text that appeared on the sled's tiny control screen:

PRIMARY RENDEVOUS COMPROMISED. EMERGENCY RENDEVOUS CANCELLED. MOVE INLAND TO BEST COVER. WILL ADVISE EXTRACTION PLAN. GOOD LUCK. DONNEGAN

"Well, at least the boss remembered us," Dulkowski commented drily. "Kind'a wish he would'a told us about the change in plans before we took our little swim."

"It is what it is," Ward answered, engaging one of his dad's favorite summations. "Let's trim these things for floating out here and wait for sunset."

Ψ

The stifling, humid blast of tropical air surged through the plane as soon as the doors swung open. TJ Dillon's shirt was plastered to his back before he even followed the other passengers off the jet. Jose Marti, Havana's airport, was just about what he expected—shabby and gray with little in the way of modern conveniences. At least Aeromexico had not lost his bag, even during the hectic plane swap in Cancun. Customs and Immigration were surprisingly easy and uneventful. The bored Cuban official waved him through with barely a nod.

Dillon stepped out of Terminal Three into the steaming tropical sunshine. Storm clouds hovered in the distance and he could hear the rumble of thunder above the hiss and hum of traffic. He hailed a cab and headed toward his hotel on the Plaza de Armas, all the while checking to see if he could discern anyone paying him any undue attention.

The Hotel Santa Isabel, chosen by Josh Kirkland and his CIA crowd, was a huge ornate pile in the heart of Old Havana that harkened back to the city's halcyon pre-Castro days. It did not take too much imagination to picture the other nondescript buildings on the thoroughfare in their heyday, their neon signs blaring, announcing music, dancing, gambling, and the street full of people enjoying the city's famous nightlife. Before Castro, of course.

He checked in at the front desk and, without even making a move toward the bank of wheezing elevators beyond the lobby, headed out a side entrance onto Casa del Conde de Santavenia. Dillon walked several blocks, ducking into shops and doubling back a couple of times. Apparently, no one was interested enough in him to bother with a tail. Or they were very, very good at what they did.

He hailed another cab at a corner and, in his reasonably good Spanish, told the driver to head for the newer Hotel Nacional de Cuba over in the middle of Vedado. The Hotel Nacional was much closer to the central government buildings on the *Plaza de la Revolución* and was a common haven for European and South American businessmen trying to hack their way through the intricacies and corruption of the socialist paradise's dense bureaucracy.

It was time for TJ Dillon to disappear into the business and tourist crowds. Cuba was much too controlled to hope to slip away for any length of time, but there was no sense in making it easy for them. He would return and check for the promised message under the door at the original hotel later. For now, though, he did not want the supposedly friendly folk in Havana to know where he was any more than he did the less friendly ones.

He checked into this second hotel and, with no bellman visible anywhere, lugged his bag up to his room. Nicely appointed with pseudo-French modern furniture, the accommodations seemed comfortable enough and overlooked a park across the street that looked almost pleasant and well-kept. After a quick inspection, during which he found the obvious listening device in the bedside lamp, Dillon decided it was time for a quick shower before he started scouting around.

He was just rubbing his thinning brown hair dry when he heard a knock on the door. Grabbing the waiting white terry robe from the closet, he opened the door for an old, stooped-over bellman that held out one hand with an envelope and the other with an open palm for a gratuity.

TJ handed him a couple of coins and then closed the door before tearing open the white envelope. Inside was a business card with a handwritten note on its back. He was not expecting contact yet, and, to his knowledge, no one should yet have a clue that he had relocated to this particular hotel. He already had instructions to make his presence known in a subtle and pre-planned way the next morning, with a specific breakfast order at a particular café nearby, and then he would be contacted in some obvious way.

The card was one of the old European-style embossed ones and contained the name and address of a café. The message on the back was written with a fountain pen in precise letters.

"We are on for coffee at the Café Vedado tomorrow at three. Ask the concierge for directions. Jose Manuel."

"Jose Manuel" was the code word for a change in plans. Whoever the author of the invitation was worked for The Company. And God only knew who else sent that person memos.

Thomas Jefferson Dillon settled back on the surprisingly comfortable king bed. So much for nobody on the island knowing where he was spending the night. Still, he had received the message as promised. He would keep the unexpected appointment the next day. But he would do so very, very carefully.

Without even planning to do so, he was quickly, deeply asleep.

Ψ

Captain Alejandro Ramirez stood proudly on the sail of his battered submarine as it moved against the seaward flow of the muddy tropical river. Hazy golden early-morning sunshine, already promising a scorching hot day, illuminated the scene in an amber hue. Standing in front of the raised periscopes and well above everyone else, Ramirez was certain that he cut a dashing figure. It was his day of glory. By the time the sun set in the evening, he would be hailed over all of Venezuela. He checked one more time to make certain that his uniform was immaculate. It was so hard to keep a proper-looking uniform on this pigsty of a submarine.

Lieutenant Armando Vasquez stood in the *Almirante Villaregoz*'s bridge cockpit, passing orders to the helmsman, who was hidden ten meters below in the submarine's control room. His oily, dirty coveralls reeked of diesel smoke and the stink of unwashed men. His face was still swollen and bruised from the torpedo's near miss and the injuries suffered during the collision with the reefs of *Bahia de Cochinos.*

"All stop," Vasquez ordered. The submarine's twin screws stopped churning the water astern. The big boat drifted forward, slowing in the river's torpid current. It came to a halt exactly at their berth on the long pier beneath a massive canvas canopy that shielded it from anything that might fly or orbit overhead.

Only a few workers stood on the pier, lazily taking the submarine's lines to the gigantic, ancient iron bollards deeply embedded in the decaying concrete. Ramirez looked around, searching. Where were the cheering crowds he expected? Where were the brass band and all the media? After all, he was the new hero of the motherland, the one who dared challenge the bullies from the USA.

Ramirez hurriedly ordered the brow lowered even as the handlers struggled to double-up the mooring lines. The steel brow connecting the submarine to the pier had barely touched the boat's steel deck, still dangling from the crane, when Ramirez dashed across.

Still no cheering, adoring crowds. Not even an official greeting party. Where were they? Only a beat-up old Chevy staff car waited at the far side of the parking lot. A big man slouched against the front fender, idly smoking a cigarette. The man looked up, spied Ramirez, and waved him over.

It was Jorge, the admiral's man.

The submarine captain felt a slight chill up his spine as he quickly crossed the parking lot. Jorge slowly stood and waved toward the open passenger door.

"Get in," he grunted. "The admiral wants to see you immediately."

Ramirez had no choice except to climb into the car. Oh well. The admiral often dispensed with formality. This was undoubtedly his ride to the meeting at which he would be honored for his skill and bravery in challenging the American submarine.

The driver slammed the door shut. The car shot off in a spray of gravel, heading for the main gate of the Navy base.

Ψ

General Almirante Juan Valdez was still fuming. His face was blotchy, his fists clenched and rigid at his sides. The admiral's willpower and his iron-hard self-control were clearly being tested as he fought his rage, trying to avoid reaching out and throttling Captain Alejandro Ramirez the instant the half-pint sub commander strode into his office, his chest out and a silly grin on his pinched, rat-like face.

Captain Ramirez took a step back when he saw his commander's expression. He had jumped from the staff car still fully expecting a hero's greeting. Instead, he now feared, based on his boss's obvious anger, that he would not leave the compound alive.

"Captain Ramirez," Valdez finally said, using a low, quiet tone that managed to rock the submarine captain far worse than if the admiral had screamed his name. "Do you have any idea in that peacock brain of yours just what trouble you have caused with your unbelievable stupidity?"

"But...but," Ramirez sputtered before finally finding the words. "My Admiral, I sank an American nuclear submarine. The same one we shot at last month and that deliberately attacked us in international waters. The one that has been so boldly intruding on our sovereign territorial waters. Why are you angry? I have spat in the face of the would-be dominators. I have made us heroes of the revolution!"

"You simpleton!" The old admiral roared the words this time. He slammed his fist down hard onto the mahogany desk. "You have probably brought the wrath of the American Navy down on our heads. You shot at a submarine in international waters. In peacetime, you fool!"

Ramirez's self-control was slipping fast. His knees began to shake. His hands quivered uncontrollably.

"But, sir, our leader has told us…"

"And the worst part is that you could not even accomplish such a colossal misstep correctly! Our spy in Norfolk reports that the submarine you attacked is pulling into Port Canaveral, Florida, even as we speak. Our only hope is that the Americans can never tie this unbelievably stupid attack back to us or they will fill every inch of the Cuban Deep with warships, just when we need them to avoid the area."

Valdez stepped back behind the desk and plopped down into his chair as if overcome by the absurdity of what his charge had done. Ramirez tried to sink into the parquet floor and disappear. Now was the time for the admiral to pronounce his death sentence. Or, more likely, pull out the famous pistol—a vintage Colt Navy revolver—from his desk drawer and actually carry out the execution himself, right then and there.

"You are very, very lucky that I need someone in command of our beautiful *Almirante Villaregoz* who actually knows her systems and capabilities. Your first officer is a far better submariner than you will ever be and would make a far, far better commander. But I cannot rely on his loyalty for so much as a second. You, on the other hand, are too weak and craven— and too dim-witted—to ever be disloyal to me."

Admiral Valdez waved his hand dismissively, as if he hardly had the strength to lift it. "Get back to your boat. And do not even defecate without first calling me for permission. The next time you do something so imprudent, you will be dinner for the caimans." He looked the little officer up and down. "Or, I should say, little more than an appetizer."

Ramirez could barely find his feet as he stumbled out of the office. Outside the building, he slumped against the old brick wall and vomited for a while, until there was nothing else left in his heaving stomach. Tears rolled down his cheeks.

Finally, he wiped his lips and forehead with his handkerchief and tucked it back into his uniform pocket, then stood up as tall and straight as he could manage and marched as boldly as possible toward the waiting staff car. At least he was still alive. Still alive and still captain of the *Almirante Villaregoz*.

Jorge did not even try to conceal his amused expression as he opened the door to allow the chastised submariner to climb inside.

13

Bruce deFrance stepped from the blazing Caribbean sunshine into the petroleum exploration ship's dimly lit information center. The blast of cool air felt chill after the tropical heat on the main deck. Now, he was supposedly about to see what all these expensive geologists were so bloody excited about.

The *RV Deep Ocean One* was slowly cruising back and forth —"mowing the lawn," as the crew called it—in the very deep water some fifty miles southwest of the Cuban coastline. The main deck looked oddly empty with all the air cannons and streamer arrays now deployed behind the ship. A cat's cradle of thick cables stretched out behind, disappearing into the waves a few hundred yards astern. The air cannons, all twenty of them, were pounding away somewhere far behind them and deep down in the sea. Their high-intensity, low-frequency noise pulses penetrated far into the Earth's crust. Then they bounced back up to be heard by the geophones in the twenty-five streamer arrays that *Deep Ocean One* towed even deeper and further astern. From that data, the geologists could determine just what fruits lay below the sea floor, ripe for the picking.

The expensive ship and crew had been out there working for

the better part of a week. At over a million dollars a day, deFrance was certain he could feel the money slipping through his fingers. It would all come back a thousand-fold if his gamble paid off. Still, it would be a hard sale to his stockholders. And to the petty dictators and third-world politicians to whom he had to bow and scrape in exchange for their allegiance.

The fact was he would have to close the sale soon. Very soon. deFrance mentally reviewed the unpleasant picture that his accountants had painted for him at their last meeting. The cash flow problem was growing acute. The Arabs and the Russians were deliberately lowering prices on the world market to squeeze him, and a few others like him, out. If Samson Petroleum did not announce a major find soon, if he was not able to attract some very deep-pocketed investors, and if he could no longer bribe key government officials with cash and the imprecise promise of even more riches in order for them to grant him unobserved access to this region, he would be forced to take drastic measures to save the company. That would almost certainly cost him his job.

At the mere thought of what was riding on the success of this project, Bruce deFrance felt a trickle of sweat roll down his back, even in the frigid atmosphere of the ship's information center.

The head geologist, a short gnome of a man with a shiny bald pate, waved deFrance over to the huge central flat-panel display. The wavy lines and swaths of bright colors were something that one might expect to see framed and hanging on the wall of some ultra-modern museum, not in this mass of computers, wires, and flashing LEDs.

The picture was meaningless to deFrance. His expertise was finance, especially the way he applied the discipline to the purchase of strategic influence. Whatever the colors meant, though, clearly had the geologists excited. That was a good sign to the oil executive.

"Right here! Right here!" the fat little man shouted, reaching up to tap a patch of bright orange that blotched across a large stretch of the screen. "I've never seen anything like it!" deFrance's perplexed look seemed to baffle the scientist. "It's only the largest, best-defined pre-Cambrian salt dome that I've ever seen."

"So?" deFrance said flatly.

"Mr. deFrance, allow me to explain. There is always oil and gas under these salt domes. And with the size of this dome, we are talking about a lot of oil. An amazing amount of oil!"

deFrance's face brightened with the barest hint of a smile.

"Great," he said. "That is very good news. Very good indeed." His brow furrowed and his face darkened as a worrisome thought came to him. "But this area has been surveyed before, many times, by exploration teams from practically every nation in the hemisphere. Why is this just showing up now? Are we sure that this is real? It isn't some kind of false return or whatever you rock heads call it?"

"It's very real," the scientist answered. "We are using recently developed equipment—purchased through your generosity and foresight, sir—and algorithms that allow us to search at depths never before possible. The find is at a little over ten kilometers down."

This was far deeper—almost twice as deep beneath the surface of the ocean—than had ever been successfully drilled before.

deFrance had risen to the top of the company through marketing, not engineering. Though he was typically uninterested in technology, he knew that greater depth almost always created insurmountable problems. "Deep" meant "expensive." And risky. He was a financier. He loathed risk.

"So what you are telling me, Doctor, is that you have found the pot of gold at the end of the rainbow. Despite the fact that we can see the pot of gold clearly, it is far beyond our reach. Thank you. Thank you for nothing!"

Point made, the oil baron turned, stormed out of the compartment, and slammed the door hard behind him.

Ψ

Night fell suddenly. One minute, the four SEALs were floating in the Caribbean in bright, burning sunlight. The next they were alone in the dark. One by one, dim yellow lights blinked to life on the Southern Cuban shore a couple of miles away. The island was slowly winding down another day.

It had been mid-morning when they received new but cryptic instructions from Donnegan. They were to go inland after nightfall, then move to the mountains that ran down the spine of the island. He had supplied a lat/long. There, near a big hilltop ranch house, they were to lie low and wait for a contact to tell them where and how they were to be extracted. Though they would be traveling in relatively desolate territory, they should be extremely cautious. Cuban military were always in this area, and American SEALs were absolutely not supposed to be.

They were not to be captured. That was the bottom line.

The sleds had died several hours before. They had been jettisoned, along with most of their gear. The men only kept what they absolutely needed for survival. The rest of the gear joined the sleds on the bottom of the green Caribbean.

A long swim was next on the agenda. Fortunately, the seas had been relatively calm, and other than a fishing boat that had come within a mile or so of them about noon, they had seen nothing but seagulls and pelicans all day.

Now, if their luck just held out.

It was time for a few minutes' rest. All afternoon, they had been swimming for forty-five minutes out of every hour and resting for fifteen minutes. Although they were young and superbly fit, the growing exhaustion was starting to tell. The four floated together with their partially inflated buoyancy control vests holding them just above water.

Ward checked his compass. With the east-northeast current, they were making pretty good time, but that same helpful push would peter out as they swam closer to shore.

"Looks like a course of three-two-zero keeps us pretty much heading due north," he reported.

"I'm thinking a big, cold mojito would be just the thing to wash the salt out of my mouth," Tony Garcia muttered, spitting seawater to make his point.

"I'll call ahead and have the barkeep meet us at the beach," Jed Dulkowski answered. "How about a side order of plantain chips?"

"Just so it's not one of the Cubans' little welcoming committees and a spray of AK-47 fire that greets our asses," Sean Horton chimed in. "I don't plan on being a long-term guest of the revolution."

"Guys, pipe down," Ward ordered. "We've got some planning to do. Let's head for that red light. See it, just to the left of the headland?" He raised his arm clear of the water to point it out.

"Yeah, Skipper, we see it," Horton answered. "Maybe a degree or two to the left of it so we land in the dark area. Looks like it's quite a ways to the hills from the beach."

"Best as I remember, it's at least ten clicks," Ward confirmed. "Mostly swamp with a scatter of villages and old haciendas up against the foothills."

"Well, time's a'wastin," Garcia piped up. "Let's get to swimming. I'll take first point."

The short Latino from Philadelphia moved out, taking long, smooth strokes. The other three fell in line behind him, drafting in his wake. They each took a five-minute turn in the lead before slipping to the back of the train, smoothly rotating through the familiar, well-practiced pattern.

Forty-five minutes later, time for the next rest period, found them a half-mile from the low white surf line barely visible in the growing gloom. They could just hear the faint burble of the waves breaking gently on the warm sand.

Garcia rolled over on his back and spat a stream of water into the air.

"Almost there," he said with a giggle. "Sure hope…"

Ward elbowed the SEAL in the ribs.

"Shhh, quiet," he hissed. "Look."

A platoon of a dozen or more soldiers had suddenly appeared on the beach, making their way around the headland, heading directly toward the SEALs' planned landing spot. The Cuban soldiers were moving slowly, the barrels of their guns held low, their eyes scanning sand and water. It did not look as if they were on a carefree after-dinner walk on the beach. This bunch meant business.

The SEAL team knew they were all but invisible a half-mile or more out in the water, but the conclusion of their swim had just been delayed. They could not risk moving any closer until the Cubans were well clear of the beach.

The soldiers fanned out into a rough, ragged line abreast. They were taking their time, being very careful and thorough as they searched the beach, looking for signs of any disturbance in the sand not caused by a crab. The most seaward one walked right at the water's edge, while the furthest inland soldiers moved in and out of the low sea grape and salt grass.

"Who are they looking for?" Horton hissed to Ward.

The SEAL team leader shook his head.

"I haven't the slightest. I only hope it ain't us."

The platoon continued slowly down the beach. The moon

was high in the sky when they finally disappeared around the next headland.

Ward signaled the team to swim on in. This time they were spread out over thirty yards or so. The four once again stopped at the surf line and waited, just four dark spots in the small breakers. The casual beach stroller, if he even happened to see them in the dark water, would only discern some unidentifiable flotsam.

They floated that way for an hour, waiting and watching, being extra cautious just in case someone was hidden in the beach scrub with an unwelcome greeting. Finally, Ward rose to his feet and scurried low across the beach, his 45ACP clutched in his right hand. He dropped at the base of the sea grape. A minute later Garcia joined him, followed by Horton and then Dulkowski.

Ward checked his watch. Already well past midnight. Time flies, he thought.

They couldn't possibly traverse the swampland and find a hiding place up in the hills before sunrise. With the Cuban soldiers patrolling the beach, hiding there was not a choice. The exhausted team's only option was to hope they could find some dry land further inland, somewhere in the swamp's thick vegetation and stagnant pools of water.

"Come on, time's a'wastin'," he grunted. "Let's see if we can find a place to get some shut-eye."

Garcia wisecracked, "I'm thinkin' a nice king-size bed in a corner room with a gentle sea breeze to caress my brow. Maybe a swimming pool with poolside service…"

"Forget the damn swimming pool after that swim we did today," Horton grumbled. "I'd like a king-size bed under a ceiling fan. But, hey, I'd settle for some dry sea oats and a breeze."

"We have to get far enough inland and hide our tracks well

enough that we can safely hole up for a day or so. We don't need to show up twenty-four hours early at the extraction point. It's supposed to have even more military protection than here. Let's quit woolgathering and get some of this swamp between us and the coast," Ward ordered.

The SEALs melted into the wall of vegetation, already knee-deep in foul-smelling, brackish black water.

14

Joe Glass swung the Type 18 periscope around in a circle, trying vainly to see whatever was up there on the surface. The thin silver cylinder bucked and jumped against his hands, slapping him in the forehead as he tried to keep his right eye stuck to the eyepiece. What with the motions of the 'scope and the *Toledo*'s spirited pitching and rolling, Glass's entire world seemed intent on making his task more difficult. He doggedly hung on to the periscope's training handles, bracing himself as best he could against the stainless-steel railing.

Wave after wave crashed over the head window, thirty odd feet above where he stood. When the green-black water cleared enough to see, a reddish-yellow sun barely illuminated the tumultuous scene. Huge waves, their tops torn away by the howling wind, stretched as far as the eye could see. Then the periscope's view was obliterated by the next frothing wave.

"'Scope's under! Can't see a damn thing anyway," he muttered. Then in a louder voice, Glass called out, "XO, what does the METOC report say?"

Brian Edwards, holding on to the chart table with both

hands to keep from being thrown to the deck, read from the message board.

"Those weather guessers say the storm center should be a hundred miles to the southeast, traveling west-northwest at twenty knots. Winds here should be forty knots, gusting to seventy knots. Not quite hurricane strength. Seas to sea state eight, confused but generally from the east."

"Full of crap," Glass muttered. "That's a full-blown hurricane up there right now if I ever saw one. I can't figure out why they wanted us out of there so bad they ordered a surface transit through a damned hurricane."

Edwards started to say something but then he suddenly grunted, grabbed a nearby green trash bag, and buried his head in it. In retrospect, ham and eggs before a ride like this had not been a good idea. The XO's retching set off a wave of puking in the control room's tight confines. The helmsman and planesman, Josh Stedman and Will Brownson, simultaneously reached down and grabbed their buckets. Sam Wallich groaned in despair, his face tinged green. "One of you two idiots needs to keep your hand on the wheel." Then he stuck his own head in a trash bag and heaved loudly.

The submarine took a particularly vicious roll to starboard before pitching her nose high in the air. Coffee cups, manuals, stray tools, and anything else not firmly tied down went crashing noisily into the after starboard corner. The air was heavy with the smell of vomit and sweat.

Wallich lifted his head just long enough to weakly report, "Depth seven-one feet and coming up. Skipper, we need more speed to maintain depth."

Glass ordered, "Ahead two-thirds. Master Chief, that's going to have to do it. With these seas, I'm afraid any more speed may bend the scope."

The 7MC announcing circuit blared to life.

"Starboard steam generator high-level alarm." Jeff Clay's voice was strained and tinged with fear. "Port steam generator low-level alarm!"

It was the young ensign's first watch as a qualified engineering officer of the watch. The propulsion plant alarm siren could be heard screaming in the background.

The sub suddenly rolled dizzyingly to port and then pitched downward.

"Starboard steam generator high-level alarm clear. Port steam generator low-level alarm clear," Clay reported. Then, a few seconds later, "Port steam generator high-level alarm, starboard steam generator low-level alarm."

Pat Durand, desperately clutching the BYG-1 fire control panel, called out, "Skipper, we'd better go deep. This is getting dangerous! That was a fifty-degree roll and a forty-degree down angle!"

Sam Wallich called out, "Depth three-nine feet, we're broached."

"Conn, Maneuvering," Ensign Clay squeaked. "The evaporator is flooded. Securing the evaporator."

Glass called out, "XO, get a quick message off to SUBLANT, info squadron. Tell them unable to surface transit into port due to sea state. Unsafe to surface. Request submerged op area until weather clears."

Edwards nodded weakly. "Got it, Skipper."

"And hurry it. I want to get deep where my stomach won't think it's on the 'Mean Streak' at Cedar Point," Glass called out at the retreating figure. He hoped pleasant memories of the Ohio amusement park coaster would take his mind off the tightening spasms in his gut.

"Injured man! Injured man in the galley!" The 4MC emergency announcing circuit had abruptly come to life. "Corpsman, lay to the galley."

Bill Dooley, the chief of the watch, grabbed a JA handset and muttered into it, then turned and yelled, "Cookie reports Seaman Jones got burned. Steam kettle. Doc McIntyre is on the scene."

More ominous crashes sounded from below as equipment broke loose and skidded across the decks. The XO's carefully crafted rig-for-sea plan was coming apart. It simply was not up to this level of torture.

"Loss of number one R114," Ensign Clay called out. "Loss of air conditioning. I don't have anyone who can get to engine room middle level to start another R114."

"That's it," Glass called out. "Let's go deep before we really hurt somebody. We'll ask for forgiveness later. Dive, make your depth six hundred feet."

The relief in Sam Wallich's voice was palpable. "Full dive on the bow planes! Full dive on the stern planes. Give me a ten-degree down angle."

"Depth six-five feet, coming to six hundred feet. Depth seven-zero feet."

The big boat slipped beneath the sea, leaving behind the tumult of the roiling sea's surface.

Joe Glass, still clinging to the periscope for support, called out, "'Scope's under. Lowering number two scope." He slapped up the training handles and reached into the overhead to rotate the big red 'scope control ring.

Bill Dooley checked the status lights on the ballast control panel and called out, "Speed twelve, all masts and antennas housed."

Toledo was passing through two hundred feet before the pitching and heaving finally, mercifully, stopped.

Brian Edwards emerged from the radio room, his face looking a little less gray than when he went in. "Skipper, we just got the message off before you went deep. Got a satellite receipt but no acknowledgement from SUBLANT."

"Thanks, XO." Glass nodded. "For now, we'll just assume they got it. And that they approved our request." He looked around the chaos that until a few minutes ago had been a well-stowed, ship-shape submarine control room. "Guess we'd better schedule a field day and look at that rig-for-sea plan again."

Brian Edwards chuckled weakly.

"Right after the doc looks at your eye. My guess is you're going to have one beaut of a shiner."

Ψ

Jim Ward watched the ever-darkening clouds building high in the eastern sky. Lightning flashed and thunder reverberated off the mountains behind them. The wind had already picked up, bending the palmettos and swamp pines until their tops almost brushed the ground.

Watching the racing clouds, Ward figured the storm's full fury would hit them in less than an hour. The SEALs' hiding place, little more than a low mound of grassy mud in the middle of the low-lying swamp, would be very vulnerable to any storm surge or even flooding from heavy rains in the mountains as the water rushed for the lower ground. It was not advisable to remain there. Time to head for altitude, whether they wanted to or not.

It had also occurred to Ward that they were lying in the mud somewhere in the vicinity of one of the most humiliating defeats in his country's history. He had studied the Bay of Pigs at the Academy. Now he knew what those men must have felt like as they lay pinned down in this bog, their fates sealed.

Sean Horton, the team's unofficial enlisted leader, antici-pated his commander's next order and rose from the grass.

"Think we'd better get moving, Skipper? Sure don't want to be out here when that storm hits or it'll wash us all the way to the Yucatan."

Ward nodded. "Yep, I'd rather be up on the hills, somewhere on higher ground. Let's saddle up and get a move on."

The first big drops of wind-driven rain splattered across the muddy water.

"Sure hope those Cuban patrols are smart enough to come in out of the rain," Tony Garcia mumbled as he emerged from beneath a brushy shrub, wiping sleep from his eyes. "If we're going to be out in this crap, just as soon not have to crawl through the mud on my belly, ducking bullets."

The four SEALs slipped into the chest-deep water, slogging their way across the coastal swamp, heading in the general direction of the inland mountains. Jed Dulkowski took lead first, moving about ten yards ahead of Ward. The others followed at ten-yard intervals, crouching low and near the shore while slipping silently through the muck.

The water, shoved sideways by the howling wind, seemed to gain a life of its own, the droplets pelting them like bullets. It was all but impossible to see more than a few feet ahead in the deluge. Palmetto fronds, huge slabs with knife-sharp edges blown free by the driving wind, shot across the swamp.

The team pushed forward, toward the promise of drier land, or at least firmer footing. They finally entered the low-growing mangrove thicket that protected the saltwater swamp's shoreward edge. The thickly entangled roots were all but impenetrable, but at least they provided some protection from flying debris in the cavern of brush.

The exhausted SEALs carefully threaded their way through the dark maze of slippery vegetation. It seemed that one step forward cost two sideways and a slide into the stinking mud.

The sky was almost dark by the time they were finally free.

Ward was not sure if the dearth of light was the storm reaching new intensity or just night falling. It really did not matter. The wind still howled across the tropical landscape, still drove a blinding rain so thick it made breathing difficult.

Emerging from the underbrush, the team found themselves on a narrow dirt road, barely more than two parallel ruts in the sand separated by a narrow strip of weeds. Probably some hunter's track into the swamp or the remains of some old sugar plantation road, though it seemed to head off in the general direction that they wanted to go, toward the foothills.

"Let's get a couple of miles inland and then find a place to hole up until this blows over," Jim Ward yelled over the shrieking wind and a deafening clap of nearby thunder. The other three nodded as they headed down the road at a trot. Each man's muscles cramped, threatening rebellion. They had treaded water all day, and now they were swimming again, this time through palm fronds, limbs, and beating rainfall and wind.

After following the road for half an hour, they came to a fork. The main road, if it could be called that, headed off to the left. The path to the right seemed much less used, so overgrown that it appeared abandoned.

Without hesitation, Jim Ward led off on the right fork. Two hundred yards down the track, it narrowed to a single-file trail. Another thousand yards of fighting through the overgrown underbrush and they stumbled upon a tin-roofed shed. One wall had collapsed and half the rusty roof was gone, likely blown away by past storms.

Ward crawled over the fallen and rotting timbers, making his way carefully into what was left of the shack. Horton, Garcia, and Dulkowski followed him in. At least they were finally out of the wind and most of the rain.

They could get nourishment, rest, and get ready to hit the road again. But they were far from safe. If anybody else was out in this weather, they might decide to seek some shelter in the shack, too. And that "anybody" could just as easily be some of the soldiers they had seen earlier on the beach.

They ate, they rested, but they listened hard for the sound of wet footsteps emerging from the jungle.

Ψ

TJ Dillon paid the cabbie and then jumped out of the ancient Ford hack and into the midst of a tropical deluge. Even though it was only a short dash into the Café Vedado, he was soaked to the skin by the time he made it inside. A popular gathering place for the government crowd and businessmen, both local and foreign, trying to deal with them, the café featured a large street-side veranda, perfect for a relaxing afternoon cup of coffee while lazing in the warm sunshine.

But this day the outside tables were wet and deserted. Inside was a crowded, noisy beehive of activity. Dillon shouldered his way through the heavy mahogany and glass double doors. The hostess immediately handed him a thick dry towel before leading him to a table in the far back corner of the crowded main room. He ordered a *café con leche* and *pastelito de guayaba*.

Dillon leaned back, sipped the hot sweet coffee, munched the guava pastry, and gazed out the windows at the gray skies and wind-driven rain. According to the message, "Jose Manuel" was supposed to find Dillon and make contact, whether that person was being brushed by the fringes of a tropical storm or not. Dillon only needed to sit and wait, looking every bit the harried businessman called out to a meeting on a miserable afternoon and who was now cooling his heels, waiting for some thoughtless government minion to get around to keeping his appointment on Cuban time.

"*Senor* Dillon, a thousand apologies." The short, dapper

young man gave the merest suggestion of a courtly bow before extending his hand. He was well-dressed, solidly built, with dark, expressive eyes and a close-trimmed mustache. He spoke English with only a touch of an accent. "I'm very sorry that it was necessary to meet on such a day as this. And to be late is simply unforgivable on my part."

Dillon rose and took the offered hand.

"Not at all, Jose. It is a pleasure to see you again."

"Jose" had offered a firm grip and a real-enough smile. He sat down across from Dillon and signaled the waitress, who knew already what he wanted. She scurried over with a steaming cup of coffee.

TJ had no idea who this man was or where he fit into the game they were playing, but he appeared to know all the right passphrases. Somebody in the CIA's vast labyrinth had determined that it was important for these two operatives to share a cup of coffee on a stormy Havana afternoon.

"How was your flight, *Senor* Dillon? I'm sorry to hear that you did not find the Hotel Santa Isabel acceptable. It is one of our oldest and finest *turista* hotels." Jose spoke over the rim of his cup. He paused to blow on the hot liquid, took a tiny sip, and then said, "But of course the Hotel Nacional de Cuba is much more convenient for your purposes. Most visiting business-people prefer its amenities. Isn't it so?"

Dillon nodded noncommittally.

"The flight was comfortable, thank you. Just another business trip. And the hotel is fine."

"Of course, of course," Manuel said quickly. "I fully understand. The rest of your trip is arranged. I have a car that will take us to the Santo Domingo sugar plantation first thing in the morning. *Senor* Riveras is most eager to discuss your business proposition and appreciates your interest in the business relationship you are offering our country and its people. We are excited to pursue any opportunity to bring a better standard of living to our dedicated workers and to assure the revolution is finally able to reach its promised glory. *Senor* Riveras promises to have his key assistants available to address any questions or concerns you may have about doing business with our country."

Dillon nodded and smiled. This came as a surprise. Kirkland had not said anything about a trip to a sugar plantation. He was here to try to find out what was going on with the national government. That meant snooping around Havana. Why this jaunt out into the country?

"I understand that you like to ride," Manuel went on. "*Senor* Riveras maintains one of the finest stables in all of Cuba. Please bring your riding clothes. We will certainly have the opportunity to ride up into the mountains as we conduct our business discussions. You must see the real Cuba, away from all this, some of which remains from the corrupt times before the revolution."

He gestured around broadly, taking in the whole neighborhood. Curiously, he ended with his finger just touching his ear and lingering there for a telling moment.

"Sounds like it could be a productive and enjoyable day," Dillon responded.

Clearly Manuel was concerned about their discussion being overheard and was making sure Dillon was aware of the possibility. The café would almost certainly have more listening devices than spoons and forks. Dillon figured that anything said in public in this backwater police state would end up being scrutinized by some government snoop somewhere in those faceless gray buildings he had passed on the way to the hotel.

Then he suddenly realized the reason for the diversion on horseback. What better way to get away from prying eyes and sensitive ears than on horseback on some jungle mountain?

Jose Manuel rose abruptly.

"I must depart now. I will meet you at your hotel tomorrow morning. I am afraid that it is a rather long journey, so we must depart early, say six o'clock? I promise we will have hot *café con leche* prepared for the trip. And perhaps more of the *pastelitos de guayaba*." He nodded toward the plate, empty except for crumbs.

The Cuban then spun on his heel and walked out of the café, immediately jumping into a waiting car and disappearing into a cascade of pounding rain.

15

The storm finally slackened and blew over, but not until well after midnight. After the rain's incessant drumming on the tumble-down shack's rusty tin roof, the sudden silence was deafening. The SEALs slowly crawled out of the ramshackle hut, easing their cramped legs and shaking the water from their ponchos.

Jim Ward looked around carefully. The meager moonlight, veiled by wispy dark clouds quickly scudding across the sky, barely illuminated the jungle scene. The place smelled of dank earth and rotting vegetation. He caught a whiff of something dead and decomposing.

"Let's saddle up," Ward whispered. "Nothing here, and we have a lot of miles to cover if we intend to hitch a ride out of here."

The little group snatched up their packs and slipped off into the jungle. Water cascaded from every tree leaf, making a secondary rainstorm, further drenching the already cold, soaked men.

After backtracking to the fork in the trail, they headed off on the route they had bypassed before. The trail was open and easy to follow but mostly flooded from the night's downpour.

By the time the moon slipped below the mountains, the team emerged from the swampy jungle into the adjacent farmland, acre after acre of thick-growing sugar cane. The going was much easier as they simply followed dirt roads through the towering cane. The roads, although slick with mud that seemed to stick to everything, were empty at that hour, and the rain had washed away any tracks on the well-worn course. Morning would bring out the farmers, quickly obliterating any indications of the SEALs' passage.

Chance discovery by someone out early was not a likely threat. The SEALs would see their light well before there was a risk of being spotted. Then, if they did happen upon some early-rising farmers checking on their crop after the storm, they merely had to move off the cane road. The sugar cane grew so thick that anyone moving a couple of yards off the road totally disappeared.

The dogs were the real problem. Every little village or isolated farm would be home to several. Their yipping and snarling in the middle of a quiet night was enough to rouse even the deepest-sleeping farmer.

The dogs forced Jim Ward's exhausted SEALs to make wide detours around anything that remotely resembled civilization. They simply could not afford to be discovered idly strolling here in the middle of the night. The locals would take a dim view of unexpected guests and would not hesitate to turn the SEALs over to the Cuban secret police. Then they would end up dead, imprisoned, or maybe—even worse—on *NBC Nightly News*.

By the time the eastern horizon started to turn pink and gold, Ward's team was only a couple of miles from the foot of the nearest mountain. Another hour and they would be up on the slopes, well away from the farmland and chance discovery.

Better yet, the GPS informed them that they would almost be at their rendezvous point.

But traveling those last couple of miles in the awakening day was far too dangerous. Ward signaled the team off the road, into the cane. The thick growth was already steaming with heat. By the time the sun reached its zenith, the field would be one large sauna, without even the hope of a cooling sea breeze finding them in that thicket.

As the team moved fifty yards through the cane, the sun climbed to well above the horizon. Sweat poured off the men as they shoved their way through, penetrating by brute force.

"Okay, that's surely far enough," Ward gasped. "Let's bed down and get some rest." He dropped his pack and slumped to the ground.

Tony Garcia pulled out his combat knife and sawed off one of the towering canes. He cut a foot-long hunk and tossed it to Sean Horton before cutting pieces for each of the other SEALs. They chewed the sweet, tough fibers, drawing out the refreshing sugary juice.

Ward swallowed a wad of cane and then ordered, "Sean, you take the first watch. Jed, relieve him in an hour. I'm going to dream about somebody far better-looking than you bastards."

Ψ

The sun was just peeking over the eastern horizon, painting the sea and sky in Technicolor. The *RV Deep Ocean One* bobbed and pitched in the last gasps of the tropical storm.

Bruce deFrance, fresh from a long, soothing shower, chose his clothes carefully. Today was an important day. The rose-colored Egyptian cotton shirt and lavender cravat would be the perfect touch of color to complement his cream linen tropical suit. Just the look he needed—a self-assured, powerful international businessman.

He had just tucked the silk cravat into his collar when he heard the high-pitched whine of an approaching jet helicopter. deFrance took a final sip of coffee without even tasting it and left his stateroom for the ship's bridge. It was important that he maintained the appearance of a busy oil executive in touch with his vast empire even as he floated out here in the midst of the Caribbean aboard this impressive research vessel.

The big Jet Ranger was flaring out for touchdown on the *Deep Ocean One's* forward helipad when deFrance walked into the enclosed bridge.

"Good morning, sir," Captain Savoir greeted his employer. "I hope that little storm did not disturb your sleep."

"Not really." deFrance helped himself to a cup of coffee and fresh pastry from a small buffet that had been set up along the after bulkhead. "As you mariners say, I do believe that I am getting my sea legs."

Savoir gestured with his cup toward the helicopter that had just landed, its door opening.

"I'm sure you have noticed that your guests have arrived. They will find a very nice breakfast awaiting them below. The geology team is standing by in their lab for a demonstration."

deFrance merely nodded as he watched the visitors descend from the helicopter and scurry aft across the forecastle.

They were a motley bunch. He recognized the two men dressed in London's latest version of tropical power suits. Samuel Brown and Harold Smyth were two of the most powerful oil executives in Europe. Together they represented most of the European Union's petroleum interests, and they reputedly—and almost certainly—had hidden ties with the big Middle Eastern players.

deFrance did not recognize the other two men. They were a

much different sort—hulking big men, much rougher and less refined, and obviously dangerous. deFrance had no idea who they were or why they were here, but he knew that he did not like having their type aboard his ship.

General Almirante Juan Valdez of the Venezuelan Navy, and representative of his country's president, was last to emerge from the chopper and marched straight toward the superstructure. He glanced up at the bridge for a second before disappearing through the hatch.

Bruce deFrance walked out the back of the bridge and climbed down the ladder toward the ship's wardroom, moving slowly. He was in no hurry to meet his guests, but it was a requirement. He stepped into the wardroom, the largest single space onboard. The smartly appointed compartment served as a combination dining room, officers' lounge, and meeting room. It filled most of the main level—which Captain Savoir insisted on calling the O-1 level—a few feet aft of deFrance's stateroom.

Samuel Brown and Harold Smyth were already politely nibbling on pastries and idly chatting. The two others—the large, dark men in their ill-fitting suits—were gobbling down the food, chewing with their mouths open while following everything happening around them with darting, suspicious eyes. These two were very clearly not executive types.

Valdez stood alone in the center of the room, regally surveying everything and everybody. His tropical khaki uniform was smartly tailored and pressed. His black boots glistened in the wardroom's soft light. He wore the barest hint of a disapproving scowl as he glanced at the two gangster types.

deFrance walked over to the admiral and extended his hand.

"My dear Admiral Valdez, it is so very good to see you again."

Valdez nodded but did not acknowledge the offered hand.

In a voice too low to be heard by anyone but deFrance, he asked, "Did the package arrive?"

deFrance murmured, in an equally low voice, "Yes, it is safely stowed in the bottom of the cargo hold. There is no trace of it anywhere in the ship's papers."

"Good, very good." Valdez nodded. "You are capable of following directions." Then, in a louder voice, so that everyone could hear, he added, "*Senor* deFrance, it is most kind of you to invite us out to see your little research ship. I hope that you have some very good news to share with us this morning."

The oilman let his hand drop. He had extended no invitation to Admiral Valdez. The call, late last night, informing deFrance of the admiral's presence at this meeting, had come as a complete surprise. One of the most powerful—and, as deFrance had witnessed, violently dangerous—men in Latin America had decided to invite himself along for the visit on a most important day for the project. It would be absolutely unthinkable not to allow him to attend and appear to be pleased about it.

deFrance ushered the group to seats at the center table.

"Gentlemen," he opened, with a nod and a tip of his coffee cup. "Welcome aboard the Research Vessel *Deep Ocean One*. This is the most advanced geophysical research ship in the world. She was very specifically designed and built to carry out geological research in the ocean's very deepest waters. We are currently engaged in extensive geologic exploration in the Cuban Deep. So far, at great expense..."

"Cut to the chase, deFrance," the larger of the two rough men growled from the far side of the table. "Is there oil beneath our asses or is there not?"

Bruce deFrance's jaw dropped. He was not accustomed to being spoken to in such a manner.

"We'll get to that soon enough, Herr Jurgen," Harold Smyth interjected, smiling weakly. "I know your type...your people... tend to be impatient with us more traditional business types, but we would like to see and hear what our initial investment has bought us so far."

"Nonsense!" Jurgen shot back. He rose from his chair, leaning forward menacingly and resting his massive weight on his fists. "You English tight asses can play games all you want while this bastard flushes your money down the shitter." He slammed his fist onto the table. The cutlery jumped, one of the china cups crashing to the deck. "My people aren't so forgiving. They really expect return on investment, not fancy yachts disguised as deep-sea exploration ships."

Smyth's face flushed. His smile disappeared.

Valdez stood and raised his hands, palms extended out. The admiral's voice was coaxing, soothing yet exuding firm control, as he calmed the tense situation.

"Gentlemen, there is really no reason to do anything but hear what Mr. deFrance has to tell us." He shot the large man a tight, menacing glare.

Jurgen sat down quietly, his face switching from angry red to ashen gray. The admiral had, in only a few words, made it very clear that he was in charge of this particular breakfast meeting.

"Bruce, please continue," Valdez continued. "We are most interested in your findings, but please understand that our time is limited. And our expectations are quite high."

deFrance smiled wanly. He walked toward the door.

"Gentlemen, since you appear to be on a tight schedule and you are much more interested in the results rather than the details of the search, let us proceed immediately to the laboratory."

The visitors followed him into the passageway and down a ladder to the next lower deck. They walked aft a few feet before entering the brightly lit laboratory space.

The spacious room glistened with polished metal. Large flat-panel displays hung from the overhead in every conceivable place. Papers, books, and humming computer processors filled all the available horizontal space. Powerful fans throbbed as they pushed chilled air into the room to keep the gear cool and properly functioning.

The geologists, all ten of them, stood in a tight huddle against the far bulkhead.

The head geologist stepped forward as the group entered the room. deFrance could not help but think of the Swiss lawn gnomes that had become so popular with Britain's garden set. The short, squat man pulled a remote control from his lab coat pocket and clicked it toward one of the large-screen video displays. It burst into life, showing the charts and graphs that had so mystified deFrance yesterday. The geologist proceeded with the same explanation that he had given his boss then.

Samuel Brown was scribbling some figures on a small calf-skin-covered notepad. When the geologist reached the end of his presentation, Brown looked up, his eyes wide.

"Doctor, do you mean to say that any expected oil and gas are more than ten kilometers down, in water that is over three thousand meters deep?"

"Yes, sir. That is what I am saying. This is very exciting. We have never found reserves at such depths. And we postulate several billion barrels of oil. Billion with a 'b.'"

Brown shook his head. "We are talking a very, very large investment to bring this in." He scribbled some more. "I'm guessing more than ten billion Euros and at least five years before we see any returns."

Jurgen stepped forward again, his face red.

"You must be joking! My syndicate has already laid down several hundred million. Now you thieves are telling me that this is only going to be the...what do you call...the 'down payment?'"

Valdez shook his head slowly, holding up a hand to dismiss further discussion.

"Gentlemen, we need to regroup and discuss this possibility in some detail. We have been presented with a very large opportunity, but it is wrapped in a very large risk. I suggest that we all fly back to Caracas and consider our options in comfort while our friends here continue their important work."

"Options?" Jurgen growled. "My first option is to call my investors and tell them to pull the plug on this glorified craps game!"

Valdez nodded but did not reply. Instead, he turned to deFrance.

"Bruce, I suggest that you accompany us."

But there was no suggestion in his words. deFrance understood that he had no choice in the matter, so they all moved to the helicopter.

The six men quickly settled into their overstuffed leather captain's chairs as the Jet Ranger spooled up to lift off the research ship's deck and turned away over the shimmering Caribbean water. By the time Bruce deFrance looked out the window, the *Deep Ocean One* was little more than a small toy boat bobbing in the sea far below them.

Once they were leveled off and pushing southward, Admiral Valdez suddenly stood and pulled from his holster his old Navy revolver. He waved the barrel, clearly ordering Jurgen to stand. The big tough understood perfectly and seemed not at all surprised, as if he had been in such spots many times before and survived. He slowly, warily pulled himself erect. His partner tensed but remained still.

"Jurgen, I'm very sorry that you will not be able to join us in Caracas," Valdez said.

The hulking gangster cocked his head and looked questioningly at the old admiral. The pilot simultaneously actuated the side hatch open and pulled hard on the collective. Wind whistled through the open doorway as the Jet Ranger pitched over, banking hard to starboard.

Caught off balance, Jurgen was thrown toward the hatch, but he managed to grab the emergency strap over the doorway. Valdez fired once, instantly turning Jurgen's right knee into a bloody mass.

Off-balance and screaming in pain and terror, the big man disappeared out of the helicopter. For the barest instant, Jurgen caught the hatch lip with his fingertips. Then he slipped away, still screaming as he plummeted toward the sea.

"Now," the admiral said, loud enough to be heard over the roar of the wind and the chopper's engine. "Anyone else have doubts about the possibilities of our amazing petroleum discovery?"

16

Over half a century had passed since the old taxicab had rolled off Detroit's production line. Once it had been a shiny new example of American manufacturing prowess, a prestigious automobile. But it had clearly and long since seen its better days.

TJ Dillon held on to the panic strap as the ancient vehicle bounced and jolted up the steep, narrow mountain road at entirely too great a speed. The Guamuhaya Mountains were not Cuba's highest, but they were certainly steep and treacherous enough, with some peaks topping out at over three thousand feet above sea level.

Dillon dared to glance out the side window, then immediately wished he had not. There was nothing except misty mountain air between him and the green jungle canopy several hundred feet below them. No berm, no guardrail, nothing, just an impossible drop into a deep ravine.

The car's bald tires spun wildly, desperately searching for the barest traction, as the cabbie slid around another switchback. Dillon tightened his iron-hard grip as the cab teetered on the very edge, gripping the rain-slick road at the last possible instant before shooting uphill toward the next twisting turn.

Dillon dared another peek. Far below, the Agabama River snaked its muddy brown course through the mountains, foaming and crashing on the rocks, cutting the mountain range in half as it headed toward the Caribbean many miles south. A picture flashed through Dillon's mind of the crumpled cab resting down there on those rocks. It would be weeks before anyone found their mangled bodies.

Amazingly, Jose Manuel snored quietly in the seat next to him, peacefully slumbering as Dillon contemplated fiery death.

The cabbie turned off what Manuel had euphemistically called the "boulevard" and onto a still narrower lane which led them to a high metal gate. As they approached, the gate creaked open just wide enough for the cab to slip through, then slid shut with a clang.

Dillon thought he caught the barest glimpse of an armed guard hidden back amongst the trees. He had spent too many years on too many missions and had been trained too well as a SEAL sniper to miss the well-hidden gunner or to not feel a rifle scope trained on him.

Dillon's finely tuned antenna went on full alert. Why would a simple sugar farmer need armed protection? This trip promised to be a whole lot more than a quiet horseback ride in the mountains and a briefing from Manuel as they rode.

Jose Manuel woke and stretched as the cab leaped forward, climbing toward an impressive hacienda that was just becoming visible on a hilltop beyond the trees. The lane wound around as it climbed, the landscape changing abruptly from jungle to carefully manicured lawn and well-tended gardens. The hacienda, all glistening white stucco with a deep-red tile roof, was left from a different age, a time of Spanish colonial *patrons* and vast riches. Whoever called this place home had found a way to get the most traction from his country's pallid economic engine.

The cab skidded to a stop, spraying freshly raked gravel across the lawn. Jose Manuel hopped out, stretched—they had been riding for more than two hours—and grabbed his small bag from the trunk. Dillon followed the young agent to the front entrance. The massive mahogany double doors silently swung open as they approached.

Dillon gawked as he took in the expansive foyer. The cool, shadowy interior was straight out of some sixteenth-century Spanish castle, complete with the ancient suits of armor and old swords above the massive oak mantel. Thick Moroccan rugs were spread over blood-red Saltillo tile floors. A sunlit courtyard glistened invitingly through French doors at the far end of the room, and there Dillon spotted the blue-tinged water of a large swimming pool.

"Wow." Dillon whistled. "Some little farmhouse."

Manuel smiled as he nonchalantly tossed his bag onto what looked to Dillon to be a very old and expensive chair. He cupped his hands to his lips and called out loudly, "*Hola. Estamos aqui.*"

A barefoot old man, dressed in a white peasant singlet and loose-fitting trousers, slowly shuffled through a side door off to the left.

"*Don* Jose," the ancient servant croaked as he made his way toward the young Cuban and hugged him. "You are late. Your father is expecting you in the solarium."

Jose Manuel seized the old man in a bear hug that threatened to break his brittle bones, then bussed him on both cheeks.

"It is good to see you, too, Pepito," Jose answered as he lowered the old man to the floor.

"Your father?" Dillon questioned. "Did he say, 'your father?'"

"*Si.* Welcome to the *Casa de la Roche,* my family home," Manuel said. "My ancestors once owned everything that you can see from up here. Now we hold only this house and a few thousand hectares of sugar cane land. Much changed under the Castros. Much will change again." He walked toward the courtyard. "Come, it's time you met the *patron* and learned the real reasons for your visit."

Dillon was not sure what he expected as he entered the sunlit room, but a large, grizzled old bear of a man in green fatigues was not exactly it.

"*Senor* Dillon." The old man's voice was as deep and powerful as a foghorn. "It is good of you to visit us. I see that you have enjoyed a long journey with my son, Jose Manuel de la Roche. Allow me to introduce myself." He drew himself up even taller. "I am Ricardo Martinez Manuel de la Roche." He spread his arms wide. "Welcome to our modest home."

TJ Dillon was not easily caught off-guard, but this entire turn of events was unexpected. The elder de la Roche looked every bit the aging revolutionary, as if he had stepped out of the army Castro led down out of the Sierra Maestros in 1959. But he sounded more like an unrepentant *capitalista*, and they had been an endangered species in Cuba for more than a half century.

"Please, have a seat," the *patron* said, waving his hand toward a comfortable-looking overstuffed leather reading chair. He slowly lowered himself onto the adjacent matching couch. Jose Manuel pulled up a side chair.

"You have many questions, I am sure," the elder man told Dillon. "But first, let me tell you a little story."

Senor de la Roche opened a small ornate wooden box sitting on the side table. "Would you like a smoke?" he offered Dillon. "These are some of Cuba's finest. I have them specially rolled from carefully selected tobacco."

Dillon extracted a fat green cigar from the offered box, inhaling the heady aroma of finely cured tobacco. The three men slowly completed the ritual clipping, warming, and lighting before settling back in clouds of fragrant blue smoke.

"Ah," the *patron* sighed. "I find a good cigar really enhances a pleasant conversation. Don't you?"

Dillon nodded. "An excellent blend, very smooth," he offered, and meant it. "Even at 8:00 a.m."

The elder de la Roche took a series of puffs and went on.

"Our ancestors came to Cuba from Spain many centuries ago. Our family was among the very first plantation owners in the Caribbean. We built this island with the sweat of our brow and the power of our hand. When Spain rotted away from the inside, we fought to free ourselves from the corpse. America was there to grab the pieces before we could finish the task on our own. They promised us independence, but it never really came."

The old man puffed again on the cigar for a few seconds, collecting his thoughts. "Then Battista and his cronies, backed by the Americans, tried to make this even more of an American colony. We fought alongside the Castro brothers to try to free ourselves from Battista's decay and graft and corruption. We rid ourselves of him and the Americans, but in the process, we made a serious mistake. We underestimated the Castro brothers. At first, we really believed that we were building a better democratic Cuba, an independent Cuba, and that we were doing it together, every economic stratum of our people, and all would benefit."

de la Roche coughed and spat out a bit of tobacco.

"The de la Roche family was in the inner circle. My brother was one of Fidel's most trusted advisors, or so we thought. We were his bankers and his link to the rest of the *patrons*."

Ricardo Martinez Manuel de la Roche's face was growing red with anger. He was almost shouting by the time he finished the next few sentences.

"Then the purges began. We turned on many of our fellow

patrons. Those that could not escape or were not willing to give up all they had worked so hard to accumulate and bow to the revolution disappeared into his bottomless prisons. Their riches went straight into Fidel's coffers. We de la Roches were, by then, hated by our own class. And I must say that I do not blame them."

de la Roche paused for a breath before launching into the story again, as if the telling of it was sapping most of his strength. "Then one day the *Direccion de Inteligencia Nacional* came for us. Do you know the DINA, *Senor* Dillon?"

TJ nodded. Castro's secret police had a very well-earned reputation for terror and torture.

"It was my brother's turn to disappear into the prison at Jaguey Grande. And disappear he did. We cannot even weep over his grave." Tears were rolling down Ricardo's cheeks. "I alone escaped the country and Castro's wrath, first to Haiti, then on to Venezuela. We lived in exile there until the Soviet Union fell and Castro lost much of his international support. Then we became valuable again, an asset necessary in rebuilding some of Cuba's economy. I did what was necessary to regain my family's land.

"Now the Castros are gone. But there is really very little change. Those in power allow us to eke out a meager living as long as we feed their insatiable appetite for dollars and keep a very low profile. They care not about our politics, only the dollars we generate from what is left of our dominion."

The old man looked Dillon squarely in the eye. "Now do you see why we brought you here?"

Dillon shook his head and answered honestly, "Not really."

With some difficulty, de la Roche pulled himself erect. "It is almost time." He paused for a few seconds. "It is almost time for us to take Cuba back, to seize what is ours, our birthright. The world will soon know the major change in our little country, and we must be ready to take advantage. But we need some minor assistance. That is where you and your CIA puppet masters come in."

"You want us to back a revolt?" Dillon asked.

"No, no." de la Roche shook his head. "We don't want another Bay of Pigs. That would serve no purpose. The world stage is different now. There are too many large, powerful players who want a piece of Cuba. We need to be able to play them off each other. China and that pompous fool Gutierrez in Venezuela are our largest threats. They both want Cuba's oil and our strategic proximity to the USA, and they will do anything to get it."

"And you want us to shoulder them aside," Dillon conjectured. "Very covertly, of course."

"Exactly," the old man answered. "But I must warn you that there are some, even in your own CIA, who are not who they seem to be. Even the one who sent you here may not understand the full measure of what is about to happen or the role he thinks he is going to play. He and others in your government, too, want to have a hand in determining our fate, just as your country once did with Batista. I will tell you more so that you may be prepared for what must eventually be done there as well."

The old *patron* leaned forward and touched Dillon's knee. "We want your help to free Cuba just as your father once tried to help the freedom-seekers in Nicaragua."

TJ Dillon's eyes went wide open. His ears tingled.

The old man stood slowly and hobbled to a wide window at the rear of the room. It afforded him a view of what remained of his plantation below, and then the thickly-vegetated plain that stretched from the base of the mountains twenty miles to the Caribbean Sea. Dillon watched him, still stunned to silence by the unexpected mention of his father.

"Many have been waiting for the Castros to meet the devil,"

de la Roche continued. "They hope to take our island in the resulting breach and turn it their way. Gutierrez and his minion, Admiral Valdez, some within your own CIA, and other snakes coiled up in their nests in those decaying government hovels in Havana all want our unique location an hour's speedboat ride from the shores of the USA. There are other interests who crave the oil that rests beneath the waters off our coast, a trove that is still unknown to most of..."

de la Roche coughed deeply, the effort of the speech almost too much for his old lungs. He finally turned to face Dillon. "You were ostensibly sent here to learn about those snakes that are coiled in their holes in Havana. But at least one in your CIA wanted you to learn more about me as well. About the small militia I have built to be ready for the coming day of reckoning. About our motives, our numbers, our plans, and most importantly, about our loyalties. They know that we have invited you here, but we cannot allow you to report back at this strategic moment. Soon, though, we will ask you to help us. And then, we will share what we know about the specific snakes within your CIA and you can deal with them as you wish. See, *Senor* Dillon, we have begun our own revolution in a much subtler way than Fidel ever did. The time approaches when we will have to back up our methods with our weapons and bravery. In the meanwhile, we cannot allow anyone else in the world—or anyone on our beloved island—to know just what has happened. I am afraid that includes you. You will remain our guest for a little longer, Master Chief. Then it will all be made clear to you for your report to your superiors. You will possibly be our main conduit to those in your government, but not necessarily to the one who sent you. Soon. Very soon."

de la Roche picked up and rang a small bell. Instantly, two uniformed men charged into the solarium from the courtyard. Their AK-47s were at the ready, aimed directly at Dillon's heart.

He jumped up, but there was no way to escape or fight his way clear. He did not even have a weapon on him.

Dillon submissively raised his hands.

"Do not be alarmed, *Senor* Dillon, but we must take all precautions at this point. Take our guest down to the dungeon," de la Roche ordered. "It is time he met our other houseguest, and then he will understand some of the things he has heard and experienced this day."

TJ Dillon was helpless as he was ushered from the room. But his thoughts were elsewhere. His father? This man, a veritable double agent, knew about his father.

Knew more than even TJ was supposed to know.

17

The morning dawned surprisingly bright and clear. A gentle breeze blowing out of the west carried the faint sweet scent of orange blossoms. The cobalt blue sea dipped and slid up *Toledo*'s smoothly rounded bow before crashing against the forward edge of the sail and sliding back down along her flanks. A pod of Atlantic bottlenose dolphins frolicked on the bow wave, leaping and diving, inviting their big brother of the deep to play.

The low Florida coast was just visible on the horizon. The massive NASA Cape Kennedy Vehicle Assembly Building dominated the view. Small fishing boats and coastal freighters dotted the scene off in the distance.

From his position standing atop the *Toledo*'s tall sail, Joe Glass felt like he was on top of the world, the commander of all he saw. The dolphins were a good omen. He sipped a cup of coffee and savored the moment. A single waist-high steel safety line connected to four temporary stanchions formed the "playpen," which afforded Glass some security in his perch. Old Glory snapped in the breeze over his shoulder.

Glass could easily make out a bright red tug idling a couple of miles ahead, just outside the entrance to Port Canaveral.

Closer still, a smaller boat made its way out to greet the black submarine, bobbing easily in the light chop.

"Captain," Ensign Jeff Clay interrupted Glass's sightseeing. "The pilot boat requests permission to come alongside, starboard side."

The young ensign held a bridge-to-bridge transceiver to his ear. He was standing his first under-instruction officer of the deck surfaced watch. He and Doug O'Malley, the actual officer of the deck, were crammed into the submarine's tiny bridge cockpit along with Seaman Will Brownson, the lookout.

Glass glanced over at the little black and white boat flying the red and white "Hotel" signal flag, with a broad "PILOT" signboard stretching the length of the cabin. A man stood easily in the cabin door.

"Very well, Mr. Clay," Glass answered. "Have the COB lay topside to assist the pilot. Ask who the pilot is and inform the XO."

"Mr. Clay, come to ahead one-third," Doug O'Malley instructed the young officer. "You don't want the bow wave to wash all the way back and drown the COB when he swings the hatch open. A wet chief of the boat is an angry chief of the boat."

Jeff Clay nodded. "Sorry, Eng, I didn't think of that." He snatched the 7MC microphone from its holder on the bridge suitcase and ordered, "Ahead one-third."

Down in the control room, Fireman Apprentice Josh Stedman, the helmsman, replied, "Answering ahead one-third," as he spun the engine order telegraph so that the arrow pointed at "Ahead One-Third" and the throttle man, back in Maneuvering, answered.

The big boat dropped speed like they had put on the brakes. The bow wave subsided to the barest ripple and the dolphins disappeared, bored now that there was no large wave to surf.

Glass glanced aft over his shoulder just in time to see the

heavy forward escape hatch swing up and open. Master Chief Wallach's bulky form, made even more bulky by the fat orange life jacket, emerged onto the main deck. He clipped his harness to the deck traveler, firmly connecting him to the submarine. Two crewmen, equally encumbered, climbed up after him and clipped themselves to the deck traveler.

The pilot boat moved alongside the submarine, easily matching its pace. The captain kissed his little craft up against the submarine's round steel side. Wallach grabbed the pilot's hand as the man leaped to *Toledo*'s deck, pulling him safely onboard. The boat smoothly eased away as the pilot disappeared down the hatch. The whole maneuver had taken less than a minute.

"Mr. Clay, you might consider having line handlers lay topside and rig topside for surface," Doug O'Malley instructed with just a hint of sarcasm. He pointed at the red tug, which had just belched a cloud of black smoke, white foam churning under her stern. "That tug over there is not going to be happy if he has to wait to tie up. And stationing the Maneuvering Watch might be a good idea."

Jeff Clay nodded again. There was a lot to learn.

"Officer of the Deck," the 7MC speaker boomed as Dennis Oshley, the leading quartermaster, spoke from his station at the plotting table down in control. "Suggest course three-two-one, ahead two-thirds to conform to navigator's track. Pilot to the bridge. Pilot's name is Captain Patterson."

Jeff Clay ordered, "Right full rudder, steady course three-two-one, ahead two-thirds."

Glass leaned down and spoke to the young officer. "Mr. Clay, always look at the rudder when you have ordered a course change. That way you know the helmsman didn't get confused. Not a serious problem out here, but once we're in the channel, you don't have much time or room. Remember, this channel is only two hundred feet wide, and we are three hundred and sixty feet long."

Clay nodded. "Yes, sir." He looked aft to see the rudder swing to the right.

"Steady course three-two-one, answering ahead two-thirds," Stedman reported. *Toledo*'s nose stopped swinging, steady on the new course. Her white wake broadened and lengthened as the massive screw bit into the water and the submarine picked up speed.

A gray head appeared in the bridge hatch. The pilot laboriously climbed up the steel ladder, ducking his head to miss the whistle linkage as he emerged into the already crowded cockpit.

Glass squatted down and extended his hand. "Welcome aboard *Toledo*, Captain Patterson. Come on up here and join me."

Patterson smiled and grasped the captain's hand. Many years of exposure to the sun and salt had tanned the man's skin to the color of old leather, and squint lines deeply etched his weathered face. He smiled easily as he answered in a thick Southern drawl, "Thank you, Captain." He clambered up into the playpen. "Welcome to Port Canaveral. You'll be tying up port side to Delta two in the Trident Basin. I'm bringing the *Annie M* alongside now. I suggest a power moor forward."

Glass nodded and repeated, "Port side to Delta two in the Trident Basin. *Annie M* in a power moor forward starboard. Mr. Clay, did you hear all that? Please pass it to the XO and navigator."

Pointing to the young ensign, Glass commented, "Mr. Clay is making his first landing today."

The elderly pilot nodded and leaned down. Placing one weathered hand on Clay's shoulder, he quietly drawled, "Don't be worryin' about anything a'tall, Mr. Clay. Together we'll get her tied up safe and sound. We might even learn a thing or two."

Patterson glanced up and saw the tug moving closer, then spoke into the microphone clipped to his jacket collar. "*Annie M*, power moor starboard side forward."

The tug answered with one short toot of her whistle and pulled alongside the submarine. Deck hands forward and aft tossed heaving lines across to waiting sailors standing topside. The sub sailors pulled the heaving lines across, followed by heavy Kevlar mooring lines, which were attached to cleats on the submarine's deck.

"Now, Mr. Clay, do you know how a power moor works?" the pilot asked.

Ensign Clay shook his head. "No, sir. I've never used one. It looks complicated."

Patterson chuckled. "Not at all, son. This here's a classic for pushing a big boat like yours around. It's all in them vectors." He pointed down at the tug. "See how she's tied up all snug alongside and that line heading from her nose to just aft o' your sail is taut?" The elderly pilot did not wait for an answer. "That allows the old *Annie* to move just like she's part of y'all's ship. She can push or pull right in line. If'n we slack the stern line and swing her out perpendicular like, she can push you sideways. Think you can remember all that?"

Clay nodded. It did not seem so complicated after the pilot had explained everything—just a simple vector analysis.

The 7MC blared to life. "Bridge, Navigator, passing Buoy Papa Charlie to port. XO reports Maneuvering Watch stationed below decks, ship is ready to enter port. Harbor control has given us permission to enter port. Channel course is two-seven-zero. Suggest coming to channel course."

Ensign Clay clutched the microphone and answered, "Bridge, aye. Helm, left full rudder, steady course two-seven-zero." He then turned and watched the big rudder swing as he repeated everything to Glass.

Glass nodded. "Mr. Clay, now that we are entering restricted waters, how do you think we would be able to stop the ship if we had a steering casualty?"

Again Ensign Clay shook his head. "I don't know, Captain. Drop the anchor, I suppose."

Glass smiled. "Good answer, Mr. Clay. Don't you think you'd better make it ready? Set snubbing scope for thirty fathoms."

The young officer spoke into the mike. "Make the anchor ready for letting go, snubbing scope thirty fathoms."

Seconds later the reply came back. "Bridge, Anchor Watch, anchor ready for letting go, snubbing scope set at thirty fathoms."

The *Toledo* proceeded down a channel between two lines of buoys, red ones on the starboard side and black ones on the port. Outside the dredged channel, the water faded from deep to pale blue as it became shallower. A finger of stone breakwater projected out from the shore on either side, leaving a narrow opening into the harbor. A crowd of tourists and fishermen stood on the rocky breakwater, waving and enjoying the rare close-up view of a submarine.

The pilot said to Ensign Clay, "I think it's time to turn into the basin. See them ranges down at the far end. Line up on them, real slow and easy like. Might want to come to 'All Stop' and coast around the turn."

Clay picked up the microphone and ordered, "All stop." He glanced down at the compass repeater and read the bearing to the range. "Right two degrees rudder. Steady course three-two-zero."

The sub slowly swung around to the new course but was steadying up way to the left of where they needed to be.

O'Malley leaned over to the young ensign. "Probably need to use full rudder here. You're trying to make a big turn with no power. You need a big rudder."

"Not a problem," Patterson offered. "You need to turn around, anyway, so that you are headin' out. Let me show you what old *Annie M* can do."

The pilot spoke quietly into his transceiver microphone, and the tug answered with a toot of her whistle. White water surged up around the vessel as she backed down. The submarine's bow started to swing more rapidly around.

The pilot waited for a few moments before suggesting, "Now, Mr. Clay, if you would give her a quick kick at 'Ahead One-Third' then come to 'All Stop,' we'll twist right around, sweet as you please."

The combination of the powerful little tug and the big submarine spun them around so that they came to a stop right alongside their berth. Only a few yards of open water separated them from the shore.

As the submarine's little outboard motor pushed the stern sideways, the *Annie M* easily matched pace, pushing *Toledo*'s bow. She slowly and gracefully moved sideways until the huge rubber camels that lined the dock groaned under the pressure of the massive submarine pushing against them. Line handlers on the pier passed mooring lines over to Master Chief Wallach's topside crew. Within minutes, *Toledo* was safely tied to the pier with lines doubled.

"You may secure the main engines," Glass said as he climbed down into the cockpit. "Not a bad landing for the first one. Nobody died, and we don't have to call Norfolk and tell them we broke their submarine."

With that, the skipper grinned, winked at the young officer, and disappeared down the hatch.

18

Simon Castellon was uneasy, itchy. Something was just not right, but he did not know what. From long experience, the seasoned guerilla fighter knew to trust his instincts. They had saved his life more times than he could remember. Those instincts were now screaming.

Something was wrong. Very wrong. Only what was it?

He was always on edge when he was in the city, away from the mountainous jungle that he knew so well. Up there he knew every rock and tree, every snake and bug. Down here the snakes walked upright and were much more deadly. Like chameleons, they disappeared in their surroundings. And their deadly bite often came without warning or provocation.

Castellon leaned back, propping himself against a brick wall and trying to appear calm, his battered, sweat-stained straw hat drawn low over his eyes. He was a day worker waiting patiently for some menial task, standing as far back into the cool shade as he could get. A half-dozen of his men were mixed with the rest of the jobless peons, disguised as struggling workers trying to scratch the merest existence from Gutierrez's socialist paradise.

Castellon spent the interminable wait working out his strategy —his plan for survival. Gutierrez was the only game in town. He had the money and, more importantly, the power. It was best to play the shouting fat fool's game as long as he had the guns on his side.

Castellon was not fooled by *el Presidente's* promises to make life better for everyone, to bring real equality. The *revolutionario* had been around too long and had seen too many bullying dictators use the peons' misery to grab power, then rely on their continued frustration to maintain control over them. There was no way for him to place any trust in Gutierrez despite the convincing rhetoric. Certainly *el Presidente* needed Castellon's drug sources and his guerrilla fighters. But Castellon did not hold any illusions. Gutierrez would turn on him for the slightest incentive from elsewhere.

A wise soldier always hedged his bets. He always had options to play, risks and rewards to weigh. This meeting might be one of those options. But it could also be a trap. Castellon knew that he was a dead man if Gutierrez—or worse, Admiral Juan Valdez—caught any hint of the consultation in which he was about to participate.

The sleepy, sun-dappled *piazza* spread out in front of him. Late afternoon heat shimmered off the cobblestones. Most everyone with a respectable job was home, enjoying a quiet *siesta*. The only people out here were the occasional tourist not smart enough to come in out of the sun, and working men desperate for a few *pesos* to feed their starving families.

"Pardon, *senor*." The tourist's Spanish was broken, with a horrible *Yanqui* accent. "*Direcciones a Cathedral de Santa Maria?*" The man read from an English-Spanish dictionary.

Castellon instantly tensed. The American tourist was giving the recognition code. Surely this old American in loud, tacky Bermuda shorts and a Hawaiian shirt was not his contact. He was supposed to be meeting someone from the Chinese Embassy, not the American CIA.

"The cathedral, it is not far," Castellon answered in halting English, working very hard to hide his Harvard education. "But the way, it is complicated. I will be happy to show you and to point out all of the sites along the way. For ten thousand *bolivares*."

The old American hesitated a beat, pretending to do the conversion in his head, and then pulled out a wallet, peeled off some notes, and handed them to Castellon. It was a bit over two US dollars.

The erstwhile tour guide motioned for the tourist to follow him as he headed down a narrow, ancient street lined with shuttered shops. After a couple of blocks, he turned left, then left again, into progressively narrower and more dilapidated streets. The pair did not exchange a word, the *turista* always staying a step or two behind the guide. Twenty minutes later, the strange pair ducked into a small, dark *casita* and plopped down at one of the roughhewn tables. They were the only customers in the bar.

"Now, *Senor* Castellon, let me introduce myself. My name is Josh Kirkland. I represent the United States of America, and I think that we need to talk."

Ψ

Admiral Juan Valdez rubbed his tired eyes and continued to carefully read the lengthy report opened on his desk. The heavy technical jargon and complex equations were meaningless, just gibberish to the old sailor. The many graphs and drawings were not much help either.

The real message was clear. A tremendous amount of oil lay miles below the Cuban Deep, untold wealth that was more than enough to make Venezuela the richest, most powerful nation in the Western Hemisphere. And to make him the most powerful man in Venezuela, if not the Americas.

But there was a serious problem. It would take a tremendous effort to tap those riches. And that effort would cost money. Serious money. Even with the billions from all of Venezuela's current producing wells, and all the money from Castellon's drug operations, he still was not even close to having enough capital to bankroll such an investment.

The old sailor scratched his chin and yawned. He rose from behind his ancient, battered desk and stepped over to the mahogany sideboard. A taste of cognac and a good cigar always stimulated the thought processes.

He had just lit the Havana when his assistant, Jorge, walked into his office.

"*Pardon, Almirante, el Presidente* is on the phone," Jorge told him as he moved toward the desk. His movements were surprisingly quick and cat-like for so large a man. He picked up the phone and handed it to Valdez so his boss would not even have to lean forward to get it.

"I will prepare the automobile," he said over his shoulder as he silently left the room, as usual anticipating his commander's needs.

Valdez heard Cesar Gutierrez's almost feminine voice on the telephone.

"Juan, I heard about the unfortunate accident on your flight." The leader almost giggled. "It must have been a terrible shock. A hatch malfunction? Who would ever expect such a thing? Sad, sad."

Valdez could easily picture Gutierrez shaking his large head, the heavy beetle brows deeply wrinkled, feigning concern.

Valdez downed a slug of cognac and grinned. "I'll pass your heartfelt condolences to *Senor* Jurgen's employers." He took a slow puff of his cigar before continuing. "Now, *mi Presidente*, how can I serve you?" He exhaled, blowing a perfect smoke ring.

"*Almirante*, there are things that we must discuss. Soon. I am particularly concerned about our co-investment with our Cuban friends. I fear that our window of opportunity there could be closing." A short pause followed, as if Gutierrez was gathering his courage to ask a question. "I am concerned with the Americans and your plans on how you will be able to keep them away from our business in the Cuban Deep. And how we assure that the Cubans will still be our willing partners if the *Norte Americanos* really turn the screws down hard. Please meet me at the presidential palace to discuss my concerns at your earliest opportunity."

"I will leave for the palace immediately," Valdez replied. But the line was already dead.

This was not good. Not good at all. The fool had probably been listening to one of his lap dogs again, sycophants interested only in sucking up to power. These hangers-on could not be trusted, always thinking of ways to make themselves look good at someone else's expense. There was no telling what hare-brained plot they could have come up with. And Gutierrez was not adept at sorting out the truth from self-serving fiction. He simply believed them all.

Valdez stood and strapped on his mirror-polished black leather holster with the Navy Colt. He also slipped a tiny .25-caliber Beretta into his trouser pocket. He would have to surrender the revolver to Gutierrez's guards, but the Beretta would get by them. No one would dare search *General Almirante* Juan Valdez.

He strode confidently out of his study and into the enclosed courtyard. Jorge was waiting beside his black Mercedes. Hopefully he had used his secret sources to find out what was happening at the palace and would brief him along the way on what to expect from his president. Jorge's contacts with the staff and servants and his ability to get information were astounding.

And such assets had been most beneficial to the admiral on more than one occasion.

Ψ

Jim Ward struggled up the last stretch. Climbing in these jungle mountains was difficult enough, with every rock coated with slick moss. The pitch-black night made it even worse. It seemed that every step forward meant a painful slip and slide back down. He could easily hear the storm-swollen river crashing and churning against the rocks far below him.

A warm, misty rain still fell gently, soaking everything and adding to the SEALs' discomfort. The rain clouds obscured even the stars, making it all but impossible for Jim to see his hands, let alone keep an eye on the other team members strung out above and below him as they attempted to scramble up this treacherous slope.

Sean Horton was only a couple of feet above, but mossy rocks that cascaded down were the only sign that the big man was there. He could hear Jed Dulkowski and Tony Garcia growling and cursing softly below.

Horton grunted and came sliding down. Ward reached out and grabbed the SEAL, halting his descent.

"Thanks, Skipper," Horton grunted. "Damn moss. Tell me again why we are out for this evening stroll in the park?"

Ward smiled in the dark. Only a SEAL could describe an all-night scramble up this mountain that way.

"We are supposed to rendezvous with some locals at a hunting camp at the top," Ward gasped. "Best that I can figure, we've got another three miles to cover."

"I reckon we've made maybe a mile since dark," Horton

replied. "At this rate, we might get there tomorrow night, if we're lucky."

Ward shook his head. "Not sure that's good enough. I don't know how long the locals will stick around. It's got to be way risky for them. And there's no place to hide our asses here on this slope either."

Jed Dulkowski scrambled up from below.

"Hey, who picked this particular garden path anyway? I'm spendin' more time slidin' downhill than climbing up."

"That would be me, brother," Sean Horton shot back. "Don't blame me if you are having a problem keeping up, toad."

"No problem," Dulkowski retorted, "but I'm suggesting some remedial orienteering be added to the training schedule for certain members of our team."

Tony Garcia climbed up.

"How come nobody told me we were taking a bitch break? You guys dissing the local Latino?"

"All right," Ward interjected. "Enough sitting around bull-shitting. Tony, take point for a bit. Pretty much straight up, so you should be able to find your way. Keep us heading north-northeast if you ever want to taste a cheeseburger and French fries again."

The SEALs scrambled up the steep, rocky slope as the drizzle became more of a moderate rain. Small rivulets ran between their feet and down the mountain, making the rocks loose and even harder to grip. Another half hour of slipping and sliding brought the team closer to the top, but first they had to work around an even steeper pitch. Past that, they finally emerged into a small stand of short bushes that clung to the edge of the bluff. Just beyond was a narrow mountain road that wound upward to the next summit.

Tony Garcia stood up straight for the first time in hours.

"See, I told you. Don't disrespect the Latino. Finding the easy way over mountains in the dark is natural for us. It's in our blood."

"Lots of experience," Horton shot back. "How many times did you have to sneak across the border, anyway?"

"Easy for you to say," Garcia chortled. "At least your people came over from Africa in a boat."

"Yeah, in chains, guests of the agrarian economy," Horton answered.

"You two about done comparing family trees?" Dulkowski chimed in. "You may be interested to know that we've got company coming."

Sure enough, they could see the occasional flash of headlights and just hear the growl of diesel engines, complaining in their own way about the hard climb up the steep mountain road.

Faced with a vertical rock wall above and a sheer slope below, the selection of potential hiding places was slim. The four dove back over the edge and clung precariously to the bushes and what rocks they trusted to hold their weight as the truck lights appeared full force from around a bend in the road.

Ward risked raising his head just enough to peek through the bushes. Three heavy military trucks rumbled past, each carrying heavily armed troops. Probably thirty or more, at least platoon strength.

He lowered his head.

"Not good," he said. "I'm guessing our rendezvous is compromised. That platoon of soldiers isn't out here for a picnic."

"Now what, Skipper?" Dulkowski asked.

"We find a place out of sight to hole up for a bit," he answered. "At least until we figure out the next move. I'm getting real uneasy about the Cubans always being one step ahead of us."

First the fishing boat. Then the unusual appearance of soldiers on the beach as they swam that way. Now, three truckloads of violent death that just happened to be headed the same way they were.

Coincidences could only account for so much.

The rain picked up even more as Ward led his team back to the mountain road and started looking for a rabbit hole.

19

The presidential palace guards nonchalantly waved Admiral Juan Valdez's car through the heavy iron gates without even a cursory search. The massive old cement structure loomed ahead, ablaze with lights from nearly every window. Ground lighting illuminated the lawns and gardens, dramatically highlighting the shrubbery and casting feathery fingers of light high up on the walls. Valdez could just make out the shadowy figures of the roaming armed security patrols moving around the grounds.

Jorge swung the car under the white-columned portico that shielded the private entrance. One of the official guards, resplendent in his red, gold, and black dress uniform, swung the rear door open and snapped to attention. He managed a stiff salute as the admiral slowly pulled himself from the big Mercedes.

Valdez charged through the open palace door without acknowledging any of the pomp and stomped right through the security check. The guards knew better than to attempt to hinder the old warrior without explicit direct orders from

Gutierrez. This time, they did not even bother asking him to surrender his Navy Colt.

He swung right and then headed down a passage before angling left to a hidden recessed cubicle. Admiral Valdez swiped his ID card and impatiently punched in the password. The door slid open, revealing a small but richly appointed private elevator. The carpet, mahogany millwork, and small chandelier in the elevator car probably were worth more than the entire hovel and furnishings of the country's typical resident. There was no control panel, no choice of floors. The door slid shut and the elevator automatically whisked him up to the third floor so quickly he had to hold onto the gold-plated rail that ran along the back of the car.

The door opened directly into President Gutierrez's private office. The burly leader of the People's Republic of Venezuela strode toward him across the vast expanse of deep-piled carpet.

"Admiral, so good of you to come on such short notice," he effused. "I really must apologize for meeting so late in the evening. Most uncivilized."

Valdez waved away the short speech.

"No problem at all, *mi Presidente*. I assure you that I am at your service at any time, day or night."

There were none of the normal cordialities for such a meeting, no offer of drinks or cigars. Just a quick handshake and a perfunctory wave toward the overstuffed divan. Valdez took a seat and carefully arranged the legs of his uniform trousers to maintain their knife-sharp creases.

Gutierrez dropped into the wing chair on his left with no mind to his own wrinkled, ill-fitting business suit. His silk tie was loose, his collar button open. For a moment, he silently glanced out the large window at the lights of Caracas.

General Almirante Valdez could sense the president's hesitation. He purposely chose to allow his leader to sweat. Whatever was so important to cause this summons, to disturb his evening, would soon be revealed in Gutierrez's own stumbling, bumbling way. The admiral had little respect for his president. He was convinced he would make a far superior leader for his country, and, of course, planned for such a thing to be a reality someday soon.

Finally, after what seemed an interminable wait, Gutierrez cleared his throat.

"Juan, we have been friends since boyhood. We grew strong together in the slums, *verdad*?" Valdez started to answer, but Gutierrez raised his hand to stop him. "We worked the revolution as a team. When I seized control of the Army, I gave you control of the Navy. Even today, I look to you as my friend and my strong right arm."

Valdez nodded, pretending modesty, even if the clown's words were mere false flattery. The president was convinced that he alone had made everything happen, that he alone pulled all the strings that brought him to the palace. Valdez well knew that *el Presidente* would have long ago found himself resting in a shallow grave had it not been for Valdez's help, guidance, and protection.

"If what I say is true, my dear Juan, then why do you not come to me with your ideas?" Gutierrez held his hands out, palms up, as if the admiral would actually place in them an answer. "I know of deFrance's discovery. This could be the most important find in the history of Venezuela. We can use this as leverage to control all of Latin America. And yet you choose to hide its enormous magnitude from me."

"My President," Valdez began. "You are a very busy man, with many heavy and important matters weighing on your mind. Your illness, as well. I know it claims your strength even as God heals you. There was no reason to bother you with this matter until all the facts had been verified and the possibilities analyzed."

The ornate antique phone on Gutierrez's desk jangled, interrupting the conversation and startling the president. He grabbed it and fairly shouted into the mouthpiece, "Yes! Yes! What do you want?" Then he fell silent, holding the earpiece close to his head, listening intently. Finally he dropped the handset back onto its cradle and leaned back in his big chair, rocking for a moment.

"Most interesting," he muttered to himself, as if the news he had just received had caused him to forget Valdez's presence. "Most interesting, indeed. It seems our old friend the CIA operative has been very interested in some of our own people. *Senor* Kirkland has been meeting with our friend Colonel Castellon. We shall have to see if the colonel deems it prudent to report to us what they have found of mutual interest." Gutierrez turned back to Valdez. "Now, Juan, where were we?"

"I was just about to discuss our challenges regarding how we will be able to capitalize on *Senor* deFrance's discovery. But this news you have just received—and of which I was already aware, by the way—offers possibilities. *Presidente*, it occurs to me that *Senor* Kirkland and Colonel Castellon may be able to assist us in overcoming some of the considerable obstacles we face in capitalizing on the Cuban Deep discovery. They can help us, whether they intend to or not."

It was time to have Jorge use his very talented blade on the old guerilla. Castellon was the only other person who had all the pieces to tie Valdez's plot together. It was far too risky to allow him to get chummy with the corrupt CIA operative, one who couldn't stay bought even if he was very expensive.

"I will keep you posted on my progress in this matter," Valdez told his commander-in-chief. "Now, with your permission, sir, I will do what I must to see what this meeting means to you and the nation's security."

Gutierrez could only stare back blankly. It had just occurred to him that the admiral was well ahead of him on this development and that he, the president, had absolutely no choice in how the matter might proceed.

Even as he steered the conversation back to the possibilities and problems of the Cuban Deep discovery, Gutierrez still considered just how little control he really had anymore. The thought of it all scared him to death.

Ψ

Jon Ward pulled himself out of the gray-black cloud that lately passed as sleep. The jangling phone. He had to answer it before it woke Ellen, his wife. Groggily, he swept his arm across the nightstand to grab it. He smacked his hand against something. The offending instrument crashed to the deck.

Ward muttered to himself as he stumbled out of bed and reached under it, finally locating and clutching the bellowing phone.

"Ward here."

"Sorry to pull you out of bed, Jon. I know you haven't been getting much sack time lately." Admiral Tom Donnegan's deep growl of a voice was unmistakable. "We need to talk on a secure line. Can you switch to the STU?"

"I have to go downstairs," Ward answered, now fully alert. Admiral Donnegan did not often call in the middle of the night. When he did, it was rarely good news. "Let me call you right back on the STU."

Ellen was wide awake and staring him in the face.

"It's Papa Tom. Business," Jon Ward told her. She still had no inkling that the business he mentioned involved their son. "I'll tell him you send your best." He patted her on the arm. "Go back to sleep, honey."

He rushed down to their home office and pulled the red secure phone from its locked drawer in his big oak desk. He inserted his security token, punched in his passcode, and dialed the familiar number.

"Donnegan."

"Good evening, Admiral. I hold you secure."

"I hold you the same, Jon."

"Ellen is getting suspicious. She hasn't heard from Jim in a week," Ward said. It had already occurred to him that this late-night call could bring bad news about their boy. "She knows me too well. She's starting to put two and two together."

"As if you're not worried, son," Jon Ward's mentor and surrogate father answered softly. "They're okay down there. We had a brief communication this evening. He's fine. We're trying like hell to extract his team, but the damn Cubans seem to be one step ahead of us every way we turn. They can't know anything, Jon. This office and a single CIA guy we had to bring in to this thing are the only ones that know what is going on. Look, Jimmy's a grown man now, and a well-trained SEAL team leader. He can take care of himself and his guys. This is what he has been trained to do." Donnegan paused for a second. Ward knew he was worried, too, but would die rather than admit it. "Look, I've been working this out in my mind. I don't like how it all adds up. There have been way too many coincidences on this mission. One or two bad encounters on a mission can be attributed to 'shit happens.' But some of this stuff looks like somebody has been reading our minds."

"We have a leak?" Ward almost whispered. The most dreaded possibility for a covert intelligence operation was to even suspect that they had a leak. Operations were compromised, sources lost, and men killed. And one of those men just happened to be his son.

"Very possible," Donnegan answered. "As of this evening, I've stopped all coordination with any other agency, even though that son-of-a-bitch Art Schmidtmegan is trying to bust my chops. Only a couple of people on my staff have access to what is going on, and I don't think 'Shit-megan' can bring down enough grief to change that right now. Operative words: 'right now.' If he even thinks this is some kind of power play or that we are deliberately going around him, he is in a position to bust this thing wide open. And I don't put anything past him, including going semi-public, if it makes his ass look good. He wants to be president, you know."

Ward rubbed his chin, deep in thought. The only sounds were the soft hum of the secure telephone circuit and the ticking of Ellen's beloved antique mantel clock. Donnegan remained silent, waiting.

"I wonder," Ward finally said. "I wonder if your leak could be tied to our problems with *Toledo*. Someone seems to know exactly what we are doing and where we will be at every turn. If they know that, they might make some assumptions about her being off Cuba."

"That would certainly explain some of this horse manure, but not all of it," Admiral Donnegan agreed. "You know things are rarely that neat in this game. I'm hoping your son and his guys can figure out what the hell is going on down there. Or at least give us a clue. Something's up, though. Something big." Donnegan paused just long enough to take a breath. "Why don't you haul your butt down to Port Canaveral? Arrange for a little at-sea time for yourself. Give Joe Glass my best. I'll have Bill Beaman meet you there. He knows how SEALs think and may be some help getting Jimmy out of that hell-hole."

"Just like old times," Ward grunted.

"Yep, pretty much a class reunion," Donnegan answered. "Now, get back upstairs and kiss Ellen and tell her that we need to do dinner at Sequoia as soon as you get back. I've been craving those crab cakes."

"Maybe we can include Jim."

"Yes. Great idea. You, Ellen, Jim. My treat. Soon as we get this deal over and done with. We'll have plenty to talk about over a platter of raw Chesapeake oysters."

Ψ

It took a moment for TJ Dillon's eyes to grow accustomed to the room's dim light before he recognized the person strapped to the gurney. That was because the man scarcely resembled the pictures of Marco Esteban, head of the Cuban DINA, that Josh Kirkland had shown him at their meeting in Crystal City. This was a pasty-white old man lying unconscious, an IV strapped to his left arm, a monitor beeping to confirm his vital signs were within tolerance. He surely didn't look like the most dangerous, deadly spymaster in the Western Hemisphere. The dim white hospital light in the far corner of the room reflected off cold, dark stone walls.

Ricardo Martinez Manuel de la Roche stood at Dillon's elbow.

"*Senor* Dillon?" he asked. "You, of course, recognize our guest?"

Dillon nodded. What the hell was happening here? How did this old pseudo-guerilla come to have one of the most powerful men in Latin America—the most likely next leader of Cuba—as his prisoner? What was this game into which he had suddenly been thrust?

"We are using some interesting enhanced interrogation techniques that we learned from your employer," de la Roche bragged. "We wake him at random intervals, but about every couple of hours. He receives hints of time passing when he is awake. Between the drugs and the temporal disorientation, *Senor* Esteban now has no idea what day or month it is, but he is firmly convinced that it is far in the future."

Dillon stared hard at the helpless old man. He had killed Dillon's father as surely as if he had personally pulled the trigger and deprived TJ of any hint of a normal childhood. He was surprised at the long-repressed rage he suddenly felt for this old man.

Revenge welled up, hot and pure. It would be so easy. A couple of quick blows and Cuba and the world would be the better for it.

de la Roche seemed to sense his emotions and grabbed Dillon's tensed arm.

"Not yet. He is still useful to us," he said. "When the time comes, you can have him. You and your government will be able to 'rescue' him. In the meantime, we will be glad to give you the benefit of the information we learn from him. But now is not that time."

"What?" Dillon shook his head, shaking off the sudden, unexpected killing rage. "What are you doing? What is your plan?"

"In good time, my friend. All in good time," de la Roche answered. "I will explain your role and how…"

Just then, one of the old guerilla's men rushed into the room and pulled de la Roche aside. He whispered a reply that Dillon could not hear before the man scurried out as quickly as he had come in. The old man grabbed his hat and moved toward the door.

"We must hurry," he said. "We have guests arriving and they are a little earlier than expected. We must prepare for them."

"But I thought…"

Dillon had assumed he was being held prisoner as well. The guns, the show of force to get him downstairs. Then they had left him in a stone cell for most of the night, waiting.

"We just did not know if you would follow us willingly. Nor do we totally trust you yet with the information that you are learning. But now...soon...we have no choice. And we require your unique skills, my friend, as we set the rest of the plan in motion. You will have much to report to your CIA. Much that will affect the relations between our countries for generations to come."

He practically shoved Dillon out the doorway. The heavy iron door clanged shut behind them. They quickly climbed the long stone stairs that led up from the dungeon.

"Who are these new unexpected guests?" Dillon asked as he drew alongside de la Roche.

"You are most impatient," de la Roche answered. "Very much like my son. He also asks too many questions, all of which will be answered satisfactorily at the proper time."

"I just like to know what's going on when I see rifles and troops." Several uniformed and armed men jogged past them, heading for the tree line to their left.

"Soon. Soon it will be clear." de la Roche handed Dillon a Beretta 9mm. "I doubt you will require this, but better to have it and not need it than to need it and not have it."

He smiled, but Dillon recognized the worry in the old revolutionary's deep, dark eyes.

20

They came at sunrise. Three trucks packed full of troops. Humberto Marquesa Garcia, the DINA Chief Inspector, rode shotgun in the lead truck, trying valiantly to keep his eyes open. The nighttime trek over treacherous mountain roads from the south had been very tiring, but certainly necessary. The enemy was always most vulnerable at daybreak. It was a proven tenet of DINA practice.

The trucks ground to a halt in front of the great old iron gates that guarded the hacienda. The rather officious chief inspector climbed down out of the truck and stomped over to the intercom box bolted to the stone wall alongside the gate. Just as he reached out to punch the red button, the heavy gates slowly swung open.

Garcia looked around warily, trying in vain to spot the hidden watchman or camera. Nothing in sight, only the open iron gate and the narrow drive stretching toward the rising sun. Garcia shrugged and waved for the troop transports to enter.

The trucks lumbered through the gate, making their noisy way toward the hacienda still hidden beyond the trees. The gates swung shut with a firm clang once the last vehicle was past.

The small convoy ground to a halt in a rough semi-circle on the hacienda's sweeping drive. The men slowly, stiffly clambered out of the back as Chief Inspector Garcia once again climbed down out of the cab.

Ricardo Martinez Manuel de la Roche met his "guests" at the old house's massive oak entry doors.

"Chief Inspector Garcia, how kind of you to grace us with your presence," de la Roche said with a courtly but exaggerated bow. "You should have called ahead. I would have wakened the cook and had breakfast ready. As it is, I am afraid you will have to wait now for the coffee."

Garcia scowled as he stomped over and stood in front of de la Roche. TJ Dillon, watching the scene from an upstairs window, had to work to restrain a laugh. He had visions of Sergeant Garcia from the old *Zorro* television shows. Now, if the chief inspector would only snap an awkward palm-out salute.

"Don de la Roche," Garcia stormed, trying to force his voice deeper than it actually was. "We have orders to search your house and grounds."

Garcia's troops, still rubbing sleep from their eyes, moved into a rough military formation behind him.

"And what would you hope to find by conducting such a search?" the old guerrilla asked in a mocking tone. "You should know that I am a simple farmer struggling to cultivate a meager existence from the earth."

Garcia stomped his foot. "Still, we will search."

"I hope that you have checked with your DINA masters," de la Roche said with a smile. "And that they, in turn, have checked with their masters." The threat was very thinly veiled. de la Roche had powerful friends in high places. A lowly regional chief inspector would be well advised to tread gently in such matters.

Garcia could not hide a triumphant grin. For once, he had the backing of *Habana's* full force of power.

"Oh, everyone is aware of our mission, and from the absolute highest levels," he shot back. "You are suspected of hiding enemies of the state. We will find them and we will lock you away in the process. For a very, very long time."

With a quick gesture, the obese policeman called his men to attention, set to begin marching toward the house to proceed with their planned search.

Don de la Roche's eyebrows arched up. As he had feared, this would not be a simple matter of swatting away an annoying fly. Garcia and his troops had shown up many times before—always after de la Roche had been tipped off well ahead of time—with orders to search the hacienda or question the plantation's master about one or another of his activities. But always a bit of bluster had been all it took to send him and his trucks of soldiers back down the mountain to their pitiful little base on the southern coast near Cienfuegos.

But this rain-cooled morning, the fool actually believed that he could come up here, threaten him, and blaspheme the hacienda with his sweaty stink and his troops' muddy boots. And someone somewhere had emboldened him enough so that the usual threats had not sent him off.

Garcia simply could not be allowed to search the hacienda. Not with Marco Esteban drugged and locked away in the lower basement. In the back of his mind, de la Roche wondered if someone had tied the abduction to him and his network and knew where Esteban was being held.

"And what enemies of the state am I hiding up here?" de la Roche queried, playing for time.

He did not fear that these troops could storm into the

hacienda should they decide to attempt such a thing. Nothing short of an anti-tank rocket could blow the doors open. They did not yet realize it, but Garcia's men were surrounded and targeted by a team of expert snipers. When the shooting started, they would all be dead in seconds. The real problem, the one de la Roche could not solve, was how he would disguise the disappearance of an entire platoon of DINA troops. Such an occurrence would kick over a hornet's nest long before he and his associates were ready to deal with it.

"Don de la Roche," Garcia scolded. "Please do not play me for a fool. An American SEAL team has been reported coming ashore and are supposedly marching directly to your hacienda. We tracked them to the base of the Guamuhaya Mountains, and our sources inform us that they arrived here last night."

de la Roche could barely believe what he heard. An American SEAL team? Impossible! Why would American SEALs be interested in him? Was this a set-up by Dillon, his CIA guest? But how could Dillon have even known where he was going when he left the city the previous morning? Or was this another phony DINA story to justify locking him away? Answering these questions would require a careful probing of the right sources and piecing together many snatches of information, but he simply had no time to do that with the present situation taking place on the front lawn of his hacienda.

First, these DINA fools would have to be dealt with. And if Garcia insisted on throwing his weight around, de la Roche would have few options.

"Inspector Garcia," de la Roche said, his voice soothing and conciliatory. He raised his hands, palms up. "We seem to have a problem. You have orders to search *mi casa*. Honor forbids me allowing that. A man of your sensibilities certainly understands my position. I am sure that we can reach a mutually profitable solution to this dilemma."

"You dare to offer me a bribe!" Garcia shouted, reaching for his pistol. The troops, now fully alert, snapped their AK-47s to the "present arms" position.

But then, the quick crack of a shot rang out, its direction of origin masked by the echoes. A small red dot magically appeared precisely in the center of the DINA inspector's forehead. He had a surprised look on his face, then a quick, odd smile before he dropped to the gravel-covered drive, dead before his bulky body hit the ground.

The DINA troops began firing their rifles wildly toward the woods on either side of the roadway as well as the hacienda. Some scrambled for cover beneath their trucks.

de la Roche took a round in the gut in the first burst, then another 7.62mm bullet in his chest. He, too, was likely dead before he crumpled to the earth.

An all-out firefight erupted, the DINA troops firing blindly from what little cover their heavy Russian-built trucks gave them. The hidden snipers in the thick woods began exacting a heavy toll. Ten of the troopers, unable to make it to the vehicles, lay silent, unmoving, on the cobblestones.

Jose Manuel, firing an M-4 from the hip, ran into the courtyard in a vain attempt to pull his father to safety. Since he was the only person the troops could actually see, he immediately drew most of their fire. The young man was cut down as he charged forward, knocked backward by the awful impact of the bullets. He somehow managed to get to his feet again and attempted to keep moving, still firing, before another burst knocked him down again. Manuel crawled forward, leaving a bloody trail. Inch by agonizing inch, he pulled himself by force of will toward his fallen father. A third burst slammed into him just as Manuel reached the elder de la Roche. He died there, reaching out to put his hand on his father's still chest.

TJ Dillon could not believe what he was watching. A quiet

early morning had suddenly erupted into all-out firefight. He saw one of the DINA troops pull some sort of tube from the truck. He recognized at once that it was a shoulder-launched RPG anti-tank rocket.

One of the snipers in the woods saw it, too, and the soldier was immediately cut down. But somehow he was able to pull himself to his elbows and launch the rocket. Trailing white smoke, the missile arched directly toward the massive oak doors just below where Dillon stood near the window. The deafening blast left only splinters and shards of the heavy double doors dangling from their hinges.

From somewhere behind the trucks, a second and then a third rocket arched up and flew into the building's second-level windows. Smoke billowed out the door and from the shattered windows as flames started to lick from the eaves above the upper stories.

Still the shooting continued unabated. Two trucks burst into flames, sending the DINA troops scurrying across the courtyard. Some of them made it through the hailstorm of bullets, charging through the open entrance and into the great hall, firing wildly.

Dillon had pulled back from the window when he saw the first rocket aimed in his direction. The second two knocked him off his feet, so he crawled on his belly down the second-floor hallway. There was no telling how this battle would end, but it was obvious that he should not be around when it did. He quickly checked that the Beretta 9mm was fully loaded and that the safety was off.

A wall of heavy black smoke poured out when Dillon opened the doorway to the stairwell. There were four flights that would eventually lead him to the cellar, and hopefully out a back entrance. He coughed heavily as he crawled with his face as close to the floor as possible, looking for breathable air. He could feel hot flames licking at his heels as he moved forward. The centuries-old heart pine floors and walls were tinder-dry and easily fed the flames.

Dillon crouched low as he started down the stairs. Just as he reached the main floor, the door in front of him—the one that led from the main hallway—suddenly blew open. Someone in a brown DINA uniform charged into the stairwell, shooting wildly up and down. Great oak splinters torn from the ancient timbers rained down around Dillon. Before the trooper could get off a lucky shot his way, Dillon fired twice, the double tap knocking the DINA trooper down the stairs as if jerked by the strings of a marionette.

Still fighting for breath, TJ raced down to the lower basement. Escaping from there would put the house between him and the battle going on out front, giving him a better chance of making it to cover. But something else drove him that way, too, something not clear to him at that moment.

The smoke was even heavier in the basement. There were no windows, but light from somewhere gave the smoky air a dim yellowish-gray glow that looked otherworldly.

Fluorescent lights. He remembered them now. The electricity was still on. He had to move quickly before it was cut and the cellar would be completely dark.

Someone was screaming in terror from behind one of the doors. He tried the knob but it was locked, so he slammed a shoulder into the door. Solid. There was no way he could hope to force it open. He placed the pistol's barrel where he assumed the bolt would be and popped off two quick shots, shattering most of the jamb. Then, a hard football block tore it the rest of the way open.

The room was filled with flames. Burning timbers fell from above like a rain of fire. Through the hellish inferno, he could barely see Marco Esteban, still tied to his bed, writhing in terror as the world burned around him.

Fighting the very real urge to let the bastard burn, Dillon untied the cords that held him down. Then he snatched up the old man, threw him over his shoulder, and headed back through the doorway and down the hall that appeared to lead toward the back of the house. There had to be an exit down here somewhere. An exit to breathable air and the nearby woods.

He had to drop to his hands and knees once again, dragging Esteban along behind him. Dillon crawled forward slowly, trying to find good air.

The lights flickered, flickered again, and then went out.

The former SEAL had been trained to work in total darkness. It was nothing new. But the thick, stifling smoke was something else.

Dillon shifted to touch and hearing. His right shoulder brushed the cement wall as he moved forward, then his progress was blocked. A door. He could feel fresh air whistling around the edges as the fire above him hungrily sucked it in.

Dillon yanked the heavy door open. He could see outside into the cool morning light, the sun just appearing over the far horizon. He grabbed Marco, shouldered him again, and ran up the slippery stone stairs, across a short stretch of open ground, and toward the jungle beyond.

He could still hear the sharp, staccato crack of gunfire and the pop and roar of the flames behind him as they consumed Ricardo de la Roche's proud hacienda.

Whatever agenda the old revolutionary had in the works was dead now, along with him and his CIA-operative son.

But that was not top of mind for TJ Dillon at the moment. Still struggling to breathe, he just wanted to put as many pines, palms, and other trees between himself and the soldiers—from both camps—as he could manage.

There would be time to piece the stories together once he got off this damned island.

Ψ

Jim Ward slipped easily through the jungle. Movement was a whole lot easier and quicker up here on top of the mountains, away from the sucking mud, mosquito swarms, and walls of thorny vegetation. According to his GPS, they should only be about half a mile to the rendezvous point. He still had no idea who to look for, or how they were going to get him and his team out of Cuba without the Cuban DINA, *The New York Times*, God, and everybody else knowing about it.

To make matters worse, the sun would be coming up soon. Such meetings were far better carried out under the cover of darkness. The light of day stole the SEALs' advantages of stealth and concealment.

Ward signaled his team to make a wide, sweeping turn around the rendezvous point. They would, of course, scout out the terrain carefully before entering an area where they might be seen.

Sean Horton moved up to point, advancing one cautious step at a time, carefully sweeping the scene for any sign of ambush. Tony Garcia slipped to the rear, erasing all traces of the team's passage and watching for followers.

The team moved around a large rock outcrop that loomed above them and out to the edge of a small grassy meadow. They hid behind several tall palms.

"Wow, where did that come from?" Horton gasped as he looked up at the hill in front of them where an old Spanish hacienda commanded the entire mountaintop.

"Now that's what I call a hunting camp," Dulkowski murmured as he crawled up alongside Horton.

Then, suddenly, the snap and rattle of gunfire broke the pre-dawn stillness. The SEALs rooted even lower into the ground and automatically spread out into a loose defensive position, each man facing a different point of the compass.

The firing seemed to be coming from somewhere near the house. The angry growl of AK-47 rounds, mostly in full automatic, and the continuous short bursts from something lighter confirmed this was not simply someone taking early-morning target practice or bearing down on a twelve-point buck. Those were shots fired in anger, and it was clear a lot of people were very, very mad.

"Somebody is sure having a disagreement," Horton said.

"Sounds like a typical day in Little Italy back in Chicago," Dulkowski added.

"I just hope to hell that ain't our rescue party getting shot up," Horton said.

"Well, it could just be another amazing coincidence that has nothing to do with us and our taxi home," Ward told them. "But something tells me it is going to affect our lives in some measure here shortly." He thought for a moment. "We may as well see what's going on. But stay back under the tree cover. And under no circumstances do we get involved since we don't know the good guys from the bad guys. Hell, they may all be bad guys. Just our luck!"

The four SEALs moved a little further back in the heavy undergrowth and started to slowly circumnavigate the meadow in the general direction of where the woods came closest to the hacienda.

Then, halfway to their destination, heavy RPG explosions ripped through the morning, drowning out even the continual snap of rifle fire. Smoke quickly began to swirl from the big house's windows and beneath the eaves near the roof.

Ward did not have to tell his team anything. They instinctively knew to pull back a few feet deeper into the shadows. A serious war was going on up there. Maybe they ought to let it play out just a little more before they tried to identify who wore white hats and who wore black ones.

Then, as they watched, a man suddenly broke out of the shrubbery below the house and ran a zigzag across the open ground, making his way directly toward the SEALs' hiding spot. And he had someone on his back in a fireman's carry.

The running man collapsed at the jungle's edge, dropping his burden as he struggled for breath. Then, dragging the other man, he slithered around behind a large mahogany tree, peering back toward the house to see if he was being followed. His chest heaving, he pulled an automatic pistol from his belt, held it ready, and watched for pursuers.

The firefight continued, only slightly less fierce than before. Apparently, no one up there had noticed the man's escape. Flames licked out of several windows and a portion of the tiled roof caved in, emitting sparks and more clouds of thick, black smoke. The house was going up unbelievably quickly.

The man was positioned between where Jim Ward lay hidden under some low brush and where Jed Dulkowski was sprawled behind a fallen log. Ward gave Dulkowski a quick signal to stay low. In the process, his hand brushed a bush just enough to cause it to move.

The man jerked around and aimed his pistol directly at Jim Ward's breastbone.

"Come out very slowly." The accent was pure mid-America. "Keep your hands where I can see them." Then he repeated the command in perfect Spanish.

Ward slowly stood, his empty hands wide.

"Take it easy," he said, his words low so that only the man could hear. "We're Americans."

"Who are you?"

"Americans. Who are you?" Ward answered. "And what are you doing here?"

The man dropped his gun to his side and sighed.

"Judging from your attire, I'd say you are a SEAL. That means there are three or four more of you bastards on your bellies out there, and I would have figured that anyway since you said 'Americans,' plural." He grinned. "Boy, am I glad to see you! I'm TJ Dillon, former SEAL Team Four. I am not even going to ask what you are doing here because I know you wouldn't tell me. We need to beat feet out of here. No telling who is going to crash that little party up on the hill. I, for one, don't want to be anywhere near here when it happens."

"Who's your buddy?" Ward nodded toward the unconscious man spread-eagled at the base of the mahogany tree.

Dillon reached down and grabbed the old man by the scruff of the neck.

"Let me introduce you to Marco Esteban, the head of the Cuban DINA and *numero uno* on the list to be this little island's next boss man." He ignored the young SEAL's shocked expression and paid little attention to the other three men emerging from the shadows. "We need to get somewhere so that I can contact The Company. They are going to be real keen on hearing all about this interesting turn of events."

21

Joe Glass sat at his submarine's stateroom desk, a tiny, cramped fold-down table heavily laden with paperwork. He rubbed his aching brow. The form-filling never seemed to end, report after endless report.

The knock on his door was barely audible. Glass looked up and said without hiding his irritation, "Enter."

Lieutenant Eric Hobson stepped into the closet-like stateroom, closely followed by Master Chief Randy Zillich. They plopped down on the tiny settee that filled the stateroom's outboard bulkhead. The little table separating the two was piled high with its own stack of files.

"Skipper," Hobson started. "Since we're scheduled to be in-port here for a few days while the nukes replace the main engine bearing, it's a good time to knock out some URO maintenance requirements. Sonar needs to inspect the towed array operating mechanism and fairing. Request permission to tag out the fat line towed array for maintenance."

"Let me see the MRC card," Glass answered.

Randy Zillich riffled through his stack of papers and culled out an Unrestricted Operations Maintenance Requirement Card and handed it to Glass. "Skipper, the whole thing will take two days, tops," he said as Glass read the card's very detailed instructions. "We remove the stow tube fairing and inspect everything for damage and corrosion. Lube the rollers, paint and preserve, then button her back up. Pier crane is all set up and scheduled to go in about an hour."

Glass nodded his okay, then added, "Just be ready to restore everything in one hell of a hurry if our orders change."

Hobson looked quizzically at his skipper.

"We expecting to head out of here in a rush or something?"

"Don't know, Weps. Sometimes, I just get these intuitions."

Ψ

"We're ready for your inspection, Eng," Machinist Mate First Class Clarence Swift announced as he emerged from the clean tent. The gangly young submariner wiped oil from his hands and stood upright. "The access covers are unlocked. My guys have everything staged. As soon as you're ready…"

The pair stood on a narrow catwalk outboard the massive reduction gears in the after part of the *Toledo*'s engine room. The reduction gears and their casing all but filled the space, with just enough room left for the catwalk.

The compartment was cool and quiet now, not hot and noisy as it was when the steam-driven main turbines were driving *Toledo* through the depths. The only sounds were men talking and joking as they worked. A pair of Swift's machinists were unpacking and cleaning the replacement bearing. The heavily taped cardboard box lay on the deck as the pair struggled to remove layer upon layer of tape and greased packing paper that protected the bearing halves.

Engineer Doug O'Malley observed, "They sure packed this

sucker. It'll take another few minutes to get this crap off, then we gotta clean off the Cosmoline."

The white clean tent looked out of place amid all the piping and metal machinery, as if it belonged on a lawn awaiting a party, not in a gray, steel engine room. Still, it performed its purpose well. By being carefully sealed all around, it kept any foreign objects from accidentally falling into the exquisitely machined reduction gears. Even a few grains of sand would interfere with the minute tolerances. The team had spent hours hanging and sealing the tent over the access covers before cleaning everything inside until there was not even a speck of dust adrift.

"How long you figure to replace the bearing?" O'Malley asked.

Swift rubbed his chin for a few seconds.

"Can't be too sure, Eng. None of us have ever done this before. Best guess is a couple of days to get her all buttoned back up and ready for steam."

O'Malley nodded. "About what I figured. I'll tell the skipper we should be ready to test her day after tomorrow. That'll give you a little breathing room."

Ψ

Brian Edwards stuck his head through the captain's stateroom door.

"Skipper, you got Commodore Ward on line one."

Joe Glass nodded and grabbed for the phone, remembering the words of advice that Jon Ward had given him when he was XO on the old *Spadefish* and Ward was his skipper. A good XO never allowed his skipper to answer the phone, no matter who was on the other end. He had passed that lesson on to Brian

Edwards, who had gone so far as to disconnect the ringer on his phone.

"Joe Glass here, Commodore," Glass said. "What can we do for you?"

"Good morning, Joe." Jon Ward's deep, matter-of-fact voice was unmistakable. "Let's go secure."

Glass pulled a Common Access Card from his pocket and inserted it into his phone. After punching in his passcode, he listened as the phone chirped and whistled for a few seconds, shaking hands with Ward's phone. Then the light shifted from red to green.

"I hold you secure," Glass said.

"I hold you the same," Ward replied. "How are the repairs coming? You getting everything you need?"

Glass nodded, even though he knew Ward could not see him. "Yes, sir. We are replacing the final reduction bearing right now. The engineer tells me that he'll be ready to put steam to the main engines by end of day, day after tomorrow. In the meantime, we're knocking out some URO-MRCs that are due. We're pulling and inspecting the towed array fairing today."

He could hear Ward chuckling.

"I just love it when I see my training in action. We both know that rolling a main engine bearing takes a day. O'Malley probably added twelve hours to the estimate for cushion. Then you added another twelve, just to be sure."

"Can't fool the teacher."

Ward's voice instantly turned serious.

"Joe, I need you all buttoned up and ready for sea by tomorrow evening. We have a midnight underway."

"We?" Glass asked.

"Yep. This is going to be like old home week. Bill Beaman and I are flying down. We'll be going out with you. Can you have a duty driver pick us up at Melbourne Airport this evening. Our flight lands at twenty-one hundred. I'll brief you on the op tomorrow morning, first thing."

"Roger, sir," Glass answered. "We'll be ready."

The line went dead.

Glass did not take time to consider this development. He shouted through the open door to Brian Edwards's stateroom.

"XO, grab the Eng, Weps, and Nav. We've got some planning to do."

Ψ

The sun was a low, hazy orange orb out on the eastern horizon, but the air was already heavy with humidity. It would be another hot, humid Florida Space Coast day. A flight of brown pelicans glided low over the water, searching for breakfast.

Jon Ward charged along the beach, staying on the hard sand just inches from the water. The running was easier here, and he needed every edge he could find to keep up with Bill Beaman. The tall, lanky SEAL moved effortlessly across the sand, easily staying on Ward's shoulder.

"Why are you SEALs...so attracted to running...in the damn sand?" Ward huffed. The pair ran past an elderly couple out for a morning beach walk, he with his metal detector, she with some kind of fluffy dog on a leash.

"Just so we can make you bubbleheads suffer," Beaman quipped. "And besides, in case you hadn't noticed, the best-looking girls are out on the beach."

"This is just like...old times," Ward answered, changing subjects. "Emphasis on...'old.'"

"Yep," Beaman replied. "All we need is one of Ellen's hot breakfasts when we get back."

"I expect that breakfast will be the finest that Patrick Air Force Base VOQ has to offer," Ward shot back. His watch suddenly let loose with a shrill chirping. "Halfway point. Time to...turn around. We need to head back...or we'll be late."

The pair executed a one-eighty and headed back down the beach.

"Speaking of Ellen, does she know anything at all about Jim's situation?" Beaman asked.

"All she knows is that I haven't...mentioned him...and he hasn't...called in days. She's been around...all this long enough... to know something's up. And she's worried."

"I hear you," the big SEAL replied. "You know we're doing everything we can to extract Jim and his team. For him, you, Ellen. But mostly because we can't afford for the Cubans to catch those boys and make an example of them."

"That's what Admiral Donnegan said. And I gather that's why you're here."

The pair ran on in silence for a few minutes. The sun rose steadily higher and more tourists streamed onto the beach, bearing blankets, coolers, and umbrellas, reeking of SPF50.

"What's your plan?" Jon Ward broke the silence once they had passed a clump of sun worshipers.

"Not sure. Since General Schmidtmegan put the kibosh on any activity in Cuba, we sure won't be using official channels." Beaman's voice was almost a whisper. "And since Donnegan is worried about a leak, most of the covert ops channels are off limits, too. Everything is going way, way deep."

"Doesn't leave much," Ward retorted drily.

"Pretty much you and me, big guy." Beaman punched Ward on the arm. "As you so correctly noted, just like old times."

Ψ

"Master Chief, what's this?" Seaman Will Brownson called

out. He was pointing to a small, nondescript gray box fastened underneath the towed array stow tube.

The towed array fairing made a hump on the starboard side of *Toledo*'s hull that stretched from well forward of the sail back to the after ballast tanks. The fairing had been removed and stacked on the pier. Master Chief Zillich had the entire seaman gang topside, inspecting every inch of the towed array stowage tube, a six-inch-diameter pipe normally hidden under the fairing.

Zillich sauntered back to where Brownson stood, all the way aft, just above the waterline. He squatted down to inspect the box, which was attached to a support strut under the stow tube and painted so it blended in. Only someone doing a very close and thorough inspection would ever have noticed it.

With a frown, Zillich reached down and tried to pull the box away, but it would not budge.

"Damned if I know what that is," Zillich mumbled. "There shouldn't be anything back here but pipes and struts. Whatever it is, it sure don't belong to our boat." He put his hands on his hips and studied the box for a moment.

"What you think, Master Chief?"

"I think you better get me the handling gear tech manual. And have somebody call the skipper."

22

Port Canaveral's broad, isolated Trident Turning Basin was calm and quiet. The dark waters reflected and scattered the glare from the high overhead security lights into shards of gold and white. The only sign of life was a small group of sailors working topside on *Toledo*. Jon Ward and Joe Glass stood back a few feet from the group and watched them.

"You know we really need to get out of here as quietly as possible," Ward said, his voice almost a whisper. "We don't want it broadcast to people who shouldn't know we've left."

Glass barely nodded.

"Agreed. We'll slip out in the middle of the night. Nobody will know until they wake up in the morning. By then we will be long gone."

Doug O'Malley emerged from the forward escape trunk and walked a few feet aft to where the two stood. He snapped a near regulation salute.

Glass casually returned the salute and asked, "What you have, Eng?"

"Skipper, Commodore." O'Malley nodded toward each. "Completed bearing replacement. We have the reduction gears all buttoned up and jacking normally. Everything looks good so far. Bringing steam into the engine room now. We'll bring the turbine generators on-line, divorce from shore power, then test the mains out in the turning basin."

"How much time you need to test the mains?" Glass asked.

O'Malley rubbed his chin as he mentally added up the time.

"Well, figure half an hour for normal main engine warm-up. We'll monitor the bearing during that, grab some sound cuts to analyze. I'd like to extend the warm-up at least until we've analyzed several sound cuts and everything has stabilized. Should be about an hour total, I figure. The real test will come when we're out in the channel. Then we can put on some turns and see how she acts."

Now it was Joe Glass's turn for some quick calculations.

"Indian River has no real current here except tidal. High slack tide is at midnight. Figure a half hour either side of that so we don't have to worry about that. You ready to go at 2330 local?"

O'Malley nodded. "Potable water and sanitaries are already disconnected. Divorcing from shore power as soon as the TGs are on-line. Shore phones will go with the brow. No problem with a 2330 underway, sir."

He snapped a quick salute and disappeared back down the hatch just as a man in dark coveralls left the small group of sailors and headed their way. The man had graying hair and a grizzled gray beard. The patch on the breast of his coveralls read "Naval Undersea Warfare Center, Newport."

"How's it going, Dr. Jacoby?" Ward asked.

"Your sonar guy is real sharp," Dr. Wilford Jacoby answered. "That box was very well hidden. We went over the circuitry pretty carefully. Very advanced stuff. Not anything we have, for sure. Probably Russian. I'd really like to take it back to the lab and reverse engineer it."

Ward shook his head.

"No time for that now, Wil. Maybe later. Besides, we have a use for it before everybody else in the US Navy knows we have it."

Jacoby nodded and shrugged.

"I understand. But I got dibs when you get through with it. I've made the modifications you wanted. As soon as I finish testing them, we'll button up. We should be all done and ready to go in about an hour."

As Jacoby returned to his work, a white Dodge pickup truck screeched to a stop right at the end of the brow. Captain Bill Beaman, dressed in jungle cammies, jumped out of the passenger side door. Brian Edwards slowly unwound himself out of the other side of the vehicle.

Beaman threw back the tarp covering the truck's cargo box, revealing a full load of boxes and crates.

Edwards called across the brow, "Topside watch. Call below decks and get us a ten-man working party up here ASAP."

Glass and Ward walked across the brow to where Edwards and Beaman stood.

"You get everything?" Ward asked.

Beaman grinned. "It wasn't easy. The Air Force didn't want to part with some of the hardware and I doubt we could have found what we needed at Wally World." He pointed a thumb toward Edwards. "Skipper, I'd be real careful with your XO, if I were you. He has larceny in his heart. Hopefully those Air Force weenies won't figure out what he was doing back in their ware-house while I was raising a ruckus with them out front." He smiled broadly and cuffed Edwards on the shoulder. "Them supply types were being real protective of their gear. Must have been real concerned about a SEAL making off with it. They totally forgot the shy, unassuming sailor while I was calling their mommas bad names. Next thing I know, I hear the horn blaring and there's your exec with a full truckload. I expect we just made it out the gate before the Air Force knew they had been taken."

"I object to the term larceny," Edwards said with a grin. "I prefer to describe it as a priority-based redistribution of assets."

"Fine, XO," Ward said. "Whatever we call it, let's get this stuff below and stowed double quick. Then lose the truck down by the main gate somewhere. Just in case the Air Force objects to your priorities. We're on a tight schedule and we don't need those guys mucking up our underway."

Ψ

Joe Glass climbed the long vertical ladder up the access trunk to the submarine's bridge. It had been a long, hard day. He pulled himself up into the bridge cockpit and then to the top of the sail.

"Where are we in the pre-underways?" he asked Jeff Clay.

The young ensign was balancing a black notebook in one hand as he checked off each item with a grease pencil.

"Nav reports that Ops Department is ready for underway. Weps still needs to verify BYG-1 fire control alignment. He reports another ten minutes on it. Chop reports that the Supply Department is ready for sea."

"What about Engineering?" Glass prodded.

Clay grabbed the 7MC microphone and made a request.

"Maneuvering, Bridge, report status of ready-for-sea."

The answer was immediate.

"Bridge, Maneuvering, this is the engineer. Engineering Department ready for sea with the exception of main engine retest."

Glass listened to the exchange and nodded. Then he asked, "Mr. Clay, you sure that you know what you're doing for this?"

"Yes, sir." The answer was immediate. "Lt. Durand and I worked it all out."

Lt. Pat Durand stood at the far side of the cockpit with a smile on his face.

"Okay, then. Let's get this show on the road. Rig out the outboard and shift to 'Remote.'"

Jeff Clay responded, "Skipper, the outboard is already rigged out, in 'Remote' and trained to port nine-zero."

The 7MC speaker interrupted their conversation. "Commodore to the bridge."

Glass nodded to acknowledge that Jon Ward was now making the long climb up to join them. He turned to Pat Durand. "Have the messenger of the watch bring a pot of coffee and cups to the bridge." He yawned. "It's going to be a long night after a long day."

Jon Ward emerged from the upper bridge hatch and climbed up the steps to the bridge cockpit before lifting himself up to join Glass on the top of the sail.

"Evening, Commodore," Glass said. "We're just about ready to get underway."

Their vantage point gave them a bird's-eye view of the pier and topside of their submarine as well as a night sky filled with shimmering stars. Master Chief Wallich was standing aft of the sail, giving his line handlers last-minute instructions. The only thing connecting *Toledo* to land was the five mooring lines stretching across to the pier.

"Fine night for an underway," Ward commented. "Cup of coffee would just about top it off perfect."

Joe Glass smiled. After all these years sailing together, Jon Ward was pretty predictable. "Coffee is on its way up. Meantime, would you observe Mr. Clay doing this underway for his quals?"

"No problem," Ward answered immediately. One of the best

parts of the job was teaching young officers how to drive submarines.

Ward squatted down so that he was level with Jeff Clay, who was standing in the cockpit. "Okay, Mr. Clay. This should be interesting. Underway with no tugs and no main engines. You got it figured out?"

"Yes, sir. I think so." Clay swallowed hard.

Ward smiled. "Well, let's see what your plan is. The outboard will swing your stern away from the pier. That's easy. How do you propose to swing your bow out without a tug?"

Jeff Clay hesitated for a few seconds before replying, "Well, sir, we still have a bit of a flood tide running. The current should be enough to get the bow swinging out. Once we're clear of the pier, I can use the outboard and rudder to swing us out into the center of the basin."

"That should work," Ward answered. "Let me give you a trick to make it easier." He pointed down at the big inflated camels that kept *Toledo* from scuffing against the pier pilings. "Those Yokohama camels are like big beach balls. If you push up against them, they will push you back out. Use that to get a little momentum and then use the tide for the rest of the way."

"Yes, sir. I think I can do that. I'll hold number two spring line, then jog the outboard. The spring action should pull in the bow when it surges ahead."

"Just a few seconds on the outboard, though," Jon Ward advised. "Your captain will get real upset with both of us if we scrape the paint on the sonar dome."

"Bridge, XO," the 7MC blasted. "The ship is ready to get underway."

As the last thread connecting *Toledo* to land slipped into the dark waters, Dennis Oshley broke Old Glory from the mast and blew his whistle. The ship was officially and legally underway.

They could only hope the wrong people had not noticed.

Ψ

Joe Glass, Bill Beaman, and Jon Ward walked into the *Toledo*'s wardroom together. The tiny space was packed. The sub's officers and chiefs filled all the available seats, except three places at the head of the table. Late arrivers stood in the narrow passage between the table and buffet.

As the SEAL captain and two senior submariners wormed their way through the mass and took the empty seats, a seaman stepped out of the tiny wardroom galley and placed a cup of coffee on the table before each of them.

The *Toledo* rolled gently in the seaway. Glass glanced up to his left at the ship's display panel. Course zero-nine-zero, speed twelve knots, depth thirty-five feet. He estimated that they had an hour before they got to the dive point.

"Eng," he said to Doug O'Malley. "How are the mains testing out?"

"Doing fine, so far," O'Malley answered. "Normal temps and flows. We ain't findin' nothin' in the purifier baskets. I sure would have liked more time to test them before we left port."

"We all would," the skipper said. "But it wasn't going to happen. Eng, tell your team that they did good. Making those repairs and buttoning up early was professional."

Jon Ward spoke up. "Skipper, since we are all on the same cruise together, I think we'd better let the cat out of the bag now. We've got a lot of work to do over the next thirty-six hours."

Glass nodded, then glanced around at the attentive faces. The room was completely silent. Every eye was on him, every man waiting to see if the scuttlebutt and outright conjecture that had been running rampant on the boat were true.

"Guys, we're going back to Cuba," he started. "We left some unfinished business. There's a SEAL team down there in need of a ride home. We're the ride."

Jon Ward took over.

"Captain Beaman and I will be going ashore about where you guys got ambushed last time. We intend to find the SEAL team and bring them out." Ward calmly took a sip of coffee. "This time, we have some advantages. Thanks to Master Chief Zillich and a very alert seaman gang, we now know how it came about that you were ambushed last time. The NUWC engineer weenies have verified that the box Seaman Brownson found was a very advanced command-activated acoustic beacon. Whoever hid it knew what he was doing. The beacon transmitted on a very narrow frequency right into our baffles and only when commanded by a coded sonar pulse."

Master Chief Zillich, his eyes wide, blurted out, "You mean some son of a bitch had the drop on us from the beginning? But how come we didn't hear the command pulse?"

"Yes, Master Chief, they were very smart," Ward answered. "The command pulse would sound like a whale call."

"Biologics!" Zillich all but shouted. "They used whale farts!" He slammed his fist onto the table.

"That's right," Ward answered. "But this time, we'll play dirty. The beacon is still out there, but we made a slight change in the circuitry. Instead of sending a beacon signal out when he command-activates it, it'll tell us someone is pinging."

A truly evil grin appeared on Zillich's face.

"You mean we'll know up which whale's ass to stick an ADCAP torpedo?"

"Yep, and this time the damn whale won't know we're there." He looked around the room. Everyone was staring intently at him. "Now, Nav, if you'd show us the track."

Jerry Perez spread a large-scale chart out on the table of the Florida Channel and Northern Caribbean. A green line stretched from their current location down around the eastern tip of Cuba and then west to their previous hunting grounds.

"We'll go to patrol quiet as soon as we dive," Glass announced. "Full war footing when we're abeam Miami. XO, COB, set up the watchbill for port and starboard battle stations watches. I'll take the port section. XO, you'll be command duty officer of the starboard. If our farting whale shows up, we'll close to within six thousand yards and shoot the bastard."

Glass turned to Ward.

"Commodore, you want to add anything?"

"Only to remind everyone that this is a very highly classified operation," Ward said. "We have real good evidence that there is a leak somewhere in our organization. There are other reasons we don't want anybody—most of our guys or somebody else—to know where we are or what we are doing. As of right now, we are completely radio silent. Not a signal leaves *Toledo*. For anyone off this boat, we have ceased to exist for all practical purposes."

Ward glanced around the room one more time.

"Anyone have questions?"

Sam Wallich spoke up.

"Commodore, scuttlebutt has it that the SEAL team leader is your son. Is that true?"

Ward nodded and, with only a slight pause, answered the chief's question directly.

"Yep, COB, that's true. Jim is out past his curfew. With your help, Bill Beaman and I are going to bring him home to answer to his mother."

23

Simon Castellon knew that he was in trouble. Deep trouble. Hiding a secret from Admiral Valdez was practically impossible. The man's tentacles were everywhere, and he was a supremely suspicious man. Castellon well knew that his own organization was riddled with Valdez's informants. So many that it was useless to try to smoke the vermin out. Most of them were, by nature, loyal only to the last person who gave them a bribe or threatened the lives of their children.

That left the veteran revolutionary in a quandary. How should he deal with Josh Kirkland's contact and his bizarre request for assistance? The CIA spy had placed him in an impossible spot, most probably by design. Such a meeting had likely accomplished the American spook's goal just as surely as assassination would have.

If he confessed to Valdez about the rendezvous, the old war horse would instantly question Castellon's motives in agreeing to meet the American in the first place. His response to these types of questions' answers was all too often a quick bullet to a knee and then, if the admiral felt especially merciful, another quick one to the back of the head.

On the other hand, if he tried to cover up the meeting, Valdez would almost certainly find out. Death would then be certain, but neither quick nor painless.

Castellon paced back and forth. The rattling old ceiling fan tried vainly to stir the merest hint of a breeze from the stifling air in the so-called "safe house." Three paces from the lice-infested bed to the door. Turn, and then three paces back. The bare bulb hanging on a chain from the ceiling tried to push back the darkness, casting moving shadows in the corners as the breeze from the fan caused it to sway hypnotically. The dim bulb didn't give enough light to even frighten away the roaches.

Castellon's recent failures in meeting the admiral's demands only made the predicament worse. If he had been successful in producing the revenue required from the cocaine, Valdez might have magnanimously chosen to believe the meeting with the American was not his idea, and that Castellon was merely learning what the CIA man had in mind.

As Castellon saw it, he had only two choices. One was to escape across the Colombian border and then slip into a self-imposed exile further south until things cooled off a bit and the current events played out. Ecuador or Peru. Chile would be even better—he had contacts there. But if he fled, his days of struggling to free his people would be over forever. Castellon had a fleeting image of himself as another broken, lonely old man in a decrepit cantina, telling tall tales to which no one listened.

His other option would be to play Kirkland's very dangerous game. The CIA man had offered protection, but that was certainly worthless if he remained here in Venezuela, and probably anywhere else on the planet.

But Castellon had to admit the American's final offer had been of some interest. It was access—virtually a free pass—to the very, very lucrative American and European drug markets. Kirkland was offering him the chance to leverage the CIA's vast network to bring his product to market, all in an effort to stymie the Mexican drug lords, who had grown far too big and practically invincible. What the CIA man was proposing was not merely a matter of buying off a few dirty cops to look the other way when a shipment came through. This was using the American spy agency to actually carry the shipments, tons of cocaine at a time.

But such a deal required a very heavy commitment by Castellon.

He gazed out the fly-specked window at the scene beyond his tiny bedroom. A few lonely street lights illuminated the dreary urban decay. Across the railroad track and the dirt path that was generously dubbed a street, tin and tarpaper shacks stretched up the hillside as far as he could see. Flickering light streamed out of a few open windows as early risers prepared for another day of despair and struggle to exist.

Kirkland had said they only wanted information in return. Information about Gutierrez and his minions. About his relationship with Cuba and those who would deign themselves to be the power brokers in that evolving shit storm. About others in the hemisphere who now advocated distancing themselves from *los Estados Unidos* to align with other emerging powers elsewhere on the planet, like China and the oil-rich Middle East. About rumors that petroleum in the Caribbean might be the chit that would buy that influence and alignment.

Kirkland wanted to be able to covertly meet with Castellon on occasion, to hear his story and to freely present his own. No spying, no bombings or assassinations, not even any attempts at subversion. A simple business meeting with reports and Power-Points. It all sounded so simple and easy.

Too easy. Castellon's instincts were screaming.

First question: was Kirkland doing this on his own, using his contacts to feather his own nest, or was this a sanctioned CIA operation? It really did not matter much to Castellon. In either case, the moral rot was appalling. Even worse than Gutierrez or Valdez. At least those two openly raped and robbed their own people. These rogue CIA types did the same under a cloak of righteousness. Despite his dirty hands, Castellon still had what he saw as noble intentions. He believed his trade would eventually result in a better life for his people. So what if Gutierrez grew rich? Or the CIA skimmed off money from his production and exporting? If he could bring medical attention and a chance at a better existence for his people—a future—then he would have achieved his primary goal.

Castellon shook his head. It was a deal with the devil. But it was the only deal on the table. He was on shaky ground already with Valdez and was not foolish enough to believe that the CIA deal came with no strings. But a few strings were infinitely easier to deal with than a bullet to the back of the head.

A freight train roared by, mere meters from the greasy apartment's dirty window. The whole room shook.

His mind made up, Castellon slammed his fist onto the table and stood up. If this was the way it must be, then it was time for action. He strapped on his old Walther pistol and grabbed his haversack, then stepped out the door and disappeared into the pre-sunrise darkness.

It was difficult to see anything in the dark alleyways. No streetlights in this neighborhood. So Castellon could not see Jorge, Valdez's assistant, as he kept to the shadows a block or so behind him.

Nor could he see Josh Kirkland in an alley on the other side of the narrow, rutted street as he put away his night vision scope and ambled back to his car.

Ψ

The idea had first come to *General Almirante* Juan Valdez in a brilliant flash of insight. It really was a stellar plan. Elegant and simple. Why had he not thought of it earlier?

The key, of course, was Cuba. The embattled island, isolated for two generations from her large neighbor to the north, would provide just the leverage he needed. All he had to do was control Cuba's bureaucratic government without anyone finding out. And now, with the power vacuum that existed at the top, and with the imminent announcement of the Cuban Deep oil deposits, the timing could not have been better.

The germ of the idea had been in the back of his mind for a while, and the report by deFrance was the trigger. Speculation reported from his operatives in Cuba confirmed that now was the time to act.

Of course, he would need to actually be in Cuba, to meet face-to-face with just the right people. Not Gutierrez, who was so visible, and whose trips there for cancer treatment were almost comical. Cuba? For advanced medical care? Laughable! And as cunning as the president was in snookering his own people, he could not even begin to make the proper moves that would be required in Cuba in the upcoming days, in the shadow of the USA, who probably had their succession plans in place for the government there as well.

The admiral knew that he must get there quickly and with absolutely no one knowing he was on the move. Once he explained about the possibilities of the oil discovery and his country's ability to actually bring it to market, the Cubans would immediately see the path to taking full advantage of what it— and the renewed and strengthened ties to Venezuela—could accomplish.

Valdez rubbed his chin and thought for a minute. He grabbed a cigar from the humidor and lit it. As he deeply inhaled the fragrant smoke, a smile flitted across his face. It would all fit together. Bruce deFrance's little device now ensconced on his exploration vessel would need to be quietly moved to the *Almirante Villaregoz,* but that was not a problem. They could make that move in Cuba without raising any interest from prying eyes. And *Senor* Buorz would be introduced as a technical expert on the submarine. That was all that idiot Captain Ramirez needed to know. Then it was only a matter of getting all the pieces in the right place at the right time.

He reached across his desk for the telephone and dialed in a number.

The phone pulsed a dozen times before it was answered. A man's sleep-heavy voice growled, "If this is not *muy importante,* then I will have your *cojones* nailed to the periscope."

"Captain Ramirez, you are even more unpleasant than usual at this hour," Valdez said, coming as close to a joke as he ever did. He almost chuckled when he imagined the little man's sudden terror when he realized who he was talking to in such a manner. "Say goodnight to your *puta* and get down to your submarine. The *Almirante Villaregoz* will be ready for underway for a war patrol at zero-eight-hundred. Do you understand?"

Captain Alejandro Ramirez, the greasy little submarine commander, was positively groveling as he responded, "Admiral, ten thousand apologies. I had no idea it was you. I thought it was my idiot first lieutenant. Only he has this number."

There was a short pause. Valdez could hear the faint rustling of bedclothes and a giggling, high-pitched voice momentarily raised in protest.

"Admiral, an underway in just four hours, and for a war patrol, is impossible," Ramirez went on. "There is much too much to do. Supplies to load, repairs to finish. The crew must be summoned. I need at least three days."

"You and your submarine will be ready at zero-eight-hundred as I ordered, or that 'idiot first lieutenant,' as you called him, will assume your command. I am confident he will take the requests of his commander far more seriously than you appear willing to do."

"But where are we going?" Ramirez blathered on. "What is our mission?"

Valdez strained to control his temper.

"You really are the illegitimate spawn of a retarded jackass," he said, his voice surprisingly controlled. "Have you any concept whatsoever of security? Do you not realize how easy it is to listen in on these conversations? Now, for the last time, let me very clearly give you your orders. Be ready for a zero-eight-hundred underway. If you and your submarine are not ready, it would be best for you to be very far removed from the pier when I arrive."

The old admiral slammed the phone into its cradle before Ramirez had a chance to reply.

24

Simon Castellon moved easily through the slum's early morning shadows. This was his natural time. While the sheep slept, the jaguar prowled. Besides, it was his territory. The place where he grew up, where he learned how to stay alive, among the people with whom he most closely identified. Not the politicians or the military types or the clandestine operatives with their inconsistent loyalties.

The shantytown was almost completely silent at that early hour. Only the occasional barking from a stray dog broke the quiet. Castellon could easily hear the rats scratching as they scurried deeper into the darkness as he passed.

And, at times, the slightest hint of another similar sound, one that suggested someone may be following him.

The guerilla leader made his way slowly up a hill, following the tight, twisting dirt paths that wound through the patchwork of huts, shacks, and ramshackle sheds. Castellon had been born here but it had been many years since he left these slums, since he escaped into the world of leftist revolutionary politics as a hot-headed young tough. Left for intense training in some of the best camps in the old Soviet Union, Central America, and Cuba, already selected and groomed for leadership. Harvard followed. Ironically, he was the beneficiary of some well-meaning Wall Street mogul who assuaged his guilt by providing scholarships to the children of the Third World. In the Ivy League, Castellon learned the enemy's ways. Next was "graduate school" in the best conservatories for learning terrorism, matriculating in Afghanistan and Pakistan.

Castellon kept to the deep shadows, relentlessly moving up the hill. As he slipped around the corner of a shack, he sensed more than saw just the barest hint of movement several meters behind him.

He upped his pace without giving any indication to his follower that he might have seen something, darting ten meters down the path and then stepping behind a rusted-tin shed. He crouched there, watching the path, his hand on the butt of his Walther.

Five minutes. Ten minutes. Then fifteen minutes and nothing. Castellon shook his head. Imagining things. This thing with the CIA man and Valdez. His nerves were on edge, and that was not like him. Being nervous caused mistakes. Mistakes got people killed. Castellon moved back onto the weed-infested path and continued up the hill.

Jorge showed his usual patience as he waited in a dark doorway for his prey to resume his walk. It was not time yet. He would do Valdez's bidding farther up the hill, where he could more easily slip to within a better killing distance. Jorge, of all people, understood how difficult dispatching someone of Castellon's skill and experience would be.

Before he had gone thirty feet, Castellon felt the hairs stand up on the back of his neck. Someone was definitely back there. It was more than simply a case of the nerves. His sixth sense had never failed him before.

Admiral Valdez certainly knew of his meeting with Kirkland.

The bastard was not even going to wait for an explanation. He had sent one of his killers out. The assassin was behind him now, and Castellon was certain he knew who it was. Jorge. And if it was Jorge, the attack would be by knife. Castellon had seen Jorge at work. He had the skills of a surgeon with his big blade.

The guerilla still did not want to let his trailer suspect that his presence was known. He walked at a fast pace down a side path, then turned and dashed up another, narrower path before turning again. The old guerilla was far more familiar with the mazes of the slums than Jorge would be. He turned right or left at random, never staying on one path for more than a few seconds. One muddy trail followed another, always different but always the same. Always uphill. The jungle and its relative safety were just over the top.

Jorge watched as his rabbit disappeared into the warren of paths and trails. There was no way to safely follow him without being seen. Or becoming hopelessly lost. But he had no reason to do so. Jorge knew by now where Castellon was headed. Being a creature of habit was very dangerous.

Instead of following his meandering quarry, Jorge took the wider path straight up the hill. Once there, he chose his ambush carefully. Half a dozen of the narrow alleys merged together at the macadam access road that led down the other side of the hill, out of the slums and into the countryside. The juncture came in a sharp curve at the very peak of the hill. From there, the road dropped steeply, plunging down the backside of a shanty-covered hillside. Castellon was almost certainly bound for his jungle command post. He would have to exit here. There was no other good choice.

Jorge moved silently, slipping into the perfect vantage point where he could easily command the area.

He had barely settled himself behind a twisted old acacia tree when he spotted fleeting movement coming his way. And heard the ragged breath of a man who had been all but running for the past forty-five minutes.

Simon Castellon was moving carefully, slowly, flitting from shadow to shadow as he checked behind and ahead, his pistol at the ready. He reached the acacia tree and stepped right past Jorge, never seeing him crouched in its deep shadows.

Catlike, the assassin rose and pounced. At the last instant, Castellon's instinct once again served him well. He felt the attack coming and spun around to meet it, barely deflecting the deadly cobra strike of Jorge's fighting knife. The blade missed his spine by an inch but plunged deep into Castellon's shoulder.

The old guerilla innately lashed out with a vicious, sweeping kick as Jorge struggled to pull his knife free from his victim's body. Castellon had his Walther in his hand, but the knife had severed nerves. He dropped the pistol.

Jorge dodged the first kick, but a sudden spin and another kick hit home, cracking ribs. He grunted and fell back but managed to bring the bloody knife with him. He then crouched and circled Castellon, moving the weapon in a slow, hypnotic circle as he prepared for the next strike. The fatal strike.

Castellon was suddenly finding it hard to breathe. His head was swimming and blackness was intruding on his eyesight.

With sudden blinding speed, Jorge thrust low, moving to disembowel his quarry with one arching swipe. Castellon barely evaded the deadly jab, but he was off-balance for the counter-strike. Jorge suddenly flipped the knife to his other hand and thrust hard toward Castellon's unprotected jugular. No chance of missing this time.

But the knife suddenly flew from the assassin's hand. So did two fingers.

Jorge looked with disbelief at his mangled hand. Then, no longer in possession of his weapon, he grabbed the spurting hand with his good one and dashed away into the shadows.

Someone with a gun. A silenced gun. Someone had made a very good shot. And it had been a fortuitous shot for Simon Castellon.

But then the blackness claimed Castellon's eyesight and he collapsed to the cobblestones. He was simply too exhausted from the fight and too weak from the blood that spilled from his shoulder to move.

A black car screeched to a halt beside him. The passenger side door flew open.

"Hurry, get in!"

Castellon looked up, shaking his head. It was Josh Kirkland, the CIA man. A sniper rifle lay across his lap.

"Get in, dammit!"

With great effort, Castellon crawled up into the car and collapsed onto the seat. Kirkland hit the accelerator, and the quick start swung the door shut. He steered the car over the crest of the hill and down the road that led toward the thick cover of the jungle.

Kirkland tossed a compression bandage into Castellon's lap.

"Take that and press it tight to your shoulder. I can't have you bleeding to death in my car. It's a rental."

25

Tom Donnegan stared hard and long at the picture, an overhead image of a tropical scene. Palm trees lined the wide, empty road running along a mud-brown river. Warehouses and industrial buildings filled the broad plain on the other side of the road.

The satellite, one of the new KeyHole birds, had passed one hundred and sixty-two miles over Venezuela less than ten minutes before. Even though it was pitch black outside, the image was so clear that Donnegan could easily discern the make of the cars parked on the Caracas Naval Base pier. The guard at the end of the pier appeared to be sleeping.

It was not what appeared in the image that grabbed Admiral Donnegan's interest, but rather what was conspicuously absent. Two days before, a Russian-built *Kilo*-class submarine had traversed the river and been tied up at the pier beneath a covering.

Today, on the orbiting bird's image, that same submarine could be clearly seen heading back toward the sea.

"Tim, get in here," Donnegan yelled through the open door.

Lt. Tim Schwartz, Donnegan's flag aide, stepped into the cluttered office. "You need something, sir?"

"Get Joe Glass on the horn," Donnegan growled as he held up the picture. "We need to tell him to expect company. It looks like *Almirante Villaregoz* has slipped her leash. And get me Admiral Greene. About time for FLEET FORCES to do another quick-response ASW exercise in the Caribbean Basin."

Ψ

The flight line at Naval Air Station Jacksonville was bustling with activity. Normally a Sunday afternoon at NAS JAX was pretty quiet. Most of the fliers and aircrews would be out at the beach with their families or lined up at the Navy Exchange for the weekend bargains. The P-3C Orions would be parked in neat rows, waiting for Monday's training missions.

But not today. Maintenance teams crawled all over four of the aging white birds while fueling crews topped off the wing tanks with JP-5 jet fuel. Weapons carriers loaded down with green warshot Mk 54 ASW torpedoes protruded from beneath each of the four aircraft's bomb bays. Aviation ordnance types strained to load the lightweight torpedoes up into the planes and connect them so that they could "talk" with the onboard computer processors.

A few feet further aft, just forward of the tail, another crew was loading sonobuoys into their launch canisters. One type of passive sonobuoy could be dropped in lines to listen for passing submarines. Active sonobuoys used active sonar to ping for quiet submarines. Finally, bathythermograph buoys measured the environment to see how sound traveled through the water, all to better calibrate the other devices.

Lieutenant Bill ("Bull") Braddock, the mission commander for this flight, and LCDR Samuetta ("Smedley") Winnowitz, the plane commander, walked out of the ASW Tactical Support Center and into the bright Florida afternoon sunshine. Jason

("Bucko") Schwartz, the copilot, and Jane ("Blondie") Biondi, the tactical operations officer, or TACCO, were a few paces ahead. They sauntered together down a sidewalk lined with precisely placed whitewashed stones, heading for the gray crew-cab pickup truck idling at the end of the walkway.

Bull and Smedley, dressed in identical green flight coveralls and carrying matching green helmet bags, could not have appeared more different. Bull Braddock was five foot six and one hundred and twenty pounds soaking wet. He barely made the Navy height standard for flying. Smedley Winnowitz was a drop-dead gorgeous six-foot-tall redhead—a former competitive volleyball player—who filled her flight suit in all the right places.

"Bull, this stinks," she grumped. "What Pentagon numbnuts would call for an all-out fast-reaction training mission on a Sunday afternoon? I had fifty-yard-line tickets to the Jaguars–Redskins game."

"It does have a certain aroma, but I'm thinking the smell comes from a different vector."

"Huh?"

"I'm thinking that this exercise mission is not all that it's portrayed to be," Bull answered, his voice much lower. "You ever fly an exercise mission off the southwest coast of Cuba before? I sure haven't. Nobody wants to thumb our nose at the Cubans just for some drill. And you see those warshot 54's they're loading. That ain't for practice."

"Anything special in your mission brief?" Smedley asked, intrigued by Bull's line of reasoning.

"Not really." He shook his head. "But we'll see a lot more when we load the mission computer and come up on the net with the TSC."

The two climbed into the back seat, barely getting the doors shut before the vehicle shot down the street with a screech of its tires. The four crewmembers looked at each other. The unusually tight-lipped driver was not typically in such a hurry. The run out to the flight line took five minutes, the truck slamming to a stop immediately in front of their plane.

The P-3C Orion, a much-modified version of the '50s-era Lockheed L-188 Electra passenger plane, was nearing the end of its service life. This particular bird, although packed with the latest in ASW technology, had rolled off Lockheed's Palmdale, California, assembly line several years before either of her pilots was born.

Braddock and Durham climbed up into the bird and immediately began downloading data into the AN/USY-1(V) Single Advanced Signal Processor System mission computers. The rest of the eleven-person crew was already aboard, checking out their equipment and stowing gear for the twelve-hour mission.

"Tower, six-four-seven, request permission to taxi," Smedley said into her throat mike.

"Six-four-seven, taxi to take-off position runway zero-niner. You are cleared for immediate take-off. Departure zero-nine-zero, climb to angels ten. Shift to Navy Control, channel seventeen, for further direction."

Smedley shook her head. That was unusual. Even on a Sunday, it was rare to be cleared out even before she started to roll. And she had never heard of Navy channel seventeen.

Meanwhile, Schwartz, with a curious look on his face, was already riffling through his books to try to figure out who the hell they would be working for on this odd little flight south.

Ψ

Jim Ward cautiously led the now-expanded group of men into the abandoned shed, the same one where they had sheltered during the baby hurricane a couple of nights ago. Ward knew that it was bad practice to ever reuse a campsite. Too much chance of being discovered. But the abandoned, falling-down structure made too good a hiding place, especially now that they had extra company and needed to hole up while he figured out their next move. Having a wounded addition, and especially one as important as Marco Esteban, added a whole new layer of complexity to the mission.

The team slumped down in exhaustion. Even the meager shelter seemed a palace after what they had been through since last being in the shed.

"Dillon, looks like your buddy is coming around," Ward said, nodding toward the man the SEAL had just carried most of the way down the mountain.

Sure enough, Marco Esteban was coming out of his drug-induced haze, blinking, glancing from face to face. TJ Dillon reached down and pulled the gag from the man's mouth.

"*Donde esta?*" Esteban asked, then defiantly jutted out his chin. "I demand that you free me, in the name of the sovereignty of Cuba!"

Dillon leaned closer, his face only inches from his captive's.

"Doesn't seem to me like you got a whole lot of room to demand much of anything at the moment, Marco," Dillon told him quietly, speaking in perfect, unaccented Spanish. He pulled the man up so that he was sitting upright against the rotting, falling-down wall, then kneeled in front of him. "The way I see things, either you are our ticket out of here or we turn you over to whatever is left of de la Roche's revolutionaries. Either way, it is not in our best interest for us to turn you loose at this moment."

The master spy stared hard at Dillon for a moment before an odd grin passed across his face. He shook his head slowly from side to side, both in disbelief and recognition.

"So the reports are true. I did not believe it when our old

CIA friend told us to expect a family reunion of sorts during the next few weeks. You are very much like your father, *Senor* Dillon," Esteban continued. "You have his eyes. His face. You are so very sure of yourself, even if for no good reason. Very foolhardy."

Dillon's jaw dropped. The spy's words stunned him.

"What...what do you know about my father?" he gasped. He grabbed Esteban by the lapels of his smoke- and sweat-stained dress shirt. "How do you know who I am? Tell me!"

"Let him go," Jim Ward ordered. "He's just goading you."

Esteban looked hard at the young SEAL. Then he smiled.

"Ah, yes, the young Ward is part of this family get-together as well. How history comes full circle. It really is quite amusing. And a coincidence of immense proportions."

Esteban laughed softly, still shaking his head as he studied Ward and Dillon.

"And what is so amusing?" Ward questioned. Suddenly the SEAL team leader's curiosity was on par with Dillon's.

"You are, of course, too young to be the son. You must be a grandson," Esteban said. "Yes, Jack Ward's son would have to be at least in his fifties by now. Yes, you are the grandson."

It was Jim Ward's turn to be stunned. His grandfather, Jack Ward, had died in a submarine accident over forty years ago, when Jim's dad was a kid. Why would the head of the Cuban DINA know his father's name?

"I don't know what..."

Esteban's dirty, smudged face broke into an even broader grin. He spread his hands before him, palms up.

"This is too delicious," he said. "Thomas Jefferson Dillon's son and Jack Ward's grandson, back in Cuba, here in this shack, trying to overthrow the legal government. And now, here we all are, not far from the very same spot where their forebears eventually met their end. I would show you their graves, but there really are not any." The grin on Esteban's face became decidedly evil. "We fed the bodies to the crocodiles. Good, well-fed Cuban crocodiles. And soon, we will do the same with you."

Dillon quickly seized Esteban again and threw the old man hard against the dilapidated wall, which almost toppled outward from the force. Sean Horton grabbed Dillon and pulled him away before he badly hurt their prisoner. Esteban collapsed into a heap on the dirt floor, trying to find some air.

Sean Horton released his hold on Dillon, asking, "Don't they teach you spook types to stay cool, no emotions?"

Esteban chuckled as he worked to right himself, rubbing his ribcage.

"You know I shot them myself," he gloated. "Executed them both. After weeks of torture, of course. I had to admire them. Neither cracked. Good men trying to deny a just cause. On the wrong side. But we had to be sure that we had finally rid ourselves of such foolish but dangerous men. And we could not allow them to become martyrs to those exiles who fled our country after the revolution and those who continue to plot its downfall."

It was Jim Ward this time who made a move toward Esteban, jerking him by the collar into a sitting position.

"Tell us more about them. What do you know about my grandfather? And how could you possibly know who I am? Whose grandson I am?"

Esteban leaned back against the wall.

"It all started in Nicaragua. I was personally leading the DINA revolutionaries, helping our fellow socialist fighters build their country. The Sandinistas had just overthrown the Somoza government and were well on their way to exterminating the last of the so-called Contra revolutionaries. That feckless peanut farmer you had for a president was inadvertently giving us everything we needed. Victory in Nicaragua was at hand, and with that, all of Central America. Honduras, Guatemala, El Salvador—we would have had them all in a few months. But suddenly a new resistance appeared on the Mosquito Coast. They fought like tigers but were very smart. We were caught completely by surprise—flat-footed, as you *Americanos* love to say."

Esteban paused to take a swig of water.

"Rumors started to feed back to us in Managua. Rumors of a *Norte Americano* who was advising this band of Contras. He seemed to be everywhere, outsmarting the Sandinistas at every turn. They would report him trapped in Li Dakua, only to have him burn an ammo dump in Francia Sirpi. It was nothing to have simultaneous reports of him leading raids in Slimalila, Santa Marta, and Klingua, all the same night. None of our sources, even the ones buried deep in your government, could find any information. We only knew that he wore a Marine officer's uniform. He became known as *espectro marino de las colinas*: the ghost marine of the hills."

The old man shook his head, obviously remembering the frustration and embarrassment that this one man had caused the revolution.

"He was operating totally alone. Even your CIA had abandoned him, as they did others in that bloody, sordid affair. In fact, they were the ones who eventually gave him up. We finally captured him because your spies...how do you say? They 'outed' him?" Esteban looked from one man to the other. "I have no qualms in telling you his name since none of you will ever escape my country. I think one of you may even know him. And I know his usefulness to us is now concluded. It was a young agent named Kirkland who gave Dillon up to us."

TJ Dillon's gasp was audible in the fetid shack.

"Josh Kirkland?" Dillon asked, wide-eyed.

Esteban paused for a moment and then smiled.

"I see you are indeed familiar with this man. I had to admire his boldness if not his scruples. He provided us with much valuable information, for which he was paid well, both in money and return information with which he was able to advance his career within the Agency. And, I might add, we have continued to maintain this exchange with him, as recently as the last few weeks. Yes, that is the name. He is quite adept at playing all sides of any issue. Quite adept, making him both an asset and a liability."

TJ Dillon sat back, quiet, confused, pondering what the Cuban spymaster was telling them, trying to make sense of it. Jim Ward looked hard at Dillon.

"How do you know this guy, Dillon?"

"Let's just say that I would not be here in the middle of this hell if not for the bastard."

Esteban wriggled about, trying to find a comfortable spot.

"We learned that our '*espectro*' was named Thomas Jefferson Dillon. When we were unable to learn anything of value from him in Managua, we brought him back to Cuba and threw him into the prison at Jaguey Grande. There we could more easily apply what you scrupulous Americans call 'enhanced interrogation methods.' We simply call it *tortura*. That is where he met the de la Roche brothers. Somehow, they all managed to escape up into the mountains again, but some of them were seriously wounded. From there, they were able to make contact with the *Norte Americano* military. Your Navy sent a submarine to rescue them. The rendezvous was at a beach just a few kilometers from here. The submarine captain was foolish enough to come ashore to help the wounded. We caught them all—the de la Roche brothers, Dillon, and the submarine captain, Jack Ward."

Esteban smiled at the memory as he looked at Jim Ward. Now it was the young SEAL's turn to settle back with a dazed expression.

"It was a great day," Esteban went on. "We ambushed them on the beach. They did not have a chance. de la Roches died there. Dillon was badly wounded. So was Ward. They died later, of course, but in a great deal of pain. The only thing we missed was the submarine, which got away. We did not yet have the capabilities we have today. Maybe this time history will be even kinder, and this ironic reenactment of history will get even better. This time, we will get the submarine, too."

Jim Ward shook his head.

"There isn't any sub. We're on our own to get out of this mosquito pit." Ward's jaw was firmly set. "We've been debating what to do with you. Now we know. You are coming with us to answer for the murders of TJ Dillon and Jack Ward."

"We have no fears from *los Estados Unidos* so long as you continue to underestimate us, as you have done all along," Esteban scolded. "Your CIA may be treacherous, but your Navy is not. There is a submarine out there, all right. Probably even as we speak."

Ψ

Smedley Winnowitz pulled back on the control yoke as Bucko Schwartz drew back on all four quadrant levers, feeding fuel to the big, hungry Allison turbines. The old warbird climbed into the sky, clawing its way up from the wave tops. Cuba's southern coast appeared as a fine green line on the northern horizon. Winnowitz eased back on the yoke as the altimeter spun past ten thousand feet. She carefully adjusted the trim tabs for a broad, slow turn to the south, setting up a wide orbit around this bit of ocean.

"All buoys are hot." Jane Durham's voice crackled over the ICS, the Intra-plane Communications System. "That's our last set."

Schwartz throttled back and feathered the number four engine.

"That's good. We'll be bingo fuel in three hours."

Bull Braddock, sitting in the TACCO station just behind Schwartz, stared at his APS137 radar screen for a few seconds. A dot had suddenly appeared out to the north, over Cuba. It was moving toward them. And fast.

"Guys, we got company coming. Fast mover from the north. Coming out of Jaime González Air Station. Bogey vector zero-one-seven. Current range thirty-five miles, angels twenty and climbing." He paused for a beat. "They've split. I now make two bogeys, mach point six. Not squawking."

Braddock called out the info as fast as he saw it. The APS137 was even faster computing the bogey's tracks. The hostile planes were heading their way all right, and they were coming high and fast.

Winnowitz looked out her windscreen, craning her neck to see the incoming flight, but they were still too far away for a visual.

"Can't see the bastards," she grunted. "Bull, where they at?"

She flipped the autopilot off and pushed down on the control yoke, trading altitude for speed. Meanwhile, Schwartz grabbed the quadrant levers and powered all four of the big Allisons to full throttle. The old gray bird jumped ahead.

"Angels twenty, vector north, range ten." Bull Braddock rattled off the data on his flat-panel display. "They've gone supersonic. Coming real damn fast."

"Bull, tell the ASWC we got company. Make sure they have log on our posit and see how far away help is," Winnowitz instructed as she pushed the P-3C down on the deck. "Let's see how these bozos like it down here with us slow freights."

"Already on it," Braddock shouted back. "You concentrate on keeping us in the air, I'll take care of the fighting part." He paused a few seconds and then added, "ASWC has good copy on our LINK. Nearest help is a flight of F-16s scrambling out of Eglin. At least half an hour to intercept."

The P-3C was down low, barely skimming across the wave tops, close enough that the big propellers were tossing up columns of salt spray behind them. And their only help was just coming off the deck up in the Florida Panhandle.

"Okay, let's haul ass," Winnowitz said. "Vector me out of here. I want as much space as I can get between us and those bogeys, international airspace or not."

"Both bogeys diving. They're comin' down to play. Almost dead astern. Still supersonic," Braddock shouted. "Standby, they're going to fly right up our ass!"

Smedley Winnowitz tightened her grip on the control yoke as she pulled up hard. She needed some altitude for what she knew was going to happen next. The airspeed dropped quickly as the altimeter started to creep up, but airspeed was not the important thing now. Those Cuban jets had over a three-hundred-knot-speed advantage on them.

Suddenly two MIG29 FULCRUMs flashed by, one on either side of the P-3C, barely a hundred feet away. The Cuban fighters were almost level with them, but their supersonic speed meant that they were kicking up a seawater rooster tail that reached hundreds of feet in the air behind them. They passed ahead and crossed over as they climbed away.

The combination of the twin rooster tails and the sonic turbulence smashed into the much slower ORION from both sides. The big plane bucked and heaved, groaning under the twisting, grinding load. The old bird side-slipped toward the gray-blue sea. Winnowitz and Schwartz fought together, pulling back on the twin control yokes and kicking hard on the rudder pedals in a last-ditch effort to pull the bird upright.

Sweat poured off their faces as they clawed for altitude. Still the altimeter wound down. Finally, just feet above the wave tops, they pulled out and began to climb back toward the clouds.

Winnowitz, her voice still shaking, called out, "Where are those rude-ass sons of bitches? Bull, talk to me!"

"Climbed back to angels ten. Coming around for another pass off our nose," Bull Braddock called out. "Let's haul ass outta here!"

"I'm trying! I'm trying!" Winnowitz shot back.

Suddenly the radio crackled.

"*Yanquis,* go!" The accent was thick. "Leave our water! Head vector two-two-zero. Climb to angels five and clear Cuban air space. If you do not comply, the next pass will be hot."

Winnowitz keyed her throat mike.

"Up yours, Fidel, and your donkey-assed mother."

"Oh, a *puta,*" the Cuban pilot said with a laugh. "The *Americanos* have a *puta* flying their spy plane. It is a shame our orders are to chase you away. I would have enjoyed a much closer encounter."

"In your wet dreams," Smedley Winnowitz shot back.

Despite the tough talk, she well knew that they had no choice but to follow the Cuban's orders. The modern FULCRUMs, designed for supersonic air-to-air combat, were much more than a match for her defenseless turbo-prop. She reluctantly swung the nose around to the ordered course and climbed toward five thousand feet.

Bucko Schwartz tugged at her sleeve and pointed at the fuel gauge.

"Boss, we're bingo fuel."

Winnowitz nodded.

"Ease back on the throttles, set economical cruise. We've done our job, so let's go home."

Jane Durham spoke up.

"I didn't want to say anything while you jockeys were playing fighter pilot, but we have a trace. I got a few seconds of a line just before we lost comms with the buoys. Best guess it's a submerged diesel submarine."

Ψ

Joe Glass swung the scope around. They were all alone in this patch of ocean. The night was pitch black, the heavy overcast hiding even the brightest stars. He made another, much slower sweep. Still, there was nothing, just the deep black sky and the even blacker ocean.

"Conn, ESM, no threat signals. Picking up a land-based surface search radar. Signal strength low. Equates to that Russian-made S-300 we know is at Cienfuegos. Not evaluated a detection threat. Also hold an airborne civilian radar transponder. Distant. Probably the Delta Caracas-to-Miami flight." RM1 Sam Seidiman was making a very careful search of the electromagnetic spectrum. Cuba lay just over the horizon to the north. It would not do to get caught with their pants down tonight.

Glass heard Pat Durand give his reply: "ESM, Conn, aye. We hold no visual contacts. Keep your ears open for surface search radars in the threat spectrum."

"Skipper," Durand started to report. "We have—"

"I heard," Glass interrupted. "Make sure the commodore and Captain Beaman are ready to go. I don't want to spend any more time on the surface than necessary."

The control room was midnight black. Only the occasional weak glimmer of a red lamp illuminated some vital indication. The tiny space hummed with the quiet activity of a dozen men, one group controlling the submarine, another navigating, and still a third searching all their acoustic and electronic sensors for any sign that anyone was looking for them. Despite all the activity, there was very little noise. Even conversations were low, lest they miss some important signal.

Durand spoke into a sound-powered telephone for a few seconds before turning to Glass again. "XO reports that both are in the escape trunk and ready to go. They are ready to surface. The ship is ready to surface."

Glass digested the report while making another rotation with the periscope. Still nothing out there. He turned toward Sam Wallich, sitting in a nearby chair, and ordered, "Diving Officer, surface the ship."

Wallich immediately snapped his reply.

"Surface the ship, aye, sir." Turning to his ship control team, he ordered, "Full rise on the bow planes, full rise on the stern planes. Maintain a seven-degree up angle."

Stedman and Brownson hauled back on their control yokes. Wallich called out the depth as it wound down, "Six-two feet, five-nine, five-five feet, five zero."

Toledo shot to the surface, emerging from the calm waters; first the masts, then the black sail, and finally the broad round deck.

Wallich reported, "Depth three-nine feet and holding. Chief of the Watch, start the low-pressure blower on all main ballast tanks."

Bill Dooley flipped a switch on the ballast control panel. One of the green bars indicating lights shifted to a yellow circle. He announced, "Head valve in AUTO. Indicates open. Starting the low-pressure blower on all main ballast tanks."

He turned a switch on the desk section. A few feet aft, in the fan room, the low-pressure blower, a very large fan, sucked air from outside and exhausted it into the six massive main ballast tanks that made up most of *Toledo*'s bow and stern. The air forced seawater out through large grates deep under the sub, down by the keel. As the air displaced the seawater, *Toledo* gradually rose higher.

"Depth three-seven feet," Wallich called out. "Coming up."

Glass half listened to the normal reports as he peered through the periscope.

"Depth three-five feet. Coming up."

Glass could easily see the main deck and the rudder further back.

"Depth three-four feet and holding," Wallich reported. "The ship is surfaced. Secure the low-pressure blow."

Unseen in the dark control room, Glass nodded. "All stop. Mr. Durand, open the upper escape trunk and send people topside."

He watched through the periscope as the upper escape trunk hatch on their topside deck swung open.

Bill Dooley called out, "Upper escape trunk hatch indicates intermediate." That report was followed seconds later with, "Upper escape trunk hatch indicates open."

Men appeared on deck, hauling bags of gear topside and arranging them on the slick, wet surface. Quickly the shapes took the form of two sea kayaks loaded with equipment. Glass watched as men filled the forward seat and cargo compartments of both. Then two of the men broke off from the rest, each plopping down in the after seats of his own kayak. The rest of the men disappeared down the hatch.

Glass glanced at his watch as he heard Dooley announce, "Forward escape trunk upper hatch indicates intermediate." They had been on the surface for ten minutes. "Upper escape trunk hatch indicates shut."

Glass glanced out at the two men, alone now, sitting in their kayaks on the submarine's main deck as if out for a nice day of white-water.

"XO reports last man down, hatch shut and dogged," Pat Durand called out. "The ship is ready to dive."

"Very well," Glass acknowledged. "Diving Officer, stationary dive the ship to six-two feet."

Wallich repeated, "Stationary dive the ship, aye, sir. Chief of the Watch, two blasts on the diving alarm. Dive the ship."

Bill Dooley reached up and grabbed a green handle, swinging it to the right and holding it there for a second. The diving klaxon blasted through speakers all over the sub. He repeated the alarm, grabbed the 1MC microphone, and announced, "Dive! Dive!" Then he repeated the two blasts on the diving alarm before immediately reaching over and flipping up the main ballast tank vent toggles. The green bars turned to red circles, showing the vents were open.

Glass watched enormous plumes of water erupt from the vents as the trapped air rushed out of the tanks. The two men in the kayaks held their hands over their ears as the twelve huge air horns sounded.

"Three-seven feet," Wallich called out. "Three-nine, four-one."

Glass watched through the periscope as the waves lapped up and over the main deck. He called out, "Decks awash."

"Four-four feet."

The kayakers quietly paddled away from where the sub had once been beneath them.

"Depth five-zero feet."

"Depth six-two feet," Wallich called out. "Chief of the Watch, pump two thousand from after trim to depth control."

The submarine settled out at periscope depth. Wallich turned to Glass and reported, "Depth six-two feet, trim sat." The ticklish little maneuver of diving *Toledo* without being in forward motion was completed.

"Ahead one-third," Glass ordered. "Steer zero-nine-zero. Now for the fun part."

Tension in the control room picked up markedly. Brian Edwards came in the back door, still wet and sweating from working topside. He stepped up beside Glass on the periscope stand.

"Did everything go okay, XO?" Glass asked.

"Like clockwork so far," Edwards answered. "But the commodore doesn't relish paddling thirty miles to the beach tonight."

Glass half smiled.

"If this works, he won't have to. Keep an eye on the plots and the monitor."

"Aye, sir," Edwards answered. "You ever do a snag and tow before?"

Glass shook his head.

"No. You?"

"Me neither," Edwards said. "But I guess it's time we learned how."

Edwards positioned himself so he could see the quartermaster's plot and the periscope monitor. The scope was locked on the two kayakers disappearing into the darkness astern.

Glass waited for a minute while the sub picked up some headway before ordering, "Right full rudder."

"Right full rudder, aye," Stedman called out. "My rudder is right full. No course ordered."

Glass kept a careful eye on the two kayakers, now much more difficult to see. They each had an infrared ChemLight attached to their helmet. Without the tiny beacon, they would be totally invisible in the darkness.

Stedman called out, "Passing one-two-zero, passing one-three-zero, passing one-four-zero, passing one-five-zero."

As Stedman called out a heading of sixty degrees from the previous course, Glass ordered, "Shift your rudder."

Stedman swung the wheel around to the left. "My rudder is left full."

"Very well, steady course one-eight-zero." Glass was performing a classic Williamson turn, a maneuver developed by a destroyer skipper named Williamson for use in recovering a man overboard. It quickly swung the ship around so that at its completion, the ship was headed back down the exact track, but on the reciprocal course. If everything worked out, the man in the water should be right there.

Glass had a different reason for the maneuver. He could see the two tiny pinpoints of light a thousand yards ahead.

He swung the scope so that the crosshairs lined up with the left-hand light. "Bearing, mark," he ordered as he pushed the red button on his right scope handle.

Pat Durand read the bearing for the BYG-1 combat control system: "One-seven-nine."

Glass swung the crosshairs to the other light. "Bearing, mark."

"One-eight-zero," Durand shot back.

Glass called out, "Steer one-seven-nine-point-five."

Toledo swung imperceptibly to the left.

He swung the crosshairs to the left light again.

"Bearing mark."

"One-seven-eight," Durand announced.

Glass swung over to the right light.

"Bearing mark."

"One-eight-zero."

The kayaks were drifting slowly to the south. Must be a little wind up there, Glass thought. He ordered, "Steer one-seven-nine."

It was a slow, iterative process as they approached the tiny

boats, taking bearings on both and steering to split the difference. Gradually, as they got closer, the two kayaks became more
distinct. They had separated by about fifty feet, not moving
except for bobbing gently in the sea. They had a line stretched
between them.

Glass steered the submarine to exactly split the difference
and went between the two, purposely snagging the line on the
periscope fairing.

The two kayaks swung around astern of the periscope,
coming together. Glass watched as Beaman and Ward lashed the
kayaks together behind them.

The squawk box above Glass's head came to life.

"Momma, this is Baby One." Glass could clearly see Ward
talking. "Snag completed sat. Thanks for the lift."

Glass laughed. "One Nantucket sleigh ride, coming up."

Ψ

"This sure beats paddling." Bill Beaman leaned back against
the padded kayak seat and stretched his arms high behind his
head. He glanced over at Jon Ward sitting in the other sea kayak.
The two boats were tied together, being pulled through the
water toward the Cuban coast by a rope looped around the
Toledo's periscope.

"Yep," Jon Ward answered with a grin. "I didn't know you
SEALs had it so easy. This is the life. Chauffeured delivery right
to the beach."

"Yeah, this is a bit of a switch." Beaman laughed. "I'm used to
you being down below, all snug and warm sipping on a cup of
coffee, while I'm out here in the cold."

The two sat back and watched the slim periscope barrel
gliding through the water ahead of them with barely a ripple.

The night was still, with only the water's gentle burble as the kayaks cut through the dark sea.

"How long until we get dropped off?" Beaman asked.

"Well, we started this little jaunt about thirty miles from the coast, so we would be well over the radar horizon from those surface search radars at Cienfuegos," Ward explained. "If *Toledo* is making seven knots or so, then we have about four hours to get to the twenty-fathom curve. They can't tow us in any closer. That'll give us an hour of darkness to paddle the last mile." He pointed at the sky. "That's Polaris, the North Star, right there in front of us. We're heading almost due north."

Beaman laughed and held up his wrist GPS.

"Yep, making seven-point-two knots good. ETA to the drop point is three hours and forty-two minutes." Beaman shook his head. "Still steering by the stars? I thought you submarine sailors were up on all the latest technologies."

They chatted most of the ride in, talking about their plan once they got to the beach and once again rationalizing why the admiral insisted on only the SEAL and the former submarine skipper doing this little excursion. Both men suspected Donnegan sent them for two reasons: he wanted people he trusted to go ashore and try to get Jim Ward and his men out without talking about it afterwards, and he knew nobody else would be quite so determined to make it a successful extraction, for all the obvious reasons.

"How you figure we're going to find Jim and his team?" Ward asked. "Cuba's a pretty big island and we can't exactly place an ad in the local paper."

Beaman went silent for a bit, thinking before he answered.

"We haven't had any comms with them since they missed the rendezvous a couple of nights ago. The one where Josh Kirkland's guy was supposed to be. You saw the imagery. That place is completely burned out, DINA trucks and ambulances all over the place. Bodies being carried out, people sifting through the rubble. It looked like they were searching real hard for something. But, on the good side, no signs that Jim's team was anywhere in the area. And God help Kirkland's operative."

"They're SEALs," Ward noted. "They'd have to really screw up to leave any signs that a satellite would pick up."

"True enough," Beaman answered. "But we would have heard if they had been taken. Not something the DINA could or would want to keep hidden. My bet is that Jim is moving down off the mountains and back toward the beach. By now, he has figured out that the only way to get off that island is to do it himself."

"So, we figure out which fishing boat he is going to steal?" Ward questioned.

Beaman chewed on an energy bar and took a generous swig of water.

"Pretty much. Not necessarily which boat, but at least which pier. Not many will work. Has to be pretty small and out of the way. And it has to have a boat that they can use to get across the Caribbean, at least as far as Jamaica."

"Okay, how many towns does that leave?" Ward asked.

Beaman took another bite and chewed a bit while scratching his chin.

"Maybe a dozen within an easy march. Another dozen or so if they really push."

"If you weren't such a good friend, I'd smack you right now. How you figure we can cover two dozen little fishing piers, just the two of us, a couple of American military guys where no Americans or military guys should even be? Planning some kind of SEAL cloning experiment right after we land?"

"Not exactly." Beaman chuckled. "The world couldn't handle more than the pair of us. I'm playing a bet. One of the best places for Jim to extract from is right on the path he took inland in the first place. I'm betting that he figured that out and is heading there."

"So we simply sit on the end of the pier with a line in the water fishing until they show up?" Ward asked.

"Not exactly, but pretty damn close."

26

Captain Alejandro Ramirez paced back and forth in the narrow space between the periscopes and the plotting table in the *Almirante Villaregoz's* control room. The cramped area seemed even more confining with Admiral Valdez sitting in front of the sonar display, idly watching the waterfall as it visualized all the sea noise around the silent submarine. In a few hours the irascible old man would be Cuba's pain. Captain Ramirez gave a silent prayer of thanks.

Lieutenant Armando Vasquez stepped through the water-tight hatch from the after compartments, wiping his hands on a greasy rag. Ramirez often wondered why his first officer spent so much of his time back there. The spaces contained only the engine rooms and crews' berthing. Nothing but dirt, grease, and stink. Certainly nothing of interest to an ambitious, rising naval officer with his eye on command.

Vasquez was, as usual, dressed in a pair of grease-stained coveralls. His hands were dirt-encrusted and smudges of grease covered his dark jowls. He stepped up to where Captain Ramirez continued to pace.

"Captain," he began. "We have...."

Ramirez, growling in anger, interrupted, "You will come to attention when you address me."

The control room fell silent. Even Admiral Valdez turned to watch the exchange.

"I have had all of the disrespect and slovenliness from you that I can handle," Ramirez raged, half watching the admiral's reaction to his bold demonstration of leadership. "You will immediately change into a clean uniform of the day and report back to me for an inspection. Dismissed."

"But..." Vasquez stammered.

"I said 'dismissed!'" Ramirez bellowed. He turned his back on his first officer.

Vasquez stalked out of the control room, shaking his head in disbelief. Admiral Valdez stood and followed the young lieutenant. Once in the passageway, he tapped Vasquez on the shoulder.

"Lieutenant, I will have your report now, if you please."

The first officer snapped to attention.

"*Si, mi Almirante,* but please excuse my appearance."

Admiral Valdez waved his hand dismissively. He suspected there were problems aboard the vessel, and if the executive officer deemed them serious enough to do a portion of the work himself, they could threaten his cruise to Cuba.

"Never mind that," the admiral told him. "You have been working, doing what is necessary to assure your ship's reliability, unlike that strutting little rooster in the control room. Now, tell me what you think is so important."

Lieutenant Vasquez hesitated. Reports about his submarine should be made to his captain. Somehow, it felt disloyal to speak directly to Admiral Valdez, even if Ramirez had so curtly dismissed him. Still, Admiral Valdez was his commander-in-chief, and this report could directly affect their mission.

Finally, he spoke. "It's the main induction valve. The linkage assembly is not working correctly. It was very difficult to close it when we dove. We have been working to repair and realign it, but we do not have all the tools onboard to actually repair it." Vasquez shook his head in frustration. "It has been an ongoing problem. We were scheduled for the Russian technicians to work on it during this in-port period. My crew had it all disassembled and ready to work on. Please understand, sir, that I am not complaining, but we did not have time to do anything. Barely got it buttoned up before we got underway. No time to test or adjust anything."

"How will this main induction valve cause us difficulties?" Admiral Valdez asked, though he suspected the answer.

"Maybe nothing at all." Vasquez's tone clearly indicated that he did not believe his own words. "But if it should fail at the wrong time, it would be critical. Possibly fatal."

"Please explain," Valdez ordered.

"Admiral, as you know, the main induction valve allows outside air to feed the diesel engines when we are snorkeling. It is shut when we are operating on the batteries, when we are submerged. If it fails closed, we would not be able to operate the diesel engines. We would only have the batteries. Or, if it fails open, we would not be able to dive and would be stuck on the surface."

Admiral Vasquez rubbed his chin for a few seconds. "What do you need to correctly fix this problem? Can you fix it?"

Lieutenant Vasquez had obviously given this question a good deal of thought. He answered immediately.

"More than anything, we will need the Russian technicians. They have the specialized tools to align the linkage. It's all lying on the pier back home. Two days' work and we would be as good as new."

Admiral Valdez grunted, "I will arrange to have the linkage flown ahead to Cienfuegos. I think we can arrange a few days for you in port, but for many reasons, you should not linger beyond that. Get your men ready."

With that, he stalked off toward the control room.

Ψ

"Getting near first light," Jon Ward murmured. The pair of black kayaks gently bobbed in the swell a couple of hundred yards off a deserted beach. The two men were all but invisible in the night, but that cover of darkness would be waning soon. The night was so quiet that they could hear the sound of the surf gently rolling onto and subsiding from the beach. Voices would easily carry for hundreds of yards in this pre-dawn stillness.

"Yep, we ought to get ashore quick," Bill Beaman agreed.

The two intruders had been idly drifting while they observed the Cuban coast for the better part of an hour, watching for any sign of human life, patrol craft, or any other threat. Nothing had changed along that stretch of sand.

Jon Ward nodded, more to himself than in expectation that Beaman could see him in the murky blackness. It occurred to him then that from here on out, he was in Bill Beaman's world. As much as he was at home playing underwater games in that massive steel cylinder of a submarine, this was Bill's playing field. Bill's and now his own son's.

Beaman aimed his tiny kayak straight at the beach and paddled hard until its nose was well planted up on the sand while Ward followed as closely as he could. The pair piled out of their boats, then dragged them across the beach and into the swampy wetlands on the other side of the narrow spit of sand. Without even pausing to take a breath, Beaman grabbed a fallen palm frond and tossed it toward Ward.

"Jon, brush back our tracks while I get these kayaks hidden," he whispered.

Ward grabbed the makeshift broom and trudged back to the waterline. The frond made quick work of erasing their footprints but the deep gouges left by the boats took more time to obliterate. Ward was almost to the crest of the first low dune when he heard voices, barely more than whispers, coming from somewhere off to his left. Whoever it was, they were still obscured behind the point of land but obviously heading his way.

Ward dropped to the ground and slithered toward what little cover the tree line offered. The voices were getting louder, closer. He could make out three or four people in the foggy darkness. He had to get hidden before they came around the point. No time left to be subtle. He jumped up and dashed toward the trees, keeping as low as he could.

Ward made a leaping dive under a sea grape just as a patrol of Cuban soldiers rounded the point. He counted six soldiers walking casually down the beach, more or less in a line abreast. They appeared more like tourists out for a stroll, bantering back and forth in fast Spanish, but they carried rifles with barrels pointed downward, ready to fire.

Ward burrowed in, praying that they did not notice any tracks that he had failed to cover. It would not be good form to be caught even before their rescue mission got going.

Ward raised his head a millimeter. The nearest soldier, a wicked-looking AK-47 hanging loosely in his hands, was marching directly toward the former submariner's hiding place. Ward slithered a few inches further back and mentally thanked Bill Beaman for slathering him with so much of the green and black camouflage paint before they left *Toledo*. At least his face— pitifully pale from too much time spent in the office and not enough on the sail of a submarine—would not be a shining beacon for the scouts.

The soldier stopped not three feet from Ward's hiding place.

Scuffed and mud-spattered boots were all that Ward could see. He closed his eyes and waited for the shout of discovery, the first burst of automatic weapon fire that would put out the lights.

The soldier suddenly shouted something. Ward held his breath, wishing that he had been more enthusiastic when Ellen talked about taking language classes together. Eyes still tightly closed, he heard the soft buzz of an opening zipper. Then he felt a warm stream of water hitting him squarely in the back.

Jesus. Piss.

He could just make out the soldier muttering something about a "*cantina*" and "*mucho cerveza anoche*." The damn scout was pissing away the results of the previous night's cheap beer.

The soldier finally stopped and zipped up. The boots turned and disappeared. Ward waited a long, long time before daring to lift his head for a peek. When he did, the patrol was no longer in sight. Their tracks led further up the beach and around the next point, out of sight.

Ward jumped up and made his way back toward where he figured Beaman was hiding in the swamp, careful to brush out his tracks with the palm frond.

He found the SEAL dozing under a low bush. Beaman grunted as he woke up, alerted by only the slightest sound of Ward's step on a dry frond.

"What took you so long?" He sniffed. "Whew! You smell like a beer hall urinal after Octoberfest."

Jon Ward frowned. "You've heard it's better to be pissed off than pissed on? I can testify that is a correct assessment."

Ψ

Jim Ward crawled slowly, deliberately through the salt grass and sea grape, making his way toward a small hummock and what appeared to be better cover. The morning sun was just coming over the horizon, a thin gold line against the blue-black sea to the east. That whole segment of the sky would be ablaze shortly, bathing the swamp with full light. The slight sea breeze brought the salt smell from the ocean, a welcome change from the swamp's fetid aroma.

Ward slithered until he was in the shadows of a scraggly salt pine. It would afford him some scant cover while he watched a tiny fishing pier that stretched about ten feet from the bank at the mouth of the bay out into the black, oily water. A rusted old fishing boat was tied to the pier, bobbing easily in the slow, ebbing current. Barely fifty yards of open water separated Jim Ward from the ride off this isle.

Those fifty yards, though, meant that the SEALs would have to wait until dark that night—one long half-day—before they slipped into the water and swiped the vessel. Until then, he would just have to lie there and watch the boat, keeping an eye out for passersby.

Oh well, he thought. Might as well make myself comfortable.

Just then, an old man ambled out of the boat, stepped off the deck and onto the pier. He stretched, nonchalantly unbuttoned, and urinated into the water. A flight of brown pelicans flew past in perfect formation, scanning the water for breakfast. Wading birds scurried up and down the beach, finding their sustenance at the water's edge. An occasional fish jumped out of the brackish water to claim a low-flying insect. The humming of insects sounded like a distant machine of some kind, and the occasional call of a tropical bird echoed through the swamp.

Ward burrowed down in the meager shade of the salt pine and settled in to watch. It would be a long day before he could safely move back to where the rest of the team was well hidden.

The sun was high overhead, baking the young SEAL, sending rivulets of sweat down his forehead and into his eyes until they burned and stung. Then he heard a new sound. A rumble that could not be any kind of animal. And if it was, he wanted nothing to do with it. Crocodile?

But the noise grew louder. It was something akin to the chugging of a muffled diesel engine, like a far-off train. He dared to raise his head above the sand dune to peer beyond the old fishing boat and out into the mouth of the bay.

He could not believe what he saw entering the harbor. A black submarine!

Ward immediately recognized the distinctive rounded sail of a Russian *Kilo*-class diesel boat. Two men, the shorter one appearing to be much younger than the taller one, stood high on the boat's sail. The older, taller man was clearly and loudly berating the shorter one, jabbing the man in the chest with his finger.

Ward rummaged in his pockets until he fished out a tiny digital camera with a powerful lens. This could be a real intelligence gold mine. It wasn't every day that a *Kilo*-class submarine visited a remote Cuban naval base.

If he could just identify the two characters, maybe he would have an idea of the boat's origins or mission.

The submarine steamed past him and disappeared in the distance further up the broad, shallow bay. Jim Ward, thankful for the welcome break in the monotony, settled back down, burrowing in once more for his long day of waiting.

Ψ

Bruce deFrance read the email one more time just to be sure the words said what he thought they said. Admiral Valdez could not possibly want him to travel to Washington and meet with the Director of the US Environmental Protection Agency about the oil find in the Caribbean. The EPA was a tremendous pain in the posterior for anyone trying to work in US waters, but it had no power to interfere with Samson Petroleum's operations in either Venezuela or in the Cuban Deep, no matter how much they persisted in claiming otherwise. But that was exactly what the note said.

"Go immediately to Washington. Meet with the Under-Secretary for Maritime Environments. Inform him that Samson Petroleum plans to drill in international waters off the northwest coast of Cuba. You will not be asking permission. No permission from the USA is requested or required. You are merely informing the US as a courtesy.

"This is most important. You will do everything you can to anger the Under-Secretary. Be your normal annoying self. We want the EPA to take a close interest in any drilling activity in the area. We want them to make it personal."

Why in hell would Admiral Valdez want him to visit with and then personally annoy the US bureaucrat? It simply did not make any sense. And why tell them that the drill site was off the northwest coast when it was actually well to the southwest of Cuba? Even for someone as cunning and devious as Valdez, his instructions just did not add up.

deFrance grabbed his glass of scotch, a nice Glenmorangie Eighteen Year Sherry Cask, as it started to slide across the drop-down table. He glanced out the window, annoyed that the pilot could not keep the flight smooth, even on a perfectly sunny early evening with a sky filled with puffy but non-threatening clouds. The Virginia countryside spread out below the big Gulf-stream V. deFrance could just make out the Shenandoah Moun-tains, painted gold by the setting sun, off to the west of the green valley below. The pilot announced that they were on final approach to Dulles International Airport. Would Mr. deFrance please buckle his seat belt?

The plane kissed the runway with the barest hint of a bounce.

A limo moved out from the general aviation terminal as they quickly taxied up to a stop near it. Bruce deFrance climbed down the ladder, scotch whiskey still in hand, but he was stiff from the flight and felt as if he might be coming down with a head cold. The quick change from the Caribbean's sultry humidity to Northern Virginia's cool air only made him feel woozier. The limo's deep black leather interior smelled of luxury and comfort and cow leather. He settled back as the driver closed the door behind him, hurried back around the car, and slid in behind the wheel.

In a few seconds Dulles disappeared in the rear window as they sped down the Dulles Airport Extension and out onto I-66. But just as abruptly, their forward movement ground to a halt amid a sea of red brake lights. The oilman fretted impotently as they barely crept forward, a foot or two at a time. His time was too important, too valuable to sit there amongst all these working-class drones, struggling to get to their miserable little homes in the suburbs only to rise the next morning and go right on back to their desperate workaday lives.

"I should have hired the helicopter," he muttered under his breath. "No surprise. It is this way anytime I am here. But usually I have a reason to be here and endure this odd bit of American self-flagellation called 'rush-hour traffic.'"

deFrance's cell phone jangled, interrupting his thoughts. He glanced toward the driver, confirming that the privacy window was up, before answering the call.

Juan Valdez's deep, guttural growl was unmistakable. As usual, the old military man jumped right in without even the hint of the normal pleasantries.

"Were my instructions clear enough? Any questions?"

The line crackled and popped a great deal more than normal. deFrance struggled to hear the old man through the interference.

"Admiral, I'm having a hard time hearing you. You sound as if you are far away. Where are you?"

"Never mind where I am," Valdez barked. "Just pay attention and do as you are instructed. You are to annoy the under-secretary into taking action. Do not, under any circumstance, give any indication whatsoever about the actual Cuban Deep find."

"I understand," deFrance shot back. "I can handle this. And perhaps I should remind you that I am not one of your minions but the chief executive officer of a major…"

But then he realized that he was speaking to a dead line. Valdez had already hung up.

Ψ

Admiral Juan Valdez slapped the cell phone shut, ending the call. Hopefully that strutting fool would do as he had been told. It really did not matter too much anyway. deFrance's mission was little more than a simple diversion designed to keep the oilman out of the fray until Valdez needed him next. deFrance would be part of the sleight of hand, the move to deflect attention while things of historic nature played out elsewhere.

The old admiral walked down the pier, away from the submarine, toward a small helo pad at the landward end. He strolled past a portable crane swinging a long, heavy crate out over the *Almirante Villaregoz*. A small group of workers were slowly loading boxes of tools and assorted gear onto the submarine's round deck. Admiral Valdez could just make out the Russian curses being passed back and forth. These must be the technical experts to fix the recalcitrant induction valve. Valdez wondered if Buorz was among them.

An ancient Russian Mi-8 Hip transport helicopter, carrying the distinctive white star in a red triangle surrounded by a blue circle of the Cuban Air Force, sat waiting for him, its rotor turning in a slow arc. The corroded old relic spooled up immediately as Admiral Valdez marched toward it.

He had just stepped in and settled down in the cargo net seat when the bird smoothly and loudly lifted off, climbing and rotating as it headed on a vector northwest of the miserable little coastal town. The crew chief strapped Valdez securely in the uncomfortable seat as the bird climbed out, then handed the admiral a flight helmet. A tiny boom microphone dangled annoyingly in front of his face.

Sitting in a cacophony of noise, the scheming admiral had a few minutes of solitude, an opportunity to think. He leaned back and closed his eyes, pretending to sleep. No one would be so foolish as to disturb him until they were ready to land. Finding time just to sit and think, to work out all the delicate intricacies of this complex plan, was too valuable to squander on idle talk with a simple flight crew.

The problems were not insoluble, just challenging. If that annoying fool deFrance could irritate the US agencies as much as he irritated everyone else, the agencies, well known for their vindictiveness, would go out of their way to stalemate him. So would the media who so loved to demonize Big Oil, and deFrance was the poster boy for Big Oil.

The EPA should have the American media—famously easy as they were to be manipulated to a near fever pitch—worked into a frenzy just in time for Buorz to do his work. That would literally throw gasoline on the fire!

The *Almirante Villaregoz* would deliver deFrance's robot submarine close to one of the exploratory drilling sites in the deep water off America's Gulf Coast. Five hundred kilos of C-4 remotely detonated around the wellhead would totally obliterate the blow-out plug while looking for all the world like a massive gas explosion. It would be years before any new drilling took place in the area. That meant Cuba and Venezuela—in reality, the mastermind of the plot, Admiral Valdez—would completely control the oil access in the entire Caribbean Basin. And he would do so from his new home base, Cuba.

Then there was the really big problem: accumulating the staggering sums of money necessary to finance the initial wells in the Cuban Deep. Now that Jurgen had met his unfortunate fate, the rest of his consortium of banks seemed much more willing to help in the effort. Venezuela and its money-hungry leader would do what it could. Cesar Gutierrez craved any advantage he could get in his quest to be the figurehead leader of all Latin America, and that amount of oil on his doorstep certainly would help. Those sources Valdez could rely on.

There would, on the other hand, be little assistance from the drug trade and smuggling operations. Simon Castellon had failed miserably. There would still have to be changes there. Not as soon as he had hoped, after Jorge's aborted effort. But it would happen eventually. Even a savvy guerilla like Castellon could not hide from him forever.

These developments only made this trip all the more crucial. Soon the world would know what was happening in this back-water socialist republic. There were loose ends. There were other factions trying to fill the power vacuum in Cuba's communist hierarchy with their own replacement. There were no clear leaders within Cuba, but none had the advantages or the head start that Admiral Juan Valdez had.

It would not be easy, but Valdez would not hesitate to use any of these advantages to achieve his goals. And the crisis of leadership in Cuba would allow Valdez to use the country and its strategic location in the middle of so much oil to his purposes. On behalf of President Gutierrez and the people of Venezuela and Cuba, of course.

The beat-up old helicopter bounced and lurched to the left. Valdez opened his eyes and glanced out the window. Nothing out there but blackness. The crew chief, sitting in the aft-facing jump seat in front of Valdez, smiled reassuringly and started talking. The words crackled and hissed in Valdez's headset.

"Just clearing the ridge tops. The updrafts can cause it to be a little bumpy sometimes."

Valdez allowed a tiny smile to crease his face as he nodded that he understood, that he did not hold the crew chief responsible for the rough ride. He leaned back and closed his eyes again to avoid any more possibility of useless conversation.

The US had stubbornly forbidden all drilling in the Gulf for over a year after the accident at the BP well in 2010, and they were even more stupid to include international waters. Even now, years after that disaster, the US erected a bureaucratic nightmare to any company foolish enough to even think of drilling a new well.

If they tried that again after this next "disaster," or even worse, tried to ban all deep-water drilling, then the Cubans would be even more enthusiastic about accepting Admiral Gutierrez's offer to help develop the new find. That, of course, was the key piece to the scheme. Convince the Cuban government that the United States was taking its embargo against Cuban economic growth to a new level with its arbitrary drilling ban. One that would effectively deny the island nation and its poor, downtrodden citizens a stake in the most significant oil find in history.

In their anger, they would be very willing to form an even stronger alliance with Gutierrez to ban all American oil drilling in the Caribbean Basin. There was a slight chance that the two countries could make it stick, at least for a while. But more importantly, the oil markets would be thrown into chaos. With the continuing unrest in the Middle East, the unceasing internecine warfare, crude oil prices would only spiral upward. Investors would be very willing to put big money into development projects. And especially a project like his historic find in the Cuban Deep, a find so close to the oil-thirsty North American market yet so near Venezuela and Cuba.

It was a complicated plan, one with a lot of moving parts. Admiral Valdez smiled to himself. Despite the complexity, it was coming together. There had been snags. Castellon. The idiot submarine captain and his obsession with his American counterpart. Jurgen. Fidel hanging on for so much longer than Valdez or anyone else could have ever anticipated. His brother, Raul, so quickly abdicating leadership to others whose motives and methods were not so well known. The duplicitous CIA agent Kirkland and whatever his intentions were.

But so far, he had shunted aside all these distractions. Even turned some of them to his own advantage. Now, the plan was unfolding.

Admiral Juan Valdez had a good feeling about this. A really good feeling.

27

It was finally time to move. The night was about as dark as it would ever be. A thick cloud cover blotted out what meager starlight there might have been. A misty rain soaked the thick undergrowth, adding to the gloom but helping to dampen any noise. The ubiquitous tree frogs served to cover any inadvertent heavy footfall.

Jim Ward rousted his little group from their hiding place at the edge of the coastal swamp. A rather vague dispatch received not long after leaving the burning hacienda had confirmed Ward's initial hunch that they were to return to the area of their original landfall. The dispatch also hinted that they were to do whatever was necessary in order to escape the island and their "cruise ship" would be waiting near the previous coordinates.

The SEALs bent to the immediate tasks of breaking camp, covering their existence, and moving toward the coast. Sean Horton took charge of their prisoner, assuming he would be going with them when and if they escaped from the island. He securely bound Esteban's hands with a thin, pliant vine that he had found growing outside the ramshackle shed. He stuffed a sock in the old spy's mouth and then yanked on the knotted vine, making certain it was secure. That would have to do for the time being.

Jed Dulkowski and Tony Garcia carefully scoured the campsite, removing all traces of their existence.

"What's the plan?" TJ Dillon finally asked Ward as the pair gazed warily out over the swamp. Dillon knew the young SEAL had to be acting on instructions received, but those had not yet been shared with him. That was to be expected. Dillon knew he was still not fully trusted. Had he been in Ward's position, he would have had the same hesitation.

Ward looked at Dillon for a moment.

"I need your help since we're a little bit bigger of a parade than we expected. We head out to the coast south of Cienfuegos, near the mouth of the bay," the SEAL team leader murmured. "We should get to the beach in an hour or so, if we're careful. The tricky part is going to be getting across the river to where our ride out of here is tied up. There was an old fishing boat at a pier there when we arrived. If it happens to be gone when we show up, we'll have to go to plan B, which, by the way, I haven't come up with yet." Jim Ward rubbed the growing stubble on his chin, allowing his understatement to hang there for a moment.

"But if it is still there, we really need to get to it and head out to sea without anybody seeing us. Those fishermen are going to be real unhappy about us borrowing their boat. I'd sure like to be well out to sea and maybe even touring a real live submarine before they find out the vessel's been swiped."

"How are we getting our friend across the river?" The CIA agent nodded toward Marco Esteban. "He isn't likely to be cooperative, and swimming with his hands tied might be a problem."

"Yep," Ward agreed. "That's the reason you stay on this side. We'll pick you up on the way out. And I need your word that nothing will happen to him."

Dillon smiled at the irony. Both he and this young SEAL

commander had had their lives changed for the worse by Esteban. Now, here they were, with the bastard captured, and the kid was asking for his word that he would protect the son of a bitch. It would be so easy to agree and then toss the old man to the crocs, just as he had boasted about doing with Dillon's father. Easier to explain to the world later, too. Unfortunate.

Dillon nodded. "I know you are not obligated to believe it at this point, but we are on the same side."

Ward's dirt-streaked face showed neither agreement nor disagreement.

With their tracks covered, the SEAL team quietly headed down the game trail, on the way to hopefully pick up their ride back to the world.

Ψ

Jon Ward awoke from what could only loosely be described as sleep. Bill Beaman was shaking his shoulder. The big SEAL motioned for him to be silent.

"We've got company," Beaman whispered. "Eight or nine shooters slipping in down by the beach. Looks like DINA to me. Not military from their gear."

"They on to us?" Ward mouthed.

Beaman shook his head.

"I really don't think so. They're digging in facing the fishing pier. If I had my guess, I'd say they are setting up an ambush for somebody."

"So they have the same idea we do," Ward whispered. "Wait for Jim and the boys here. Did they guess this place, too? Or has somebody tipped them off?"

"They probably have these traps set at every little fishing village along this stretch of coast, assuming the SEALs will leave the way they came in," Beaman replied, then gave him a crooked grin. "Unless Admiral Donnegan himself is tipping them off, nobody would know the exact point where they came in or plan to leave. But they probably have plenty of information, too. They have a pretty much infinite manpower pool and a couple million spies. Even the guys who hate them will snitch on their grandmother if that's what it takes to keep their testicles attached."

"So what do we do?"

Beaman grabbed his M-4 and screwed on the sausage-shaped noise suppressor. "We stay very, very careful as we get out in front of these guys."

He slid the action to quietly chamber a round.

Ward grabbed his own M-4 and followed Beaman as they moved off toward the river.

Ψ

The old Soviet military helicopter had barely squatted down on the tarmac when Admiral Valdez swung out of his seat and hopped down from the bird. He was almost to the decaying concrete structure that served as the base operations building before the pilot had a hand free to tell ops that his VIP passenger was loose and on the prowl.

The gruff old admiral barged through the door, catching the honor guard as they scrambled out to meet him. The sergeant major was still apologizing to Valdez's back as the old man charged through the lobby and directly into the ops center.

"Who is in charge of this pigsty?" he demanded.

A pimply-faced young lieutenant leaped to his feet, stammering, "I am, Admiral! Lieutenant Jose Garcia Lopez, at your service, sir. How may we—"

"Get me transportation to Federal Palace, immediately," Valdez shot back, cutting the hapless lieutenant off in mid-sentence. "And I need a secure landline to the Minister of Resources."

The lieutenant made an instinctive decision. With no instructions or guidance to depend on, Garcia could feel that keeping this visitor happy was very important to his well-being. And discretion was important to the admiral.

"The base commander's car is available for your use," Garcia answered. "I will personally drive you." He ushered Valdez into a small closet of an office. "This is my personal office," he said as he backed toward the door. "The phone on the left is a secure landline. Does the admiral need assistance in making the call?"

Valdez ignored the offer and was already dialing the number from memory. Garcia took the hint and quietly shut the door.

The phone was answered on the second ring.

"Hermando Guanayca here."

"*Senor* Guanayca, it is good to hear your voice," Valdez said, his usual growl greatly muted. "Is everything set for our meeting?"

Guanayca, the Minister of Resources and arguably one of the most powerful men in Cuba, hesitated for only an instant.

"We have a small problem that may delay our plans a bit."

Valdez immediately became wary. Guanayca never concerned himself with small problems. Something serious was afoot. He chose to remain silent and let the Cuban bureaucrat explain.

"*Senor* Esteban will not be able to attend our meeting as planned," the Cuban began.

"That is not a problem," Valdez answered. "We will merely reschedule our discussions for another time today when he is available."

"You do not understand," Guanayca said. "We do not know where he is. He has disappeared and we have not been able to locate him." The minister's deep gulp of exasperation was plainly audible, even over the secure phone line.

"What I am about to tell you is known by only a handful of people. Esteban has been missing for several weeks. We have not the vaguest idea of his whereabouts but fear foul play. The DINA has reported rumors, ones that we cannot substantiate, that *nationalista* guerillas may have kidnapped him. Acting on a tip, they stormed a location where it was believed he may have been held, but he had been moved ahead of our arrival. We fear they plan to either assassinate him or spirit him out of the country, perhaps to hold him hostage in the hopes of claiming power over the government. We are all very concerned, as you can imagine, Admiral. But we must not let others—and especially our neighbors to the north—know of this development."

Valdez's mind was working at whirlwind speed. This was, of course, not news to him. He knew the Cuban spymaster had been kidnapped. And that he had been taken to the de la Roche compound. And that there had been fighting there. If Guanayca knew of Esteban's disappearance, then other low-level bureaucrats would know it as well.

Admiral Valdez had to act quickly. No time to confer with that strutting bantam rooster in the presidential palace in Caracas.

"All of Venezuela's resources are at your disposal," the old admiral said. "Allow me to suggest that you and I meet immediately so that we can help you in your efforts to assure the peace and stability of your country as you work through this crisis. I am sure you and your DINA are aware that no one else in the hemisphere will be as good a friend to Cuba and her people during this trying time than the people of Venezuela and her president, *Senor* Gutierrez."

On a deeper level, both men understood that Valdez was not

only offering support to Cuba but also promising to support Guanayca in his inevitable grab for his country's highest office.

"Yes, we should certainly meet, Admiral, so that we may speak frankly and completely," the bureaucrat said. "But discretion is an absolute necessity. These are very dangerous times. Many are lurking to seize any opportunity to control our country and its people now that the Castro brothers are gone. And we must maintain the revolution begun by our beloved leader and his brother."

"I fully understand," Valdez answered. "Discretion and trust. Is there a private entrance to your office? I can meet you there in an hour. Very quietly and very discreetly."

Valdez gently put down the telephone even as Guanayca was effusively thanking him, and before the man could even begin wondering how Admiral Valdez could get to a meeting at his Havana office so quickly from Caracas. Valdez stood, smoothed the wrinkles from the front of his uniform trousers, and marched out of the cramped office.

"Lieutenant Garcia, I require your car and accept your generous offer of services as my driver and assistant." As the two climbed into the base commander's car—the admiral in the back seat, the young officer behind the wheel—Valdez leaned forward and tapped the driver on the shoulder. "Garcia, you are not aware but your life is about to change. If I can depend on your loyalty, you will be very amply rewarded. If not, well…"

The lieutenant understood immediately. He nodded as he looked at the admiral in the rearview mirror. "Good," Valdez said. "Very good."

The lieutenant shoved the old limousine into gear with a grinding sound, released the clutch with a clank, and took off with a spray of gravel and a fog of oily blue smoke.

28

Jim Ward assumed the point as he led his team through the clutching undergrowth. The thick foliage made for maddeningly slow going. Esteban's added weight did not help. The old spy moved only reluctantly, no longer physically fit for marching. Sean Horton and Tony Garcia took turns lugging and prodding their prisoner down the narrow trail. Jed Dulkowski followed along behind, carefully erasing any signs of their nighttime passage.

"How much farther?" TJ Dillon whispered to Ward. He was still wearing casual clothes and a pair of deck shoes, fit more for the horseback ride he was promised than a forced march through jungle terrain. They had just finished working their way through a ribbon of reeds that surrounded a small salt marsh. Mosquitoes dive-bombed them in constant swarming squadrons. The swamp's rotten stench was enough to make breathing difficult. Methane and hydrogen sulfide bubbled up under their noses as their boots disturbed the pond's mucky bottom.

"Another mile," Ward answered. "We'll be out of this crap in a few minutes, then it's pretty much beach dunes the rest of the way. Not as much cover, but at least the sand won't be trying to suck our boots off." He glanced down at Dillon's feet. "Or whatever we happen to be wearing."

Ward felt more than saw Dillon's frown as he slipped further into the murky water and was quickly more than waist-deep. He barely made a ripple on its surface.

Dillon grunted and uneasily followed after the SEAL, holding his weapon high over his head. His instincts were telling him that something just was not right about this situation. The hairs on the back of his neck were standing up, and he had the unmistakable sense of being watched. He stopped for a moment and very carefully surveyed his surroundings. Nothing seemed out of place. He could not see or hear anything suspicious, just the drone of the mosquitos, a few distant cries of night birds, and the other muted sounds of nighttime in the jungle.

Then he noticed that the tree frogs had stopped their harmonizing. His hunches about such things were very rarely wrong.

Dillon followed Ward into the water, and they crept along as close to the muddy, reedy shore as they could manage. The moonless night and eerie silence did nothing to allay the sensation of being watched.

There was a sudden splash behind him.

Too dark for him to see what caused it, Dillon figured that the two SEALs and Marco Esteban were now wading in the muck somewhere back there. Probably not more than ten feet back, but he was unable to make them out.

The pond was getting progressively deeper, now well up on his chest. Hopefully it would not get any deeper. Swimming would cause more noise than he felt comfortable creating. Still, he waded on, following Ward, trusting the young SEAL to find the way out of this sludge.

Dillon thought he could see just the first hint of a lightening sky back to the east through a sliver of space in the veil of the undergrowth. If they did not get to the beach soon, they would have no time to steal the fishing boat before daylight overtook them. It would be difficult indeed to keep this group—and especially its reluctant guest—hidden if they had to hunker down for a full day.

Dillon pursed his lips. It would be tempting a really ugly fate to spend another day in this stinking hellhole.

At long last the bottom began to taper upward. Dillon could feel the mud turn to sand under his feet. He stumbled onto a narrow shelf and almost stepped on Jim Ward. The young SEAL was crouched down, all but invisible among the reeds at the edge of the jungle.

Ward signaled Dillon to ease down and lie prone beside him.

"I don't like this," Ward whispered. "It's too damn quiet."

"I've had the same feeling for the past hour," Dillon answered, nodding, though the young SEAL could not really see him in the darkness. "I feel like we're being watched."

"Yeah." Ward pulled his 9mm. "I'm going to circle back a little. You stay here and get the others under cover."

"Roger." But Dillon was speaking to himself. Ward had already slipped into the blackness.

Ψ

Jim Ward headed back, making a wide circle around the little track they had just traversed. If someone was trailing his ragtag team, their attention would likely be concentrated in the direction of the trail, not out further afield. Moving parallel to the pond, he stayed hidden in the heavy undergrowth. Movement was slow as he slithered and slid from shadowy tree trunk to half-submerged log. In twenty minutes, he had barely moved fifty yards. It was far more important to stay hidden than to cover ground. Whoever was out there would come to him soon enough.

Finally, he slipped under a low bush. This would be the perfect hiding place to watch for the watcher.

Ward had barely gotten himself hidden when he heard the slightest rustling of branches, the sound of a limb being quietly moved aside. Two black shapes, more shadowy apparitions than solid forms, appeared. It was obvious that they were men following the SEAL team's trail. The pair of shadows worked like well-trained pros. They moved with careful ease, silently slipping forward a few feet then hesitating while they surveyed the area. Ward could just make out the night vision goggles that obscured their faces.

Professional and well-equipped. That did not bode well for the inevitable ambush. It would have to be quick and silent. If there was gunfire or screams from either or both of them, the whole south end of Cuba would hear it and be on them in minutes. Ward quickly ran through his options.

Knife. Garrote. Silenced gun, quickly applied in turn to the backs of the stalkers' heads the instant they passed him.

He decided the pistol would be fastest and surest. The blade or strangulation could only take care of one of them quickly enough, and the other could fight back or make enough noise to get them all captured.

Then, as the pair drew closer, Ward noticed something that made him wonder. There was a familiarity about these two. Maybe it was the way they carried themselves, their body language as they crept from shadow to shadow. He fought to not allow the sudden bit of shady intuition to cause him to hesitate too long.

Then they paused only a few feet in front of his hiding place. Jesus!

Ward had to stifle an audible gasp. The two nefarious

stalkers were people he knew very, very well—his father and Bill Beaman. But why were they here?

The young SEAL realized that he had to say his hellos very carefully. Beaman could easily cut Ward's throat before he even had the chance to give his greetings.

Maybe his gasp of recognition had been audible after all. Maybe they heard the sudden rapid beating of his heart. Something alerted the pair, for they instantly dropped into a crouch, their menacing M-4 carbines aimed directly at where he lay beneath the bush.

Ward burrowed into the jungle floor as he barely whispered, "You better have brought me some of Mom's pineapple cheesecake."

One of the shapes fairly jumped and sprinted the few feet to where Jim Ward lay hidden. He jumped on the young SEAL and enveloped him in a massive bear hug.

"Jimmy, son, am I glad to see you!" the older Ward blurted out in a raspy whisper. "Your mother is worried sick about you."

Jim Ward grinned as he hugged his father. He had a fleeting thought. If TJ Dillon or another of his team had made the circle-back to see who was following them, he would not have had that last-second recognition. And both men would likely be dead.

And another thought: his team and the other SEALs in his squadron must never know that the first words from their rescue team had been, "Your mother is worried sick about you!"

Ψ

Josh Kirkland was worried. He had too many balls in the air to juggle effectively, and time was running out. But he was getting very close to the monstrous score he had so long anticipated, the one that would finally set him up for a lavish existence in the South of France, away from the world of cutthroat politics and ruthless international skullduggery. The little villa on the high cliffs overlooking the Mediterranean beach far below, the good wine and willing women. It was all so very close. All he had to do was manage to bring in this one last job, complicated and convoluted as it had become.

Kirkland glanced over at Simon Castellon. He had done what he could to stop the bleeding. Jorge's deadly blade had come within a millimeter of instantly ending the old revolutionary's life back there in the slums. Even then, Castellon had come close to bleeding out that night. Only Kirkland's emergency field dressings and a couple of liters of plasma had kept him alive.

Kirkland shook his head, trying to drive away the sleep that was weighing down his eyelids. Too much important work to do to fall asleep now. He needed to keep Castellon alive for a few more days. The revolutionary was Kirkland's only key to the cocaine, and the coke was his only way to get Juan Valdez. The admiral was where the big money lay. His "South of France" money.

Simon Castellon stirred, twitching about in some drug-induced dream. Kirkland glanced back over his shoulder at the wounded man stretched out across the Land Rover's backseat. It wasn't comfortable, but it would have to do. Kirkland figured he had shot so much morphine into the guy that he would dream through a cyclone. The hallucinations must have been vivid ones. The revolutionary groaned again, his jaw working as he gave orders to nightmarish minions and shouted threats to dreamscape enemies.

Kirkland squinted forward, trying to see through the muddy, bug-encrusted windscreen. The narrow jungle road was difficult to make out in front of the vehicle, barely more than twin ruts stretching ahead of the running lights' glare before disappearing into the gloom. Heavy brush and limbs swished against the

Land Rover on either side like a million arms clutching, trying to grab them, stop them.

The rebel camp could not be much farther. Kirkland had studied the CIA's satellite imagery very carefully before he headed out into the jungle. The camp and the surrounding coke factories were very well hidden, invisible to any normal aerial surveillance, but they stood out in great detail on the satellite's hyper-spectral images.

The track in front suddenly disappeared into a solid wall of green. Kirkland barely had time to react to the sudden turn. He braked hard and sawed the steering wheel brutally to the left, throwing the truck into a skidding, swerving turn. The big off-road tires spun and slipped, desperately grasping for a bit of traction in the wet dirt.

Despite his best efforts, the truck slid off the road, eaten up by the underbrush. A tree limb crashed through the passenger side window. Glass shards went flying like shrapnel.

Kirkland over-corrected, shooting back up onto the rough road and almost off the other side, where the ground dropped away sickeningly to who-knew-how-far down. But with one final jerk of the steering wheel, he managed to get the Rover under control and straightened back up onto the twin ruts of the path.

Just as suddenly, he jumped onto the brake and clutch pedals. Several logs were stacked across the path ahead, and jutting out from behind those logs were the unmistakable muzzles of a dozen or more guns. AK-47s pointed his direction by some very determined-looking men.

Kirkland took a deep breath. He and his patient had arrived at their destination. This was obviously the rebels' first line of defense.

Now, he could only pray that they would not shoot him to death before they bothered to ask him who he was and why he had dared come to this place.

And before they took a look at his passenger laid out in the back seat.

Ψ

"What's the problem, XO?" Joe Glass rubbed the sleep from his red-rimmed eyes as he stepped into the submarine's brightly lit control room. There had not been much chance to catch up on sleep since they had left Port Canaveral. "Got contact on our mystery sub?"

Brian Edwards did not even try to smile as he shook his head.

"I only wish. Eng just called. He's back aft. The high-pressure end bearing is on the fritz again."

"Damn," Glass grunted. "That ain't good. Does he have any idea what the problem is this time?"

"Not yet. He says he's still investigating," Edwards answered, but he was already talking to Glass's back as the skipper headed out the control room's back door.

Glass slid down the ladder into middle level. The mess decks were normally empty at this hour of the mid-watch, but tonight a gaggle of machinist mates were huddled at one of the tables, poring over a tech manual. They looked up for a second and then bent back to their studies. So the engineer was already putting together a work package to repair the main engine. That certainly did not reassure him about the extent of the problem.

Glass hurried into the side passageway that led past the reactor and back into the engine room. Doug O'Malley met him at the top of the ladder just outside of Maneuvering. Deep worry lines furrowed the engineer's brow. That, too, signaled bad news.

"Skipper, it ain't good," the Eng blurted out as soon as he saw Glass coming up the ladder, confirming the captain's fears. "Temperatures are rising on the high-pressure end bearing again. Sound cuts look like so much gravel in a rock crusher. Either we put in a bad bearing or there's some kind of misalignment."

Glass nodded and scratched his chin. "Not much we can do to fix it out here. You thinking of running single main engine?"

"Already have the machinists breaking out the clean tent and the gear," O'Malley replied. "I figure it will take the best part of today to get set up, get into the reduction gears, slide the coupling, and then button back up. I've got a team up forward writing the work package."

"Good work," Glass said with a nod. He could tell his engineering officer was taking this personally. "Let's make this as quick as possible. I don't want to leave our friends high and dry on the beach if they need help, and I sure want to be ready if our submarine friend with the nasty trigger finger shows up again."

"We'll be limited to twelve knots while we're running with the port side shutdown," O'Malley answered. "Then twenty-five once we have vacuum back in the port condenser and the port turbine generator on-line. We could try to gut it out and pray this thing holds together. It's a big risk, but if we babied her along we might be okay."

Glass scratched his chin some more, but there really was no decision to make. There did not seem to be any better alternative. Disconnecting the port main engine right away was the best bet. What the Eng said was true—they might be able to baby it along for a while, but there was too much chance that it would fail at the worst possible time.

Glass headed down the ladder, calling back over his shoulder, "Okay then. Disconnect the port main. I'll go tell the XO we're not going anywhere fast."

29

Juan Valdez leaned back in the seat and tried to relax as the ancient Buick labored up a hill, bouncing along on the potholed road that led back to the airbase just outside Havana. He pulled a cigar from its silver filigree case. Lighting the choice Habana, inhaling deeply, and then expelling a cloud of blue smoke, the old admiral allowed himself just an instant to imagine the power and wealth that would soon be his. He would be the principal powerbroker of the entire Caribbean Basin, and he would do it from the best possible place—behind the scenes, pulling the strings of two very powerful puppets. He would have all the real power—and the wealth that came with it—while Guanayca and Gutierrez got all the limelight and the heat that it would inevitably generate.

The meeting with the Cuban Minister of Resources had gone very well. Hermando Guanayca was going to be the perfect inside man in Cuba. Extremely ambitious and ruthless, yet just witless enough to be used by someone with far superior intelligence. Juan Valdez smiled. The man already envisioned himself as the next "Great Liberator of Cuba," the worthy successor to General Castro and his reluctant brother. And he already openly accepted Valdez as his trusted ally. The man was more than willing to squander the potentially vast oil reserves somewhere under the Cuban Deep in exchange for getting his hands on immediate and tangible power on this blighted little island "empire" of his.

There was just one minor glitch. He still had to keep the United States preoccupied and out of his way. His contact within the CIA was, of course, totally aware of the situation, but he, too, had an agenda that assured he would not share that information with anyone else in his organization until the time was right. With the package on the way to the oil wellhead in the Gulf of Mexico, and with the almost certain capture of the SEAL kidnappers now imminent—and the "unfortunate" death of Marco Esteban in the resulting firefight—then all pieces to the puzzle would be in place.

It was time to see how successful Bruce deFrance had been in riling the American Environmental Protection Agency. Valdez had to admit that sending the Brit there was a master stroke. The bastard could piss off a saint. Any EPA bureaucrat would be in apoplectic rage within seconds of deFrance crossing his doorsill.

Valdez pulled his cell phone from his uniform pocket and chose a number near the top of the list of often-called contacts. The phone buzzed and chirped for a few seconds before Bruce deFrance's Oxford accent oozed from the speaker.

"Good evening, Admiral. And how are you this evening?"

"I trust that I found you at an inconvenient time," Valdez fired the opening volley. "What happened with your new Washington friends?"

"Admiral Valdez, how very pleasant to hear your voice so late in the evening," deFrance shot back, but the wry British humor was totally lost on the Venezuelan admiral. From the male voices and tinkling music in the background, it was plain deFrance was entertaining. "I left the EPA with a heightened sense of their power. The under-secretary went to great lengths to impress upon me both his and his department's reach as well as the opposition that he had for any expanded exploratory drilling in the Gulf or the Caribbean. He was most certainly not happy when I informed him that my visit was merely a courtesy and that his jurisdiction did not extend to Samson Petroleum and most decidedly not to our activity in the territorial waters around Cuba." The oil executive was working himself into a high state of dudgeon. "He fairly threatened me. He actually dared to use the term 'court of world opinion.'"

Valdez could not help chuckling as deFrance recounted the conversation with the American bureaucrat. He could picture the image of Bruce deFrance's red-faced, nostril-flaring indignation as he sat across the desk from the righteous Washington functionary. It would have been a sight to behold, the two effete snobs slapping each other with virtual white gloves.

The old Buick lurched around a turn. Valdez was thrown against the side window as the vehicle's worn shocks failed to keep the big car on an even keel. Lieutenant Garcia got the car straightened out and heading down the street, and then shot a worried glance over his shoulder, making sure that his VIP passenger was still with him.

Valdez nodded nonchalantly toward the Cuban officer and continued his conversation.

"The pompous fool didn't waste any time taking advantage of his connections," deFrance continued. "This morning both *The New York Times* and *The Washington Post* had feature articles relating the dangers of more deep-water drilling. The Associated Press picked it up and it will be in every daily in the US by tomorrow morning. According to them, we are going to turn the entire Caribbean and the US Gulf Coast into oil-soaked wastelands, murdering millions of pelicans and Spanish mackerel.

Typical quotes from the Sierra Club and the rest of what the Americans call 'Big Green.' All very nasty stuff. Very inflammatory."

Valdez took a puff on his cigar, relishing its taste.

"Perfect," he replied. "Any idea what we expect for a response?"

There was a momentary hesitation on the other end of the call, as if deFrance was carefully measuring each word before he uttered it.

"From the responses that I've seen from the talking heads on television, I would not be surprised if we were met by a squadron of US Navy warships if we venture out of port with anything that looked like a petroleum exploration vessel."

"Just as I thought," Valdez said, more to himself than anyone else. In a louder voice, he ordered, "Get back down here as quickly as possible. I want you and the *Deep Ocean One* steaming around northwest of Cuba. Let's give them a show of our intentions that they cannot help but notice."

He punched the button on the phone's screen before deFrance had any chance to reply. Valdez leaned forward to speak with Lieutenant Garcia.

"Once we arrive at the air base, we will leave as soon as possible."

Garcia smiled in the cracked rearview mirror.

"Yes, sir. I took the liberty of having the flight prepared while we were at the minister's office. It will be ready to depart immediately."

Ψ

Jim Ward very carefully and very slowly raised his head, but only as high as he needed to in order to peer over the sea grass.

He was half expecting a spray of 7.62mm bullets to be spit at him by a dozen or more AK-47s.

His little team had made a wide circle to the west around the fully expected DINA ambush and had approached the moored fishing boat from down the beach. The extra trek had eaten up most of what little remained of the darkness. If they were going to escape without having to hunker down for yet another day, they needed to move very quickly. And carefully.

They still had to get across the channel and steal the fishing boat before daybreak. The rest of the group lay hidden in the sea grape with the taller salt grass a few yards behind them, waiting for Jim Ward's all-clear signal.

The DINA combat team was spread out in front and a few feet below where the SEAL lay hidden. Ward could spot fourteen gunners, and if these guys were as well trained as he suspected, more of them were probably hidden in the brushy undergrowth protecting the flanks. They were arrayed to chew up anyone who might be coming down the swamp trail with a vicious crossfire. While they were facing the wrong way, expecting someone from the other direction, their presence still blocked Ward's team from crossing the narrow channel to reach the fishing boat. Even if Ward could somehow get his team across the waterway, they still had to steam the fishing boat right back out in front of the shooters.

That would be very tricky. But it also appeared to be their only hope of getting the hell out of Cuba.

Ward snaked back to his team. Bill Beaman was the first face he saw at the edge of the sea grape.

"Just like you said," Ward whispered. "At least fourteen shooters, certainly more I can't see."

"How are you planning to get past them?" the older SEAL queried. This was Jim Ward's mission. Beaman would give him his head—to a point. "Sure wish we didn't need that boat, but with the extra passengers...well, damn!"

Marco Esteban was the real problem. There was no way to swim all the way out to Joe Glass's submarine with him along. Even the short swim across the channel would be a problem for the old spymaster. The man had not really taken care of himself and the long hike had worn him out. And Beaman had no way of knowing TJ Dillon's capabilities.

"I think the only way is to swim around on the seaward side of the fishing boat," Ward whispered. "I'll take my team. We'll steal the boat. Horton and Garcia can pass for Cuban at that distance. That gives us a decent chance of faking our way past the DINA if they challenge us. You and Dad take Esteban and Dillon out in the kayaks. We'll meet you after we're clear of the channel."

Beaman smiled. Young Ward had the cool head of his father, and, as Beaman had fully expected, he was turning out to be one fine SEAL team leader. Or at least, in the next few minutes, he sure as hell had better be.

"Sounds like a plan, Jim. Let's coordinate GPS points. Then you need to get a move on unless you were planning on looking for souvenirs in the gift shop," Beaman told him.

The two SEALs slipped back into the sea grape to put their hastily developed plan into action.

Jim Ward, Dulkowski, Horton, and Garcia scuttled across the narrow beach on their bellies and slid reptile-like out into the warm surf. Within seconds their dark heads disappeared into an even darker sea, even as the first tendrils of blood-red sunlight illuminated the clouds in the eastern sky.

After swimming straight out from the beach for a couple of hundred yards, the SEALS changed course to parallel the sandy promontory. Twenty minutes later, they turned back inland.

Ward imagined that he could feel the DINA eyes on them as

they silently swam up the narrow channel. Only thirty yards of open water separated them from discovery and death by the platoon's blazing guns. The team barely made a ripple in the water as they swam hard against a surprisingly brisk current.

Ward halted in mid-stroke when he saw movement on the western shore. One of the soldiers ambled over to the water's edge. Ward was certain that they had been discovered, but if so, the soldier seemed very nonchalant about telling the others.

There was no place to hide. Even a quick underwater swim would not help. They would have to surface after only a couple of dozen yards, and the movement would surely be noticed. The only thing to do was remain absolutely still and do their best impression of pieces of driftwood as they treaded water.

The wait was excruciating. Surely the soldier had seen them. They watched as the man slung his AK-47 around his shoulder, unbuttoned his fly, and urinated into the channel. Finishing his business with a flourish, he buttoned up and sauntered back to his hiding place along the trail.

"That was way too close," Garcia whispered. "These bastards sure piss a lot."

"You're telling me. I think I can feel the water getting warmer," Ward replied. "Now, let's get swimming. Daybreak's going to be here in half an hour." The glow on the eastern horizon had already changed to orange and the wave tops appeared to be flecked with gold.

Ten minutes later the four SEALs lifted themselves up over the side of the fishing boat on the opposite side from the Cuban soldiers. They had barely gotten aboard when they heard voices bantering in Spanish, growing louder as they came out of the woods and down the rickety old pier that jutted out into deeper water from the weather-beaten tin shanty. Ward dreaded looking. It could well be soldiers coming their way.

But it was three fishermen, heading out for a day's work on

the water, walking down the pier toward the only boat moored there, the one on which the SEAL team now hid.

Ward and his team did their best to disappear among the ragged fishing gear laid out on the boat's deck.

Garcia whispered, "They're talking about the soldiers. It's got them worked up. Evidently there's another team up the road on this side. Story is a bunch of smugglers might be trying to steal fishing boats. The DINA is out here protecting the poor fishermen. But they know there is more to it than..."

Ward held a finger to his lips.

A leg appeared over the gunwale just forward of where Ward lay behind some rusted bait buckets. No time to wait. They had to grab the men quickly, before they could alert the soldiers.

Lightning quick, the SEALs overpowered the fishermen, silencing them with hands over their mouths. It was two teenaged boys and an ancient man, all barefoot, dressed in ragged shirts, shorts, and well-beaten straw hats.

Garcia tried to assure the terrified trio as Horton and Dulkowski bound them.

"*Mis amigos*, we are not going to hurt you," he whispered in Spanish. "We only want to charter your boat for a few hours. We will pay you much better than you could ever make fishing."

The older of the boys tried to sit up, his eyes wide, trying to speak around his gag. Garcia loosened it enough to hear what he was saying, signaling him he had best not be loud or try to call for help. The SEAL's knife at the boy's throat was enough to keep him from screaming.

"*Norte Americanos*," he said. "What do you want with us? We have done nothing to you."

"We are not going to hurt you," Garcia assured the boy, but kept the knife at his neck. "We are just trying to go home."

"You lie," the boy hissed. "You will slit our throats and feed us to the fish. And you will steal our boat." Tears welled in his eyes. "Our family will starve, and they will never know what happened to us. The *policia secreto* have warned us about you *Norte Americanos*."

The old man grunted and tried to speak. Garcia put the gag back into the boy's mouth and loosened the one that silenced the old man.

"There are many things you do not yet understand, *nino*," he said to the boy, then turned and whispered to Ward in halting English, "It has been many years since I saw American soldiers in Cuba. Long gone, better days. Take our boat, but please do not hurt the boys."

Ward nodded and told him, "We aren't going to hurt anyone. Just like Tony said, we need to rent your boat for a few hours. We must leave now. Please lie down in the bilge so you won't be seen."

It was the old man's turn to nod. He muttered to the teenagers in rapid-fire Spanish. The SEALs watched warily as the two boys climbed down and hid among the fishing gear below the deck. The old man sat down on the deck, then looked up and said, "You will need help running our boat. I will tell you what to do."

Garcia looked at Ward as if to ask if he was really going to trust the old Cuban. Ward simply shrugged.

At the old man's direction, Garcia stepped into the tiny cockpit, pushed and pulled the choke lever as suggested, and then started the engine. The rusty old motor coughed and wheezed until it finally came to life in a fog of blue exhaust smoke.

Sean Horton grabbed one of the tattered old straw hats and jammed it onto his head. He removed his shirt and shoes and then rolled up his pant legs. From a distance, he could have easily been mistaken for one of the boys. He tossed another hat to Garcia before he cast off the lines that tied the boat to the pier.

Ward and Dulkowski crouched low in the boat so they could not be seen from the shore. The old vessel drifted out into the channel, mostly carried by the current, and then slowly pointed toward the sea beyond the point of land at the bay's entrance.

Ward clutched his 9mm. In ten minutes it would all be over. Either they would be clear of the ambush and free, or they would be shark chum, chewed up by DINA bullets. And the rest of their group would be floating at sea, stranded.

He could see Horton and Garcia tense as they came abreast of the troops on the shoreline. Several of them had stood and were stretching, taking note of the fishing vessel easing past.

"Skipper, we got a problem," Garcia whispered. "They want to throw a bon voyage party for us. At least half a dozen of them. One of them is waving for us to come over closer to them."

Ward could hear one of the soldiers calling out to them.

"Miguel! Miguel! You going fishing today all by yourself? Where are your boys?"

That was it. They were done.

If the DINA was aware that this boat belonged to Miguel and the two teenaged boys, there was no way Garcia could bluff his way past them. They would either be captured or go out in a blaze of gunfire.

Ward checked the ammo clip on his 9mm to make sure he had a full load and tensed to jump up shooting. He glanced over to Jed Dulkowski, who was mimicking his team leader's moves, tensed to go on the attack, surprise their only advantage.

An instant before he jumped up to begin the fight, the old fisherman suddenly stood and waved to the troops. Ward whipped his weapon around and put his finger on the trigger, on the verge of putting the old man down to buy them a few seconds.

"*Capitan* Alverez, *buenos dias*! No, the boys are home today.

These are my cousins from Cienfuegos. Times are hard in the city. They need fish for their families, too."

Mouth open in surprise, Ward took his finger off the trigger and exchanged glances with Dulkowski.

The DINA captain lowered his weapon and shouted back, "*Si*, times are bad everywhere these days. Bring back some fish for our families, too, *por favor*." The soldier and his little squad turned and sauntered back up the beach.

Jim Ward's hand shook as he brushed the sweat from his brow. The old man smiled as he squatted back down.

"My tiny moment of defiance for the eventual freedom of my homeland, *Senor Americano*," he said.

30

The two black kayaks were relatively easy to find, almost exactly at the GPS coordinates two miles offshore. With the morning sun climbing higher in the sky behind them, the kayaks and their four passengers stood out in stark relief against the pale blue-green water. Any aircraft patrolling the shore would certainly spot them if they remained too long in the brightening daylight.

Tony Garcia was actually enjoying himself at the helm as he brought the old fishing boat to a stop only a couple of yards from where Jon Ward and Bill Beaman were waiting. The two pushed their passengers aboard the vessel and then scurried up after them. Horton and Dulkowski next slid the kayaks up on deck and quickly covered them with a ratty old tarp and some salt-encrusted floats.

"Glad you could make it," Bill Beaman told Jim Ward as he slumped down onto a fish net. "We were wondering if you might have gone hunting instead of fishing today." He caught sight of Miguel and the two boys huddled in the bow. Excess baggage and a potential complication, he thought. "See you brought some company along."

Jim Ward glanced over at the big SEAL.

"Fishing guides. Miguel owns this boat," he explained. "Normally he fishes out here with his grandsons. We arranged a charter deal with him this morning. Miguel came in real handy when the DINA wanted to ask questions."

Tony Garcia suddenly interrupted them with a shout.

"Guys, we got company coming!"

He pointed back toward Cuba. There, on the blue-green surface of the Caribbean Sea and heading straight toward them, was the improbable but unmistakable narrow black silhouette of a *Kilo*-class submarine. Jim Ward told Beaman and his father it was likely the same one they had seen enter the harbor before. The boat was still a good five miles away, so they had some time, but they had no chance of evading the menacing vessel. They had almost certainly been spotted already, and the sub could easily out-race the ancient fishing boat if they decided to make a run for it.

The old man immediately took charge once again.

"Quick, under here," he directed the SEALs as he pulled back the cover on the fish hold. "We need to hide your white gringo skin." He grabbed Marco Esteban by his shirt collar and shoved him toward the hatch. "Hide him, too. And stick something in his mouth."

Sean Horton jammed an oily rag into the old spy's mouth and unceremoniously dropped him down into the hold. Jed Dulkowski pulled out his razor-sharp fighting knife and held it where Esteban could readily see a sliver of sunlight glint off its blade. "One noise, even a squirm, and I'll gut you like a pig," Dulkowski threatened. Esteban nodded and sat down quietly and obediently. The fight had long since gone out of the man.

Miguel was not finished, though. He looked at Tony Garcia.

"You will pass as my nephew," he said, "as long as they don't get too close and you keep your mouth shut. Your Spanish sounds too much *Americano*, not so much *Cubano*."

The submarine was drawing closer every minute. They could plainly see three men standing up on the high sail. Miguel waved a greeting to the onrushing boat. One of the men held up a radio, pointed at it, and mimed talking. Clearly they wanted to use the radio to talk to the fishermen and not have to come too close.

Miguel shook his head with exaggeration and raised his empty hands high in the air. He was a poor fisherman who could not afford such a luxury as a radio.

The submarine moved closer, into hailing distance. Garcia could easily see that two of the men on the sail held very wicked-looking weapons. The guns were held loose and easy, but Garcia well knew that in seconds they could turn the old fishing boat and its crew into a sea full of floating splinters and fish food.

The third man on the submarine's bridge cupped his hands and yelled, "On the boat, come alongside. We want to talk with you."

Garcia started to reach down to grab his 9mm. There was no way that he could allow anyone from the submarine to board and search the fishing boat. Not now. Not with the people who were aboard her. Not when they were so close to the rendezvous with their rescue submarine that would get them out of this place.

"No! Wait!" Miguel grunted at him, then turned and shouted back at the sub, "What is it that you want, *senor*? We are only poor fishermen trying to feed our families and your ship will scare away all the mackerel for miles."

The man hollered back, "There was no fresh meat when we left port. We want to buy your fish. We will pay you well for them."

Miguel shrugged and held his arms out, palms up.

"Many apologies," he shouted back. "The sea has not been kind today. We have not netted the first fish yet. Maybe the fishermen farther out in deep water have seen better luck than we."

The man on the submarine paused, thought, and then shouted back, "Maybe so. We will try them. I wish you better luck."

Miguel smiled and waved a sincere goodbye as the submarine steamed away from them.

"That was too close for my old nerves," he muttered.

As the submarine disappeared over the horizon, Miguel threw back the cover on the fish hold. Jon Ward popped up, with Bill Beaman close behind.

"Okay, how do we warn Joe Glass that a diesel submarine is roaming around out here?" the older Ward asked no one in particular. "We sure don't want *Toledo* to pop up with that bastard sniffing around."

Beaman shook his head.

"I haven't the faintest idea how to warn him. At least not until he actually shows up. By then, it'll be too late."

"Could you radio this friend?" the old fisherman asked.

"Sure, if we had a radio," Ward answered him, the exasperation heavy in his voice. "We don't have one that works anymore."

"Then use mine," Miguel offered.

"I thought you didn't have one," Ward shot back.

Miguel pulled up a section of decking to reveal an antique, tube-type radio set hidden there. He hooked up the power leads to the boat's battery, flipped a couple of switches, and within seconds, the old radio lit up and was humming quietly.

The wily old Cuban smiled. "I am not above telling a lie if it serves my purposes. God will certainly forgive me."

Ψ

Lieutenant Armando Vasquez shook his head slowly and sadly. Some fresh fish would have been a treat for the crew, a welcome change from the Bolivian canned meat that his Navy was forced to purchase from La Paz merely to prop up the Bolivian economy. But it was not to be. There just was not time to go from fishing boat to fishing boat seeking some grouper or mackerel for the mess table.

Vasquez sent the two lookouts below. It was time to dive the *Almirante Villaregoz* to test the repairs on the main induction valve. Admiral Valdez had been good to his word. The Russian technicians and the parts had been waiting on the pier when they arrived at the Cuban port. The technicians had done a fine job of repairing and adjusting the linkages. Everything had worked smoothly in port, while they were still safely tied to the pier, but the only way to really do a final test was to take the boat out and submerge. Only then would they know for sure that everything was operating correctly.

Lieutenant Vasquez was alone on the bridge for a few seconds. He loved it there, high above the sea, the flanks of his boat almost covered by the ocean, the rumble of the big diesel engines easily conducted through the steel at his feet. He often dreamed of a time when he would have a boat of his own and no longer be haunted by his present commander. He made one more sweeping scan of the horizon in all directions and took a final deep breath of fresh sea air before he, too, dropped down through the opening and swung the heavy hatch cover shut above his head. After spinning the handwheel shut, he expertly slid down the ladder without even allowing his feet to touch the rungs, dropping onto the deck in the control room below. Captain Ramirez stood nearby, all decked out in his dress uniform, as if they were about to be in a parade, not dive the boat. The captain would surely fly into one of his histrionic rages if he thought there was even a hint of a delay in following his orders to dive the submarine, so Vazquez wasted no time.

The lieutenant braced up and stood at stiff attention as he shouted out, "Last man down! The hatch is shut! *Almirante Villaregoz* is ready to submerge! The only contact is that fishing boat, ten kilometers astern."

Captain Ramirez curtly nodded just the barest of an acknowledgement.

"First Officer," he ordered, "submerge the ship."

The diesel submarine slid silently beneath the warm waters of the Caribbean. When the last wave washed over the top of the sail, it erased all traces of the killer now hiding beneath the surface. Lt. Vasquez and his team of engineers rapidly completed testing the repairs before they headed any farther out into deeper waters.

While the engineers were finishing their tests, Vasquez checked the torpedo room. He found warshot weapons loaded in all the tubes, just as he expected. Sitting on the loading tray for tube two were the two mysterious crates that they had loaded the previous day. The technician that had accompanied the crates was carefully working on removing the wooden top cover of the long one. He looked up with alarm in his eyes, the picture of a boy caught stealing candy.

As Vasquez stepped over to look into the crate, the technician moved to block his view.

"Please, sir." The technician spoke with a heavy accent that Vasquez thought might be Eastern European. His tone was somehow both pleading and threatening. "The instruments are very delicate and very expensive."

He slipped the top cover back over the crate, obscuring the contents from Vasquez. The technician searched in a breast pocket and pulled out a much-folded piece of paper which he handed to Lt. Vasquez.

The lieutenant was surprised to recognize Admiral Valdez's letterhead. The brief note stated that Anwar Sjamchan was performing important duties and should be rendered any assistance that he required, but otherwise he was to have no interference from the submarine's crew, including her officers.

Lt. Vasquez carefully refolded the note and handed it back. "*Senor* Sjamchan, welcome aboard the *Almirante Villaregoz*. How can we be of service?" He carefully backed away. With orders like that, it was best to give the man as much room as possible.

Sjamchan was no longer being polite as he growled, "You can carry out your orders and leave me alone. I will tell you when I need anything. Until then, just make sure that I am not disturbed."

Lt. Vasquez beat a hasty retreat out of the torpedo room. He was not sure how he would explain it, but he would make the room off limits until the surly technician was done and off *Almirante Villaregoz*.

His next stop was the sonar room. It was vitally important that the eyes and ears of the submarine be wide open and attentive. The sonarmen barely glanced up when the tall, dark officer pulled back the curtain. They were working their equipment, making sure that they were alone in this bit of ocean. The *Almirante Villaregoz* was ready for anything.

Finally satisfied, Lt. Vasquez knocked on Captain Ramirez's stateroom door before entering. He reported, "Retest of the main induction valve was satisfactory. Warshot weapons are loaded in all tubes and operating satisfactorily. Sonar is conducting a careful sonar search. They report no contacts. Our guest is working on something with his crates."

Ramirez glanced up from the report that he was reading. A scowl crossed his face. "Mister Vasquez, you run a very sloppy submarine. You report everything is satisfactory, always. Your standards are unacceptably low." He pointed at the china mug on his desk. "My coffee is cold and no one has brought me a refill. You will order the ship cleaned until I am satisfied that it is up to my standards and you have properly instructed the stewards. Now get out!"

Vasquez backed out of the captain's stateroom and shut the door softly behind him. The man was becoming more irrational every day. He was reminded of an American novel that he had once read about a sea captain run amok. He would not at all be surprised to find Captain Ramirez clicking together steel ball bearings and angrily inquiring about stolen strawberries.

31

Simon Castellon knew for certain that he was near death. He could feel it deep in his bones. The knife wound was little more than a dull ache in his shoulder—the morphine made sure of that. But the impressive amount of blood he lost had very nearly ended his life. It had also left him weak and woozy and on the edge of no longer caring. The knife fight with Jorge, Josh Kirkland's rescue, the emergency battle dressing, the mad dash through the jungle—they were all swimming in a gray cloud in his brain.

It took him a while to figure out what the constant roar in his ears was. Then he realized that it was a tropical rain drumming on the corrugated metal roof. Soon, the fetid, rotting jungle smell reached the small room where he lay. The sounds and smells were the first indication that he might actually live through this ordeal. But still, his body was telling him that the fight was far from over. Jorge's knife thrust had come too close to his valuable assets.

Castellon groaned and tried to lift his head. Gentle hands pushed him back down onto the cot. Reluctant to ever give up control, he fought back as best he could. He needed to communicate with Kirkland. Everything was starting to come together. He could almost fit the pieces together despite it all still being a hazy puzzle.

He finally knew what Juan Valdez's plan was and understood why the old man was trying to kill him. But now he needed the CIA man to help him put it all together. And to help do something to stop the bastard.

"*Mi Coronel,* you must lie still." Castellon recognized the voice immediately. It was Hermon Alcatel, his camp surgeon. "You will tear the sutures or rip out the IV. You very nearly did not make it back to us this time," the old medic fussed. "You really must learn to stay away from knife fights. You are running out of places for new scars."

"Hermon, old friend," Castellon groaned weakly, his voice barely audible. "Where is *Senor* Kirkland? I must speak with him."

"Soon, soon," Alcatel replied, calming him as he reached over to adjust the morphine drip. "For now, though, you must rest."

The old guerilla could feel the warm numbness slowly surround his consciousness, like a gentle morning mist. He tried to fight it but the comfortable darkness was far too inviting.

Ψ

Juan Valdez came about as close to a smile as he ever did. The grand design was finally coming together. Soon he would be the most powerful man in the hemisphere, controlling great power and immense wealth, manipulating the levers of his grand design but staying well out of sight behind the curtain. The old fool, Gutierrez, could strut around and thumb his nose at the North as much as he wanted. Valdez would be the real power, the puppet-master pulling the strings.

The old admiral leaned back in his rickety chair and gazed out the fly-specked window at the shallow harbor of Cienfuegos. The modern, smart-looking R/V *Deep Ocean One*, tied up to the ancient pier, contrasted sharply with the rest of the filthy, dilapidated port. From his vantage point high up in a third-floor office of an almost abandoned sugar warehouse, Valdez could watch as the crew made their final preparations to go back to sea. A harbor crane, shrieking, wheezing, and puffing with effort, lifted pallets of fresh fruits and vegetables onto the ship's main deck. A line of trucks waited patiently on the pier, ready to have their cargoes unloaded.

Valdez wondered where deFrance and his crew were stowing all this stuff and why they needed so much of it in the first place.

The admiral's phone chirped. He flipped it open and answered curtly.

"Admiral, deFrance." The Brit's Oxford accent and the shaky cell connection made him annoyingly hard to understand. "We are almost ready to depart. As you directed...hmmm...as you suggested, we will explore the far northwest edges of the Cuban-controlled waters."

deFrance's voice betrayed his exasperation on being sent on this fool's errand.

"Bruce," Valdez began, pausing for effect. He could see deFrance, phone to his ear, apparently dressed for yachting, lounging against the rail high on the ship's bridge wing. "I am sending you into waters that could be dangerous, so I am dispatching with you a security detail for your protection."

Almost on cue, a decrepit old bus rumbled around the corner of the building and pulled up to the brow, thick smoke billowing from its exhaust. The door swung open and a half-dozen uniformed men tumbled out. They immediately started unloading several hard polymer shipping containers and lugged them toward the ship.

"Why would we need protection?" deFrance sputtered. "We're talking about the Gulf of Mexico. If there is any place in the world where you don't need armed security protection, it is there. The US Navy makes sure of that. I do not want your soldiers on my ship. Send them away."

"Bruce, you do not understand," the old admiral told him. "You will do as I say. Those men are there to protect my interests as well as you and your crew. Now please get down from your perch and make sure that Captain Savoir is ready to depart."

Click.

Ψ

deFrance stared at the dead phone then up at the buildings shadowing the wharf. The bastard was spying on him. Now he could feel Valdez's eyes boring in like gun sights. But where was the crazy old tyrant? He could only see a maze of dark, empty windows staring blankly back at him. Valdez could be behind any one of them.

The oilman slid his phone back into the breast pocket of his suit jacket and scurried into the bridge house to find Captain Savoir.

Ψ

"What you got, XO?" Glass asked as he stepped into the radio room. *Toledo* rocked gently, riding in the calm seas at periscope depth. Another couple of hours and they would be at the rendezvous point. They had just come up to see if there were any last-minute instructions from Donnegan or an update from the men they were picking up.

Brian Edwards looked up from the flat-panel that had been claiming his attention. "Nothing from the admiral, but we did grab some very interesting signals." He glanced over at the radioman, Sam Seidiman, to allow him to fill in the technical details.

"We picked this up on an old HF frequency, one we haven't used in years," the leading radioman explained. "It sounds like an ancient transceiver, something really old. AM modulation."

Glass looked at the screen. He grabbed a headset that Seidiman offered him.

The noise didn't sound like any data transmission that he could remember. Then it dawned on Glass. The breaks in the signal? Dots and dashes.

"Is that Morse code?" he asked.

Edwards nodded. "I've been putting my old Eagle Scout training to work. Really blowing off the cobwebs, but I think I have most of it." He handed Glass a sheet of paper filled with pencil scratches.

BIG FISH BIG FISH THIS IS HEAD MAN BLACK SHARK IS FREE MEET AT HOME BASE BE CAREFUL

"That's it?" Glass asked as he scratched his three-day-old beard and tried to make sense of the terse words.

"Yep," Edwards answered. "He has sent the same message a dozen times or more, so I know I copied it right."

Seidiman nodded in agreement. "And his power is really low. The signal won't carry very far, even for HF."

"How far?" Glass asked.

"Just a guess, but I'd say we're within twenty miles of the guy. We DFed him, and the bearing line points right at the rendezvous." Seidiman pointed at the bearing readout on the BLQ-10 display.

The light finally came on in the sub skipper's head. He threw down the pad and bolted out the radio room door.

"It's from Jon Ward," Glass called over his shoulder as he left. "He's at the pick-up point, but he's warning us that our old friend, the *Kilo*, is out and about."

Seconds later *Toledo* angled down into the dark depths. The DC lights flashed three times, signaling the crew to man "battle stations/torpedo" but to do so silently. Glass could barely hear the whisper of his men scurrying to their duty stations.

Almost precisely ninety seconds after the lights flashed, Master Chief Wallich turned to report, "Ship is manned for battle stations."

Glass did not even glance away from the BQQ-10 Remote Display. He continued leafing through the sonar-grams as he quietly answered, "Very well, COB."

Edwards stepped over, murmuring into a sound-powered phone headset for a second before speaking up.

"Sonar has completed a careful sonar search. The only contact is a weak broadband, bearing two-three-seven, tentatively classified a fishing boat. No other contacts, no signal from the special receiver."

"Very well, XO," Glass answered, just loud enough for the appropriate crewmembers to hear him. "We will circle the rendezvous point at this range before we get any closer. Make tubes one and two ready in all respects. Open the outer doors on tubes one and two. If our friend shows up, we'll close to an attack position deep on his quarter before launching an ADCAP. Set safety range at four thousand yards."

The crew set to work. Watching the displays and pressing the headphones to their ears, Master Chief Zillich and his team used every tool and trick they had to search for the mysterious submarine that had twice tried to kill them.

Down in the torpedo room, Bill Dooley and his team made

doubly sure that *Toledo* and her ADCAP torpedoes were ready to deliver the final blow, if and when the time came.

Ψ

Aboard the submarine *Almirante Villaregoz*, Lieutenant Armando Vasquez looked up from his sonar repeater. All was quiet. Only that fishing boat a few thousand yards on the starboard quarter, probably the same hapless old vessel from which they had tried to buy fish. Vasquez silently wished the old man luck.

Captain Ramirez swaggered into the control room, brushing imaginary dust from his carefully creased trousers.

"First Officer, what are you doing?" he asked with all the inference that Vasquez was somehow shirking his duties.

"Captain, I am conducting a sonar search before we head north on our mission," Vasquez answered, carefully keeping his tone neutral. "The tests on the induction valve are completed. The Russians did their work well."

"Why are you dawdling here?" Ramirez snapped. "We have important work to do. Move north to our patrol area at best speed. That is an order."

Lieutenant Vasquez hesitated.

"But Captain, our special pinger is not working. The sonar technicians say that it will take another hour to complete repairs. How will we find the American submarine without the pinger? It is my suggestion that we stay here in safe waters until it is fixed, then head north."

"First Officer, you heard my orders," Ramirez exploded. "You will immediately head north or I will have you arrested for mutiny."

Vasquez had no choice. He ordered a course that would take

them around the western tip of Cuba and then up into the Gulf of Mexico.

Ψ

Toledo was five miles away to the east, but neither submarine heard the other. They passed each other like two silent ghosts in the night.

32

As the morphine-induced gray fog slowly lifted, things became clearer to Simon Castellon. Juan Valdez was a genius, albeit an evil one. The old admiral's attempt to kill him had nothing to do with his meeting with Josh Kirkland. It was because Valdez had finally realized that Castellon was the only man on the planet who could put together his bold plot.

The underwater robot. The staggering amount of plastic explosives. Buorz, the Chechen bomb expert. Cuba.

Admiral Valdez was going to blow up something. Something underwater. Something very, very big. Now Castellon knew what it was. Valdez was going to destroy a deep-water oil well.

Castellon called out, his voice weak and cracking.

"*Si, mi Coronel*. You are finally awake." Hermon Alcatel lifted Castellon's head and poured a small amount of water between his parched lips. "This will make it easier to talk."

"Kirkland. I must speak with Kirkland," Castellon rasped.

As if summoned, Josh Kirkland stepped into Castellon's view. The rebel leader could just see a pair of guards standing by the door. So, Kirkland was being held prisoner. Not that he could go anywhere, even if he somehow escaped. They were far too deep in rebel-held jungle for that.

"*Senor* Kirkland," the guerilla leader whispered. "I must get word to your masters. Admiral Valdez must be stopped before he wreaks havoc across the entire Caribbean."

Struggling for voice between slurps of the cool water, Castellon outlined what he knew and what he inferred from Admiral Valdez's recent actions.

The CIA spymaster listened quietly, absorbing the information, automatically collating it with what he already knew. It made for a plot worthy of a bestselling but implausible thriller, yet it was actually spinning out at that very moment. Clearly, the home office in Langley would be very interested in what Castellon was saying.

On the other hand, such news-telling would leave Kirkland in a very ticklish situation. If he shared with the CIA what he was learning, he would have to share the identity of the source as well. No one back there knew of his contact with the Venezuelan guerilla leader or his role in Cuba. Nor did they know of the drug deal that he and Castellon had worked out. They were certainly intelligent enough that they would figure out the details. Then, his retirement nest egg—if not his freedom—would certainly evaporate.

The old agent's mind was working at warp speed, considering the options, as Castellon droned on. There had to be a way out, a way to use this new but not totally surprising information to his advantage. He thought briefly of simply not telling anyone, but quickly rejected that idea. No gain there.

What if he informed Gutierrez? Kirkland quickly realized that, at best, Gutierrez could do nothing. At worst, he was a willing part of his top admiral's plot.

Then, as if a bright ray of sunshine invaded the room, Kirkland knew what he needed to do—reach out to Tom Donnegan. The Navy intelligence chief could put the forces in play to stop Valdez. With his SEAL team trying to escape Cuba, he probably already had some sniffs of the plot anyway. There would be no reason to elaborate on why the Cubans were always one step ahead of his every move. That would remain Josh Kirkland's final secret, one he certainly would not share with Admiral Donnegan.

Ψ

"Skipper, the only contact I see is that fishing boat. They have been sitting right on top of the rendezvous point for the last hour." Pat Durand finished his report, his right eye still stuck to the periscope eyepiece. "Sonar reports no other contacts. Looks like our friend, the *Kilo*, didn't stick around to play."

"Very well, Mr. Durand," Glass answered as he once again paged through the sonar displays. No sign of any other sonar contacts, not even strange biologics. "XO, everything ready?" Glass called over his shoulder to Brian Edwards.

"Yes, sir. The COB has his people in the forward escape trunk, ready to haul everyone aboard as soon as we're on the surface."

"Very well," Glass acknowledged. "Diving Officer, broach the ship up."

Young Jeff Clay, standing his first watch as diving officer, snapped back, "Broach the ship, aye, sir." Turning to his planesmen, Fireman Apprentice Josh Stedman and Seaman Will Brownson, he rapidly ordered, "Full rise on the bow planes, full rise on the stern planes."

Toledo popped to the surface. As the chief of the watch, Bill Dooley, gave the sub a little positive buoyancy by pumping water from the depth control tanks, Sam Wallich and his team rushed topside.

Moments later, after a hurried good-bye and well-wishes between the SEALs and the old Cuban fisherman, the team and their unexpected prisoner were all below, standing shoulder-to-shoulder on the mess deck. *Toledo* once more slipped below the waves.

Safely back in the deep, Joe Glass left the control room to greet his passengers. Jon Ward immediately pulled the skipper aside as he stepped onto the mess deck.

"Joe, we need to talk to Tom Donnegan right away. We need to know what to do with our guests." He nodded toward the pair standing a little apart from the SEALs. "The old guy is Marco Esteban, head of the Cuban DINA. The younger guy is TJ Dillon. He's some kind of CIA operative. Don't ask me what he was doing there in the first place, but somehow he managed to rescue Esteban from a firefight up in the mountains."

Glass shook his head, trying to absorb the news. Things were getting very complicated.

"Okay, let's go up to radio and talk to the boss," he said, and started back up the ladder.

Ψ

Admiral Tom Donnegan was already having an especially interesting day. First, the EPA had their pantyhose all tied in a knot, wanting him to send someone out to covertly bird-dog an oil research ship in the Gulf, all because some mid-level bureaucrat had his feelings hurt by some oil guy. Then the rogue Venezuelan *Kilo*, the bastard that was probably the crazy shooter at Joe Glass, had gone missing right in the part of the Caribbean where *Toledo* was supposed to be picking up Beaman and the SEAL team. And to top it all off, here was Joe Glass on the horn now telling him that they had none other than Marco Esteban aboard *Toledo* as a decidedly unwilling guest.

Donnegan rubbed the stubble on his chin as Glass talked. What the hell could they do with Esteban? This one was well above his pay grade, Donnegan decided. He needed to buy some time while he let Sam Kinnowitz and President Brown sort out all the diplomatic niceties.

The possibilities were curious. They could simply return the old spy to Cuba and take full credit for saving his life at the hacienda. Or they could hang onto him and prosecute him as a war criminal. Donnegan was thankful it was not his call. He would allow the president and his top advisor to untie this Gordian knot.

If it were up to him, Donnegan would take the simple tack—keep Esteban in Cuba and preserve the cover that the CIA and SEALs had rescued him from some nefarious plot to eliminate him. Since no one knew who was behind the plot, and since Esteban needed medical attention anyway, the SEALs had evacuated him to the nearest safe medical facility. The Cubans, all worried for their jobs and lives with neither Castro in charge anymore, would certainly make no big deal about American combat troops being on the ground in their little fiefdom.

Simple, direct, effective, and, above all, believable. So long, that is, as Marco Esteban did not begin screaming about *imperialistas* and kidnapping. Or the Cuban Communists did not decide to use this little incident to rally support against their constant tormentor to the north.

"Joe, make a run over to Guantanamo," Donnegan ordered. "I'll give them fair warning and they'll have a boat meet you in the turning basin. Transfer your guests off. We'll keep Esteban there while we sort everything out. Tell Jon and Bill to hightail it back here ASAP and bring this Dillon guy with them so we can figure out how the hell he fits into all this." He thought for a second, considering if he needed to say anything else, before realizing that he did not have any more instructions for the *Toledo*. He ended the conversation with, "Donnegan, out," and placed the receiver back into its rest.

He had just started to reflect on how relieved he was that all his guys were off the island, safe and secure, when there was a discreet knock at his door. Lt. Tim Schwartz stuck his head in.

"Admiral, Josh Kirkland from the CIA is on the phone. He says that it's important."

"Secure line?" the old spook asked. What the hell was coming now?

"No, on an open line. He says he is calling from Venezuela."

"Jesus. This should be interesting," Donnegan muttered as he reached across the old, battered desk for the phone.

"Admiral, this is Josh Kirkland. I'll be very brief. Let me start out by saying that my sources for what I am about to tell you are absolutely reliable and I have independently verified much of it. We have reason to believe that Admiral Juan Valdez is making a move to secure exclusive access to a very large deposit of oil under the Caribbean."

"Tell me something I don't already know," Donnegan shot back, quickly growing impatient. Kirkland went on as if there had been no interruption.

"He recently acquired a considerable amount of plastic explosives and the services of a demolition expert out of Chechnya. He also obtained a rather large underwater robot and has deployed them all on his submarine, the *Almirante Villaregoz*. Our read is that he intends to destroy a deep-water oil rig somewhere in the Gulf."

The line went dead before Donnegan could think of anything to say. He put the phone back into its cradle and took a deep breath.

Suddenly it was all fitting together—what Kirkland was

saying and what he already had learned from his people down south. The *Almirante Villaregoz* would have to be stopped before it carried out this plot or the result would be an environmental disaster of historic proportions.

"Schwartz, get Joe Glass back on the horn and then Bill Greene. It's time to go *Kilo*-hunting."

33

The sun was reluctantly peeking over the eastern horizon as if even it was having a hard time waking up. Smedley Winnowitz climbed stiffly up into her waiting P-3C aircraft. She yawned widely at the top of the ladder and took a big gulp of coffee from the Styrofoam mug she carefully held, not wanting to spill a precious drop.

"God, I hate these 'before the rooster crows' missions," she groaned as she stepped onto the flight deck. "Interrupts my beauty sleep. Did you see any sunrises on the recruiting posters, Bucko?"

Bucko Schwartz, already sitting in the right-hand seat, was working his way down the pre-flight checklist. He glanced up and smiled at her.

"Glad you could make it. What special words of wisdom did our leaders bestow on you?"

Winnowitz, the plane commander, plopped down in the left seat and grabbed her headphones from where they hung on the control yoke. She drained the last of the coffee before answering.

"It has come down from Mount Olympus," she intoned, "that we are to go forth and protect mankind from evil." Her voice became more serious as she continued. "Looks like there might be a diesel submarine on the loose somewhere in the Gulf north and west of Cuba with some kind of bad intentions that we don't necessarily need to know about. Our task is to find him and convince him that he should peacefully leave the area to the oil tankers and cruise ships."

"And if he doesn't want to play?" Schwartz replied, still scanning the checklist.

"We'll have to wait and see," she answered. "Are we about ready to get out of here before it really gets hot and humid?"

"We just got clearance from the tower to taxi out to One-Three Right. We're second in line for departure." Schwartz pulled back on the throttle quadrant levers. The big bird slowly lumbered out to join four other P-3Cs on the taxiway. "Please turn off all cell phones and electronic equipment and hand your cups and other trash to the flight attendant," he added.

Five minutes later, P-3C Tail Number Six-Four-Seven was climbing through ten thousand feet heading almost due west. The early morning sun was painting the patchwork of Central Florida horse farms, citrus groves, and subdivisions far below them in shades of rose and gold. Behind the pilot and co-pilot, Mission Commander Bull Braddock was in the process of uploading the latest mission profile into his AN/USY-1(V) mission computer when he saw a chat box pop up on his screen.

"Hey, Smedley," he called over the intercom. "We have a good link with the ASWC. We have patrol boxes Seven Charlie and Seven Bravo. Looks like we will not be lonely out there. The *Toledo* will be patrolling in and around our area, too. ASWC says that we are 'weapons tight' unless we receive further guidance."

"Roger, Bull," Winnowitz answered. "'Weapons tight.' Ask them if there is any chance of a CAP on this run. I'd sure hate to get splashed like we did last time."

Braddock typed on his keyboard for a few seconds. The reply flickered into the text box.

"ASWC says negative on the CAP. Someone wants to avoid upsetting the Cubans. If we need the cavalry, they'll be twenty minutes out."

Ψ

The R/V *Deep Ocean One* left a long, frothy wake as it slowly ploughed across the blue-green sea. All the geo array streamers and air cannons were deployed miles behind the ship, diligently probing the bottom of the Gulf for geological signs of oil.

Bruce deFrance sat on a bridge wing chair, idly sipping a cup of designer-blend coffee as he watched his corporation's revenues frittering away in this useless show of defiance that Juan Valdez seemed to think was so damned important. To add to his pique, the old admiral's security troops were disturbing deFrance's early morning reverie with their exercises on the forecastle.

Captain Savoir stuck his head out of the bridge door. "Excuse me, sir, but Admiral Valdez requests that you call him on the secure phone."

deFrance set down his coffee cup in disgust. What did the old bastard want now? Maybe Valdez could be talked into canceling this whole silly trip, or at least ridding him of the hovering security guards. deFrance stomped into the bridge house and grabbed the secure phone that Captain Savoir offered him.

"Yes?"

"Bruce, are you at 23 North, 85 West?" Valdez demanded.

The oilman glanced at the large-screen GPS display hanging on the after bulkhead.

"We're twenty miles south of there right now," he answered. "We should be surveying that area late this afternoon."

"You are a total idiot," Valdez shot back. "You were instructed to be there today, this morning. Can you not understand the simplest order? Turn that fancy yacht of yours north and make the best possible speed to get there. You have three hours. And tell the captain of your new security guards to go to high alert and to precisely carry out my previous orders."

"But 'today' is not over until…"

The line had gone dead. Bruce deFrance stared warily at the now mute receiver. He had felt the barely controlled rage in the admiral's voice and shuddered as he remembered that the only times he had heard Valdez sound like that, the target of his ire had soon suffered an awful death.

Now would not be a good time to question the admiral's commands.

Ψ

Joe Glass paced back and forth between the navigation plot and the sonar repeater. He had long since given up fretting that *Toledo* was incapable of getting there any faster. It was extremely frustrating to command one of the fastest submarines in the world and, just when he needed to use that speed, have it taken away by an unexpected engineering casualty.

"Time to turn north," Jerry Perez called out. "New course three-four-seven. We're clear of Cabo de San Antonio."

"Right ten degrees rudder," Jeff Clay, the OOD under instruction, ordered. "Steady course three-four-seven." He grabbed the 21MC microphone and announced, "Sonar, Conn, coming right to new course three-four-seven."

Master Chief Zillich's voice boomed back, "Sonar, aye. Hold no sonar contacts."

Brian Edwards stepped into control and stood beside Joe Glass. The XO was munching on a sticky bun, licking the gooey icing from his fingers.

"Umm, these are sure good," he mumbled through a mouthful.

Glass smiled. "I've been living with the smell of them baking all night while you were getting your beauty sleep, XO."

"There might still be a couple if you get down there before the Eng inhales them." The pastry finished, the XO's tone changed to pure business. "What've you got?"

Glass rubbed his tired, sandy eyes.

"It's been real quiet. We just turned north. Couple hours on this course, then turn into the patrol box."

"Any more news from Donnegan?" Edwards asked.

"Nothing since we left Gitmo. I figure we need to copy the broadcast just before we get to the patrol area to get the latest intel." Glass stepped over to the Nav chart and made a small circle around 23N and 85W. "Right about here on the southern edge. Then we go *Kilo*-hunting. I'm going to get some breakfast and lie down for a bit. Nudge me when we're in the area. This could be an interesting day, Brian."

Ψ

Lieutenant Armando Vasquez gazed out through his submarine's periscope. The eastern sky was glowing orange, red, and gold. It promised to be a beautiful morning. He had the sea entirely to himself, not another ship in sight. The *Almirante Villaregoz* was exactly where Admiral Valdez had ordered them to be, despite the fact that the first officer still had no idea why or what they were supposed to do there. Perhaps their orders would be on this morning's broadcast. He could only hope.

Captain Alejandro Ramirez barreled into the control room, growling ominously as he came.

"First Officer, why do you not have the 0700 broadcast onboard yet? You incompetent fool, you have not even raised the radio mast yet. Do I have to do everything on this ship?"

"*Mi Capitan,*" Vasquez answered quietly. "It is only 0655. I plan to raise the mast but just before 0700 to minimize our chances of being seen by the American radars."

"Always so smart, always with an impertinent answer for everything," Ramirez fumed. "Raise the radio mast immediately and establish communications. I have long since grown tired of your excuses."

Vasquez bit his lip as the radio mast smoothly slid up out of its housing, breaking the sea's calm blue surface a few feet aft of the periscope. The first officer winced as he rotated the periscope around. He could see the tall black pole every time and knew anyone else within a reasonable distance would be able to see it as well. Especially the Americans with their sophisticated radar.

The mast had no sooner broken the surface than the loudspeaker next to Vasquez's ear came to life.

"We have radio signals. Admiral Valdez is on voice communications. He will speak with the captain."

Ramirez reached up to grab the red radio receiver handset, snapping to attention as he cleared his throat.

"Captain Ramirez."

Through the hissing and chirping electronic noise, he could just make out Admiral Valdez's rough, gravelly voice.

"Ramirez, where are you?"

"*Mi Almirante,* I am in the control room overseeing my crew."

"No, no, no! Where are you in the ocean?"

"Yes, we are precisely where you ordered us to be, of course," the little sub captain answered, blushing bright red. He quickly lapsed back into the oily, fawning tone that he employed when speaking with Vasquez. "We are standing by, ready to bravely and successfully fulfill our mission, whatever it might be."

"Finally, someone who can at least follow the simplest and most precise orders," Valdez answered. "No doubt it was your first officer who was responsible. Now, for your orders. You will proceed directly to 23N and 85W. When you arrive, you will follow *Senor* Sjamchan's orders to the letter and without question. You will do this until he is entirely satisfied that the mission is complete. Do you understand?"

Captain Ramirez nodded before realizing his admiral could not see him.

"Yes. Yes, I understand completely."

He turned to his executive officer and gruffly ordered him to steer toward new coordinates.

In moments, they were on their way.

34

Anwar Sjamchan had a certain amount of well-earned notoriety, but not under his real name. He was better known to the world's press and Western intelligence circles as "Buorz, the Wolf," but no one had any idea who he actually was. At the moment, he was preparing to embark on what would be a first-time mission for him, one that would certainly reinforce his image as one of the planet's most prolific and daring terrorists. He was just finishing packing a deadly cache of plastic explosives into the cargo space of an underwater robot, a UUV. It was a tight fit, but he managed to cram in every lethal gram.

The wily terrorist grinned as he worked, amused at what was about to happen. The explosives expert had spent his entire adult life building weapons for others to use in glorious retribution against the enemies of his homeland. He had very carefully stayed deep in the shadows, allowing his colorful moniker to be his only identification. He existed only in the sometimes-true, sometimes-glorified rumors, news reports, and intelligence dossiers. Often, the Wolf received credit for attacks he had never touched. Just as often, he was the technician behind a splendid bit of vengeance for which others were blamed. He had no worries either way. Other than the terror his name struck in the hearts of his enemies, he did not seek glory or recognition. Not even money, though he never refused generous payment.

Now, finally, he was on his first assignment as an operator and was truly "under the radar." He relished the opportunity to see first-hand the result of his handiwork.

Buorz nonchalantly slid the firing circuit connector into its mate on the processor board. A few keystrokes and the thing would be armed and ready to do his bidding. He was well aware that a botched connection or a wrong bit of instruction on the keyboard would set off a conflagration that would instantly end the lives of everyone aboard the vessel. But he was just as certain that neither mistake had been made.

He screwed down the water-tight cover and made one final continuity check through the fiber optic control line. Once certain that everything operated satisfactorily, he motioned to the sailors hovering at the hatch that led out of the submarine's torpedo room. He chuckled to himself. As if they would have had any chance at all of escaping if anything had gone wrong with the massive bomb he had just assembled. Now, it was time for them to load his UUV into the torpedo tube.

As he watched the long black cylinder slide forward and disappear into the yawning mouth of the tube, the Wolf glanced at his watch. The minute hand was almost up to 1000 hours. It would be late evening back in his homeland, but outside, on the surface of the Gulf of Mexico, the sun was shining high in a clear blue sky. When it reached its zenith in two hours, this would all be over. Then, his job successfully completed and his turmoil unleashed, he would be on his way back to his beloved homeland.

Ψ

Two decks above where Buorz worked, Lieutenant Armando Vasquez stood at the sonar room door, waiting. The sonar technicians had finally finished repairs on the special pinger. The job had taken much longer than the hour they had promised. Almost two full days. It was time to employ the device to make sure the American submarine was nowhere near them. Whatever that strange man, Sjamchan, had planned, it was not something for the Americans to accidentally discover.

"Lieutenant, it is working." The chief sonar technician smiled as he gave his report. "Now we will see if that silly *Americano* wants to play games with us again."

"*Si, Alberto,* we will see," Vasquez answered with a frown. "We will see."

"First Officer, the captain wants to see you," the watch officer called across the control room to Vasquez. "And the torpedo room reports that the device is fully ready in number two torpedo tube. *Senor* Sjamchan says that it is to be launched from precisely 23 degrees, 3 minutes North, 85 degrees, 1.4 minutes West at exactly 1030 local time."

Vasquez nodded as he stepped out of the control room and headed for Captain Ramirez's stateroom. Glancing at his watch, he did some quick calculations. They had fourteen minutes to travel the last two kilometers to Sjamchan's desired coordinates, deploy whatever the frightening little man's package was, and then, thanks be to God, head home.

Ψ

"First pattern is in and hot," Jane Durham said into her mouthpiece. She settled back in her seat, ready for another long, boring flight, watching and listening. The chances of actually finding a submarine were very, very small. She would likely spend the next twelve hours watching biologics, the ocean's natural noises. She was listening to a whale at the moment, watching its distinctive audio pattern play out on her screens.

"Any sign of our friend?" Bull Braddock inquired.

"Nope, just an amorous whale and a shrimp medley down there right now," Durham answered.

"Pretty boring here, too," Braddock said. "I've got that research ship we were told to watch for at one-two-six and ten miles. Nothing else all the way to those drill rigs to the north."

"You two finished exchanging pleasantries?" Smedley Winnowitz chimed in. "I'm much more interested in whether or not we're seeing any MIG activity out of Jose Marti."

Braddock glanced at his air search panel. "*Nada*, all quiet down that way. Smedley, you can rest easy. I don't think your Cuban boyfriend is going to come out to relieve you of your virtue."

Winnowitz snorted and threw the P-3C into a hard left bank, spilling Braddock's coffee into his lap, just as she knew she would.

"Smedley, you bitch," Braddock yelled in mock anger. "You did that on purpose!"

"Aw, I'm sorry, Bull," the pilot apologized, false sincerity heavy in her voice. "We were at the edge of our patrol area. I didn't know you weren't rigged for sea yet."

Braddock was about to respond when he suddenly noticed a flicker on his APS-137 screen. He zeroed in on it right away. "Hey, guys, I got a pop-up on the periscope detection radar. Bearing one-seven-six, twenty miles. That's right smack at 23 North, 85 West, and it would be a big coincidence if somebody popped up at that exact coordinate by chance."

"I ain't seeing anything," Durham answered. She flipped through the displays, looking closely for any sign of a submarine. "If it's a real boat, it's a really, really quiet sucker."

"Alpha six whiskey, this is papa lima two." The transmission blared harshly from the speaker above Bull Braddock's head. Somebody was calling out their daily call sign. "Authenticate lima zulu four two bravo."

Braddock glanced at the grease pencil comms board on the right side of his tiny desk. He keyed his microphone. "Papa lima two, this is alpha six whiskey. Authenticate mike niner. Say again, authenticate mike niner."

"Roger alpha six whiskey, we hold you visually, bearing north, range ten miles."

Braddock smiled. For once he could tell a US submarine that he had contact on them, too, and not be lying about it. "Papa lima two, we hold you on radar bearing one-eight-seven, seventeen miles. Only other contact is a research ship at one-one-five, twelve miles from me. How copy? Over."

"Alpha six, copy all. Understand you hold no submarine contacts. Contact of interest has a special device that sounds like biologics. We think that it will sound like a whale calling."

Jane Durham's chin dropped.

"Oh shit!" she called out. "We have a whale on our DIFAR pattern right now." Flipping through the displays until she was back on the whale call, she adjusted a couple of dials. "Just north of our line, moving pretty slow. I do not have a shooting solution."

"Alpha six, that's our guy. Can you drop a DICASS pattern on him? We need a shooting solution ASAP."

Winnowitz had already thrown the ungainly bird into a steep bank even before Bull Braddock could answer. "Papa lima, roger. Going in now."

As the P-3C swooped down to two hundred feet, Bull Braddock watched the pattern play out on his geographic display.

"Standby to drop. Drop now, now, NOW!" With his last "NOW!" Jane Durham keyed the launcher command and a DICASS sonobuoy fell away from launch tubes just aft of the aircraft's bomb bay. Six seconds later, another DICASS buoy dropped away. Another six seconds and then a third fell from the plane toward the ocean below.

The buoys parachuted down to the surface. Once in the water, a small hydrophone unspooled on a thin copper wire, sinking down to four hundred feet beneath the sea's surface. A tiny antenna sprang from the top of the float, sending an encoded signal back up to the P-3C.

"I have three good buoys," Durham called out. "Going active."

Before Durham could even key the active transmitter, she saw a blip bloom on her screen. She held her earpiece tight to her ears, not believing what she was hearing. "I have launch transients!" she shouted. "That whale just launched a torpedo!"

"Jane, give me a solution!" Winnowitz demanded. "We're rolling in hot." To accent her order, the bomb bay doors rumbled open. "Come on, Jane! I need a solution!"

Durham's fingers danced across her panel, trying to find the submarine hidden in all the auditory mess. She uploaded her best shot into the computer and fed it to the Mark 54 torpedo waiting down in the bomb bay.

"Solution uploaded," she called out.

At the same time, Bull Braddock yelled into his microphone, "Papa six, bogey launched a torpedo. Say again, bogey launched a torpedo. Stay at papa delta, we are rolling in hot. Weapon set deep."

"Alpha six, Wilco. We hold transients, too. This bastard has shot at us twice before. Go get him."

Ψ

Buorz involuntarily jumped as the air-driven torpedo ejection pump slammed forward, flushing his UUV out into the

Gulf waters. His ears popped as the high-pressure air vented back inboard.

The control screen came to life, linking him with the UUV heading toward its target. Buorz went over the plan in his mind yet again. The UUV would follow its pre-loaded mission trajectory, swimming the ten kilometers to the wellhead before sinking down to the bottom and coming to a rest right next to the riser pipe and blow-out preventer. Once in place, the timer circuit would kick in, giving them twenty-four hours to safely clear the area before the glorious explosion. They would be back in Cuba when the wellhead was blown to hell. Nothing would tie them to the unfortunate disaster, the plumes of oil that would eventually foul the beautiful Gulf beaches, the blaming and caterwauling that the "accident" would once again set loose around the United States.

He only had to sit here and watch for the next few minutes, still tethered to the UUV, and make any last-minute adjustments to the tracking data. It was all too easy. By this time tomorrow, he would be the richest man in Chechnya, and all for striking this lethal blow against those who would foul sacred lands with their occupying troops.

He felt the submarine suddenly accelerate and heel over to the left. Crewmen were instantly running around, slamming doors shut. One sailor jumped to the launch control, pushing a series of control levers. Buorz's control screen went dark as the torpedo tube outer door light flickered to "SHUT." The door had severed his fiber optic line to the UUV.

Buorz sensed that something had gone wrong. Why the sudden alarm, the unintelligible panicked gibberish over the submarine's announcing system?

Then he heard a high-pitched screaming sound coming from outside the ship, through its steel hull, rapidly getting louder. Something out there was coming in their direction.

Coming very quickly. The angry scream grew to a shriek. Like a freight train flying past the station, whatever was out there flashed by and screamed off into the distance.

Buorz saw the relieved faces of the sailors around him. They were going to live!

But then the same ominous screech came roaring back, as loud as ever.

The MK54 torpedo flew straight at the escaping submarine, the *Kilo*'s speed no match for the forty-five-knot torpedo. The firing circuit initiated automatically when the weapon was five feet away from hitting the submarine's steel hull. The ninety-eight pounds of PBNX blew a superheated slug of molten copper shape-charge through the half-inch-thick outer hull and then the two-inch-thick inner hull of the sub. Buorz had a millisecond to register surprise before the superheated gas cloud vented inboard, igniting fires in the torpedo room, followed immediately by a steel-hard shaft of cold gray water pushed by the pressure of hundreds of feet of seawater. The force of it slammed Buorz across the narrow torpedo room and crushed him into a wall of pipes and valves.

The violent explosion had shoved Lieutenant Vasquez to the lurching deck. He ignored the knot on his head and the blood that flowed down into his left eye as he quickly pulled himself upright and surveyed what damage he could see. The control room looked essentially all right, but the thickening smoke and the roar of the flooding coming from below him told a tale of severe damage. A quick glance at the damage control panel showed that all the water-tight doors were shut. He was well aware that a *Kilo* was designed to stay afloat with any one compartment fully flooded—that is, as long as the bulkheads and doors were really water-tight.

"Come shallow quickly," he ordered the watch officer. They had only one option if they were to survive whatever had just happened to them. "Prepare to surface." He grabbed the announcer system microphone and ordered, "All stations, report damage."

One by one, the watch stations reported in. No damage. Only the torpedo room was silent.

A watchstander rushed into the control room, his face ashen with fear. "The torpedo room!" he gasped. "It is completely flooded, water is coming up to the middle level! We are all going to die!"

"Silence!" Vasquez ordered, struggling to maintain control of his own fears while trying to keep his crew functioning. "Our ship is built to take damage. We won't sink." He prayed that he sounded more confident than he felt.

Captain Ramirez ran into the control room from his state-room, already dressed in his escape suit.

"Surface the ship immediately!" he screamed. "We must abandon ship!" Spittle flew from his lips and drool strung from his chin. His eyes were wild with fear as he shoved people out of the way in a rush to reach the escape chamber.

Vasquez stepped into his captain's path. Ramirez tried to push him aside in his attempt to flee, but Vasquez stood firm.

"Captain, there is an American ASW aircraft up there, ready to shoot us again. We will fight the flooding here."

Ramirez babbled incomprehensibly. Fear and cowardice had driven him beyond all rational thought. He reached into one of the escape suit's pockets and drew out an automatic pistol.

Vasquez could see the wildness in the man's eyes. He reacted quickly, smashing the pistol away with his left hand while driving his right fist into that hated face. Ramirez crumpled to the deck and lay there, crying uncontrollably, praying to God.

For a moment, the first officer looked down at his captain with utter disdain.

Then, without any more hesitation, he turned and gave orders in a loud, strong voice.

"Men, let's do what we must to save our ship." He casually wiped the blood from his eye with his sleeve so he could see the gauges. "Pressurize the ops compartment to sea pressure. Come to periscope depth. We will stop the flooding that way."

A calm seemed to fall over the men inside the submarine's control room as each sailor concentrated on his job, his duty station, ignoring the increasing upward angle of the boat and the urgent shrieks and flashes from all the indicators needlessly reminding them that something was terribly wrong with their ship.

35

The R/V *Deep Ocean One* cut a broad, pale scar across the deep blue waters of the Gulf of Mexico. Bruce deFrance had just completed his late morning breakfast when he decided to work off the eggs benedict and caviar with a brisk walk around the main deck. He knew four complete circumnavigations equaled a kilometer. Five orbits would give him plenty of time to get some fresh air and exercise while he figured out the optimum way to deal with and reject the continual demands of Admiral Juan Valdez.

During each round trip, he brusquely pushed past the admiral's security force as they cleaned their weapons on the forecastle. Their leader—a man deFrance knew only as "Sergeant"—was growling out orders. The ten very rough-looking soldiers stood in sharp contrast to the research ship's small crew of professional mariners and scientists.

On his final trip around the deck, as deFrance reached the sharply jutting bow, Sergeant jumped up, looked at him, and pointed toward the horizon to the west. deFrance stopped, squinting in that direction. He could just discern the shape of an airplane swooping very low, just above the wave tops. It appeared to be one of those old propeller-driven airliners from the fifties. But what could it possibly be doing out here, lunging and diving so?

Sergeant yelled again. deFrance could not quite make out what he said, but the security guards dropped their weapons and raced aft. deFrance followed along, curious to find out what had set off such sudden consternation.

The men tore into a metal CONEX box that was lashed down to the main deck just aft of the ship's superstructure. Seconds later, they emerged with three long, ugly-looking green tubes. The soldiers slung the tubes up on their shoulders and pointed them in the general direction of the mysterious aircraft.

It suddenly became very clear to the oilman what was happening. The green tubes were shoulder-fired missile launchers, MANPADs. The security men intended to shoot down the aircraft. Bruce deFrance leaped forward, screaming at them to stop. Sergeant met him full-force with a shoulder tackle, slamming him to the deck.

Bruce deFrance lay there, gasping for breath. But even as darkness seemed to be closing in on him, he could hear the *swoosh* and see the smoke trails of the three missiles as they streaked away from his exploration vessel and headed out toward the aircraft.

Ψ

"SAM! SAM! SAM!" Bull Braddock screamed into his microphone.

With his left hand, he was already punching the ALE-47 Countermeasure Dispenser control, pushing out flares as fast as he could hit the button. The other hand was sweeping across the ALQ-78A Countermeasure set, trying to jam the homing devices on the incoming missiles. The AAR-47 Missile Warning System infrared warning blared its alarm, adding to the sudden din inside the aircraft.

Smedley Winnowitz slammed the bomb bay doors shut and pushed the ungainly old bird over into a steep dive. Their best hope to try to lose whatever was being shot at them was to hurtle the plane down to the wave tops.

"Which way? Damn it, which way?" she yelled, fighting the control yoke as the P-3C pitched and heaved, seeming unwilling to fly so close to the water.

Bucko Schwartz strained against his flight harness, trying his best to get a visual on the missiles out the cockpit windows.

"Can't see 'em!" he yelled, frustrated.

"Comin' right up our ass!" Durham screamed desperately. "Break left! Break left!"

Smedley pulled the P-3C into a hard left turn, side-slipping to keep the wingtip out of the water.

It almost worked. The first missile ran out of fuel just twenty yards short of them and dropped harmlessly into the warm water. The second missile got much closer, detonating about a foot short of the number-three engine. The weapon's shrapnel tore into the big Allison turbo-prop, sending red-hot metal spinning into the compressor unit. The high-speed turbine instantly flew apart, sending even more shrapnel up into the wing tanks and through the paper-thin aluminum skin that formed the fuselage.

Bull Braddock and Bucko Schwartz took most of the blast. A large piece of tungsten-steel turbine slammed through the mission commander's chest. Braddock was dead before he even realized what had happened.

Bucko Schwartz was not so lucky. A dozen pieces of red-hot shrapnel tore through his flight suit. Most were only painful but superficial wounds. One piece, though, ripped into his right leg, nicking the femoral artery. Schwartz looked down in horror, seeing the blood spurting before he even felt the sudden intense pain.

By the time the third missile obliterated the number-four engine, Smedley Winnowitz knew her plane was doomed. She was fighting just to keep aloft long enough to make a level, gliding crash landing, trying to not cartwheel if they hit the surface at the wrong angle.

Fire streamed far behind the starboard wing. The cabin was filling with smoke. Almost every alarm on the flight deck was screaming its warning. And her copilot was groaning in pain.

Sweat streamed down into her eyes as she fought the sluggish flight controls. If she could just get the old girl level enough to pancake into the water. Never mind pretty, just get down flat, she prayed.

The plane's tail hit first. Then the nose suddenly slammed down hard, plowing into a wave. At two hundred knots, the sea had the consistency of concrete. Smedley was stunned at how quickly the wall of water burst through the windshield, crushing her.

Then everything was strangely quiet. The surprisingly warm seawater quickly filled the cabin. Smedley Winnowitz, the breath knocked out of her, could only sit, stunned and unmoving, as the P-3C, tail number Six-Four-Seven, swiftly sank beneath the surface.

Suddenly someone jammed an SEAD air breather between her teeth. The tiny air bottle would give her a few minutes of breathable air. She breathed in and opened her eyes to see Jane Durham struggling to get her free of her flight harness.

The release was jammed. The blue water grew murkier as the dead aircraft sank like a rock. Durham somehow managed to retrieve a crash survival knife and began sawing away at the harness. Finally, amazingly, it gave way and Winnowitz was loose.

Durham swam toward where she assumed the windshield had been, pulling Winnowitz behind. Once outside, both of them stroked toward the light of the surface that now seemed so very far above them. Winnowitz glanced down once, but their airplane had already sunk deep and out of sight.

Then, just when they thought they would never get there, the two women burst into the bright daylight and sweet air. No one else was there, none of the rest of the crew. Both realized at the same instant that they were the only ones who had survived the attack.

Durham could not help it. Tears rolled down her cheeks and, even as she gasped for breath, she fought back a sob.

Ψ

"Hold the MK54 torpedo in final homing," Master Chief Zillich's voice rang out over the 21MC.

A brutal blast suddenly rang throughout the hull. The P-3C's torpedo had found its target: the pesky submarine. The son of a bitch would not be launching any more torpedoes at *Toledo*. Or anybody else for that matter.

Pat Durand swung the periscope around. He no longer needed to watch the ASW aircraft that was still swooping low, looking for debris or a broaching target. Now he wanted to observe the white ship five miles away to the east and decide if she was in these waters coincidentally or tied in some way to the rogue submarine.

"Oh, my God!" he suddenly yelled. "They just shot the P-3!"

Joe Glass jumped to the scope and grabbed it out of the young officer's hands.

"What are you talking about?"

"The ship, that white one!" Durand stammered, wide-eyed,

as he stepped out of his skipper's way. "It shot missiles at the P-3. Three of them. All fired together. I saw them."

Glass slewed the scope around to once again find the P-3C. Smoke and fire streamed far behind the aircraft, which was almost in the water. Then Glass caught his breath when he saw the huge plume of water kicked up as the plane plunged in. It was brutal.

"Quartermaster, mark this position," he yelled. "Bearing mark, range twelve thousand yards."

Brian Edwards read out the bearing repeater: "Bearing two-six-three."

Dennis Oshley, the battle stations quartermaster, marked the chart and gave the confirmation: "Marked."

Glass muttered under his breath in a cold, flat voice barely audible to the others in the control room, "Let's get that bastard."

Then, in a louder voice, he ordered, "Firing point procedures on the surface ship, tube one."

Eric Hobson's hands danced across the weapons launch panel, flipping switches and adjusting dials. He paged through a dozen drop-down menus, making selection after selection, sending orders to the MK48 ADCAP torpedo waiting patiently down in tube one.

Thirty seconds after his skipper's order, Hobson called out, "Weapon ready!"

Brian Edwards made one final check on the fire control solution in the BYG-1 system. Satisfied, he called out, "Solution ready."

Pat Durand chimed in with, "Ship ready."

Joe Glass ordered, "Shoot on generated bearings."

Eric Hobson punched his thumb down on the button to launch torpedo tube number one. A loud whooshing sound and rush of air erupted as 1500-psig compressed air slammed the torpedo ejection pump piston forward, pushing water up into the tube and flushing the ADCAP out into the Gulf waters. Forty-five seconds had elapsed since Joe Glass decided he needed to shoot, and a weapon was on its way.

"Own ship weapon running in high speed," Zillich reported. "I hold air noises on the bearing of the submarine. He may be blowing ballast."

"XO, assign tube two to him and get me a solution. We'll shoot him, too, if he so much as farts."

Brian Edwards had been staring over Eric Hobson's shoulder at the weapons control panel. He glanced up so he could be heard.

"Assign tube two to the submarine, get a solution, aye," he answered. "First fired weapon now in search, running normal."

Ψ

"Lieutenant, the *Americanos* just fired a torpedo!"

Lieutenant Vasquez was amazed that the sonar system still worked. The three atmospheres of air pressure that they had vented into the operations compartment were holding the flooding at bay, but the operations compartment was nearly half full of sea water. Regardless of their quality control in other areas, the Russians truly built a rugged submarine.

"Launch two torpedoes on the bearing to the *Americano*," he ordered. "Set them for submarines."

It was time to see how rugged this boat was. If he could still launch torpedoes, they had a small chance of surviving the day. They could not run or dive deep with the flooding continuing and the hole blasted by the American aircraft's torpedo still not plugged. Standing and fighting was their only recourse.

He was again amazed when he felt the double thud of two torpedoes being shoved out of his boat's torpedo tubes.

"Our torpedoes running normally," the report from sonar came back.

Ψ

"Launch transients on the bearing of the *Kilo*," Zillich called out. "Two torpedoes, bearing two-six-two and two-six-one. Both in search mode."

"Snapshot, tube two, on the *Kilo*!" Glass ordered without hesitation.

"Weapon ready," Hobson answered just as Glass finished.

"Ship ready."

"Solution ready."

The reports from Durand and Edwards came in rapid succession.

Master Chief Zillich shouted out, "Incoming torpedoes still bear two-six-two and two-six-one." His voice was flat and calm despite the fact that a ton of high explosives was, at that moment, racing directly at them.

"Shoot on generated bearings," Glass ordered.

Once again, Eric Hobson quickly checked the torpedo presets and then punched the launch button for tube two. A deadly mechanical bloodhound bounded out of the tube and raced away in search of its prey.

"Tube two launched, weapon normal," the young weapons officer announced just as Master Chief Zillich's voice came over the 21MC.

"Hold own ship's first fired weapon in search, second fired in high speed. Hold incoming torpedoes at bearing two-six-two and two-six-one. Zero bearing rate, still in search."

"Chief of the Watch," Glass called out. "Launch evasion devices from both signal ejectors. Reload and launch again."

Bill Dooley jammed the button down to launch the signal

ejectors. Two noise makers tumbled out into the water, floating along as they filled the area with a mass of bubbles and noise, trying to create enough bedlam so *Toledo* could hide from the torpedoes behind it.

"All stop, broach the ship to the surface," Glass ordered. "If we can't outrun those torpedoes, we'll have to outsmart them. Let's make like a surface ship, dead in the water."

"All stop! Start the blower on all main ballast tanks."

Glass stepped over to look at the geographic plot showing the best guess of the incoming torpedoes, as well as the locations of the *Kilo* and the research ship. And a downed friendly aircraft was still out there somewhere, too.

Dennis Oshley glanced up at the captain. Sweat poured off the young quartermaster's brow and his hands shook involuntarily as he tried to plot another bearing line. Still, his voice was calm as he said, "Best guess, we got ninety seconds until..." His voice trailed off.

Eric Hobson piped up, "Detect! Detect! First fired weapon in final homing!"

The 21MC blared, "Hold first fired weapon in high-speed re-attack. Second fired weapon in high-speed search. Incoming torpedoes bear two-six-four and two-five-six, still in search."

The thunderous blast created a tremendous wall of sound, even from almost six miles away. Joe Glass had only seconds to spin the scope around to see the midsection of the research ship lifting high in the air, its back already broken. The two torn remnants fell back into the water and began slipping beneath the waves.

"Detect! Detect! Second fired weapon in high-speed attack!" Hobson called out.

"Depth three-three feet and holding," Sam Wallich called out from his seat at the diving officer's stand. "Answering all stop."

"Inbound torpedoes in high-speed attack!" Zillich yelled. Now every man aboard *Toledo* could hear the screaming of the approaching weapons.

Each crewmember braced for the inevitable blast but the two torpedoes passed underneath them, roared away for a few seconds, and then turned around and came roaring back again. They circled a hundred feet below them like two snarling guard dogs unable to leap up to snap at the surfaced submarine.

Another rumbling explosion reverberated through *Toledo*'s hull.

"Breaking up noises on the bearing to the *Kilo*."

Ψ

The sound of its propeller totally lost in all the noise and mayhem behind it, the explosive-laden UUV dutifully swam on toward the wellhead and, once it arrived, sank deliberately to the bottom of the Gulf of Mexico.

In its belly, the timer did precisely as it had been instructed and began to tick down, marching toward doomsday.

36

The last torpedo launched by the Venezuelan submarine ran dry of fuel, sank into the deep, and exploded. The blast still shook *Toledo* hard, jostling the crew, bouncing a coffee cup off the plotting table to crash into shards on the deck.

Joe Glass heaved a deep sigh of relief when the reverberations finally stopped. The shooting was over. *Toledo* was safe again. The sub captain stole a quick glance around the crowded control room.

Randy Zillich was back in his normal position at the sonar room door, visibly relaxed. He threw a thumbs-up at Sam Wallich, sitting in the diving officer's chair. Pat Durand was busy talking with Bill Dooley at the ballast control panel. Something about trim system suction, but Glass could not quite hear it. If it was important, Durand would share it with him.

Brian Edwards, Jerry Perez, and Dennis Oshley stood huddled around one of the plotting tables in the aft end. Oshley slewed the electronic bug for the ECDIS nav plot around, measuring the bearing and distance to the P-3C crash site. Despite their own narrow escape moments before, they were now focused on some other folks still in peril out there.

The senior quartermaster called out, "Skipper, bearing to the crash, three-five-one, range twelve thousand."

Glass spun the Type 18 scope to look down that bearing line, but even in 24-power, he knew that he would not be able to see anything yet. Calling over his shoulder to Pat Durand, he ordered, "Officer of the Deck, come to course three-five-one, ahead full. Get the bridge rigged and manned. Have the search and rescue detail standing by at the forward escape trunk."

Sam Seidiman's voice boomed over the 21MC speaker just behind Glass's ear. "Conn, Radio. Picking up two SAR beacons, one military and one commercial. Request you raise the BRD-7 to DF."

The big black electronic sensor mast slid up from its stowage tube in the after part of the sail. Looking like a futuristic trash can stuck on top of a pole, it was crammed full of sensitive antennas designed to suck signals from the radio spectrum, sort out the desired one, and then provide a very accurate bearing line to the transmitter.

"Conn, Radio, best bearing to the military beacon three-five-zero. Equates to the P-3C. Looks like someone made it out. Bearing to the civilian beacon zero-nine-four," Seidiman reported a few seconds later. "No longer need the BRD-7. Lowering the mast from radio."

Edwards laid the new bearings down on the plot. He looked at Glass. "That second bearing cuts right through where the surface ship went down."

"Maybe someone made it off before it went down," Durand commented.

Glass grunted as he started up the ladder to the bridge, shaking his head. "They'd be damn lucky. Between the blast and how fast she sank, any survivor would have a very small window. Probably just a life jacket that floated free." Almost as an afterthought, he added, "XO, draft a message to Donnegan. Tell him what has happened. Request SAR assistance to search for survivors."

Toledo ploughed through the surface of the crystal blue sea, kicking up a bow wave that reached high on her sail before crashing back down, the seawater rolling smoothly off her round steel sides. Glass, Durand, and Seaman Will Brownson crowded into the cramped bridge cockpit, each scanning a section of the sea with their 7X50 binoculars. High above their heads, both periscopes continuously rotated so that Edwards and Jerry Perez could use the devices' powerful optics and height of eye to peer out farther.

Brownson was the first one to spot the downed fliers. Pointing their way, he called out excitedly, "Got 'em! Two points off the starboard bow. Out maybe two thousand yards."

Glass looked out where the young seaman pointed. At first, he did not see anything. Then, almost a mile away, he could just make out two objects in the water, floating close together.

"I see them," he called. Sighting through the compass repeater, he ordered, "Officer of the Deck, steer zero-one-seven, slow to one-third."

The big sub swung around toward the two downed aviators as Glass grabbed the 7MC microphone and spoke loud enough that Pat Durand would hear him, too. "XO, open the forward escape trunk, send the search and rescue party topside, rig out the outboard, and shift to remote. All stop."

The boat slowly covered the last few yards, sliding to a stop alongside the aviators.

Ψ

The black submarine was only a mile away when Smedley Winnowitz first saw it.

She pointed excitedly while yelling to Jane Durham, "Get their attention. They'll never see us! Quick! Do something!"

Struggling to search her survival vest without dunking her face in the water, Winnowitz finally pulled out a red flare. One yank on the lanyard and the little pyrotechnic arched up into the air only to slowly parachute back down, its bright red flame leaving a red smoke trail as it fell.

She looked up at the top of the submarine's sail to see sailors pointing and yelling something. The boat changed course until its rounded bow was pointed right at them. As it loomed large, a shiver of fear seized Winnowitz. The submarine was on the verge of running over them.

"Swim for it!" she yelled, breaking into a long, clumsy crawl stroke. But the submarine glided to a smooth stop with the two downed aviators only a dozen yards off the beam. Two swimmers leaped from the main deck and stroked toward the women. Within minutes they grabbed them, swam back alongside the black steel hull, and were all pulled up to the deck.

Ψ

Bruce deFrance came to, spitting out a mixture of salt water and blood. For a few seconds the oilman was unsure where he was. The last thing he remembered was struggling to free himself from Sergeant's iron grip. Then there was an awful roaring noise and he was hurtling through the air, away from his ship and into the Gulf of Mexico.

deFrance looked around frantically. Where was everyone? Where was his ship? The ocean was empty, save some trash and debris floating around him. Whatever had happened, he suspected that the loss of his ship was tied to shooting down that plane. It was all Admiral Valdez's fault, along with the henchmen he had put aboard his ship.

He grabbed an orange life jacket that fortuitously floated by. Maybe it would keep him afloat until someone came to rescue him. Struggling to get into the awkward floatation device, deFrance discovered that he had a long gash down his left leg and his expensive chino slacks hung in tatters. But as he noticed the pink mist rising from around his leg, the oilman also realized he was not feeling any particular pain.

Then fear struck him. Blood in the water meant sharks. He was certain that a great white was about to leap from the depths to devour him, to tear his body to shreds. Terrified, deFrance swam around looking for anything to climb up on, to pull himself out of the water.

That was when he saw the submarine steaming toward him. He waved frantically to get its attention. It passed agonizingly close but then steamed on by. No one had seen him. deFrance slapped the water in frustration.

Then the massive vessel swung around, completely reversing course until it was once again headed straight for him, stopping just a few yards away. He tried frantically to swim toward the sub. Then he saw men standing up on the sail. They held rifles. One was aimed right at him. They were going to shoot him in the water while he floated there, helpless.

deFrance waved and screamed in fear but then heard the crack of shots. They were firing in his direction!

Then, as he turned to desperately try to duck the bullets, he saw something else. A huge white creature—a shark—mere meters behind him. Bullets pocked the water all around the large gray dorsal fin slicing toward him.

They were shooting at the shark!

Suddenly the fin dipped and disappeared below the surface.

deFrance braced himself for the impact of the animal's maw ripping into his lower body. Nothing happened. He spun back around toward the submarine.

One of the men standing on the main deck threw what looked like a ball attached to a line in his direction. He grabbed at the line and allowed himself to be pulled toward the vessel. When he tried to lift himself up onto the sub, he fell back before the sailors could reach him. One leaped into the water and shoved him up into his shipmates' hands.

Bruce deFrance lay on the deck of *Toledo*, coughing, crying, and sputtering out weak appreciation to his rescuers.

Ψ

"Captain," Brian Edwards said into the sound-powered phone. "Admiral Donnegan wants us to stay on station here and search for any other survivors. Coast Guard will have an SAR helo here in an hour and a cutter in six hours."

Joe Glass, sitting on the bridge cockpit combing, gazed out at the blue sea.

"Roger. Tell the Nav to keep us on an expanding spiral search around datum until we are three miles out, then collapse us back to datum. How are our guests doing?"

"The two fliers are okay," Edwards answered. "Doc gave them a slug of medicinal brandy and has them resting in my stateroom. The guy we pulled out is still delirious. Probably shock, but Doc wants to get him to a medical facility ASAP. Lost a lot of blood. He has him laid out on the wardroom table, suturing up the gashes in his leg. The guy kept mumbling something about somebody named 'Valdez' and then thrashing around. Doc had to put him out just to sew him up."

"Thanks, XO," he answered. "Get on the horn and see if

Donnegan has anything new for us. Mention that name... Valdez...to him, too. I'm going to go talk with the pilots."

Glass climbed down out of the cockpit and found the two aviators sitting in the XO's stateroom sipping on tea and nibbling at a couple of sandwiches.

After a round of introductions, Smedley Winnowitz, with tears in her eyes, asked, "Any sign of the rest of my crew, Skipper? You've got to keep looking. They have to be here!" She slapped the table hard. "It's my fault. I should have saved them. They're out there! I know they are!"

Jane Durham reached across the little stateroom table and grabbed the pilot's shoulder.

"Smedley, take it easy! Captain Glass has work to do. He and his crew will do what they can." She looked up at Glass. "Did we get the sub? We got just a little bit busy after we dropped."

The captain nodded. "Yes, we heard the explosion and flooding noises just after the missiles hit you. He counter-fired a couple of torpedoes at us and we had to do some pretty fancy dancing, too. But then we got the sons of bitches that shot you from the surface vessel and finished off the sub. Found one survivor from the surface ship. He's down in the wardroom getting sewed up and I can't wait to hear his version of what just happened up there."

"One thing bothers me, Captain," Durham went on. "After we heard the initial launch transients, I didn't see any of the typical torpedo engine lines on the DIFAR display. What did you hear?"

Glass pursed his lips, impressed at her ability to continue analyzing the problem even after all she had been through in the past hour.

"Now that you mention it, I don't remember seeing any either. Sonar will have it all recorded. I'll ask the guys to take a careful look and see what they find." He shook his head. "There are lots of screwy things I want to figure out now that the shooting's all over with."

But before the words were out of his mouth, he questioned himself. Was it?

Was the shooting really all over with?

37

Admiral Juan Valdez punched the glowing numbers on his cell phone screen with mounting frustration. Where was that damn Brit? How dare he not answer his call? After a third futile attempt, the old naval commander viciously threw the phone at the concrete wall, smashing it to pieces.

"Jose Garcia!" Valdez shouted. "*Aqui. Ahora.* Come here!"

At the summons, Lieutenant Jose Garcia Lopez stepped out the French doors onto the veranda, casually dancing around the remains of the shattered cell phone. A gentle breeze carried the aroma of hibiscus and ginger across the little walled garden. The remains of Admiral Valdez's half-eaten luncheon littered a small wrought iron table. It reminded the Cuban that he had missed his own lunch. And his breakfast.

"I need to talk to deFrance immediately," Valdez grumbled. "Get him on the phone for me."

Garcia shook his head. "*Almirante*, I have tried every telephone number I know on the *Deep Ocean One*, including the bridge and the captain's stateroom. No one is answering. It is almost as if the ocean swallowed them up."

Valdez slammed his fist onto the table. Birds fluttered away from the bougainvillea at the edge of the patio, spooked by the noise.

"Then you will get your damned Cuban Air Force out there to find them. Investigate why they ignore my calls."

Ψ

Admiral Tom Donnegan's face was wrinkled with confusion as he squinted at the mass of information arrayed on the desk before him. Too many new puzzle pieces, and none of them fit together.

There was the revolutionary, Castellon, and the wild revelation that Juan Valdez was leading a plot to blow up a deep-sea oil rig. Cheap techno-thriller-movie stuff, but Josh Kirkland seemed absolutely certain that his information was legitimate and required immediate action from the highest level.

Then Bill Beaman and Jon Ward show up with none other than Marco Esteban in tow, spinning some wild story about a mountaintop hacienda shootout between some old Cuban revolutionary and the DINA, and the Cuban spymaster having been a prisoner there until some shadowy guy named TJ Dillon rescued his ass.

Oh, and there was the little matter of the SEAL team sighting a mystery submarine leaving the harbor near Cienfuegos.

And now, just to confuse the issues even more, Joe Glass pops to the surface long enough to share that he sank a submarine and sent some surface ship to the bottom of the Caribbean, but only after the submarine shot at Glass's boat and the surface vessel somehow managed to shoot down a P-3.

Jesus.

It was either a monstrous coincidence that all this crap had hit the fan in the same part of the world at the same time, or something mighty ugly was going on down there. The pieces had to fit, but how? Hard to stop a cluster freak if you didn't know who all was in the cluster and what the freak they were doing!

Donnegan tried to rub away the dull, throbbing pain that arced across his forehead. He took a swallow of coffee from his ever-present Thermos, then carefully returned it to the one spot on the battered old oak desk not littered with papers.

Then he swiveled to face Bill Beaman, who was working at the conference table.

"What's the latest from Joe?" Beaman asked. The SEAL captain looked up from a laptop where he had been typing up his post-mission after-action report. He looked very wide awake for someone who had only recently escaped the swamps of Southwest Cuba, caught a ride from Guantanamo Bay to Washington, and likely had not slept in three days. "He find any more survivors?"

"No, only the two from our aircraft," Donnegan answered, "and the one guy from that research ship. I'll be glad when he comes around and can talk again. We need the SOB to tell us why a damned petroleum survey vessel would be shooting at one of our planes in international waters. I'm betting Admiral Valdez is mixed up in this somehow, right up to his double-dealing eyeballs."

Beaman shut the laptop and leaned back in his chair.

"I'm thinking I'll take young Jim Ward and his team down Venezuela way for a scenic tour and maybe catch a chat with Kirkland for his opinion on the best places to wine and dine." Beaman rubbed the stubby whiskers on his chin. He had not had time to shave yet. "I might take TJ Dillon with us, too. Both would really like to get their hands around Kirkland's throat. When this is all over, we need to run down that dirty SOB's history with the CIA."

"Good idea," Donnegan agreed. "An idea somebody else had already."

Right on cue, one of Donnegan's staffers walked in with a thick envelope and handed it to his boss.

"This just showed up," Donnegan said. "I was about to brief you. And the decision on Dillon going has been made for us, too. Somebody at Langley has tagged him already and he's part of the team, whether you, I, or God Almighty want him to be or not. Good man or not, it chaps my ass that somebody we don't even know is mucking up our ops. I don't know, maybe he can help us figure out what Valdez is up to. We need to watch our back with Kirkland. Never have trusted that old bastard. Now Esteban is fingering him."

"Understood." The big SEAL nodded and slowly unwound from his chair. "Time's a 'wastin'. See you when we get back."

"Wait, BB." Tom Donnegan always called Beaman "BB" when he had tough news. "That same muckety-muck says you have to stay here with me. Jim Ward's got the helm on this one."

"What the...?"

"Don't know. Fact is, I need you here, too, but I would have preferred having you down south. This one could be tough, especially for a new guy. But as my daddy used to say, 'It is what it is.'"

"Shit," was all Bill Beaman could add.

Ψ

"Captain, Eglin Air Control reports flight of four bogeys outbound from Jose Marti," Brian Edwards said into the handset. He sounded short of breath. "They're fast movers, heading our way in a hurry. ETA seven minutes."

Joe Glass jumped down from the bridge cockpit combing and slammed his handset back into its holder. "Officer of the

Deck," he shouted to Jerry Perez, "get the bridge rigged for dive and get us submerged. You have three minutes."

Glass slid down the ladder into the control room. Edwards was already busy getting the big boat back under the surface and out of sight. Pat Durand, now officer of the deck, had watch-standers ready to dive. Bridge paraphernalia came down in a steady stream through the hatch.

Just as Glass's watch indicated three minutes had passed, Bill Dooley called out, "Upper bridge hatch indicates shut. Straight board."

Glass turned to Durand and ordered, "Officer of the Deck, submerge the ship," just as Jerry Perez dropped down the access trunk ladder into the control room.

"Last man down. Hatch secured and the bridge is rigged for dive," Perez informed everyone in the compartment.

Durand, his eye locked to the Type 18 periscope, called out, "Diving Officer, submerge the ship."

Sam Wallich, sitting in the diving officer's chair, reached forward and rang up "AHEAD 2/3" on the engine order tele-graph while ordering in one continuous breath, "Chief of the Watch, open all main ballast tank vents. Full dive on the bow planes, full dive on the stern planes. Seven-degree down bubble. Make your depth one-five-zero feet."

"Depth three-nine feet," Wallich called out.

Durand spun the scope around to look aft and sang out, "Decks awash."

"Four-four feet," Wallich called as the big boat slowly sank. "Four-eight feet. Five-zero feet."

"Conn, ESM, picking up a coherent pulse doppler radar. Equates to N-019E Slot Back radar carried on Mig-29A Fulcrums. Signal strength is weak but getting stronger. Best bearing one-three-seven."

"Looks like our Cuban friends are arriving on the scene," Edwards commented to Glass.

"Yep." Glass nodded. "I'm thinking that we should stick around and see what our friends are doing out here in such a hurry. Officer of the Deck, make your depth six-two feet. Come to ahead one-third."

The boat stopped its descent with just the top of the periscope sticking above the water. At this low speed, the sub was invisible to anything but a very high-accuracy periscope detection radar. The Cuban Migs would not be blessed with such fancy options.

The four jets, flying low in a loose formation, roared over the sea, passing directly over the spot where the *Deep Ocean One* had sunk, only a little over a mile from where Joe Glass now stood in *Toledo*'s control room watching them through his periscope. The jets broke formation, each flying out a different radial, still staying low.

"Conn, ESM, picking up radio comms in Spanish. Frequency equates to Cuban Air Force flight control. Sounds like our friends are looking for some ship named the *Deep Ocean One*."

Joe Glass reached for the mike to reply, but Brian Edwards tapped him on the shoulder.

"Captain, I think you need to come down to the wardroom. Two things you need to hear. The pilots from the P-3 have been talking with Master Chief Zillich about what everyone heard. And the guy we rescued is awake. He's talking, too. We may have a problem."

Glass followed the XO down to the wardroom, which now looked more like a hospital emergency operating room. The patient still lay on the table, wrapped in blankets and with an IV tube running from his arm to a bag hanging from the overhead. The buffet along the inboard bulkhead was strewn with various medical instruments. The operating lights gave the room a harsh glare. Doc Halliday hovered over his patient.

Master Chief Zillich and the two fliers sat on the little Naugahyde couch along the outboard bulkhead, heads close together, speaking in hushed tones as they reviewed some notes scratched on a wheel-book.

"Captain, meet Bruce deFrance," Doc Halliday said, waving toward the man lying on the table. "He says that he's the owner of a boat named the *Deep Ocean One*. That's who we sank."

Glass nodded toward the injured man but didn't say anything. deFrance tried to rise, but the straps across his chest and legs kept him bound in place. He started to speak, but Doc Halliday urged him to lie quietly.

Master Chief Zillich spoke up. "Captain, Lieutenant Durham and I have been trying to work out an anomaly in what we heard during the attack."

"More precisely," Jane Durham said, interrupting, "we are trying to figure out what we didn't hear. When we first held the *Kilo*, we heard launch transients, both on my gear and here on *Toledo*. That's why we dropped on it. But neither of us heard torpedo engine lines."

"We couldn't figure it out." Zillich picked up the story. "That is, until we went back and looked at the tapes. We replayed them both broadband and narrowband. We finally picked up a slow speed screw and faint engine lines heading off totally away from us. The engine lines look like some kind of DC motor."

"Yeah," Durham went on. "We laid the bearing lines down on the plot. The lines run straight from where the *Kilo* went down and appear to be on a track straight toward the big oil rigs off to the north, the Gulf, or to the beaches beyond."

Bruce deFrance waved his hand to indicate he wanted to join the conversation. His voice was weak when he spoke.

"Admiral Juan Valdez of the Venezuelan Navy had me buy an

underwater robot submarine, an ROV—for what purpose, I do not know. We delivered it to the *Almirante Villaregoz* submarine in Cienfuegos." He paused to find the strength to talk. "Captain, I can only assume that was why he had those missiles on my ship. They were to protect the robot submarine. But I swear I had no idea..."

Glass bolted out the door and sprinted down the passageway. He had to get to a radio and inform Tom Donnegan of what he had just found out.

It appeared some very nasty people were about to do some serious damage, and he and his submarine might be the only asset with the chance of stopping it.

If it was not already too damned late.

38

Admiral Tom Donnegan finally had all the pieces to the complicated puzzle he had been pondering the past few weeks. He still had no idea what he was going to do with the completed picture, though.

So, Juan Valdez had managed to plant a bomb on a deep-sea oil wellhead. Blowing up a producing wellhead—and Donnegan had to assume the blow-out-preventing device would be destroyed as well—would certainly create an unprecedented ecological disaster. The world was still very aware of such a catastrophe after BP's Deepwater Horizon blow-out back in 2011. This time, though, the damage would be a thousand times worse.

No exploratory drilling rig this time. This was a full-blown production well, currently delivering tens of thousands of barrels a day. Such an occurrence would not only do tremendous damage to the ecosystem, but it would also cause panic in the world oil market. That panic would disrupt supply, and prices would soar out of sight.

Plus, more than 250 people lived on the platform, and

Donnegan had no way of determining how much time was left to evacuate them before the bomb detonated.

Donnegan paced the length of his office and back again, wearing a familiar path in the deep-blue carpet. The sun had set and darkness had already dropped a veil on the panorama outside his big office window. A continuous line of cars filled Richmond Highway, people zipping home after a typical day at the office. Donnegan glanced out at the red tail lights heading up the parkway. It occurred to him that these same automobiles could very well be coming back the other direction before he had a chance to crawl into his own bed. And in a few weeks, the gas to fuel their commute could cost many times what it did that day, if there was even supply to fill their tanks.

It was about to be one very long night.

Tom Donnegan stopped his pacing, grabbed the secure phone from his desktop, and punched in a number he knew even better than his own. A deep voice at the other end answered, "Naval Undersea Warfare Center, Special Vehicles Section."

Admiral Donnegan got to the point.

"Don, I need you and your Large Diameter UUV on a plane heading to Tyndall. I have a mission for you."

Don Ester was head of NUWC's super-secret Special Vehicles Section, the Navy's development house for the fleet of clandestine unmanned underwater vehicles. UUVs could go many places and do many missions that a manned submarine could not. This was, Donnegan had just determined, one of those missions.

"Okay."

"I'll have a C-17 waiting for you at Quonset Point to haul you down to Tyndall Air Force Base. There'll be an LCS waiting at the pier in Panama City to haul you out to the platform." Donnegan's instructions were machine-gunned.

Ester chuckled. He was accustomed to getting calls like this from the Navy's top spook. Admiral Donnegan was far and away his best customer.

"Admiral, where is the LCS taking us and what are we looking for? It would sure make load out a lot easier if we had those details."

"Sorry, Don, here's the scoop," Donnegan answered. "All you'll have to do is find and defeat a bomb in a thousand fathoms of water. We think that it will be planted on a deep-water wellhead by a UUV. My best guess is that you might have a day or so before it is timed to go off. But I make no guarantees. Damn thing may blow up in your face."

There was only the slightest of pauses on the other end of the secure line before Don Ester responded.

"In that case, I suppose we had better haul ass."

Ψ

The sun, just taking its first peek over the horizon, found Don Ester standing on the bridge of the USS *Freedom*, LCS-1. The littoral combat ship, the Navy's answer to a high-speed, sea-going pickup truck, was making better than forty-five knots as it planed over the deep blue waters of the Gulf of Mexico. Panama City, Florida, and its blinding white-sand beaches were quickly disappearing below the horizon astern.

Ester's team of scientists and technicians were below decks, in the mission module bay, checking out all the circuits on his bright-yellow submersible. The LDUUV, affectionately if not too imaginatively named the Fat Yellow Baby, was the very latest in undersea technology. Designed to operate down to five thousand meters and powered by a high-capacity polymer membrane hydrogen fuel cell, the craft could be configured with a wide array of sensors and cargos. Originally designed for undersea exploration and to place remote sensors covertly, the Fat Yellow Baby could either operate completely autonomously or remotely by using a fiber optic communications link.

Ester's cell phone chirped with a few notes of "Anchors Aweigh." The caller ID showed Tom Donnegan.

"Mornin', Admiral," Ester said. "Got us any more details to work with?"

"Not really," was Donnegan's gruff reply. "Just head out to Exxon number six platform. They're the closest to where the sub launched the UUV. If my informant is good to his word, the bomb has to be on one of their wellheads. And the closest one is the most likely."

"Did you say 'one of their wellheads?'" Ester asked.

"Yes, they have a dozen of them, according to their records," Donnegan answered. "They are spread out over about twenty square miles. I'm downloading the charts to you, along with the plans for the wellheads and locations. Whatever you need to cut that fuse, just ask for it. What's your ETA? I can't imagine we have a lot of time."

"We should be alongside number six in ten hours; say, sixteen hundred, local time," the scientist answered. "The LCS really rocks, but it's still four hundred miles. The ol' Fat Yellow Baby will be in the water by seventeen hundred."

"Sure hope that's soon enough..." Donnegan answered, his voice trailing off.

"Why don't we just have Exxon plug their wells?" Ester inquired. "Then, even if the bomb goes off, it just blasts some wellhead hardware."

"Exxon is bucking at that," Donnegan shot back. "First, I don't think they believe us. And even if they did, plugging them all would cost them billions to re-drill and even more billions in lost production. If we can find the bomb, then that will affect only one well. They'll go for plugging that once they're sure."

"Well, you have to admire corporate priorities," Ester responded drily. "They realize they are playing with the future of oil production in the Gulf, not to mention the ecology of tens of thousands of square miles of ocean and all those pretty beaches and marshland up there, right?"

"Yep," Donnegan grunted. "It's high stakes poker for sure. I just hope we draw the right cards, Don."

Ψ

The sun was little more than a bare glimmer hiding below the western horizon. A full moon, bright orange, had started its slow journey across the nighttime sky. The *Freedom* rocked gently in the slight Gulf swell, keeping station a few hundred yards off the deep-water oil platform that towered into the air.

Down in the LCS mission module bay, the narrow CONEX box that functioned as a command center was an anthill of activity. Six men crowded into the cramped space, working to keep the Fat Yellow Baby happy and searching for the bomb. The remnants of a hastily consumed dinner and a phalanx of empty coffee cups littered the narrow desk that stretched down one long wall. A half-dozen laptop computers and several processors vied with the mess for space.

Don Ester did not have time to enjoy the astronomical show playing out overhead. He was far too busy glancing from one flat-panel monitor to another that hung in a row above him. A couple of the screens were covered with a complex display of engineering parameters monitoring the UUV's health and well-being. Another was a large bottom map showing a god's-eye view of the oil wellheads and the UUV as it moved between them. It was the last monitor, a feed from the UUV's video cameras, that ultimately held Ester's attention.

The Fat Yellow Baby had visited three wellheads already and

found nothing suspicious. Ester was now sending his under-water vehicle in for a view of the fourth one. It was a ticklish operation. He had to get the UUV deep enough to clearly see the wellhead and the bottom but avoid stirring up the fine silt that covered the sea floor. The cloud would bring visibility down to nil, making navigation around the wellhead hardware nearly impossible and giving them virtually no chance of spotting anything down there, almost a mile below them.

The high-resolution side-scan sonar was printing out on the high-definition flat-panel, developing twin swaths of the bottom picture out to a couple of hundred yards on either side of the Fat Yellow Baby. At the same time, the high-frequency gap-filler sonar filled in the area between the two side-scan displays. Together, the system pictured a boring montage of rocks and mud and the occasional curious grouper.

The UUV's bright, high-intensity lights illuminated the muddy bottom for the high-resolution video cameras as the submersible approached this latest wellhead. Slowly, the tall steel structure that formed the production tree came into view. The unit stretched almost thirty feet up from the flat, muddy bottom, with pipes leading off in various directions.

Ester leaned forward until his nose almost touched the screen. An empty coffee cup rolled off the desk and crashed onto the steel deck. Nobody seemed to notice.

There it was. Just visible, nestled up close to the tree. A black shape that did not belong.

"Bingo," was all he said.

Ester brought the UUV down closer and swung it around to get a better view. The black shape looked like another UUV resting there, not nearly as colorful or as big as the Fat Yellow Baby, but still a sizeable craft. Ester did a little quick mental math. That thing was big enough to carry a ton of explosives. It would really do a job on the wellhead if it decided to detonate.

Grabbing the radiophone, Ester said, "Exxon Six, this is *Freedom*. We found the bomb. It's right next to wellhead four. It's a big one. Better start plugging four."

The speaker behind his head crackled. "*Freedom*, Exxon Six. Roger. You sailor boys do understand that this is going to cost us big bucks, don't you?"

"Six, *Freedom*. Yes, just get the damn concrete flowing!"

"Six, roger. We're pumping now, but you realize this is going to take several hours to get enough mud in that hole to pack it, right?"

"We may not have several hours!" Ester shouted into the mike. "Can't you push it any faster?"

The answering voice's slow Louisiana drawl only added to Ester's frustration.

"Ain't nothin' we all can do to make it move any faster. That mud is gonna move like mud moves. Which is, by the way, real damn slow."

Ester knew that he would have to find a way to either move or disarm the bomb. His senses screamed that he had to do it quickly, that they may not be blessed with the several hours needed to cap the well with cement.

Only one thing left to try. Maybe he could employ the LDUUV to move the bomb. It was possible, but a long shot. And breathtakingly dangerous.

The black UUV he had discovered looked big and heavy, and there was always the possibility that it was rigged to explode if it was jostled. But maybe whoever sent the thing did not worry about that since there would have been no reason to suspect anyone would ever expect it to cozy up to a working oil well. Maybe they did not want to take a chance on such a setup going off prematurely.

Ester simply did not know for certain. If his hunch was correct, there was no time to find out.

He cautiously maneuvered his underwater pride and joy until he could snatch hold of the black monstrosity with Fat Baby's mechanical arm. Once he was certain he had a good grip, Ester opened the UUV's throttle full astern.

The image on the video monitor shook and shuddered. The power meter on another monitor pegged well into the red zone. Several alarm lights blinked red.

The interloper did not move. The bomb was still firmly planted atop the well and the millions of gallons of crude oil below.

Ester coaxed the LDUUV around a bit to see if he could get better leverage. The other craft still did not move a millimeter.

He swallowed hard and gritted his teeth, as if he actually had a grip on the black vessel with his own hands. In desperation, he moved around until he could get a straight shot at the bomb. Maybe he could simply bulldoze the bomb far enough away by ramming it with the Fat Yellow Baby. Ester knew that it was a final, desperate effort. He would have to hit the black UUV at full throttle. Even if the other craft did not move, his Fat Yellow Baby could be damaged beyond repair.

Or he could set off Armageddon down there.

Holding his breath, Ester backed the LDUUV up so he could get a running start. He carefully lined up to hit the bomb but just miss the production tree. Jamming the throttle full ahead, he muttered a silent prayer.

The LDUUV shot forward. The image of the black bomb rapidly grew larger and then filled the video screen for a fleeting second.

Then the screen went blank.

The camera, mounted on the front of Fat Yellow Baby, was the first thing to hit. No matter, Ester thought. He had probably kicked up enough silt and mud to be blind anyway.

Ester shifted his attention to the engineering monitor

displays. The electric drive motor was still going full throttle. But now the forward speed had dropped to zero. His baby was working hard to shove what appeared to be an immovable object.

Ester could not help it. He pumped his fist in the air and shouted at the top of his voice, "Go, Baby! Go!" He deftly moved a couple of controls to positions he had never used before. He was now shunting every joule of available power directly to the LDUUV's churning screws. He watched as the velocity meter came almost imperceptibly off the low peg. Something was moving, if barely. The meter wiggled slightly, still hovering just above zero. The power meter was pegged high. Alarms were blinking urgently all over the control panel. The Fat Yellow Baby could not tolerate much more of this.

Ester reached up and overrode the high-current shutdowns. At this rate, the motors would burn up in a few more seconds.

Maybe those few seconds—or a few more yards—would make a big enough difference if—when—the damn thing went off. It was moving. He could not tell how far, but it was moving.

Suddenly, all the screens blinked in unison and went blank. Something had happened six thousand feet below them. There was a distant rumble, like an earthquake.

Seconds later, the men on deck saw a huge, roiling bubble of water erupting a couple of hundred yards away, almost directly over wellhead number four, as if the sea was boiling.

The speaker above Ester's head crackled.

"*Freedom*, this is Exxon Six." The man's voice was breathless this time, and he no longer spoke in his slow Cajun drawl. "I don't know what you sailor boys just did, but you actuated all the shutdowns. The well is isolated."

He paused for an instant, as if studying something.

"But, hey, it looks like she's still there."

39

Admiral Juan Valdez was mystified, a condition in which he rarely found himself, and he hated the realization that he had lost control. He clutched the ornate phone so hard his hand cramped, and he fairly screamed at Hermando Guanayca.

"What do you mean they did not find anything? You will send them back out and you will order them to search the seas until they find something, or until they fall out of the sky!"

Guanayca, one of the most powerful men in the Cuban government and Valdez's well-placed henchman, hesitated. Having someone scream at him was just as foreign to him as the admiral's loss of control. His voice quivered as he took a deep breath and answered the irate would-be dictator.

"*Almirante,* please understand. The pilots searched every hectare. They found nothing but some scattered wreckage. There is no sign of your ship. I fear that it is sunk."

"And the submarine?" Valdez growled. "Where is the *Almirante Villaregoz*? Did it just disappear as well, swallowed up by the sea?"

Valdez did not wait for an answer, one he already knew but did not actually want to hear. Instead, he hurled the phone across the room. It, too, shattered into pieces as it crashed into the stone and stucco wall.

The *Almirante Villaregoz* was two days late to report in. By now, it should be tied up safely in Caracas harbor, far from the impending disaster he was about to unleash on *los Estados Unidos* and her tourist-strewn beaches.

But there was yet another concern. There had still been no word of the explosion and ecological catastrophe coming out of the Gulf. The news channels should, by now, be full of stories of the oily nightmare once again spreading across the pristine blue waters, set loose by an unexplained problem at another well-head. The media should already be screaming for a stop to all offshore drilling.

But thus far, only silence.

Something was terribly wrong. Juan Valdez could sense it. He called for Jorge. It was time to retreat, to hide for a while.

Jorge stepped into the room, holding a portable phone. "Admiral," he said, "it is *el Presidente*. He desires for you to come to the palace immediately."

Admiral Juan Valdez turned white. It was time to go to ground and assay the situation, and it would have to be from a place where nobody could ever find him.

Ψ

President Gutierrez, the liberator of the Venezuelan people, was just as mystified as Admiral Valdez but for a totally different reason. He had the American, Josh Kirkland, sitting across the desk from him, and the CIA agent was spinning quite a fantastic tale.

If even half of it was true, Gutierrez had a real problem before him. If Valdez was really trying to goad the Americans by blowing up a deep-water oil well, if he had tried to sink an

American submarine, and if he was trying to do more than he and the president had agreed to do to influence control of Cuba, then Gutierrez needed to put him in a box permanently. Prodding the American elephant was good, as long as the elephant did not lose its temper and crush you with its considerable weight. With what Valdez had apparently tried to do, the crushing would be assured. And playing a dangerous game of regime-change in Cuba—other than the way Gutierrez had already decided to do it—was unforgivable.

There were other ways to accomplish that, using propaganda, bribes, drug trafficking, influence, and, yes, even a tiny bit of diplomacy. All the ways with which Gutierrez was so very familiar. Not with torpedoes, bombs, and submarines. Not in this day and time.

Josh Kirkland took a series of deep draws on his cigar and then blew a perfect smoke ring. It rose toward the ceiling and gently circled the crystal chandelier.

"A most excellent smoke, Your Excellency," he pronounced with a smile. "Most civilized. Now, from what my people tell me, I have every reason to believe that the good admiral has deduced by now that his plans have collapsed. You know him better than anyone. What do you expect he will try?"

Cesar Gutierrez rolled his own cigar through his fingers as he pondered for a moment.

"It is true that I have known Juan nearly all my life," he said quietly. "He always has a backup plan behind the backup plan. He will try to run, of course. Try to save himself until he can conjure up a story to tell me. He will have some carefully prepared hideaway, some place where he will be very difficult to find."

Josh Kirkland sensed his chance. He was playing a very dangerous game, dancing on a knife edge as he played Gutierrez against his own CIA masters. If either side sensed what he was doing, the whole house of cards would fall, and he probably would not live long enough to see them flutter to the floor. But this was his only gambit if he had any chance of protecting his little illegal operation and hiding his Cuban secret.

"That's about what I figured," Kirkland responded. "Let me help you catch him and I will make sure that, so far as anyone else will ever know, he went rogue and was acting alone. There is no reason for anyone in Washington—or Havana, for that matter—to have any idea that you were involved in this unfortunate treachery."

"You can make that happen?" Gutierrez asked, his eyes wide with doubt. "No one can know that we worked together. It would not sit well with my people. With my peers in the hemisphere."

Kirkland grinned. He now knew that he had won the game. All he needed to do was close the deal and make very sure that no one was left alive who could tell any tales. Valdez had to die, of course, but so did TJ Dillon and those meddling SEALs. And they were already on the way to the party.

"With the proper positive incentive, I can make many things happen," the CIA man answered. "There is no reason that anyone needs to know we are working together, either your people or mine. Now let's discuss how we make your reprobate of an admiral go away. I have a team of SEALs heading this way. They may be very useful in this end game. Now, perhaps you can determine where the admiral might go to escape your wrath, Mr. President."

Ψ

Delta Flight 915 was at the end of a long trip. The sun was setting in the west as the airplane taxied toward gate six at Bogotá, Colombia's El Dorado International Airport. The sun had not even been visible over the horizon yet when Jim Ward and his SEAL team—plus one former SEAL—had left Dulles International, just outside Washington, D.C., fifteen hours before.

Someone higher up—Jim Ward suspected it was Josh Kirkland—had insisted that TJ Dillon go along for their upcoming march through the jungle. Ward was not sure how he felt about that, but it was not his place to ask. Still, he did not really know that much about Dillon, other than he had come loping across a clearing at them back in Cuba, carrying the country's top spy on his shoulder. And that the former SEAL's father and young Ward's own grandfather had both met similar fates at the hands of the same Cuban.

But the key fact was that Dillon was a former SEAL. That made him a brother. And so far—even for an old fart—he had earned his keep.

After all that time in a cramped coach-class seat, and with a layover in Miami, everyone was irritable. The trip had been just short of unendurable, especially for men in top athletic shape like the young SEALs. The silly romantic-comedy in-flight movie had not helped at all. Still, Dillon seemed none the worse for the wear. It remained to be seen if he was in fighting shape after such a short rest from the Cuban tour.

Ward unfastened his seat belt even before the 757 came to a stop at the gate. There was something incongruous about taking a commercial flight on a mission, more like a businessman off to a sales meeting than a crack team of well-trained warriors. But in a few hours, he and his fellow travelers would be deep in the Venezuelan jungle searching for Admiral Juan Valdez.

Ward pulled his iPhone out of his pocket and reread the latest instructions from Admiral Tom Donnegan. Admiral Valdez had disappeared from Caracas. Josh Kirkland was sure that he had gone to Cuba for a bit but was now headed to a hideout in the far southwest corner of the country, deep in the jungle and tight against the border with Brazil and Colombia. The region was a wild and largely unexplored jungle. If Valdez disappeared in there, he would be impossible to find.

Kirkland swore his information—and tacit approval for the SEAL team's mission—came from the highest level of the Venezuelan government, and he was confident the intel was correct. But the "approval" applied only if the SEALs were not detected or captured. Operatives in the country confirmed that the CIA man had visited the presidential palace the previous day.

Highest level, indeed.

Kirkland—still unaware that his colleagues knew more about his background than he could have ever suspected, and equally unaware that they knew of his real role in the last few weeks' events—was supplying them with valuable information. But was there an ulterior motive? Was he leading the SEAL team into a trap?

No, more likely he was going to allow the SEALs to solve his Admiral Valdez problem for him.

Ward and his team-plus-one were to take a Colombian helicopter in as close as they dared and then trek cross-country the rest of the way. Orders were to bring Valdez back to face trial for whatever crimes he had committed. Ward and his team did not need to know any more than that. The niceties of international borders and legal jurisdiction were not a concern worth discussing. Ward understood perfectly that the governments of Colombia and Venezuela knew they were there but did not—and, in fact, could not—assure that most elements of their military would be understanding if they determined that the men wading through their swamps were American SEALs, regardless of how many politicians had blessed their presence there.

Young Ward had just finished rereading his orders when a blast of hot, moist tropical air signaled the opening of the cabin door, welcoming them to Colombia. Ward rose and shuffled off the flight, then headed toward baggage claim with the rest of the weary passengers.

His team, along with TJ Dillon, were waiting at baggage claim, accompanied by a very official-looking Colombian Army major. Minutes later, they were hauling their packs out, walking through customs without even slowing. A Colombian Army Humvee was waiting at the curb to shuttle the team to CATAM Military Airport, just across the main runways from the passenger terminal.

"Let's load 'em up and move on out," Ward told them. He had already noticed that Dillon accepted his direction without question. There seemed to be no misunderstanding. Even though Dillon had tenure, and even though he was along by order of some high muckety-muck at Langley, Ward was the undisputed team leader.

Only room for one of those where they were going.

An hour later the team was strapped into a Colombian Air Force Blackhawk chopper, heading east-southeast. Jim Ward and Sean Horton pored over the latest satellite imagery of the Southwestern Venezuelan jungle. They spent extra time with a high-resolution, hyper-spectral image taken of an area located about twenty miles up an unnamed tributary of the Rio Casiquiare.

"Man, the hyper-spectral is neat stuff," Horton enthused. "Makes looking through a jungle canopy like peeking in through an upstairs window. See that camp?" The SEAL pointed toward a bright area at a bend in the river. "Looks about right for a hidey-hole. High ground overlooking the river. Hell-and-gone from anywhere and a day's easy walk to either the Colombian or Brazilian border."

"Yep, saw that, and it has all the signs of being occupied,"

Ward said with a nod. "I can't quite make out any people, but it's the most likely place for us to have ourselves a look-see."

"You guys have some neat toys these days," TJ Dillon shouted over the roar of the chopper engine.

"I'll take any advantage I can get," Ward answered.

"Me, too. Me, too." Dillon pointed to the image. "I've actually been in that area in a previous life. I was helping the Colombian Army root out some really nasty cartel guys who were funding and arming any guerilla group that would help them get their product to market."

The two SEALs looked up at him.

"Another advantage, I'd say," Jim Ward noted.

Ward directed the pilot to set them down just short of the border. They would hike in the rest of the way. No sense letting the racket from a military helicopter advertise their presence, particularly in an area where helicopters were very rare and almost always meant trouble. Twenty miles through the jungle would take a couple of days, but it was far better to arrive with complete surprise than sound and fury.

Ψ

Admiral Juan Valdez climbed out of the motorized canoe and began the trek to the top of the rocky outcropping that towered over a rapidly-moving stream. The river was so full of jungle mud, nutrients, and red ore that the water looked for all the world like spilled blood. It had been a very long, difficult journey, first by helicopter to Esmeralda, then by boat down the winding, twisting Rio Casiquiare to a smaller stream that ultimately led to here. The last forty kilometers into the wild had been in the rough-hewn log canoe.

He gazed with considerable interest at the deep jungle vegetation that came right up to the river's edge and slapped at a particularly determined mosquito as he listened to the jungle sounds. The rocky cairn rose almost vertically over a hundred meters out of the jungle mud, a granite fortress in the middle of nowhere.

This place was a long way from the sea, where the admiral felt most in his element. And this was certainly distant from his luxurious home in Caracas, with none of the comforts. But it was, of course, far safer. His old friend Castellon had first shown him the way here and he would certainly not tell anyone, even if he was still alive. Now, between Jorge and the small, very select contingent of naval infantry, Valdez would be safe from anything but a battalion-strength assault. That was not going to happen out here. Even if the president did somehow figure out his location and could mount some kind of an operation, the admiral's tentacles ran deep into all the Venezuelan military. Valdez would be warned well in advance and would be long gone before anyone arrived.

Reaching the camp, Valdez walked around to check the security and defenses. A pair of machine cannon guarded the trail snaking up the mountain. Gun pits dotted the camp's perimeter.

"I think you will find the security adequate," Jorge commented as he trotted along beside his commander. "The area outside the camp, both on the rock and down on the jungle floor, is monitored with the latest surveillance sensors that I could find, all installed since your last visit. Patrols go out every day. No one will approach without us knowing it, unless they are a ghost." He pointed toward a large hut nestled underneath a banyan tree. "If you step over here, I will show you the new command and communications center."

"You are certain Castellon is no longer alive?" he asked Jorge yet again.

"As certain as I can be, sir. I inserted the knife and twisted it, and I saw the blood he was losing as I fled from whichever of his henchmen tried to protect him." Jorge's damaged hand, minus two fingers, was still swathed in bandages as it healed from the gunshot wound.

An unexpected blast of frigid air greeted the pair as they stepped into the hut. One entire wall was made up of flat-panel displays showing various jungle scenes. The two naval officers who had been scanning the screens immediately jumped to rigid attention when they spotted Admiral Valdez.

Jorge slapped one man hard on his cheek and kicked the other in the butt.

"You worthless curs!" he shouted. "Your duty is to watch those monitors, not to stand around like a pair of fawning martinets. Get back to work."

Guiding an approving Valdez over to the other side of the hut, Jorge pointed out a computer, a pair of telephones, and a sophisticated radio set.

"From here you will be as connected to the outside world as if you were back in Caracas," he bragged. "That is thanks to the American communications satellites. And we have set up the phone routing so that any calls circle the world several times through myriad switches. They cannot be traced to here."

Valdez nodded as he turned to face Jorge.

"Still, we must be careful. No one will make any contact with the outside world without my permission. We must be very careful until this quiets down. I do not trust the president, especially now. I have learned that the CIA is whispering in his ear and that they see the failure of our plan as an opportunity to get closer to Gutierrez. Just as they will scramble to try to arrange to have a government in Havana that will be friendlier to the capitalists in Washington." He put his hand on his trusted man's shoulder. "Jorge, this may well be an opportunity for us too. We still have loyal men in the right places. Once the maelstrom subsides, we will give them the signal and they will convert to our strong backup plan. Then we will replace our corrupt president and bring true, disciplined rule to our country."

"I know, my Admiral."

"Someday our people will sing folk songs that tell of what we were able to do, the power we were able to wield, the freedom we won for our people, all from this little secluded spot in the jungle. The revolution that was spawned here in *la Valle de la Sangre.*"

Jorge snapped to attention.

"From *la Valle de la Sangre.*"

The Valley of Blood.

40

Jim Ward and his team made maddeningly slow progress through the constant, clinging curtain of near-impenetrable jungle. Twenty miles would normally be a quick five-hour hike for him and his SEAL team. This time, though, they had been going non-stop for almost a day and a half. Donnegan's satellite imagery did not even begin to give them an accurate picture of the cloying vines, rotting logs, or thick, sticky mud that made every step an exhausting chore. It was similar to what they had experienced in Cuba, but here, the real estate was as much vertical as horizontal, and that made it even more taxing.

"Skipper," Tony Garcia grunted, "time to check in. GPS says that we are half a click from the rock." He had been on point for the last couple of hours, leading the team through a particularly thick section of the seemingly endless jungle, but other than the sweat and grime on his face, he looked as fresh as when he had jumped from the helicopter. Garcia gestured ahead, as if the granite would be visible if they only looked intently enough through the leafy canopy.

"Okay, let's take ten," Ward agreed, waving the team to

spread out in a loose defensive perimeter. However, they had already begun their moves. Even Dillon dashed away to instinctively occupy a flank.

They were close enough to the camp now to be even more cautious. There was no telling what defenses Valdez might have out. It would be bad form to have some stray patrol stumble upon them and give away the element of surprise they so desperately needed to pull this mission off. Even worse form to show up in HD on some security monitor.

Pulling his sat phone from a pocket, Ward punched in his security code. Within seconds the latest imagery and instructions were downloaded from a comms satellite in geosynchronous orbit twenty-three thousand miles overhead. Not much had changed since the last update. Same small encampment atop a granite cairn in the middle of nowhere. The only new bit of information was a communications intercept that confirmed Valdez was up there. NSA had listened in as he sent out some instructions to his Cayman Island bankers. At least Ward knew now that their march was no dry run or useless exercise.

Sean Horton looked over Ward's shoulder at the image.

"Any idea how we get up there, Skipper?" he asked. "Don't figure ol' Admiral Valdez is going to invite us in for coffee if we stroll up and ring the doorbell."

Ward chuckled. "Suspect you're right, Sean. We'll have to find a back door to slip in. It might be a good idea to have someone ringing the doorbell while we're busy at the back, though."

"What you got in mind?" the big SEAL asked.

"I'm thinking that Joe Glass can use a couple of his Tomahawks to ring that doorbell for us. Let's get Admiral Donnegan on the phone."

Ψ

Joe Glass read the tasking order one more time, just to be sure he understood what he was being asked to do. There was no doubt. They had a job, and they had to be damn quick if they were going to get it done in time.

"Officer of the Deck, make your depth six hundred feet, come to Ahead flank and course south," Glass said machine-gun-quick to Pat Durand, who was standing beside him gazing out through the periscope. That would, at least, get them moving in the right direction while he figured out the details.

Pat Durand clapped up the operating handles, lowered the scope, and issued the series of orders that caused *Toledo* to leap ahead like an unbridled stallion. Back in the engine room, steam roared down the main lines, pouring into the turbine and driving the huge bronze propeller at dizzying speed. Reactor coolant pumps slammed into fast speed, forcing more cold water through the reactor to draw off more heat energy. Stern planes angled down, shoving the big submarine down into the deep, where they could safely race on to where they now knew they needed to be.

Brian Edwards came running into the control room as Joe Glass moved back to the navigation stand. Before the XO could even open his mouth, Glass tossed him the message board.

"Got us a job to do, XO. Admiral Donnegan wants us in a launch box a hundred miles off the Venezuelan coast, tossing Tomahawks by oh-six-hundred zulu. We are going to cover Jim Ward's job. We've got ten hours to make two hundred and thirty miles and be ready to go. Let's get cracking." He grinned and winked at his serious-faced exec. "Looks like we have yet another opportunity to avoid hanging the boss's son out to dry."

Edwards quickly read through the brief message and then

looked at the Voyage Management System display. The electronic chart showed their current position as south and east of Jamaica. He punched the coordinates for their launch basket into the VMS keyboard. The computer system instantly flashed a blue course line, complete with courses and speeds it would take to get them there.

"Skipper, VMS recommends coming around to one-nine-eight, speed twenty-five knots. Even with that, we'll be skidding into the very back edge of the basket with barely enough time to get the birds in the air. And that assumes our bearing problem doesn't get worse."

Glass pursed his lips, his serious face now matching his XO's.

"Showing up late is not an option. Pour on the coal."

Ψ

Josh Kirkland had been pondering the various solutions to a major problem. How could he make sure that Admiral Valdez did not live to tell any tales? And how could he, at the same time, make sure Jim Ward and TJ Dillon would not be around to help anybody else figure out his role in all this treachery? Last thing he wanted—what with their connected history—was for the two of them to compare notes and come to some conclusions on their own. The more he balanced the various options in his head, the more he realized that he would have to solve this one all by himself.

Dillon had done exactly what Kirkland wanted him to do in Cuba, even without knowing it—locate Marco Esteban and rescue him, if possible. Kirkland had suspected that de la Roche had something to do with the DINA head disappearing so suddenly. And he also knew the old revolutionary's son would lead Dillon right to Esteban. The whole scenario had played out even better than he had hoped when the DINA showed up and gave Dillon the chance to escape with Esteban in the confusion.

Now, if Kirkland could only use the fact that he had helped save Esteban, he might be able to pull off the true crime of the century. Not only would he have the sweet deal with Gutierrez and Venezuela, but he would also have powerful influence to parlay into even bigger and better things.

Things that smelled like sweet crude oil. And money.

The CIA man started an inventory of his resources. What could he bring to bear? Gutierrez was a key cog in the drug dealings, of course. The tin pot dictator could not be trusted with the subtleties of this new plot. Nobody on the island of Cuba—outside of Marco Esteban at Guantanamo—could do him any good. He really had no friends—or even dependable enemies—in Langley anymore. Those few bridges were rapidly being torched as he accumulated power and influence at the expense of others.

That left just one option for help in eliminating Valdez, Dillon, and that SEAL team—Simon Castellon and his ragtag army of guerrilla fighters. After all, Castellon owed him a big favor for pulling him away from Jorge and out of Caracas. And after the attempt on his life, Castellon had every reason to hate Valdez enough to cut his head off. Maybe Kirkland could count on their help. Especially if he again held up the lucrative CIA-supported US drug trade for bait.

There was no one else. It was time to set things in motion and see if he could save his ass and keep from getting caught up in this giant quagmire.

He grabbed his cell phone and punched in a number from memory.

Simon Castellon answered on the second ring. "*Señor* Kirkland, it is good to hear your voice. How may I be of assistance, my friend?"

Josh Kirkland began to lay out his scheme for the Latin guerilla.

Ψ

Juan Valdez paced restlessly as he watched another patrol disappear down the mount, crossing the little stream of blood-red water and heading out to reconnoiter the jungle that so effectively obscured his hideout. He had only been here a couple of days and he already felt like a caged tiger. How would he ever survive months of this utter and complete boredom? He would certainly go mad.

At least he could make some outbound calls. As long as he kept the calls short and used the encryption device, he assumed no one would know what he was doing.

He first dialed the number to his Lichtenstein bankers. It would be a good idea to have some liquid assets stashed where he could get to them easily, something that could not be traced and was easily portable. Minutes later he was the proud owner of a cache of diamonds worth fifty million Euros, safely stored in a vault in Durban, South Africa. And another fifty million Euros' worth of gold placed with a brokerage in Hong Kong.

Valdez felt much better, safer. Now he had the wherewithal to move anywhere quickly and still tap enough assets to maintain his power base.

Soon he would be out of this godforsaken place, his hands once again on the levers of power that would ultimately change the pecking order of the Western Hemisphere once and for all.

Ψ

Bill Beaman barged into Tom Donnegan's office without bothering to knock.

"NSA has him again. The old son of a bitch sure is talkative for somebody who's trying to keep his ass hidden from us."

"What now? Ordering a pizza? Putting a bet on the Redskins game?" Tom Donnegan grunted.

"No, even better," Beaman told him as he plopped down in one of the overstuffed wing chairs facing the battered old oak desk. "He's moving money again. Bastard bought a bunch of diamonds and gold. Looks to be about a hundred million bucks' worth, and I doubt it's a gift for one of his mistresses. Our guys are moving to intercept and commandeer the trinkets. Valdez will have a stroke when he figures out that he's paying for his own downfall."

Donnegan scratched a quick calculation on a notepad and smiled crookedly.

"Adding that to the thirty million he just freed up from the Caymans, we might be able to afford first-class tickets back for Jim and the boys." He chuckled. "As long as Valdez keeps talking, we can keep him pinpointed, too. Make sure Jim knows the admiral is still up there on that rock. Any word on how things are coming together?"

"Nothing from Joe Glass since we sent them the tasking message," Beaman answered. "But we didn't expect to hear anything. He has to make a mad dash down to his launch box if he's going to make it." Beaman glanced at the old ship's chronometer on Donnegan's back wall. "*Toledo* should be there in a couple of hours, ready to light off some Roman candles for our guys down there, but..."

Beaman trailed off. Donnegan looked at him.

"Okay, you going to go ahead and tell me what's really on your mind, Captain?"

"How much do you really know about this Dillon guy, Tom? You know it's not the usual deal to send anybody—even a former SEAL—on a mission like this. We keep our teams together and small for a reason. Somebody somewhere had a reason to tag him and send him with Jim and the boys."

Donnegan snorted.

"You think I would have stood still for a second if I had any reason not to trust him? Even if the president himself punched Dillon's ticket? I know everything about the guy. He's square. Good as they come. I knew his daddy, too. He's an asset, not a liability. He'll be part of the team. I'm certain of that."

Beaman let out a long sigh.

"I feel better now, but..."

"But what?"

"I still don't know why somebody was so determined for him to go along with Jim and the boys. They not trust Ward and his team?"

"That one I can't answer for you, Bill. Long as I'm convinced he'll help more than he'll hurt, I don't really give a damn. They'll let me know when the time is right. Or not."

Admiral Tom Donnegan stood, stretching old muscles that had cramped from sitting for such a long period. He paced across the room and ended up at the blast-proof window at the far side of the office. He stood there for a minute, looking out through the glass at the Potomac River and the brightly-lit Washington skyline.

Bill Beaman knew Donnegan well enough to read the old warrior's mind. He knew what he was thinking and who he was thinking about.

After several minutes, Donnegan asked, "Anything from Jim?"

"He checked in an hour ago," Beaman answered. "The team is moving into position. They'll be ready when the Tomahawk strike hits. You know they'll be out of communications until then. We'll have to sit here and wait to hear from them."

Donnegan glanced over at the brass ship's clock on the wall

and frowned. Then he turned back to survey the Washington Monument, whose spire was pointing to a full, blood-red moon overhead. A passenger jet wound its way down the river, lining up to land at Ronald Reagan Airport.

"Sitting and waiting," he mumbled. "That's the hardest damn part."

41

The USS *Toledo* steamed just below the surface of the placid, pitch-black Caribbean. Joe Glass peered through the submarine's Type 18 periscope, making sure that they were all alone in this patch of sea. If any stray fishermen or cruise ship were out there, they were about to get one big shock.

However, Glass could not see anything except the star-filled night sky and the flashing red pinprick of light from a passenger jet high overhead.

"ESM, Conn, report all contacts," he ordered over the 21MC.

Back in the radio room, RM1 Sam Seidiman flipped through the circuits on the AN/BLQ-10 electronic warfare system. He was effectively searching the entire electronic spectrum for anything that might indicate danger to the *Toledo*.

"Conn, ESM. Completed initial search. Only contact of interest is a distant SPY-1D, probably a Burke-class destroyer over by St. Croix," Seidiman reported. "Also hold a couple of Furuno navigation radars. Also weak and distant. Probable fishermen. No threat contacts. Continuing search."

Satisfied with the report, Glass next turned to Brian Edwards.

"Okay, XO. Let's get this show on the road." He glanced at his wristwatch. "We have three minutes until the launch envelope opens."

"Yes, sir," Edwards shot back from his position standing behind Eric Hobson, the weapons officer, who sat at the BYG-1 launch panel.

"Man battle stations, missile," Glass ordered. The words sounded odd in the quiet control room.

Sam Wallich grabbed the 1MC microphone and repeated, "Man battle stations, missile." He yanked the square handle for the general alarm, and the bong-bong-bong sound filled the sub. He repeated the announcement, "Man battle stations, missile."

The announcement was a formality, a ritual, with none of the mad rush to make the sub ready for immediate battle that foretold a sudden torpedo attack. Not like in the movies, either. The crew had been preparing their systems and weapons for the last ten hours. The COB's announcement merely told them that it was almost time to set the birds off on their mission.

Wallich listened to reports coming in from around the ship. The clock had ticked off thirty seconds when he turned to Glass and reported, "Ship manned for battle stations, missile, Skipper."

Glass nodded and glanced one last time at the sonar screen, confirming that no one was trying to sneak up on them. "Firing point procedures, Tomahawk strike, tubes five, six, seven, and eight."

Brian Edwards made one final check on the BYG-1 fire control system to ensure the right strike packages were loaded. Satisfied, he called out, "Solution ready."

"Missions downloaded to tubes five, six, seven, and eight," Hobson shouted. "Tubes nine and ten are the backup birds. Weapons ready."

The deadly Tomahawk missiles now knew where they were supposed to fly and what they were supposed to hit when they got there.

Pat Durand, the officer of the deck, made a final check to make sure that *Toledo's* speed and depth were within the launch parameters. He announced, "Ship ready."

Glass took it all in before quietly ordering, "Open outer doors, tubes five, six, seven, and eight. Commence Tomahawk launch sequence."

Bill Dooley, down in the torpedo room, flipped the switches to open the vertical missile tube hatches. Out in the number three ballast tank, forward of the crew compartment, four hatches on the main deck were pushed open by hydraulic rams.

When the "Launch Enable" light flashed green on tube five, Eric Hobson jammed down on the launch button, announcing, "Tube five launched," as the red "Missile Launched" light flashed on.

Durand, his eye locked to the periscope, watched the bird jump out of the water, a brilliant, fiery trail following it up into the sky.

"Missile away," he called out.

Seconds later, the rocket motor flamed out and dropped away from the Tomahawk. He watched as the wings scissored out from inside the body and an air scoop dropped out, too. The little turbo-fan engine spun to life, pushing the missile into level flight toward its destination.

"Missile transitioned to normal flight," Durand announced, just as Hobson called that tube six was launched. The well-rehearsed process was repeated as another Tomahawk was sent off on its way.

"Tube seven launched."

Again, Pat Durand watched a flaming arrow shoot up out of

the water. The rocket motor flamed out when all its fuel was used, as expected, but the motor did not drop away. Instead, the missile arced over and plunged back into the sea.

"Missile did not transition," Durand shouted as he watched it splash down a few hundred yards astern.

"Assign tube seven mission to tube nine," Edwards ordered, even as Eric Hobson's fingers danced across the launch panel, setting up the Tomahawk in tube nine as he continued the launch of tube eight.

There was barely a pause in the launch sequence as the last two Tomahawks raced after their brethren, off to unleash some serious hellfire.

Joe Glass couldn't help muttering to himself, "Damn! But all that training paid off." Every man knew exactly what had to happen and did it.

Ψ

Josh Kirkland sat in the front of the boat, holding on for dear life. The flat-bottomed craft was racing up the jungle river at full throttle. The dark undergrowth on either shore flashed by in a bruised blur. The CIA man looked back over the heads of the dozen heavily armed guerilla fighters. Simon Castellon sat placidly next to the helmsman, and three more boats filled with paramilitary troops followed in their wake.

Kirkland stole a glance at his watch. At this pace, they should be at Valdez's camp by midnight. That was good. He knew the SEALs would be there, waiting to use the deep night as cover for their attack. Kirkland would arrive after the Americans had wreaked their havoc, just in time to surprise them and make sure no one was left to tell tales.

The boat skittered around another bend in the winding

snake of a stream, side-slipping dangerously close to the shore as it planed around the turn. The boat's bow abruptly dropped down and the engine's scream fell to a low burble as the helmsman throttled back.

"From here on, we go slow and close to the shore," Castellon said, his voice barely above a whisper. "We sneak in on the admiral now."

Kirkland watched as Castellon's well-trained and deadly jungle fighters quietly checked their weapons. These men were professionals.

Kirkland's watch hands had just reached midnight when the boat gently nudged the muddy edge of the stream. He scrambled to follow Castellon and his band up the steep bank and into the jungle.

Castellon fell back and tugged at Kirkland's coat sleeve.

"*Senor* Kirkland, my men are trained and hardened jungle fighters. They will move fast and quietly. I think maybe it is better for you to stay here with the boats. We will be back before the sun rises."

Before Josh Kirkland could even form a phrase of protest, Simon Castellon had disappeared into the overgrowth. Kirkland knew there was no point in arguing.

He plopped down on a rotting log. Might as well be comfortable. It would certainly be a long night.

He idly watched the odd-looking blood-red water swirl away at his feet.

Ψ

Jim Ward looked at his watch for the hundredth time. Midnight. Time to get moving. The Tomahawks would be showing up at the party in just under twenty minutes. They needed to be poised, ready to strike in the resulting confusion. Snatching Valdez alive was going to be tricky. Being late would only make it more so.

He waved his team forward. Valdez's night patrol would already be heading up the trail toward the top of the cairn. Satellite imagery confirmed that they were habitual, predictable. The SEALs had to get in behind them if they hoped to snake through the hideout's electronic defenses. Otherwise, they would have to make a far noisier appearance.

Sean Horton moved smoothly into point as they headed toward the path while Jed Dulkowski took up the trail position. Jim Ward and Tony Garcia spaced themselves a few meters apart in the middle of the line. TJ Dillon followed them.

Five minutes later they came out on the edge of a well-traveled trail, right where it was supposed to be. Sean Horton signaled them to disappear into the overgrowth as Valdez's patrol suddenly emerged a hundred yards away, right on schedule and heading up the path directly toward the SEALs. The Venezuelan marines passed so close that Ward could smell their sweat and the sweet tobacco smoke that permeated their uniforms. As the group moved up the trail, the SEALs became shadows in their wake, silently following, darting through the darkness.

Ψ

"*Capitan*, I thought I saw something," the marine watching the video monitor suddenly called out.

The watch captain, bored from another tiring night, stretched and yawned before bothering to acknowledge the man's statement.

"What did you see, Miguel, and where? Are you spooked again by another great *potoo* bird?"

"On the trail, the steep part, and it is no *potoo*," came the answer.

"It is only the patrol returning to base," the watch captain said, but he rose to look over the marine's shoulder. Then he saw it, too. A shadow moving quickly, a dozen feet behind the last man on the patrol. It would have been easy to miss, but it was definitely there. Someone or something was tailing the patrol.

This stretch of trail was across and up a steep rock face, open ground and nearly vertical except for the path hewn from the rock with toe-holds for the men's boots. The captain reached for the alarm button that would send the troops in the compound out into the night to intercept whoever dared to attempt to breach their security.

"We have intruders!" he told the marine. "We will send..."

The first of *Toledo*'s Tomahawks streaked across the sky and crashed nose-first into the command hut with a deafening detonation. The marine, the watch captain, and the hut were gone in an instant, vaporized in a blinding flash and horrific roar.

Two more explosions took out the barracks hut and the mess tent as the next missiles arrived almost simultaneously. The remaining rocket was a TLAM-D carrying a cargo of 2.2-pound submunitions. It made one pass over the hilltop, spewing out bomblets as it flew by, and then turned and made a second pass. The bomblets pocked the hilltop with shrapnel, tearing up everything above ground level.

But the missile was not yet finished with its mayhem. On its third pass, it crashed into the compound, unleashing a scorching trail of flames and debris across the open ground.

As soon as Jim Ward heard the first explosion, he raced up the narrow, steep path toward the hilltop, the rest of the team in hot pursuit. The members of the night patrol had stopped, gazing in awe at the blazing night below them.

Ward bowled over the last marine in the line, sending him

flailing over the edge of the bluff. Then he laid a full-body block on the next soldier, dispatching him after his buddy. Sean Horton grabbed Ward, stopping his momentum, keeping him from following the troops over the edge.

Meanwhile, Tony Garcia slipped past and took out the next trooper with a well-placed double tap from his M-4. The man fell, already dead.

Out of the corner of his eye, Ward saw TJ Dillon grab the marine who had been on point from behind. With one quick slash of the former SEAL's knife blade, the marine's throat was open and bleeding.

The team ran up the trail, bursting into the clearing on the little hilltop, finding chaos in every direction. The burning wreckage illuminated the scene. Someone had manned both heavy machine guns, which were filling the night sky with random tracer fire, ineffective but very dangerous. The deep, growling roar of AK-47s firing off into the darkness on full automatic added to the confusion. And the peril.

Ward crouched down behind a fallen tree and listened for a second. Most of the wild barrage was coming from the gun pits around the edge of the cairn. That made some sense. The Venezuelans would assume that the attack would come from the jungle below, not from the hard-to-reach high ground.

He raised his head cautiously to look around. No sign of Valdez. Where would the son of a bitch be?

He used hand signals to tell Dillon and Horton to take out the machine-gun emplacements before some random hot junk hurt somebody. They were both immediately lost in the smoke.

Ward caught a flash of movement out of the corner of his eye. A door in a small hummock of dirt flew open, and two men came running out of what had to be an underground bunker. They saw Ward at the same instant that he saw them. Ward hit the first man squarely in the forehead with two bullets. Dulkowski took out the other one just as he raised his AK-47 toward Ward's muzzle flash.

Ward hand-signaled toward the bunker. Dulkowski took the right flank and Ward took the left as they bull-rushed the entrance. Dulkowski tossed a flash-bang grenade into the opening as Ward rolled inside the open door. The blinding, disabling roar was followed almost instantly by the pop-pop-pop of Ward's M-4. The two marines in the ante-room were down and dead before they knew what had hit them.

Jed Dulkowski raced past Ward and kicked in the next door. A large bear of a black man roared out of the room, flashing a fighting knife. The first slash caught Dulkowski across his arm and chest, and the SEAL's rifle fell from his instantly numb fingers.

Ward swung around and fired two shots. The first hit the big man in the chest. The second was just an empty click. Ward swore under his breath as he grabbed his own knife.

Damn rookie mistake, not counting rounds.

The big man did not seem to be affected at all by the .223 round in his rib cage or the growing dark stain on his dirty uniform shirt. He circled Ward to the left, flashing his fighting knife back and forth, a cobra waiting to strike.

Ward moved around to cover his wounded teammate while he watched the blade flit about. The big man kept his knife low and loose as he moved slowly, seeming in no particular hurry to gut the young SEAL.

The man suddenly made a slashing move to his left. Ward moved to block the blade with his own. Too late, the young SEAL saw the feint just as the crashing kick caught him in the kneecap. Ward fell back from the force of the blow, stumbling over a fallen chair, scrambling to get back up before the guy could follow up and strike again, but this time with the razor-sharp blade.

His leg felt like it was on fire. He only hoped that it would hold him up and allow him to react.

The black man circled slowly to the left again, his grin signaling his belief that this fight was practically over. All he needed to do was finish it. He swung the big, bloody blade forward and up, aiming to catch Ward across the chest before ramming it into his throat. Ward stumbled backward to avoid the deadly arc, feeling a sharp sting as the knife nicked the unprotected skin of his forearm.

But as he moved, the damaged knee gave way and he crashed to the floor so hard the breath was knocked from his lungs. The knife-wielding guerrilla immediately pounced on top of Ward and, in one motion, brought the knife down to rip the young SEAL commander's jugular.

The growl of the M-4 sounded like a cannon in the tiny room. The big man wavered for a quick moment, eyes wide, and then dropped the knife and fell heavily on top of Ward.

Ward crawled out from beneath the man. Jed Dulkowski, who had been leaning against the wall, was now sliding slowly to the floor. The front of his fatigues was soaked in blood. No way he could have managed a shot. He did not even have his rifle.

TJ Dillon stepped out of the smoke, grinning.

"I can't tell you how good that felt," he said.

"Felt pretty good over here, too," Ward said as he rose unsteadily, shook his head to clear it, and took in big gulps of air before moving to help his wounded man. He was just applying a pressure bandage to the wicked slash wound across Dulkowski's chest when Horton and Garcia came crashing through the door, dragging behind them a very unwilling prisoner.

"Boss, look what we found sneaking out the back while you

two were lounging on the porch," Tony Garcia said. "Let me introduce Admiral Juan Valdez of the Venezuelan Navy." The SEAL held up a big gun, a Navy Colt. "We had to relieve him of this bad boy, but once he lost his pop gun, he started begging for mercy."

42

Jim Ward fiddled with his phone as Sean Horton finished placing a field dressing on Jed Dulkowski's knife wound. The young SEAL knew that they needed to get down off this rock before any of Valdez's troops realized that there were only five of them and that the rain of ordnance from the night sky was likely done. Then they would certainly muster a rescue effort. That meant they had to move quickly, but Dulkowski had to be stabilized before they tried to make a getaway with their prisoner.

Ward nodded to TJ Dillon.

"I need you to babysit our prisoner. We're one gun short and I'm going to need all my shooters."

Dillon nodded. It made sense. Despite what had just transpired, he was still not really part of the team. He understood how carefully choreographed any operation was, and the last thing he wanted to do was get in the way. And he was impressed the young SEAL commander was savvy enough to recognize it.

Ward fished around in a pocket for a second before pulling out a heavy black zip-tie and a Syrette, a small needle already attached to a dose of liquid medication, all in one convenient unit.

"Phenobarbital," Ward said, answering the unasked question. "Enough to keep the admiral quiet for about eight hours."

Dillon yanked Valdez to his feet and spun him around. Pinning the admiral's arms behind his back, he slipped the zip-tie over the man's wrists and pulled it tight. Then he broke open the Syrette and jabbed it into the crook of the admiral's arm.

The effect was almost instantaneous. Valdez slumped to the ground.

"Okay, let's get a move on," Ward whispered. "Where's Tony?"

Garcia appeared right on cue at the dugout's back entrance.

"We figured that snake might have a back way out of this hole in the ground," he said, nodding toward Valdez. "We found a rope ladder heading down to a back trail. In another thirty seconds he would have been out there with the monkeys and the rest of the reptiles."

The ragged little group headed up the dugout steps, following Garcia. Sean Horton half carried Jed Dulkowski, helping him as he did his best to walk. TJ Dillon slung Valdez across his right shoulder, once again employing a fireman's carry to transport an important prisoner. Jim Ward brought up the rear.

Suddenly the silent night erupted in unexpected shooting from the heavy machine guns that the SEALs had taken out before. Other troops were manning them now. But as the SEALs dashed to cover, they noticed something peculiar. The tracers were not arching up into the sky anymore. Nor were they aimed at the retreating SEAL team.

The new gunners were shooting downward, into the jungle. And someone from down there was shooting back.

Ward could even see muzzle flashes among the thick undergrowth below. From all those sparks, he figured at least thirty or forty shooters were down there. Someone else wanted to storm the compound pretty badly. Ward, his SEALs, TJ Dillon, and Admiral Juan Valdez had better be long gone if these late party crashers succeeded in storming the hill.

It was a short hike to the secret escape route hidden behind the smoking ruins of the command hut. Tony Garcia tossed the ladder over the precipice and watched as it unrolled down the rock. He scurried down the vertical rock face, barely touching the granite. With Garcia tending the bottom, Horton and Dillon lowered Dulkowski and then Valdez down to the trail below before following them down the ladder.

Jim Ward was halfway down the hundred-foot drop when a bullet pocked the rock above his head and showered him with gravel. The shot had come from somewhere below him, but he could not tell precisely where. He loosened his grip on the rope, careening down in a not-quite-controlled fall. He kicked away from the granite, dropped a quick fifteen or twenty feet, then stopped his fall with his boot heels before kicking away and dropping once again.

He fully expected more bullets to tear out chunks of earth and rocks. Or to rip into his flesh. He was a relatively easy target for a good marksman as he dangled there on the cliff face. He tried to push away at a different angle each time, making himself as much of a moving target as he could manage without falling all the way to the ground.

But there was no other shot.

Finally, he collapsed onto the ground. The other men had spread out in a defensive position, but they were not yet returning fire. They could not see who had shot at them and didn't want to give away their own positions in the brush—or waste precious ammunition—by firing wildly.

"We need to get to the river," Ward ordered. "We could stay here and fight, but we'll only get chewed up. We can hope our shooter friends are more interested in hitting Valdez's camp than taking us, and I assume they don't know we already got their prize with us."

With that, he stood and charged down the narrow trail to the river, hoping that it led to safety and not a trap. The rest of the team followed their leader, moving as quickly as they could manage with a wounded man and an unconscious prisoner.

Minutes later they could see the river through the trees and hear the rushing, dark water. The path merged with a much wider, well-used trail that meandered downward toward the water's edge.

Ward sensed more than heard movement just ahead of them. He waved his team off the trail and into the brush just in time.

Ten heavily armed guerrillas, charging down the trail, almost overran them.

Ψ

Josh Kirkland clearly heard all the shooting. He had a view of the tracers arcing down from the rocks above. Valdez's body-guards were putting up one hell of a hard fight against Castellon's guerrillas, especially considering how they had been pounded by the Tomahawk missiles. With their high-ground advantage and heavy armaments, there was no way to tell who was going to win this skirmish.

Not that it really mattered.

It would be good if Castellon and his men prevailed. Then he could silence the admiral, and Kirkland would only have to meet up with young Ward and his SEAL team—plus his invited guest, TJ Dillon—and make sure none of them made it out of this jungle alive.

He saw movement at the top of the cairn. His night-vision binoculars picked up someone trying to escape down a rope ladder. It might be Valdez trying to get away. Or, more likely, the SEALs making their egress. And if it was the latter, that likely meant they had Valdez in tow.

Either way, he was now presented with the perfect opportunity to end this whole mess while Castellon and his men kept the rest busy. That would prevent many questions that could not be easily answered.

Kirkland grabbed his rifle and took careful aim at someone quickly descending on the rope ladder. It was a difficult shot, more than seven hundred yards, from a bad angle. The CIA agent took a deep breath and exhaled slightly, calling on all the training he had received way back when, before he became a field agent. The 300 Browning bucked as he squeezed the trigger.

The target fell away behind the jungle canopy, out of view. Kirkland could not be sure if he had hit him or not. If he had missed, the man had reacted with lightning-like reflexes, dropping out of sight before he could get a second round off.

Kirkland placed the rifle on the dugout floor and grabbed the AK-47 lying there. He would need its increased firepower for close-in work. He settled down in the boat to wait out the fight.

Ψ

Simon Castellon did not like the way this fight was developing. The massive explosions—what had set them off he could not imagine, but it seemed to come from the sky—had attracted the attention of the machine gun bunkers for a bit, giving Castellon some hope that they could storm the enclave. But once they realized his men were headed their way, they redirected their fire to the valley below the cliffs.

The old jungle fighter had tried to explain the difficulties of such an assault from this low angle to Kirkland, but he would not listen. Now his men were pinned down, futilely shooting upward at their well-hidden protagonists and taking the brunt of their constant barrage. If he had a small army, with airpower and artillery, maybe he could take the bunkers up there, but not tonight and not from this location. Half his men had already fallen, victims of all the random lead hailing down on them from the hilltop.

Quietly the guerrilla leader signaled his men to fall back. They would regroup at the river landing and wait for dawn. Then he could figure out whether to stay here and do Josh Kirkland's bidding or concede defeat—sometimes the bravest course to follow—and slip back to his jungle headquarters to fight another day.

His few remaining warriors moved quickly back down the trail toward their boats.

Ψ

"I counted ten," TJ Dillon whispered to Jim Ward after the last guerrilla had dashed past them. "And the guy leading them is none other than Simon Castellon. He's the head kahuna in these parts. There is something weird going on for him to be taking on Valdez and his guys. They're best buddies."

Ward nodded.

"Same guy that Josh Kirkland said was his inside source on the whole Valdez operation."

"Yep," Dillon agreed. "Suggest we mosey on down this trail and see where they're headed in such a big damn hurry."

Ward shook his head.

"No, you stay here and play host to our guest in case he comes back from Sleepytown. We're supposed to keep him warm and breathing. We'll follow those sprinters and see what we can find out."

Ward motioned for Horton and Garcia to follow him, leaving Dulkowski and the sleeping Valdez with Dillon.

The SEALs silently edged down the trail, moving from deep shadow to deep shadow as they pursued the guerrilla leader. They had barely covered a hundred yards before Ward signaled them to stop and spread out.

Ten yards in front of them, the trail ended at a narrow gravel beach. Three dugout canoes were pulled up in the mud and rocks. Ward could count eleven men standing around the boats. From the violent gestures, Castellon was arguing with someone. He looked to be a Caucasian, older and heavier than the guerrilla fighters.

Ward slithered forward, alligator-like, remaining hidden from view. Whatever Tall White Guy was saying, he was being pretty damn emphatic about it. Ward knew he needed to hear what was going on if he was to piece this mishmash together and determine if it affected him, his team, or his mission.

He was almost close enough when a shot rang out from somewhere behind him. Then someone was shouting, but Ward could not quite make out the words.

The guerrillas, Castellon, and the tall guy dispersed like sand crabs, disappearing behind the cover of the big canoes. Their AK-47 barrels popped up, spitting fire and smoke, and chewed up the meager cover around where Ward knew his team was hiding.

Then the higher-pitched reports of M-4s joined the conversation, adding to the angry rumble from the heavier automatic rifles. Ward's SEALs were fighting back.

An RPG rocket suddenly zoomed across the narrow space, exploding at the base of a tree. The guerrillas knew what they had to do. They began to spread out, giving each other cover fire as they moved to flank the SEALs. Someone was shouting instructions in loud Spanish.

Hugging the ground, Jim Ward wiggled around to the left until he had a clear shot at several of the guerrillas and took careful aim. His first shot took out one fighter, then Simon Castellon filled his sights. Ward squeezed the trigger and watched as Castellon fell hard, already twitching as he lay on the wet ground.

The shooting abruptly stopped, the short but intense fire-fight ending as suddenly as it had begun. Five of the guerrillas lay on the ground. The remaining men melted into the jungle, bound to leave the area, regroup, and wage battle another day.

One of the canoes floated free, out into the brackish, copper-colored stream, slowly drifting toward the swifter current.

Ward had dared to rise to his knees to take a look around when he heard an outboard engine come to life in the direction of the floating canoe. The dugout suddenly sprang forward, followed by a broad, white, churning wake as the craft raced around a bend in the river and disappeared from sight.

TJ Dillon came stumbling out of the jungle.

"He's getting away!" he screamed in anguish. "The son of a bitch is getting away!"

Ward stood and faced the enraged former SEAL.

"Dillon, you're supposed to be guarding the prisoner."

"Jed is watching him sleep," Dillon responded. "How did you let Kirkland get away? He's the man responsible for killing my father. And your grandfather. I'm going to take him down if it's the last thing I ever do."

Ward stood there wide-eyed for a moment and then pointed at one of the two remaining dugouts.

"Take that one. He's only got three minutes on you. We'll head toward the extraction site in the other. You know where to go. If you're not there, we'll come looking for you. You know we—"

"I know. We never leave a man behind," Dillon shouted over

his shoulder as he shoved the canoe into the water, hopped in, and cranked the engine all in a single motion. He tossed a casual wave over his shoulder as he disappeared around the bend in the stream.

Jim Ward was certain that he saw a broad smile on TJ Dillon's face.

EPILOGUE

Juan Valdez woke groggily. Bright sunshine poured in through the window. Through half-closed eyes, he could make out a sterile white room, but all he could discern was the ceiling, a straight chair, and a small steel table.

Valdez tried to sit up but his hands were pinned. He was bound to his bed by something he could not break.

He had no idea where he was or what time it might be. The last thing he remembered clearly was the firefight deep in the Venezuelan jungle and his aborted escape. He had a very vague, blurry memory of the inside of an airplane and maybe a truck somewhere, but he could not quite shake out all the cobwebs.

Valdez heard a door open, its hinges squeaking. Someone in a camouflage uniform walked over and sat down in the chair. The man spoke in perfect, non-accented Spanish.

"Admiral, welcome to Guantanamo Bay on the island of Cuba. This will be your home for a very long time. Now, since you have awakened from your long nap, I would like to begin by asking you some questions. I assure you, we will eventually get the answers we seek, and believe me when I tell you that we have inexhaustible patience. Are you ready, Admiral?"

Ψ

Josh Kirkland flattened himself against the brick wall that formed one side of the narrow, dark alley. The stench of rotting garbage, and perhaps something even worse, swirled around him while a cloud of mosquitos filled the night air. Carefully keeping in the deepest shadows, the rogue spy inched his way toward the alley's entrance and the main thoroughfare beyond.

The main drag's orange-yellow streetlights glimmered dimly, muted by a quickly gathering fog. Kirkland dared to sneak a quick peek around the corner and down the constricted street. A gentle breeze found its way down the avenue and blew away just a bit of the alley's stench, replacing it with diesel exhaust and the barest hint of salt water.

As he expected at this hour of the night, the street was vacant of cars and pedestrians. Across the way, on the other side of a tall chain-link fence protecting the piers, a container ship rested along a broad quay, filling the skyline. A few workers clustered around a truck as a yard crane lifted its last container to the freighter's deck, high above. More men stood in twos and threes around bollards, waiting to cast off lines as soon as the container was safely strapped down.

Kirkland took a deep breath, tensed his muscles, and raced across the broad street and through the open gate. No one said a word or even glanced his way as he ran across the quay and hustled up the gangway and into the ship's interior.

The old spy gasped for breath as he dashed down one ladder and then another. At the bottom, he slowed and headed forward, carefully reading the numbers written above each door. Finally, he found the one he was looking for: 5-L-121, at the very end of the passageway.

Kirkland slipped into the darkened room and locked the door behind himself. Only then did he dare to draw a deep, lung-filling breath. It looked as if Gutierrez had been true to his word. He had come through. In a few hours, Kirkland would be safely out of this godforsaken country, with enough head start, thanks to its president, to evade that damned persistent TJ Dillon.

Ψ

Dawn was a rosy glow on the eastern horizon when Dillon slammed on the brakes. The Land Rover screeched to a stop, tires smoking in protest as he sawed the steering wheel over and shot through the gate that led out onto the quay.

The pier was empty.

Dillon grabbed the 7X50 binoculars from the floorboard where they flew when he made the hard turn. He quickly scanned down the river toward the seawall beyond. A large freighter churned the muddy water as it made its way toward the mouth of the harbor and the open sea. He could just make out the ship's name painted in tall white letters across her broad stern: *Helen K II*.

Dillon pounded the steering wheel in frustration.

He had been so close, so very close to catching Kirkland. But he had escaped him for good. Dillon knew it would be very easy to find the *Helen K II*'s next port of call and be there waiting when she docked. But he also knew that Kirkland would be long gone by then.

TJ Dillon sauntered over to the edge of the quay. Several other big rigs were now being loaded, and the former SEAL watched the so-familiar activity for a moment. Would he return to the cover of steering his own big rig across the country as he awaited instructions from whoever his new "handler" would be? Would he, instead, devote his life full time to chasing bad guys and preparing others to blow up things and kill people?

Or were his fighting days now over for good?

He assumed he would find out soon enough. He walked back to the Land Rover, reached for the cell phone tucked behind the sun visor, and prepared to give a report of this narrow miss to Tom Donnegan.

Then, without even bothering to get a shower or a bite of breakfast, he fully intended to take the next flight to Miami, catch the regional jet to Tampa, and run—not walk—to the biggest hug he could manage for his wife and boy.

Ψ

Bill Beaman stood in the pouring rain, watching the SEAL team crawl out of the C-17. Steam rose in tendrils from the heated tarmac, painting the airfield with an ethereal orange-gold glow against the dark, wet night. A P-8 Sentinel screamed into the sky behind the parked aircraft.

The veteran SEAL's mind drifted back to all the times that he had returned battered and bruised from a tough mission. Maybe it was only his imagination, but it always seemed to be on a dark, rainy night at some lonely, isolated hangar at the backside of the airfield. Never a band or a cheering crowd or a line of uniformed brass to welcome them. No press or TV to record the victory. Only a quiet ride back to the SEAL compound to nurse new wounds and fresh bruises and get ready for the next mission.

Beaman knew that was what Jim Ward had in front of him. That was how it should be. It was the SEAL way.

The four young men walked slowly across the apron, water dripping from their hats. Jim Ward had brought his team home and that was certainly one of the goals. Even if they were not officially covered in glory, they could still proudly say, "Mission accomplished."

Mostly. They had captured Valdez alive. They had, at the same time, taken out one of the hemisphere's top drug smugglers and a bunch of his guerillas. But each man was disappointed that they had not brought back the rogue CIA man, Kirkland. They could only hope TJ Dillon had caught up with him.

The team stopped a couple of paces short of where Bill Beaman awaited them. Jim Ward snapped a crisp salute.

"We got our man," he reported. "But Josh Kirkland got away."

Beaman returned a crisp salute of his own.

"Yeah, I know. Valdez is safely locked away down in Gitmo and getting the VIP treatment. TJ checked in a bit ago. Kirkland gave him the slip in Caracas. Dillon's heading back while we see if we can get a lead on the bastard. For now, we need to get you back to Little Creek for a bit of debriefing." He punched Jim on the shoulder. "You know your mother is expecting you for breakfast. Your old man, too. I may even wrangle me an invitation myself."

Ψ

Joe Glass sat on the small flip-down seat, too tired to do more than watch his team do their jobs as *Toledo* glided smoothly through the deep. They had just finished a set of engineering drills, getting ready for the Operational Reactor Safeguards Exam that would be staring them in the face when they returned home to Norfolk the following week.

RM1 Seidiman stepped up on the conn, holding the metal message boards.

"Excuse me, Captain. Here is the traffic from the last broadcast. The message on top might be of interest."

Glass took the message boards from the radioman and

flipped open the top one. He glanced at it briefly, then rose and reached for the 1MC mike.

"XO, lay to the conn," his amplified voice boomed out.

Seconds later, Brian Edwards stepped through the aft door to the control room, breathing hard after dashing from the engine room, middle level, aft.

Glass extended the board to Edwards with a grim, hard look.

"Well, XO, it looks like BUPERS has finally caught up with you."

Edwards looked at his skipper in complete bewilderment as he reached for the message boards. He had no idea what Joe Glass could be talking about.

Then his skipper broke into a broad grin.

"Your orders are on the boards. Your relief will be waiting on the pier. You are off to PCO School, then a boat of your own. Congratulations, Brian!"

"Thanks, Skipper."

"No, thank you...Skipper."

ALSO BY WALLACE AND KEITH

Fast Attack

When the Russian Navy attacks a US submarine, both nations approach the brink of war.

A belligerent Russia seeks to reunite the Soviet Union—starting with Lithuania. But as the US sends military support, Russia's navy forces a dangerous face-off in the Atlantic.

Meanwhile, two US submarines become ensnared in a perilous game of cat and mouse with a mysterious Russian craft. When the US president orders all vessels back to port, Commander Joe Glass and his fast attack submarines find a way to remain at sea to engage the enemy.

But not all aboard the submarines are who they seem… and with a threatening storm bearing down, the consequences of betrayal could be deadly.

Fast Attack is the fourth book in the Hunter Killer Series.

Get your copy today at Wallace-Keith.com

ACKNOWLEDGMENTS

As with any endeavor like this, there are many people working "behind the scenes" to make this book possible. The authors would like to acknowledge the support and professionalism of the entire team at Severn River Publishing. We are especially indebted to Amber Hudock, Publishing Director and our Editor, who patiently herded us through the process and Cara Quinlan, copy editor, who showed us the finer points of the Chicago Style Manual.

We certainly owe a debt to our agent John Talbot. We could not have brought this story to life without his help.

And most of all, we acknowledge our deepest gratitude to our wives, Charlene Keith and Penny Wallace, who have faithfully and steadfastly stood by us as we indulge in our passion for storytelling.

We also want to assure readers that we strive to make our books technically accurate and the stories thoroughly authentic. Any errors in this regard are the fault of the authors and not Severn River or anyone who assisted in the editing process. We urge readers to report to us any perceived mistakes by visiting our website at www.Wallace-Keith.com.

ABOUT THE AUTHORS

Commander George Wallace

Commander George Wallace retired to the civilian business world in 1995, after twenty-two years of service on nuclear submarines. He served on two of Admiral Rickover's famous "Forty One for Freedom", the USS John Adams SSBN 620 and the USS Woodrow Wilson SSBN 624, during which time he made nine one-hundred-day deterrent patrols through the height of the Cold War.

Commander Wallace served as Executive Officer on the Sturgeon class nuclear attack submarine USS Spadefish, SSN 668. Spadefish and all her sisters were decommissioned during the downsizings that occurred in the 1990's. The passing of that great ship served as the inspiration for "Final Bearing."

Commander Wallace commanded the Los Angeles class nuclear attack submarine USS Houston, SSN 713 from February 1990 to August 1992. During this tour of duty that he worked extensively with the SEAL community developing SEAL/submarine tactics. Under Commander Wallace, the Houston was awarded the CIA Meritorious Unit Citation.

Commander Wallace lives with his wife, Penny, in Alexandria, Virginia.

Don Keith

Don Keith is a native Alabamian and attended the University

of Alabama in Tuscaloosa where he received his degree in broadcast and film with a double major in literature. He has won numerous awards from the Associated Press and United Press International for news writing and reporting. He is also the only person to be named *Billboard Magazine* "Radio Personality of the Year" in two formats, country and contemporary. Keith was a broadcast personality for over twenty years and also owned his own consultancy, co-owned a Mobile, Alabama, radio station, and hosted and produced several nationally syndicated radio shows.

His first novel, "The Forever Season." was published in fall 1995 to commercial and critical success. It won the Alabama Library Association's "Fiction of the Year" award in 1997. His second novel, "Wizard of the Wind," was based on Keith's years in radio. Keith next released a series of young adult/men's adventure novels co-written with Kent Wright set in stock car racing, titled "The Rolling Thunder Stock Car Racing Series." Keith has most recently published several non-fiction historical works about World War II submarine history and co-authored "The Ice Diaries" with Captain William Anderson, the second skipper of USS *Nautilus*, the world's first nuclear submarine. Captain Anderson took the submarine on her historic trip across the top of the world and through the North Pole in August 1958.

Mr. Keith lives in Indian Springs Village, Alabama.

You can find Wallace and Keith at Wallace-Keith.com